THE
FAITHFUL

THE
FAITHFUL

S.M. FREEDMAN

THOMAS & MERCER

Text copyright © 2015 S.M. Freedman

Published by Thomas & Mercer, Seattle

www.apub.com

Amazon, the Amazon logo, and Thomas & Mercer are trademarks of Amazon.com, Inc., or its affiliates.

ISBN-13: 9781503948044

ISBN-10: 1503948048

Cover design by Christian Fuenfhausen

Printed in the United States of America

For Jon.
You are the coffee in my cream.

AFTER

I found her amid the drifts of dirty snow, somewhere near the silenced creek. She was cocooned in rough wool blankets, which hid the sharpness of her bones.

I stopped short, watching her.

From my right came the distant scent of horses, a bit of warmth on the bitter wind. The smell was life, and it was a good reminder. It got me moving.

She was watching the jaundiced sky, perhaps searching for birds. But of course, the sky was empty.

"You must be cold." The words puffed around my face and drifted off into the silence.

She shrugged within her blankets, but her nose was red and weeping. I wanted to tell her to eat, but who was I to tell her to do anything?

"I don't understand any of this."

It was the first time she had spoken in days. Or was it weeks? I eased down next to her, and the cold gnawed at my thighs.

"Do you blame me?" I asked her.

She blinked, but didn't answer. It was answer enough. Rather than jump in to fill the silence that followed, I decided to wait her out.

One small hand made it out of the tangle of blankets. She passed me a grimy piece of paper, crumpled and damp from her hand. I pulled off my gloves and opened it. It was part of a sermon, a page ripped from a book. I scanned the page quickly, anxiety tightening my chest. No need to read it; I could have spoken the words from memory.

Humankind isn't at war, humankind is war. They rape and pillage our sacred Mother Earth, call their own brothers "enemy" and kill in the name of a God who long ago turned His back.

They are blind to the enemy that walks among them, to the deity hiding inside human skin. They move about our Earth like an infestation of cockroaches, oblivious to the coming extermination!

But the time of Judgment is upon them. The time of Brimstone and Fire. The time of Extinction.

Day Zero approaches, my children. We must walk the straight path, and remain faithful.

With trembling hands, I folded the paper. Then, in a flash of anger, I crumpled it into a tight ball and hurled it toward the trees. It landed on the dirty snow. A dirty page full of dirty teachings.

"Where did you get that?"

She shrugged. "Where do you think?"

There was a long silence.

"I'm old enough for the truth," she said.

I searched the trees, looking for some sign of life. "I don't know everything. The others—"

"They've told you a lot. And you're remembering so much now."

"Inside, then. Where it's warm."

"No."

"It's their story, too."

"No. Just you. I want to hear it out here, in the ashes."

I swallowed past the barbed wire in my throat. "Will you share the blankets?"

She opened them silently. I tucked us deep within their folds, using my good arm and moving quickly before what little warmth there was could escape.

She waited, keeping her gaze on the trees, while I struggled to find the right words to start. The words that would make her understand.

"I suppose the best place to begin is with Ryanne Jervis," I said. "A little girl who disappeared from Elkhorn, Nebraska, on the last day of school before summer vacation."

Suppressing the desire to stroke the hair matted beneath her wool cap, I closed my eyes and let that long-ago Nebraska sun prickle my roughened skin.

She was so clear now, the little girl with the red hair.

"Her mother liked to say Ryanne was a comet pulling a tail of trouble, and she was right. Because Ryanne knew things and saw things others didn't."

I felt her body tense beside me and squeezed her gloved hand in acknowledgment.

"She was always passing on information no one wanted to hear. She was awkward, skinny, and pale. Her classmates would have told you she was just plain *weird*." I pulled the blankets tighter, snuggling her up against my side. I was glad when she didn't pull away.

"They might have left it at that, unable to explain why they were so uncomfortable when she was around. They sensed she was different, but they didn't understand how or why.

"Only a few kids could have said more. Like Jimmy Fairchild, who, in kindergarten, bumped her arm in the cloakroom while reaching for his coat. Ryanne had gasped, and then blurted out she was sorry about his dad. She left him there with his coat puddled at his feet.

"His mind had probably returned to that moment again and again, like a tongue to a loose tooth, after his father died of an aneurysm three weeks later. He never spoke to Ryanne again, but every once in a while she caught him looking at her, as though wondering if his dad's death was somehow her fault.

"And there was Teresa Hernandez, who made the mistake of taking Ryanne's butterfly hair clip. Ryanne had stood before the whole class, red-faced but determined, and accused Teresa of stealing it.

"She listed, one by one, all the items Teresa had stolen: Penny Marsh's sparkle pen, Colin Purdue's Garbage Pail Kids cards, Jennifer Morrow's yellow scarf. In the span of five minutes, Teresa became the most hated girl in the school. Well, aside from Ryanne.

"Of course, after that day, Teresa hated Ryanne most of all. She followed her on the way home from school, pulled her hair when no one was looking, and threw Ryanne's art project in a mud puddle.

"None of her classmates ever tried to be her friend, or stepped forward to help her. Once she was gone, I bet most of them tried to forget her. But I hope her memory haunted them, instead.

"I hope the sound of her lonely weeping stalked her tormentors on the playground. I hope the kids who had spit wads of paper at her head found themselves transfixed by the shadow-space of her empty chair. I hope they saw her face in the dull gleam of their desks, or her tattered pink coat hanging from the unclaimed hook in the cloakroom."

I paused to catch my breath. I could feel her now; she was right there with me. The little lost girl on whom I had turned my back.

"Of course the years passed, and the world moved on, as it does. But I'd like to believe, to *hope*, she wasn't so easily forgotten . . ."

CHAPTER ONE

Twenty-five years ago, Elkhorn, Nebraska

"Ryanne Elizabeth Jervis. For Christ's sake, Phil, you know who she is!" Sherry Jervis plucked a cigarette from the crumpled pack in her purse, but her hands were trembling too violently to light it. The sheriff leaned over and did the job for her.

Josh guessed there were times when the new no-smoking regulation in the county sheriff's office simply did not apply.

"We have to fill out these forms right, Ms. Jervis, or something might get missed. Now, do you have any recent pictures of her?" the sheriff asked.

"Not on me, no." She plucked a fleck of tobacco off her lip and eyed him through the haze of smoke. "Does that make me a bad mother?"

Sheriff Lagrudo leaned back in his chair—the one that squeaked—and regarded her with weary eyes. "Of course not. But we'll need to get one from your house as soon as possible. I can have Officer Metcalf go over." He nodded in Josh's direction and she shrugged.

"Where can he find a photo?"

"In the top drawer of my dresser. Under my bras," she said.

Josh felt the heat creep up his neck. He nodded, keeping his gaze averted from the deep *V* of her exposed cleavage. They waited while she dug through her purse and handed over a key. She smelled so strongly of violets and cigarette smoke it made Josh's head ache. He pocketed the key and moved toward the door.

The sheriff cleared his throat, catching Josh's attention, and glanced at the chair in the corner. Josh was so new to the force his belt still creaked when he walked, but he'd already learned enough about his boss to pick up on the silent order. Josh sat.

Sherry Jervis had been six years ahead of Josh in school, and by the time he attended Elkhorn High, the stories about her had become legend. If even half of them were true, the sheriff was wise to keep Josh in the room. Even under the current circumstances.

Sherry got pregnant at eighteen. Although she remained tight-lipped, rumors about the baby's father had spread like wildfire. The general consensus around town was that the father was either Mayor George Buerle (and did you notice how much Mrs. Buerle started drinking right around that time?) or Thomas Bussini, the high-school science teacher who packed up and moved to California halfway through the school year.

She slouched against the corner of the desk, and her denim skirt rode up alarmingly. The sheriff's chair squeaked, but Lagrudo managed to stare earnestly at the forms in front of him, pointedly ignoring the bare thigh that thrummed with life so close to him.

Sherry had an effect on men. Josh doubted she meant half of what she did; it was just an innate part of who she was. A perfect example was calling the sheriff "Phil," rather than addressing him more properly as "Sheriff Lagrudo." It put them on equal footing, which somehow implied they were potential bed partners.

The sheriff cleared his throat. "Okay, Ms. Jervis. Run through this with me again. She would have biked home from school?"

"Right. She always does that. I work the dinner shift at Max's."

"And she usually gets home at what time?"

She bounced up and began pacing. "Jesus Christ, didn't you hear me? I *work*, Phil. I don't know. She's home when I get there."

"And what time is that, normally?"

"What's it matter?" Her eyes were red and puffy with tears.

The sheriff waited, pen poised.

"My shift ends at nine, okay?"

"So you usually get home at what? Nine fifteen, nine thirty?"

She stabbed out her cigarette on the sheriff's Coke can. Josh found himself leaning forward.

"Ms. Jervis?" the sheriff prompted.

"Does this matter, really? My kid is *missing*! Shouldn't you be out there looking for her instead of questioning me like I've done something wrong?"

"We *are* looking for her, and no one is accusing you of anything. But I do need to know what time you got home."

"Ten." She would no longer meet the sheriff's eyes. Her skin was mottled pink.

Sheriff Lagrudo put down his pen. "Ten last night?"

Her shoulders slumped. "This morning, okay? I got home and everything was locked up like when I left. No lights on, nothing. No dishes in the sink. Her bed wasn't slept in. Her bike's gone. Her backpack." Strands of red hair had come loose and were sticking to the wetness on her cheeks.

"Dammit, you've gotta find her! She's my baby. She's *all I've got*." She clapped her hands over her eyes and began to wail. Her knees gave out, and she crumpled to the floor.

The sheriff met Josh's eye and gave him a small nod. Without a sound, Josh stood and left the office.

***

The Jervis home was located where Chancellor Road formed a T-junction with Skyline Road. The house was small and pale blue with purple trim. It might once have been cheery, but the decade-old paint was peeling, exposing the rust-colored paint underneath like traces of dried blood.

Josh pulled off his sunglasses and dumped them on the seat next to him. The overgrowth surrounding the property shrouded it in permanent shade. The only neighbors were the corpses quietly rotting in Mt. Calvary Cemetery across the street.

The house was two miles south of the school where Ryanne was last seen, perhaps a fifteen-minute trip by bicycle for a girl her size. Officers had been dispatched to walk the route, retracing Ryanne's trip from school to home.

As the newest member of the force, Josh had been issued a 1978 Ford Fairmont. It rattled and moaned when pushed beyond forty miles an hour, and its shocks were no match for the gaping potholes in the Jervises' side yard. He cracked his skull on the roof as he bounced to a stop at the edge of the property.

He grabbed his radio and exited the car into the cloud of dust stirred up by his arrival. It stuck to his damp skin as he crossed the yard and climbed the stairs to the rickety porch. The door squealed on its hinges, exposing a dim and cluttered living room. Josh took one last dusty breath of summer and stepped inside.

Past the living room was a dingy, galley-style kitchen, and beyond that a narrow hallway that led to a bathroom and two bedrooms. He paused at the open doorway of what must have been Ryanne's bedroom. A Care Bears quilt was hanging slightly askew on the twin bed. Pink wallpaper with a rainbow border brightened the room, and a white princess desk was tucked under the only small window, which was barred shut with a wooden stick to prevent anyone from sliding it open from the outside.

With a guilty glance toward the front of the house, Josh stepped across the threshold. There was a ragged, worn-out doll propped against the pillow. The desk held a small pile of children's library books about space and the solar system, and a pink hairbrush matted with red hair.

Her smell permeated the small space, a heady combination of strawberry ChapStick and Johnson's shampoo that caused an ache in his chest. The room looked abandoned, like a photograph beginning to curl at the edges with age and neglect. Josh touched the doll's hair, as though in apology, and left.

The call came over the radio as Josh was exiting Sherry Jervis's cluttered bedroom. The room was strewn with lacy underthings and the rumpled sheets smelled like violets and sex. He had barely dared to breathe while searching her dresser.

His stomach cramped at the first burst of static over the radio, and he paused to listen. One of the officers was calling it in, her voice crackling with urgency. They had found the girl's bike.

***

The bike had been spotted some twenty feet off North Main Street. It was half-hidden in the scrub bordering Papillion Creek, a small stream that cut between the gravel lot of Enfield's Tree Services and the train tracks to the north.

Officers had cordoned off the area and were clustered around the yellow tape, antsy and eager to take action—any kind of action. Josh stood off to the side, trying not to transfer the sweat from his palms onto the photo of Ryanne Jervis.

"What's the deal?" the sheriff asked, placing his duffel bag on the ground at his feet.

Officer Lahoya stepped forward. "Pink bike, child's size, white basket with a pink flower. Matches the description Ms. Jervis gave us.

There's a Care Bear on the ground about five feet away." The officer swallowed hard. "I don't have a good feeling about this, boss."

The sheriff pinched the bridge of his nose, wincing. "Officer Metcalf, you find that photo?"

"Right here, boss." Josh handed it over.

Holding out the photo, Sheriff Lagrudo said, "Okay, people. Listen up! We're looking for Ryanne Jervis, age seven. She's three feet ten inches tall and weighs about fifty pounds. Her mom's not sure what she's wearing, but she has a pink My Little Pony backpack."

The other officers pressed forward to get a look. It was a glossy eight-by-ten school photo. Ryanne perched awkwardly on a stool, her hands clutched in her lap. Red hair flamed in a cloud around her pale face. Her denim dress was several sizes too big and had a red strawberry on the breast pocket. Scabbed, bony knees poked out from the hem of her dress, and dirty lace socks circled her ankles above scuffed, black patent-leather shoes. Most notable were her eyes, which seemed to take up half her face. They were Coke-bottle green and rimmed with dark circles. She looked like a girl who didn't get much sleep.

"Detective Smythe," Lagrudo continued, "canvass the businesses along North Main; check if anyone remembers seeing her after school. Start with Enfield's and move north.

"Sergeant Grant, get ahold of the school administration. I want to talk to her teacher, and as many of the faculty as possible. I want to know everything that was going on with Ryanne, and if anyone suspicious has been hanging around the school.

"Officers Lahoya and Perkins, I want a grid search done of the surrounding neighborhoods.

"Sergeant Nicholson, head back to the office. Issue a 'be on the lookout' to the surrounding counties. Contact the police in the neighboring states. I want everyone on red alert.

"All right, let's stay in contact; I want to hear any news *immediately*. Got it?" They all nodded.

The sheriff picked up his duffel bag and turned to Josh. "Come with me, rookie. We're going to have a look at that bike, and then we're going to cover every square inch of the area around it." He lifted the tape and stepped underneath, and Josh followed.

The bike was on its side, the rear tire sticking out of the scrub. The sheriff pulled a Nikon out of his bag and took some shots, explaining what he was doing as he went. Josh listened with solemn intensity.

Once the sheriff was satisfied, they slapped on gloves and pulled the bike out of the tangled vegetation. They wrapped the bike in a large plastic sheet for transport back to the office.

There was a dirt-covered teddy bear facedown on the hardpack, half a dozen feet from the bike. Sheriff Lagrudo took several shots and then slid the bear into an evidence bag.

When both pieces of evidence were stowed in his Ford Econoline, they split up and began a grid search of the brush surrounding Papillion Creek.

It was Josh who spotted it. "Boss!"

"You all right there, officer?" the sheriff called from somewhere upstream.

"You'd . . . you'd better come see this."

He listened to the rustle of the sheriff's progress through the brush, unable to move.

"What is it?" Sheriff Lagrudo's voice had a hitch in it. Josh couldn't find his at all, so instead he pointed toward the water.

The sheriff slid down the embankment, and with shaking legs, Josh followed.

A My Little Pony backpack was caught in the shrubbery at the creek's edge, bobbing gently in the current. It might once have been pink; it was hard to tell. Now it was streaked and splattered with red, like a Rorschach made with blood.

CHAPTER TWO

I awoke in a flood of tears and sour sweat, clawing my way out of the same damned dream I had been having since my early twenties. Occupational hazard. I should have been used to the dreams by now.

They occurred in many different ways, yet they were always the same. Whether I was sheltered among the red cliffs of Bryce Canyon, or running through a corn maze, or fleeing on horseback through a crisp pine forest, or trapped a thousand feet up in the Willis Tower, or stumbling up the Oregon Dunes in a hopeless quest for higher ground, it always ended the same way.

New York had sponsored the latest version of the dream. The Big Apple. Also known as the Big Melting Pot. Ironic, indeed, since New York was definitely melting.

The smell of warm urine and unwashed bodies slithered up the stairs from the subway platform. The air was so humid, my damp T-shirt clung to me like the eager hands of a teenage boy.

In my dream state, it seemed perfectly logical to be walking barefoot through the litter that swirled in the fetid air blasting out of the subway vents.

Ahead of me a woman was walking, also barefoot, her pale arms stretching toward the sky. Her dirty red hair hung in limp ropes down the back of her grubby dress.

Perhaps that's what caused my urgency. That red hair, so much like my own. I was desperate to catch up with her, desperate to see her face.

I labored forward through an endless swarm of angry New Yorkers. Again and again the crowds tripped me up, shoved me back, battered me with sharp elbows. I pushed and fought my way through them.

Eventually the damp bodies gave way to a blistering wind. I leaned in, my hands sheltering my eyes. The wind assaulted me, sucking the breath out of my lungs and clobbering me with Coke cans, empty candy wrappers, and cigarette butts.

Bit by bit, I closed the gap.

"It's coming!" she screeched. "It's coming!"

What was coming? What?

And then I saw it: A blue-white ball of fire. A raining inferno. It tore a path across the sky, unzipping the heavens.

The sonic boom ruptured my eardrums, and the world went silent. The ground rocked and trembled. The city shattered, showering glass and metal.

She turned to me. The she that was *not* me, after all. She was older. Wider in the hips and chest. Her eyes were muddy brown instead of my green. But she shared my red hair and pale skin, and the same high cheekbones and delicate curve of the mouth. It was like seeing myself in a carnival mirror: familiar, and yet different. And of course she was familiar. She was a frequent visitor to my land of dreams.

Shards of glass rained down upon her, opening up gash after bloody red gash on her face, her arms, her chest. She pointed one long, trembling finger at me. And though I couldn't hear her, I understood.

"See . . . what . . . you've . . . done!"

S.M. Freedman

On the last word, the world exploded. The woman went rag doll, flying up toward the boiling sky.

Impact.

***

My smartphone on the bedside table read 3:12 p.m.

Perfect.

There would be no more sleep for me that afternoon, and I would be dog-tired when I reported for work at 8:00 p.m. I pulled myself out of bed with a groan, tossing the twisted sheets aside, and pulled open the blackout curtains.

The stark New Mexico daylight slapped me in the face. It was a good start, and a pot of coffee would do the rest. But first I needed a shower. A long, hot, use-up-the-entire-tank kind of shower.

I ignored the image of my naked body in the bathroom mirror as I crossed the cold tiles. As a general rule I avoided mirrors. Vanity wasn't worth the risk of facing the other people I often found staring back at me.

If I didn't look, I wouldn't know there was a bloody-haired little boy reaching for me, or some creepy dude ogling my breasts, or a woman trying to untangle the noose from around her neck so she could talk to me. Definitely not a conversation I wanted to have.

The first thing I did after buying the house was remove the mirrored tiles from around the living room fireplace. I also replaced the mirrored closet doors with shuttered ones, and changed out the large bathroom mirrors for small oval ones. They were just big enough to make sure there wasn't greenery stuck in my teeth.

The second thing I did was purchase some extra lamps. Lamps were important; they did battle against shadows and dark corners.

The shower was restorative, and I trooped into the kitchen in flannel lounge pants and an old Kiss T-shirt, my hair hanging to the small of my back in a heavy wet sheet. While the coffee brewed, I cleaned up the empty ice-cream container and box of Oreos, embarrassing evidence of my nutritionally deficient dinner-slash-breakfast some six hours before.

As part of my daily routine, I vowed to start doing better. To eat more salads, and cut back on the coffee and ice cream. I would even exercise—start jogging again or something. Just as soon as I unearthed my expensive Nikes from the shoe mountain piled on my closet floor.

In my weeklong attempt to become a runner, I had learned a few things: Blisters hurt. Chafing happens in the most embarrassing places. Jogging is incredibly mind-numbing, and really hard work. Maybe I would take up yoga instead.

Not to be dissuaded from healthy pursuits, I chose the strawberry Pop-Tarts instead of the s'mores.

"Fruit!" I cheered.

***

"Rowan, I think we've got a fast mover," Dan said as I pushed into the trailer, balancing two takeout coffee cups and a box of doughnuts. As usual, his belongings were scattered from door to desk chair, eager to trip me up. I kicked his gym bag out of my path and dumped the coffee and doughnuts on the desk, pushing aside a pile of paperwork with my arm.

"What's the velocity?" I asked, moving to the bank of monitors.

"It's looking like zero-point-five degrees a day."

"Whoa. Okay, convert it to MPC format and send it off with an NEO flag on it."

Finding an NEO, or Near Earth Object, with that kind of speed was not a nightly occurrence. It would be processed at the Minor Planet Center as a high priority. The lower-velocity asteroids were observed for several nights before they were sent to MPC for categorization.

"You got it, boss." Dan turned back to his computer and started pecking away at the keyboard.

Standing in front of Bertha, our largest computer monitor, I tracked the fast mover and sipped coffee. After several minutes the newest CCD images of the night sky came in, demanding my attention.

I ran through the standard detection algorithm, which included registering the images, suppressing the background, and clustering and filtering by velocity.

Once the newest detection list was ready, I went through the star catalog match and made my final observations. The nightly results would be sent to Hanscom AFB Lincoln Laboratory at the end of my shift.

I left the trailer to check on the two GEODSS, or Ground-Based Electro-Optical Deep-Space Surveillance, telescopes. The night air was silky against my skin, and I paused to take a few deep breaths. The sky was completely clear, stars twinkling above my head. It was a perfect night for capturing CCD images.

The telescopes were owned by the US Air Force, and as such were located behind the security checkpoint on the White Sands Missile Range, or WSMR. It was a quiet place to work, when they weren't testing missiles.

MIT's LINEAR program, or Lincoln Near-Earth Asteroid Research program, was charged with doing large-coverage searches for Earth-crossing and main-belt asteroids. In other words, we searched for near- and deep-space asteroids that posed a risk to life on Earth. We were funded through NASA and the US Air Force.

Both telescopes were functioning well inside their metal domes, so I headed back to the trailer. A chocolate cupcake with a single lit candle was waiting for me on the desk.

"What's this?"

Dan turned away from his computer and smiled. His hair was a mess of curls in which brown and silver fought for supremacy. He had docile brown eyes surrounded by smile lines, and charmingly crooked teeth flashed white inside his bushy beard.

"Don't you think we should celebrate, *Doctor?*"

To my dismay I felt the prickle of tears, and my words clogged in my throat.

He sighed theatrically. "Don't get all girly on me, Red. Blow out the candle!"

I giggled, wiping a fist across my wet cheeks, and then did just that. "Dan . . . thanks. Really," I managed.

"Are you kidding? I've been waiting for this day *forever*. Please tell me I'll never have to hear another word about the *Phenomenology Analysis of Experimental Prototype ISR Systems?* Talk about a buzzkill." He rolled his eyes, and I laughed.

"Okay, I promise." I pulled out the candle and licked the icing off the bottom. "Share it with me?"

"What? Take chocolate away from you? I'm not suicidal." He turned back to his keyboard, and then grinned over his shoulder at me. "There are five more in the fridge. By my count you've only had two doughnuts tonight. Gotta keep those sugar levels up."

I had just shoved the last bite into my mouth when my gaze fell on a small envelope with a Hallmark logo. It was half hidden within a mountain of paperwork, and I wondered how long it had been there.

"What's this?"

Dan glanced in my direction. "A card from Lincoln Labs, I guess."

"They sent flowers to my home."

"Dr. Rowan J. Wilson" was typed across the front. No address, no stamp, nothing else. Had it been delivered by hand? Who had made it past the armed guards?

I slipped a fingernail under the seal and pulled the card free. It was a simple piece of white card stock. In bold black letters were two words:

RICORDARE
RITORNARE

"What in the world is that?" I hadn't heard Dan come up behind me. The card fell from my trembling fingers. It floated and flipped in elegant circles, a butterfly testing its wings. I watched it land at my feet.

"It's Italian." My voice sounded very far away. "It means 'Remember, Return.'" My vision was going dark. I watched in astonishment as the floor thundered up to meet me.

CHAPTER THREE

The last leg of Sumner's journey back to hell began with a Great Lakes flight from Denver to Cheyenne. The flight itself was uneventful and over way too quickly. He spent the forty-five minutes nursing the one glass of Jim Beam he had allowed himself, monitoring his alarmingly unsettled intestines, and wishing for an in-flight emergency of the crash-and-burn variety.

Sumner shook his head and swallowed the last trickle of courage, letting it sear his throat and tickle his nostrils. They called for him and he came running, like a good little soldier.

"You're a chickenshit patsy," he grumbled, crunching ice between his molars and steadfastly ignoring the raised eyebrow of his seatmate. He was making quite the impression on her. She was blonde and frighteningly thin, buffed smooth by expensive surgery. She smelled like oranges and had no sense of humor. Certainly not his type, but he wouldn't have complained. Any port in an emotional storm.

Initially, she'd sized him up with a predatory hunger reserved for *Desperate Housewives*–type females approaching the wrong end of forty. But any chance he'd had at joining the mile-high club had vanished when his stomach gave a very ill-timed, threatening rumble. There was only one thing he was going to be capable of doing in the bathroom and she clearly didn't want to join him for it. Rather than bask in her wide-eyed look of disgust, he beat a hasty retreat to the front of the cabin and christened the blue water.

Upon his return, he saw that she'd pulled a lipstick-pink e-reader out of her purse. Sumner noted the title on the top of the screen, *How to Snag a Husband in Ten Simple Steps*, and found his mouth opening against his will, a not uncommon occurrence.

"Any woman determined to make one poor bastard miserable instead of many happy has lost my good opinion."

Her cool blue eyes focused on him, causing him to stammer.

"It's, uh, John Wayne . . . in *North to Alaska*."

She obviously didn't share his obsession with late-night TV. Perhaps she had better things to do between midnight and 4:00 a.m. Like sleep.

Without reply, she turned back to her e-reader. For the rest of the flight she pointedly ignored his existence.

As the plane angled down for its final approach, he took the last few chunks of ice into his mouth and crunched hard, avoiding her sharp glance and trying to ignore the churning anxiety tightening his gut.

But his intestinal distress was becoming alarming. Like a freight train roaring toward its destination, there was no stopping it. By the time the plane touched down and began its roll toward the gate, he was in a sweaty stew of agony.

Thunderous noises erupted from his belly, causing his seatmate to wrinkle her nose in disgust. She turned to him with her best bitch-face, probably expecting him to get his rioting intestines under control. Damn, he wished he could. But her rudeness couldn't go unpunished.

He leaned toward her and lowered his voice seductively. "So, can I call you sometime?"

Her jaw dropped unbecomingly and her cheeks flamed. That only encouraged him.

"Come on, sweetheart. You can't deny the chemistry between us." With excellent timing, his stomach chimed in with a threatening gurgle. That did it; she turned away, her gaze fixed on the window.

The plane eased to a stop and he watched the seat-belt sign with desperation. The moment it went out, he grabbed his satchel and plunged forward.

"Looks like you missed your chance, sweetheart!" he couldn't help but call back to her. He pushed past a couple of old biddies, paying no heed to their angry squawking, and threw himself through the doorway and down the stairs to the tarmac.

Like Jerry Rice on his way to a touchdown, he clutched his satchel against his chest and weaved around the slower passengers. Pushing his way into the airport, he said a silent prayer that he would find the men's room before he soiled himself.

And there it was! Twenty feet ahead, the bathroom sign beckoned him to safety. Moaning with relief, he crashed through the door and barricaded himself in the only stall.

Some time later Sumner emerged, unsteady and bathed in sweat. His belly was still rumbling threats. Placing his satchel on the counter, he splashed cold water on his face and neck, soaking the front of his T-shirt. He scooped several handfuls into his mouth, washing away the bitter taste of bile and booze.

His temples were pounding in time with his heartbeat, but the cool water flowing over his wrists calmed him. Eventually, he turned off the tap and scrubbed his face with a rough paper towel.

After a nervous glance in the smudged mirror, he let out a shaky breath. He was alone. There were no silent grinners, no bloodied soldiers, and none of his bogeys.

Good. That was good. His bowels unclenched a bit.

Sumner felt like he had aged twenty years in the six months since that letter in his mailbox had started his awakening. But the man in the mirror was still in his prime. Well, almost. His sandy hair had more silver and some weight had dropped off his already-slender frame. His clothes would soon be hanging on him. He'd always considered his eyes to be his best feature, with their intense, crystal-blue clarity. But at the moment, they were bloodshot and bruised-looking.

You're starting to look like a corpse, he thought. *Walking Dead*, eat your heart out.

And, right on cue, his ears started ringing. A bogey was approaching. His teeth clenched convulsively.

Dammit, not now!

It was a familiar spirit, too. He could feel it. Was it *Coach*? Or *Loretta*? Or worst of all, *Soapy*?

"Not now!" Sumner growled.

It was *Soapy*, he was sure of it. *Soapy*, with his oily counsel and intrusive good cheer. *Soapy* was trouble, and Sumner already had that in spades. But the ringing grew louder, drowning out any other noise. His bogeys could not be stopped. Sumner curled over the sink, groaning and clutching at his ears. The noise was bad, but *Soapy*'s caved-in grin and beetle eyes would be way worse.

"No! Not now!"

And then a miracle happened. *Soapy* disappeared. He didn't fade away, or ease back into the blackness from which he had come. Poof! He was simply gone. Sumner blinked, letting his hands drop as he processed the inexplicable, deafening silence.

"Dude, you okay?"

Sumner screamed like a fifties housewife who had just discovered a dead mouse in the flour canister. The teenage boy near the hand dryer screamed with him, showing off a mouth full of metal. Something about that flash of braces made Sumner realize the kid was real. He was wearing a Denver Broncos hat and his skin was pink and pimpled. Sumner couldn't help but stare. The boy was perfect in his gawky, storklike pre-manhood. He was gloriously *alive*.

But for how long?

That thought pushed Sumner over the precipice upon which he'd been teetering, and into a decision. His shoulders squared and his stomach unclenched. The boy was frozen against the garbage bin, probably scared that any movement might set the crazy dude off into a murderous rampage. Sumner was equally scared. Not of the boy, of course, but of what he was about to do. After all, it was likely to get him killed.

"Sorry," Sumner muttered. Grabbing his satchel, he moved around the boy, giving him the widest berth possible. He could almost hear the kid's sigh of relief as the door closed between them.

With renewed urgency, Sumner entered the main part of the airport. He spied a UPS drop box thirty feet away and moved toward it.

Keeping his gait loose and his eyes straight ahead, he surreptitiously scanned the people around him. They would be nearby, but for the moment he couldn't spot them. He was feverishly hoping to avoid their scrutiny for the next couple of minutes.

Along with a Bic pen, Sumner slid the envelope out of his satchel. His hands were shaking as he found the appropriate label and filled out the address and payment information. As he stuck the label to the envelope and watched it drop out of sight, the noose tightened around his neck.

He spotted her on his way to the Hertz counter. She was sipping from a takeout coffee cup at a two-person table beside the Peaks Cafe. Blonde and voluptuous, tight with youth, she had tanned legs that took an impossibly long journey from the edge of her frayed denim skirt to the rims of her high-heeled cowboy boots.

Her cowgirl-gone-whore ensemble was attracting plenty of notice, but she seemed immune to the ogling of the barista behind the counter and to the suits who hovered hopefully around her. Her gaze was fixed on Sumner, but he doubted she'd fallen victim to his animal magnetism. Unless she had daddy issues, which, come to think of it, she probably did.

There was no mistaking her. Even dressed in the uniform of American youth—it was like the entire generation was experiencing a critical fabric shortage—to Sumner she might as well have had *I Fidele* stamped on her forehead.

He took a deep breath. All right, he thought. Game on, cowgirl.

Doing his best to ignore her surveillance, Sumner moved casually toward the Hertz sign. At the same time, he took stock of his mental defenses and bricked up the imaginary wall inside his head. The last thing he needed was her picking up on his thoughts. That would be a death sentence.

There were no customers at the kiosk, and he was served immediately. He chose a Ford Edge for its four-wheel-drive capabilities, paying the extra for it without a second thought. October in the mountain passes was unpredictable.

Grabbing the keys, he managed to laugh almost naturally at a joke the attendant made, and left the counter.

A casual whistle as he walked by her. She was standing at a tourist rack, feigning interest in a brochure on trail riding. He passed so close he could smell her skin, an intoxicating mix of soap and musk.

She was green and wide open, and it was impossible to resist a small peek, despite the risk. He picked up her name—Ora—and a few other tidbits. Most interesting was her preference for female companionship. That almost stopped him in his tracks.

I Fidele Doctrine preached against homosexuality. It was considered an abomination, a strict bit of religious philosophy Sumner figured was actually based on pragmatism; those unwilling to reproduce weren't of much use for populating the New World.

But if she was so easy for him to read, how had she hidden her sexuality from the Fathers? It seemed impossible, since he had effortlessly snatched that little nugget from her defenseless mind. He was under no illusion about his limitations.

With some effort, he avoided her gaze and made his way to the glass exit doors and the parking lot beyond. She followed too closely behind him, and he repressed a nervous laugh. She may have been smoking hot, but she made a terrible secret agent.

She watched him from the other side of the glass doors as he drove out of the parking lot. He tightened his grip on the wheel, fighting the urge to give her a cheerful wave as he passed, or maybe flip her the bird. As he moved toward the exit, he congratulated himself on a brief moment of self-control.

The Ford Edge had less than a hundred miles on it, and it drove like a solid, boxy dream. He fiddled with the satellite radio until he found the E Street station. Springsteen's bravado washed over him—damn, that dude could rock!—and he cracked the window so the crisp fall breeze could tickle his face. "Thunder Road" was playing, and Sumner joined in at full volume.

He caught the grin on his face in the wing mirror. It erased at least a decade. If today were the last day of his miserable life, at least he was going into battle with The Boss by his side.

"Bring it!" he shouted into the wind, feeling young and strong and alive for the first time in forever.

But his rush of confidence was short-lived. By the time he reached the town of Encampment, Sumner was filled with quiet dread. The dark fingers of *I Fidele* were scrabbling at him, trying to hook in their claws and reel him in. It would take another hour and a quarter to reach The Ranch, and dusk would be setting in.

Like a kid afraid of the dark, he was overwhelmed with fear at the notion of being stuck at The Ranch overnight. He was kicking himself for his lack of foresight. An earlier flight could have delivered him to The Ranch in the early afternoon, giving him a chance to get out of there before nightfall.

He briefly fantasized about finding a hotel in Encampment. About ensconcing himself in hotel blankets, six-pack at his side, the room dark, save the flicker of the TV. He would lose himself in a cult classic on Turner Classic Movies, or maybe he would escape into John Wayne's swagger in *True Grit* or *McLintock!* The Duke was never afraid of anything.

But the weather was fair and dry. The forest road that led to The Ranch would be clear. It would do no good to delay. Other than living to see another sunrise, which would be nice. His best chance of survival was to follow orders. And pray that cowgirl hadn't seen him put that letter in the drop box.

There was a Conoco on Sixth Street, and Sumner stopped to fill up the Ford. While it was filling, he went inside to use the facilities and buy a huge cup of bitter coffee, to which he added four creamers and three sugar packets. He glanced longingly at the Coors on display in the fridge, but drinking was considered a weakness at *I Fidele*. There had been plenty of weakness in the last six months. Perhaps it was best if he didn't show up with beer on his breath.

He paid cash for the gas and coffee and climbed back into the SUV. Route 70 cut west through the grasslands of southern Wyoming before hacking an endless, rugged path through the Routt National Forest. It was the perfect place to disappear into the wilderness of another time, especially since Route 70 was closed during winter months.

Six miles past Encampment, he slowed for the turnoff onto Forest Service Road 550, a gravel lane that cut south and west into the belly of the forest. Sumner gritted his teeth and slowed to a crawl.

CHAPTER FOUR

As soon as Sumner was out of sight, Ora pulled her iPhone out of the back pocket of her skirt and punched in the code to unlock it. She pressed the next numbers from memory; there were no contacts stored in her phone.

Father Narda answered, his voice gravelly, before the first ring was complete.

"He's on his way. Driving a gray Ford Edge," she said, dumping her tepid coffee in a bin by the automatic door.

"How does he look?"

"Like shit. Like he hasn't slept in six months."

"Do you think he's fighting against his programming?"

"How should I know? He came off the plane like his ass was on fire. Went straight to the john. He was in there for almost twenty minutes."

"And then?"

"And then nothing. He came out looking like a man who'd just dropped a huge load. He rented a car and took off."

"Hmm." His voice was so rough she could feel its vibration, and she instinctively pulled her ear away from her phone.

"Do you think he made you?"

Ora snorted. "Are you crazy?"

Well, it wasn't really a lie, just not a direct answer. Sumner most certainly *had* made her, just as she intended. But her dad didn't need to know that.

"Okay." The line went dead. No thank you, no good-bye.

"Where's the love, fucker?" she muttered, deleting the call history and tucking the phone into her back pocket. She reached into her cleavage, glaring at the trucker who slowed to catch a glimpse, and pulled out a prepaid Samsung. As it powered up, she moved back to the Peaks Cafe.

"Hey, it's me. I'm on my way back. I've just got to lift a letter out of a UPS drop box."

CHAPTER FIVE

"Who'd you have to sleep with to make senior special agent?" Special Agent Carl Robertson's voice was crackling before Josh even had the phone to his ear.

"Your mother," Josh retorted. No different from in the schoolyard, there was unwritten FBI protocol to follow: when in doubt, always insult a fellow agent's mother. Josh waded through the necessary banter and then asked, "What can I do for you, Carl?"

"Think I've got another one for your collection," Carl said, his tone turning serious.

"Oh yeah? What's the story?" Josh sat up and grabbed a pen out of the FBI coffee mug on his desk.

"Nine-year-old boy in Clatsop County, Oregon. He went missing from a cyclo-cross competition on the county fairgrounds."

"What in the world is that?"

"Some kind of bike competition. Anyway, he wasn't competing; he was there watching with his dad. Dad says he went to get a hot dog and disappeared into thin air. That was four days ago."

"And the dad?"

"I met him today. I doubt he's involved. He's a drunk, but with reason. Wife committed suicide last Valentine's Day. His son is all he's got left."

"What makes you think it's one of mine?"

"Remember that Kerry case a couple years back?"

Josh swiveled in his chair. They stared back at him. Forever frozen. Forever lost. Forever pinned to his mural of tears. Some of the photos were almost fifty years old, curled at the edges with age. The most recent was from four months ago.

Josh scanned the photos until he found her, low down on the left. Jessica Kerry, a six-year-old who was snatched from a mall in Portland during the Christmas season almost three years before. She was blonde and freckled, captured with one bottom tooth missing.

There were exactly 778 photos on the wall, and Josh knew each one by name. It averaged out to fifteen or sixteen new cases a year, although some years there had been almost no disappearances, and other years, like 1998, there had been more than thirty.

On the surface there was nothing to link the cases, other than the fact that they all disappeared without a trace. The kids were black, white, Hispanic, and Asian. They were from every part of the country and every socioeconomic class.

On top of that, all the cases were flimsy on evidence. More often than not, there were no witnesses. When someone *had* seen something, the description of the suspect was always different. One time it was an older white man with silver hair. Next it was an African-American woman in a business suit. Then it was a twentysomething hippie type with dreadlocks who smelled like patchouli and BO. Always different. The suspects were as varied as the kids who went missing.

Before computers caught up, and before Josh came along with his deep and never-ending personal obsession, law enforcement had never connected the dots between the cases. There were only a few connections, but they were there.

"Yes, I remember," Josh confirmed.

"Well, there was blood found at the scene. We typed it. It's not human."

"Lamb's blood?"

"You got it."

Josh's gaze traveled across the wall of faces until he found her. The red hair. The Coke bottle–green eyes. More than two decades later, Ryanne Jervis's kidnapping still haunted him. "I'll see you in about five hours."

***

According to Hollywood, FBI agents travel by special jet. In reality, they are subjected to the same traveling schedules and frustrations as the average American citizen. They even fly coach.

The earliest flight he was able to book was on Alaska Airlines, and it didn't leave Dulles until 5:10 p.m. With the time change he would get into Portland, Oregon, just before 8:00 p.m. He choked back his frustration and booked the flight online, then called Special Agent Carl Robertson to let him know when he would arrive. Carl offered to pick him up and drive him the hour and a half to Seaside.

Josh left the office at 2:30 and headed to his Falls Church, Virginia, townhome to pack a bag, take a quick shower, and change his suit. He was back on the road twenty minutes later, and made it to the airport in less than thirty minutes.

The metal briefcase that held his Glock 22 firearm and ammunition had to be checked, and he waited while it went through the security screening. Once it cleared, the officer handed back the key to the protective case, and Josh found a Starbucks.

He bought a large coffee and a *Washington Post* with which to pass the time until boarding, and a blueberry-bran muffin and a fruit-and-cheese platter to take onboard for his dinner.

The flight was uneventful, but after almost six hours of cramming his six-foot-three frame into a coach seat, he was stiff and fighting a dull headache. Carl met him at baggage claim and led him through the short-term lot to his company-issued Chevy Suburban.

Josh placed his bags in the trunk and took a minute to load his Glock, which he holstered against his rib cage. Once ensconced in the passenger seat, he asked Carl if there were any new developments in the case.

"There's been nothing. The vendor remembers Jack. Says he was alone. Bought a couple of hot dogs and drinks. We found the dogs and the two spilled drinks about fifty feet away, covered in blood. One of the dogs had a bite out of it."

Carl paused as he paid the cashier, then pulled through the gate and navigated the twists and turns toward the on-ramp for I-205 South. Once they were on the freeway he pulled a file folder out of the center console and passed it to Josh.

"It's all in there, if you want to catch yourself up."

Stapled to the inside page was a photo of the boy. Jack Barbetti was a good-looking kid. He had light-brown hair cut close to his head and large, almond-shaped brown eyes. His crooked teeth would require expensive orthodontic work. Smooth-skinned, his cheekbones were just starting to push out with the promise of the man he would become.

Would have become. Josh felt the familiar ache in his chest. If Jack Barbetti was case number 779, he would never be seen again.

***

The Barbetti home was on a small street of clapboard, single-level homes, a block and a half off the beach. It was painted a bright yellow with pale-blue trim, and the yard was artfully appointed with tufts of sea grass and driftwood.

The front door had a two-foot-square inlay of blue-and-white sea glass, which surrounded the word "Welcome" in shades of green. The windows were aglow, making the home look incongruously cheerful.

A makeshift shrine surrounded the mailbox: a pile of wilting flower arrangements still in their plastic, a few teddy bears, and a large sign that said "May God bless Jack and bring him home safe!"

The smell of brine and rotting fish assaulted Josh's nostrils as he emerged from the vehicle and stretched out his long frame. He could hear the waves crashing against the shore. Patches of beach were lit by the dim glow of streetlamps, and beyond lay the vast black of the Pacific.

He tightened his tie and buttoned his suit jacket, then followed Carl up the path. A battered red Ford F-150 was tucked into the left side of the carport; the other side was vacant save the oil stain on the cracked concrete.

There was a tinfoil-wrapped casserole on the stoop, and Carl picked it up and took a peek at the attached card. It smelled like noodles and cheese.

"I let Mr. Barbetti know we were coming," he said quietly as he knocked on the door.

They heard shuffling inside, and a moment later the door opened. Keaton Barbetti might once have been a handsome man, but grief and alcohol had taken their toll. His sandy hair was tangled and sticking up on end. His blue eyes were bleary and puffed with tears and lack of sleep.

He was barefoot, wearing gray sweatpants and an Oregon Ducks T-shirt with a rip near the left armpit. A week's worth of scruff covered his face and the scent of whiskey rippled off him in waves, like cartoon stink lines. Josh did his best not to wrinkle his nose.

"The FBI is bringing me food now?" His voice was raw with grief.

Carl gave him a half smile. "Trust me, you wouldn't want anything I managed to cook."

Without another word, Mr. Barbetti stepped back from the door and headed into the living room, leaving the agents to close the door and follow him in. Carl left the casserole on the hall table on top of a pile of unopened bills.

The living room was a mess of scattered bottles, newspapers, and takeout wrappers from Taco Bell and Subway. Mr. Barbetti sat down on the couch and reached for a glass of amber liquid in which a couple of ice cubes were melting. They clinked against the side of the glass as he took a long swallow.

Despite its more recent neglect, it was obvious a woman had once lived in the home. The late Mrs. Barbetti's touch was everywhere: in the seashell lamp on the side table, the overstuffed yellow cotton couch and chair, and the rainbow rag rug that covered the hardwood floor.

The walls were decorated with paintings of ocean and forest scenes. Josh spied an "EB" neatly scripted in the lower corner of the nearest painting, a beach scene in which a young boy was building a sand castle.

It took him a moment to realize the artist must have been the deceased wife, Emma Barbetti. To his untrained eye, she'd had talent. The ocean was deep and mysterious, the waves somehow alive, and the curve of the boy's back managed to capture the brief innocence of toddlerhood. He wondered if the boy was Jack, and his chest tightened with frustration.

How many more? How many more innocent children would disappear into the abyss while he chased after them in utter futility? Would he go to his grave still chasing these shadow children, never knowing what had happened to them?

He turned back to Mr. Barbetti, yet another frantic and terrified parent in another sad living room looking at him with the same desperate hope. And once again, he had no hope to give. He never did. It was his life, and he felt like the worst kind of failure.

"Mr. Barbetti, I'm Senior Special Agent Joshua Metcalf of the FBI. I'm here to help find your son." He tried to sound calm and authoritative, like an FBI agent should, but he felt like such a fraud.

"Oh yeah? And how are you going to do that?"

"The first thing I'd like to do is hear what happened the day Jack disappeared."

"Look, I appreciate your help." Mr. Barbetti dropped his empty glass onto the coffee table with a clumsy clatter. "I really do. I hear you came all the way from DC. But I don't see how going through the whole story for the millionth time is going to really do anything."

"New details often emerge during the retelling," Josh explained. "And one new detail can make all the difference."

Mr. Barbetti studied Josh with bleary eyes, debating. Josh closed his mouth and waited. In his experience, people felt compelled to talk after a tragedy. They needed to tell the story. It helped to process the horror and grief, to make sense of the unthinkable. Mr. Barbetti was no different.

With deliberation, he refilled his glass. "Don't think I don't know what you're thinking, Agent whatever-your-name-is. I can handle plenty more than this before my lights go out."

"I'm glad to hear it," Josh said.

"Lots of experience," Mr. Barbetti said, nodding into his glass. "Years and years . . ."

"Mr. Barbetti," Josh said when the silence had stretched too long, "why don't you start with that morning? When did you wake up?"

He made a noise that was more sob than sigh. "Nine, maybe? It wasn't any different from any other morning . . ." He looked up, meeting Josh's eyes with apparent effort. "I'd caught quite the Irish flu the night before."

"Meaning you were drunk."

Mr. Barbetti tipped his head in acknowledgment. "Yessir. That I was. Good old Jimmy Beam's like a neighbor that keeps comin' over and then ignoring the cue to leave at the end of the night. So the morning started with my head in the toilet."

Jack was eating a bowl of Cheerios when Mr. Barbetti finally entered the kitchen, wearing yesterday's sweatpants. It hurt his heart, he admitted, to see the quick once-over his nine-year-old gave him.

"He's too young to have eyes that old, you know?" he said, and Josh nodded.

Shoving the previous night's empty bottle into the garbage bin, he'd asked his son what was on tap for the day. But his attempt at cheeriness had fallen flat. Without a word, Jack had shoved a Costco bottle of ibuprofen across the counter and poured his dad a glass of water.

"I was thinking maybe we'd gotten to the point where he just wouldn't talk to me anymore. But I kept pushing until he told me about those cyclo-cross races going on at the Clatsop County Fair. He loves those damn races . . ." Mr. Barbetti stopped, choking up.

"Would you like some water?" Carl asked, but he shook his head and took a sip of amber liquid instead.

"Jack was so excited when I said we could go," he said hoarsely. "It's been so long since he acted like a kid . . ."

"Since your wife passed away," Josh said quietly.

"Yeah. Emma . . . maybe marrying her was a mistake; she was only just out of high school. But we couldn't keep our hands off each other, and you know, being Catholic." He shrugged. "My mom used to hold her rosary in one hand while she beat me with the other. Marriage was the only option."

And he'd loved Emma, he told them. He'd loved her deliriously and blindly, and with his whole damn heart. For a time, they'd been happy. She'd painted, and he'd worked at the sawmill—and if he had too much to drink on occasion . . . well, in the early years it was under control.

"But Emma, she had her demons, too. Some days she seemed happy with our life; other days she wanted to move to an ashram in India or live 'off the grid' in the Ozark Mountains or some damn thing.

Out of the blue, she'd disappear. She'd go for groceries and not come back for days." He stopped, blinking into his glass.

"That must have been difficult," Josh prompted.

"I was out of my fucking mind, thinking she was dead in a ditch or something," Mr. Barbetti agreed. "But she always came home. She'd be bruised, exhausted, covered in filth . . ."

"Any idea where she'd been?" Carl asked.

Mr. Barbetti looked down. "I learned not to ask. But that was all before Jack came along. She was a good mom to him . . ."

"I'm so sorry for your loss, Mr. Barbetti," Josh said softly.

He shuddered and drained his glass. "They found her car in the Barview Jetty off the 101. She drove full bore across the damn beach and straight into the water."

"Mr. Barbetti," Josh redirected as gently as he could. "Can you tell me about the cyclo-cross races? You said Jack was excited to go?"

He scrubbed hard at his face, pushing his hair up into spikes dampened by his tears. "Yeah, Jack was really excited. But I knew it was a mistake the moment we got there. It was so loud and hot in the arena."

They had found seats at the back, and Mr. Barbetti had rolled his jacket into a ball and used it as a pillow.

"I was just trying to get through it without puking," he admitted. "The next thing I knew, Jack was asking me for money to buy a hot dog." He rubbed his eyes again. "I gave him a twenty, asked him to get me a Coke. I didn't even watch him leave . . ."

After a moment, Mr. Barbetti turned glum eyes on Josh. "That's everything I remember."

"Thank you." Josh glanced at Carl, who gave a small nod of encouragement. "This might seem like a strange question, so bear with me. Is your son, um, special in any way?"

"Special? What do you mean?"

"Does Jack have any abilities that would be considered abnormal?"

"He's really smart. Tested at a genius level. The school keeps talking about skipping a grade, but he doesn't want to move past his friends. Like that?"

Josh frowned. "That might be significant. But does he have any, um . . . psychic abilities? Like mind reading, or predicting the future, or being able to move objects with his mind?"

"Moving objects with his *mind*? Can people seriously do that?"

"You'd be surprised."

"No," Mr. Barbetti said with a smirk. "He doesn't read my mind or change the channel without the remote."

"What about when he was younger? Did he ever talk about dreams that came true, or ghosts visiting him, or anything?"

That seemed to stop him cold. He blinked at Josh, cheeks going pale. "Shit. Yeah, he did."

Josh leaned back in the chair and closed his eyes. No matter how many times he did this, it never got any easier. "What kind of ability does Jack have, Mr. Barbetti?"

"I don't think he *has* any ability," he said defensively. "It was a long time ago and I don't see what this has to do with Jack's kidnapping."

"Please, just humor me," Josh said.

Mr. Barbetti grumbled and reached for the bottle. It clinked against the edge of the glass as he poured himself another three fingers. He took a hefty swallow and Josh stifled the urge to beg him to go easy. Despite the amount of alcohol that must have been coursing through his veins, his eyes were surprisingly sober.

"When Jack was three, he started seeing people who weren't there. He was saying all kinds of wacked-out things about angels and demons and something he called 'the White.' We took him to a priest. He wanted to do an exorcism." He drained his glass, and Josh noticed his hands were shaking.

"Emma freaked out. She hauled us out of there, said no way was that priest getting near Jack. She told me she'd gone through the same thing when she was a kid. Spooks, she called them. They'd tell her to do or say something, and then laugh when she got in trouble. She said it took a long time to figure out no one else could see them. But she learned how to control them, shut them out. Or so she said. Now I have my doubts . . ."

"Since your wife's suicide," Josh said softly.

"My wife didn't kill herself. Suicide is a mortal sin."

Josh noted the stubborn set of Mr. Barbetti's shoulders and nodded. "All right. What happened with Jack?"

"Emma said she could teach him to block them out. I don't know all that went on between them; I didn't get involved. But Jack stopped talking about that kind of stuff and Emma was happy. She said Jack was really strong."

"Mr. Barbetti, do you think Jack was still seeing these 'spooks'?"

"He never said so. Why?"

"Do you think he would have talked to anyone else? A teacher at school, or his friends?" Josh pulled a pen and notepad out of his breast pocket.

"I don't know. Maybe. What's this about?"

"I need to talk to Jack's friends. I'll also need access to his medical and school records. Has he seen a psychologist or anyone else? If so, I'll need to talk to him or her as well."

"What? Why?"

"I want to know if anyone had knowledge of Jack's abilities." Josh snapped his fingers and made a note in his book. "The priest you took Jack to. What church was it?"

"What the hell is this about?"

"Sorry," Josh said. He took a deep breath and pocketed his notebook. "For the past decade I've been heading a large missing-children investigation. Since the 1960s, over seven hundred kids have gone missing across the US. I believe, although not everyone agrees, these cases are linked. And I think your son might be one of them."

"How? Why?"

"Because all these children have some form of ESP, whether it's telepathy, precognition, telekinesis, or something else."

"I don't know what those things are. You seriously think Jack was kidnapped because he used to talk to ghosts?"

"Yes, I do. That's not the only connection. The lamb's blood left at the scene is a major clue. Sometimes there's just a drop, sometimes more. But it's always there, like a calling card of some kind."

"Seven *hundred* kids? Are you fucking *serious?*"

"Seven hundred and seventy-eight, actually. Not including your son."

"Why is this not on CNN or something?"

"Because over fifteen thousand kids go missing *every year*. Seven hundred and seventy-eight kids seems like a lot, but over the course of fifty years it's just a drop in the bucket."

"Fifty years? This has been going on for *fifty years?*"

"Yes, sir. I believe so."

"So . . . what? Do you know who took Jack?"

"I wish I did. I suspect this is being done by a large organization. They have a lot of resources, and many people involved. The kids always disappear without a trace. I believe they are being taken because of their special abilities, but for what purpose? I just don't know. But I do know one thing."

"What's that?"

"I strongly believe your son is still alive. I think they all are. No bodies have ever turned up, not ever. Not *one*. So that gives me hope. And if we can find just one of them, I think we'll find them all."

"But you've never found *any* of them, right?"

"That's true. But it only takes one." Josh spoke with more confidence than he felt. It had been ten years since he first linked the cases, and his confidence was pretty much shot. But he would never give up.

"Somehow, this organization is finding out about these kids. Finding out what they can do. If I can figure out how they're getting their information, that just might be the bit of thread I need to unravel this whole thing."

CHAPTER SIX

"The telekinetic kids were extra special. They got taken somewhere else."

"What? Rowan . . . Red! Can you hear me?"

"They were the Inner Circle . . ."

"Rowan? You are freaking me out! Wake up!" Dan sounded like he was yelling through miles of pillowy cotton.

Slap!

Distant fire prickled my right cheek.

"Uhhhhh . . ."

"Rowan, wake up!"

Slap!

The left cheek this time.

"Whaaaaa . . ."

I couldn't open my eyes. My eyelids had bricks on them. Why were there bricks on my eyelids?

"Rowan!" Dan's worried face swam into focus, hovering over mine.

"Oh, shit. They *are* open."

"What?"

"My eyes."

"What? Can you see me? Are you all right?" Dan's worried face floated above me like a balloon.

"You have a booger in your right nostril."

"Red, seriously . . . what the *hell*?"

"Did you slap me?" My cheeks were burning.

"Yeah, sorry. I didn't know what else to do. Are you okay?"

"I could fire you for that."

"You go right ahead. Can you sit up?"

"I think so."

He helped me anyway, supporting my back and not letting go until he was certain I wasn't going to flop backward and concuss myself on the floor.

"What the hell happened?"

"I don't know. That card . . ."

"Right." He grabbed it off the floor. "*Ricordare, Ritornare.*' I didn't know you spoke Italian?"

"I don't."

"Then how did you know it meant 'Remember, Return'?"

"I don't know. Can I see it?" Dan pulled it into his chest, clearly wondering if I would pass out at the mere sight of it. Again.

"I'm okay, I promise."

He handed the card over. There was nothing else on it. Just those two words, in bold print on white card stock. How sinister could that possibly be?

And yet dread was pounding its spikes through my temples like coffin nails. I handed the card back to Dan with a shudder.

"Get rid of it for me?"

"Of course." He stuffed it into the pocket of his cargo pants and helped me to my feet. I was shaky; my legs felt like rubber. Dan shoved a chair under me and I sat down with an embarrassed laugh.

"Sorry. I really don't know what that was all about."

"Do you think you should go see a doctor? Maybe your blood pressure dipped or something. My mom gets that a lot, then she falls over just like you did."

"Isn't she in her eighties?" I lifted an eyebrow in his direction.

"Well, yeah . . ."

"Thanks, Dan. I think I'm all right."

He was still frowning with worry.

"Are the latest CCD images in?"

I waited him out. Dan was a smart man. He understood the futility of arguing with a stubborn redhead. He gave in with a sigh.

"About twenty minutes ago. Would you like me to run them through the star catalog match?"

"That would be great." I tried to stand and realized just how shaky I still was. "Maybe I'll head home early. Do you mind?"

"I think that's the first sensible thing you've said in the last hour. Go home, get some rest, do whatever else it is you do when you're not busy being a science nerd."

I laughed. "Okay, thanks."

He helped me put on my coat and handed me my purse.

"See you tomorrow night? Wait! Are you sure you don't want me to check . . ."

"I've got it." And with that he pushed me through the door and closed it in my face.

***

Like most medium-sized towns, Las Cruces, New Mexico, had been hit hard by the economic downturn.

During the real estate crash, I took advantage of a steady job and a hefty savings account to buy my first home. A year before, the house would have been way above my means. I had patiently worked through the red tape that came with buying a foreclosed home, and was proud to be in my thirties and mortgage free.

The house was located in a newer subdivision off El Camino Real on the north end of Las Cruces. The development was full of beige stucco houses with Spanish-tile roofs. In the back corner, my house stuck out like a sore thumb.

It looked like a child had put it together. Five white blocks of varying sizes were stacked in a random way and then linked by a central courtyard. The inside had two bedrooms and a den spread out across twenty-two hundred square feet.

It took almost forty-five minutes to get home from the White Sands Missile Range, but it was worth it to live off the base. I had lived on base at WSMR for six months after my transfer, and that was plenty.

After getting my masters in aeronautics and astronautics from MIT, I had moved the forty minutes to Westford, Massachusetts, to work on improving the Haystack Long Range Imaging Radar. After more than a decade of greenery, apple orchards, and New England winters, the move to New Mexico three years ago had been a huge adjustment.

Las Cruces, also known as "City of Crosses," was a combination of Old Mexico and Old West. Modern conveniences like Albertsons and the drive-through Starbucks were slapped on top of the old town like a fresh coat of paint that barely covered the rough grain of the wood underneath. The Rio Grande cut a path across the west side of the town, and to the east the Organ Mountains stood sentry like ancient guards.

Due to proximity, the city housed many employees of the White Sands Missile Range and the White Sands Test Facility, as well as students from New Mexico State University. It was through NMSU that I had just completed my PhD.

The eastern sky was aglow as I pulled my yellow FJ Cruiser into the garage. I had held it together during the drive home, but as I let myself into the kitchen, I began to shake. The walls pushed inward, threatening to collapse on top of me like a weighted blanket. Fighting the urge to escape back into the emerging daylight, I took a big, trembling breath. The walls receded on my exhale, so I did it again. And then again.

Light. I needed light.

The house was as I had left it, but as I moved from room to room turning on lamps, nothing felt the same. I kept expecting to see something out of place: a painting hanging askew, a vase tipped over, the corner of a rug turned up. But there was nothing.

I finished in the living room, looking around as though I were a guest. The couches were made of buttery leather, accented with orange and plum throw cushions. The table lamps were orange glass, and a revolving rosewood coffee table stood in the center of the room. The artwork was bright and abstract, by artists such as Darlene Keeffe and Sharon Cummings.

Most of the furniture in the house was midcentury modern, a style I found pleasing to the eye. I had purchased the furniture and artwork with studied care; through time, I'd cobbled together a collection that made me feel at home.

Yet it all looked like an illusion. Like a stage preset with furniture and props. I stood with my hands on the back of the couch, waiting.

Waiting for what?

I could feel the anticipation in the surrounding stillness, like a held breath. The air throbbed in time with my heartbeat.

What actors would step out of the wings? And what story would they have to tell?

But the stillness remained. For once there was no one lurking in the dark corners, waiting to torment me.

It was *inside*. Like that stupid slogan about being the change you wanted to see in the world. The change was happening within.

I closed my eyes, shaking my head in denial.

Ricordare, Ritornare.

There was a cesspool of toxic junk churning deep inside me. It was spinning faster and faster, threatening to spill over the sides and burn me with memories.

Remember, Return.

My jaw clenched convulsively. My tongue glued itself to the roof of my mouth. The tendons in my neck went as taut as violin strings. Was I having a seizure? I crumpled onto the couch, curling in on myself.

Ricordare! Ritornare!

"No! I'm not ready!" I screamed, terrifying myself even more. What? Ready for what?

The tinkling of wind chimes. The earthy scent of hay and horses.

"Rowan, Rowan
Under the apple tree
Rowan, Rowan
Remember, return to me!"

A child's rhyme. A skipping-rope chant. I could hear the slap of the rope hitting the ground. Again and again.

"Rowan (slap!) *Rowan* (slap!)
Under the (slap!) *apple tree* (slap!)
Rowan (slap!) *Rowan* (slap!)
Remember, (slap) *return to me!* (slap, slap!)"

The rope was red plastic. It glowed in the last rays of the setting sun, flaming for a moment as it arced up over my head, and then winking out as it dove down into the shadows.

My feet found the air at just the right moment, missing the rope as it passed beneath them. I jumped and landed, jumped and landed.

My body was light as air, small and sturdy and perfect. I was burning with childfire.

"Rowan, Rowan."

With one last devilish wink, the sun dropped behind the mountains.

"Under the apple tree."

They were green and rocky and impossibly tall.

"Rowan, Rowan."
Before my child-eyes everything faded.
"Remember, return to me!"
Leaving nothing but shadows.

CHAPTER SEVEN

The security gate eased open as if by magic. It bore no markings and was tucked eight hundred feet up a narrow path so dense with vegetation, it was unlikely to be found unless one knew exactly where to look.

First one would have to leave Forest Service Road 550 behind for an even rougher gravel track, so unused it didn't even have a name. Three harrowing miles up that road one would snake through a small opening so overgrown it was virtually invisible to the naked eye, and then risk some seriously scratched paint as one bumped and jittered eight hundred feet up the hill.

Someone who made it that far would discover a sturdy electric gate with a spiked top just waiting to impale an unwanted visitor. Any attempt to circumvent the gate would be met by an electric fence that enclosed the property. The only way in was through the gate, and one had to be granted permission to enter.

Bile filled Sumner's mouth with hot bitterness as he waited. Once it was open, he pulled through and stopped on the other side, watching the gate swing closed behind him. It closed with a metallic clatter that made him wince. He wiped his sweaty hands on his jeans, and then clutched at the wheel as if it were a life preserver.

The Ranch was spread over almost eight thousand acres of spectacular Wyoming wilderness, climbing up the western edge of Green Mountain to almost seven thousand feet and shadowed by Red Mountain to the west.

The nearest civilization was the Hog Creek Reservoir, six miles south of The Ranch as the crow flies. It filled up with campers and fishermen during the summer months but lay abandoned the rest of the year.

Sumner guided the Ford up the steep incline past thick stands of spruce, subalpine fir, and aspen. The air was thin and cool, and he found himself gasping for breath. The Main House was one mile up the dirt path, and Sumner moved slowly as the condition of the road demanded. The sharp tang of pine and rot tickled his nostrils, mixing with the far-off earthy scent of cows and horses.

Night was stretching its inky fingers over The Ranch, and as it did a new memory opened before him like a blood-black rose opening to the darkness, seeking nourishment from the absence of light.

***

Hell was a moving metal box. He'd been rattling around inside it for hours or days or years, skidding this way and that way across the grimy floor, slamming repeatedly into cold walls, and bashing his skull against the jagged handle of the roll-up door.

The crotch of his pants was icy with wetness, and his eyes were swollen shut with tears. He was six.

"Mommy!"

He cried, and screamed, and banged his fists against cold metal until they were bruised, but his mommy did not come. Eventually, he curled into a tiny ball in the corner of the metal box and Loretta came with her green

*light and sang his favorite song, the one about the little boy blue and the
man in the moon.*

"*I want my mommy . . .*"

*He whimpered against his arm, but Loretta just kept singing because
that was all she could do.*

***

The memory began to fade back into the ink from which it had come,
and Sumner gritted his teeth and tried to force it to stay.

His mother. Who was she? Who . . . ?

He wanted to follow the thread back and back and back to his
beginning, but it was gone. Life before that moving metal box was a big
black hole. It was as though he had been birthed there. Birthed from
metal. Perhaps he had been.

He was cold. He was so little and so very cold.

That same cold clamped around his adult bones as the trees fell
away and The Ranch opened out around him. The Main House loomed
ahead on the right; on the left was the dim glow of the stables. Behind
the stables stood the half circle of outbuildings that housed the cows
and pigs, and on the far end the chicken coop. Farther back, the silo
roosted over the lot of them, its tall metal doors sealed against the night.

Turning away from the pastoral scene, he bumped toward the
Main House. It was eighty-five thousand square feet of functional and
inelegant space. The exterior was three levels of weathered, unpainted
wood. The porch ran across the front and along the sides, bisected
only by the wide staircase that led up to the front door. Two additions
extended back from the main structure like the wings of a butterfly.

Sumner had left The Ranch more than two decades before, but he
could close his eyes and trace every splinter and every scratch and every
shadowed corner of the great house.

The third floor was the living quarters for all the children; the Disciples and the Chosen bunked together. The boys were in the eastern wing, girls in the western wing. Between them, running the length of the main part of the building, were the bathrooms, and a common room where the children could congregate. Boys were not allowed into the girls' wing, nor the girls into the boys'. A breach of this rule was met with severe punishment, as Sumner had learned during the testosterone-fueled summer of his fifteenth year.

The Priests rarely entered the third-floor living quarters. They didn't need to. If a fledgling was doing something wrong, the Priests simply *knew* about it. Punishments were swift and severe, and most of the Disciples lived in such fear of the Priests that acts of rebellion were almost nonexistent.

After all, the Priests not only knew what one *did*, but also what one *thought*. There was no privacy. It wasn't enough to mask inflammatory thoughts; one must not think them in the first place.

And yet the children were loved, and as long as they followed the straight path they were treated with respect and kindness. More than that, though, for the first time in most of their lives they were *revered* for the gifts that, on the "Outside," made them different from their peers.

They were no longer freaks because they could read minds or predict the future or see people who weren't there. They were encouraged to explore and develop those gifts rather than shamefully hide them away.

The Founding Fathers' Doctrine was intoxicating, and in his early years Sumner had lapped it up. They were not to feel shame, but pride in their abilities. They were exquisite beings with powers that brought them close to divinity.

As he grew, he was encouraged to immerse himself in the Doctrine. He learned that the *I Fidele* family was fashioned in the Heavenly Father's image. *They* were the Chosen People. And who was their enemy? Why, it was the human species who roamed the earth like an infestation of cockroaches, plundering the earth's resources and polluting her fragile ecosystem.

Of course, all that knowledge was fed to the Disciples slowly, over the course of many years. A new child at The Ranch wasn't thrown into the Main House with the rest of the children. They were brought to The Hut, a small cabin in the woods on the western edge of the property. During their month in The Hut, they were carefully monitored and guided by the Priest assigned to be their mentor. This was where the mind-wash began.

The day would start with an injection, the daily dose of "vitamins." Sumner had no idea what was in that powerful concoction, but it made him feel slow and compliant. About fifteen minutes after the injection, the world around him would start to throb. He would find himself staring at the intricate web of lines on the palm of his hand, comparing it to the delicate beauty of a spiderweb in the corner of the kitchen.

The days were broken into three categories. The first was learning. His mentor, Father Narda, spent hours explaining life at The Ranch, the basics of the Doctrine, and what would be expected of him on a daily basis.

The second was a long evaluation of his skills. Tests upon tests were administered. Could he move that glass across the table using just his mind? Could he light a fire in the fireplace without getting up from his chair? Could he read Father Narda's mind? Could he summon a spirit to him and, if so, could he force it to do his will? Sumner was especially proficient with the spirits, and eventually the testing focused on his skills in that realm.

The third category was one he thought of as the Moonlight Time. He was forced to drink a black liquid that tasted like a combination of bitter licorice, mint, and earth. It would take effect within minutes, burying his mind in clouds of black cotton.

The Moonlight Time was like the erasing of a chalkboard. The boy from *before* was wiped away, one stroke at a time. A month later he emerged from The Hut a newly baptized Disciple and was inducted into life at The Ranch as "Sumner," *The Summoner of Spirits*. The boy from before ceased to exist.

Ranch life was busy and exhausting. They arose before sunrise to do their assigned chores. Chores were rotated and everyone was expected to be proficient in all aspects of Ranch work. Outdoor chores included tending to the horses, milking the cows, cleaning the chicken coop, and gathering the eggs. Indoor duties included cleaning bathrooms, tidying the bedrooms, cooking, and doing endless loads of laundry.

The children were divided into four groups, and for one week each month a group was assigned to farming duties. After breakfast they would troop down to the fields on the north end of The Ranch to plow or plant or harvest, depending on the time of year.

The other three groups would adjourn to the second floor, which housed the school. They learned Latin, French, and Italian, which was the original language of the Founding Fathers. They studied astrophysics, trigonometric interpolation, algebraic topology, geophysics, and relativistic mechanics.

After lunch they would spend another hour doing chores before settling into the afternoon learning, which was devoted to expanding their individual gifts. The Priests would work with them in small classes and one-on-one. The classes usually involved three or four children with similar gifts working on a series of exercises to "stretch the third-eye muscle." Sumner spent a lot of time in darkened rooms pulling spirits to him and trying to bend their actions to his will.

They were also forced to expand on gifts that didn't come as easily to them. Mind reading and decoding of dreams were emphasized. They worked on premonitions, astral projection, and telekinesis (for which Sumner never developed a gift, although over time he did become very proficient at mind reading).

Those who did develop a strong ability to move objects with their minds, the Telekinetics, were ranked highest among the Disciples for reasons Sumner never figured out. They were usually moved off The Ranch to a place called The Command. No one seemed to know where The Command was, or what they did there, and those who went never returned to enlighten them.

Except for boys who entered the Priesthood or girls who became an *Amante*, Disciples would leave The Ranch at eighteen. Upon their seventeenth birthday, there was a ceremony in which they left the Main House and moved into the Cocoon, a small log building on the northeast edge of the property. From that moment on, they didn't associate with their younger counterparts.

Sumner had once asked Father Narda what happened in the Cocoon. His mentor smiled and told him the Disciples were being prepared for life beyond the walls of The Ranch, and one day Sumner would learn it for himself.

To Sumner this seemed more threat than promise. He had run into a Cocooner on occasion, but after the first few times he did his best to avoid them. They were pale and confused, like broken ghosts. One hadn't even recognized him, although he and Sumner had shared a bunk for several years. And then one day, that Disciple would simply be gone.

And what did he learn in the Cocoon?

Sumner felt the familiar pounding at his temples, but there was nothing but a big black hole where those memories should have been. And perhaps he was asking the wrong question. Perhaps the question wasn't what did he learn, but rather *what was he programmed to do?*

And the answer to that could drive a man to drink.

"And who trusts a man who doesn't drink?" Sumner muttered in his best John Wayne voice as he pulled to a stop by the front stairs and cut the engine.

The silence descended like a fresh blanket of snow. There was no one about; it must have been dinnertime. Was he in the dining hall? Sumner could picture him, encased in his black robes, joyful amid the heat and noise. So many young and old bodies crammed together, sharing the pleasure of mealtime. Sumner felt hollow, achy. But was it with fear, or desire?

Then he saw him. He was enveloped in the darkness of the porch. His black robes were fluttering in the evening breeze. They danced an elegant ballet around his slender frame, contrasting sharply with his stillness.

Father Narda's face was hidden in the growing shadows, a black moonscape. He raised one hand, though whether it was in benediction or in condemnation, Sumner didn't know.

CHAPTER EIGHT

"I've spoken to Father Santos at St. Mary's. He's adamant that knowledge of Jack's ghostly encounters never left the sanctity of the church." Josh sat down across from Carl at a two-person table in Dundee's Doughnuts.

"Don't you feel like a bit of a cliché?" He lifted an eyebrow at the coffee and doughnut.

"You should try one; they're the best doughnuts in Oregon." Carl took a hefty bite, leaving sugar-glaze crumbles in his mustache. Josh handed him a napkin from the dispenser.

"Just coffee for me," he said to the waitress as she approached their table. He turned over the ceramic cup in front of him, and waited while she poured. "I think the church is a dead end. It's not like all the kids were Catholic."

"But did all of them attend some kind of church? Maybe that's the link."

"I've thought of that. First of all, not all the families were religious. But even if there were no atheists in the bunch, there's no way all those families consulted a religious leader about their child's abilities. And even if they had, we're talking about a bunch of different religious organizations." Josh took a sip of his coffee, and then shook his head. "No, I just don't see it."

"I don't see a connection between these kids at all, Josh. Well, other than the ESP factor."

"They all disappeared without a trace," Josh said, ticking off each connection with his fingers. "No bodies have ever been found, they were all kids between the ages of five and twelve, lamb's blood was left at the scene of each disappearance . . ."

"No other forensic evidence?"

"Absolutely nothing. No fingerprints, no fibers, no DNA. These kids just *vanished*."

"The lamb's blood seems religious to me. Is that Catholic?"

"It's Old Testament. Book of Exodus. The Jews were instructed to paint lamb's blood on their doorposts to avoid the Plague of the Firstborn. So the firstborn Egyptian children died, while the Jewish kids were spared."

"Ah, right. Passover?"

"That's right."

"Were all these kids the eldest in their families? That might be a link."

Josh shook his head. "Nope."

"But this group you're picturing—you think they're religious?"

"That's my guess. I've never found an organized religion that links itself to supernatural powers. But maybe some kind of cult?"

"But you've never found any hint of them. What does that say?"

"Either they have enough wealth and resources to remain below the radar—"

"Sounds like a conspiracy theory. The absence of evidence proves they exist."

"*Or* they don't exist and I'm off my rocker."

"Right."

The two agents sat mulling it over in silence.

"Okay, Josh. Let's assume you're right and some kind of cult is kidnapping kids with ESP all over the country. Where are they hiding them?"

"I have no idea."

"What do they want these kids for?"

"I don't know."

"And of course, how are they finding them in the first place?"

Josh raked his fingers through his hair. "Welcome to my life."

Carl leaned back in his chair and smiled at the waitress as she refilled their cups. When she left, he looked at Josh with weary eyes.

"You know a lot of guys in Washington think you're crazy."

"Yup."

"That you're wasting your career on some kind of flimsy conspiracy theory?"

"And what do you think, Carl?"

He shrugged. "I've learned to trust my instincts, and put stock in the instincts of my fellow agents as well. You're a good agent, Josh. You earned your stripes on the Jessup case, and on the Wineheart murders. You deserved that promotion to senior special agent."

"But?"

"Well, on this one you might indeed be off your rocker. I don't know." He watched Josh for a moment. "It's personal for you, isn't it?"

Josh took a sip of his coffee and nodded.

"I was twenty, my first six months with the sheriff's office in Elkhorn, Nebraska. I'd never handled anything more serious than traffic violations and domestics." Josh pulled out his wallet and slipped the photo out of a credit card compartment. He slid it across the table. Her hair flamed in the shaft of sunlight filtering through a crack in the blinds.

"Ryanne Jervis. She was a month past her seventh birthday when she disappeared. I found her backpack in a creek a mile from her home. It was covered with blood, which of course was later determined to be from a lamb. No trace of her was ever found."

"I assume she had ESP?"

Josh nodded. "She was the outcast at her school. She knew things she shouldn't have. She talked to people who weren't there. Kids thought she was weird, spooky. Some people thought she was a witch.

"Her mom, Sherry, was a real piece of work. Sexy as hell, and she used it for all it was worth. She slept with half the town, including plenty of men who should have known better, like the mayor.

"She had Ryanne when she was nineteen. No father listed on her birth certificate, and no one ever owned up to it, although there was plenty of speculation. You know how small towns can be.

"Anyway, when Ryanne disappeared her mom went on self-destruct. I tried to save her. Hauled her into rehab three times. Kept her daughter's case going, even though there was no evidence and there were no leads. I became obsessed with finding Ryanne. I got my BA in criminology and eventually my master's as well, all to gain the skills I needed to find her.

"And then Sherry Jervis hanged herself on May 24, 1996. Ryanne's fifteenth birthday. I came home from her funeral and submitted my application to the FBI that same afternoon."

Once again, Josh pulled something out of his wallet and passed it across the table. It was a piece of paper, folded over many times and soft with age.

"That's a photocopy of the original, of course. I carry it with me wherever I go."

Carl unfolded it and read the short note inside. Josh had read it so many times it was committed to memory.

Dearest Josh,

I can't. It just hurts too bad.
If you ever find my baby, please tell her I'm sorry. Tell her I loved her.

Thank you for being my only friend. Thank you for caring about my sweet girl.
I'm sorry.

Love, Sherry

"Damn." With a shake of his head, Carl handed back the note. Josh folded it and tucked it back into its home inside his wallet, along with the school photo of Ryanne Jervis.

***

"Did they all go to public school?" Carl was shouting.

"What?" Josh rolled over and looked at the clock on the bedside table. The red numbers said 3:24. He was completely disoriented. The room was black save the glow through the curtains from the illuminated walking path along the beach.

Shilo Inn. Seaside, Oregon. Right.

Carl Robertson was breathing hard on the other end of the phone. Josh had answered it automatically, before he'd pulled himself out of the pit of his dreams.

"What did you say?"

"Did they all go to public school? Josh, is that the link?"

"Well, yes. But the school administration and teachers were thoroughly investigated in each case."

Josh sat up and rubbed a hand across his face. Something was niggling at him. His body knew before his brain caught up, and his heart began to gallop inside the walls of his chest. He forced his mind to flip through the files like a stack of cards. One by one, faster and faster, their faces flashed before his eyes.

Yes, they had all gone to public school. The schools were all different, of course. Different states, different socioeconomic regions.

But they were all *public* schools.

And was there anything that linked public schools across the nation?

"Oh my God." How in the world had he missed it?

"Josh?"

"Standardized testing!"

"What?"

Josh flung the blankets off and launched himself at the small table where his laptop sat charging. He flipped it open and waited impatiently for Safari to load.

"Standardized testing!" He propped the phone against his ear and typed frantically into the Google bar. Sure enough, there it was.

"The public school standardized testing started in 1965 with the introduction of the Elementary and Secondary Education Act. It tests all public school children yearly from kindergarten through seventh grades. 1965! The first missing kid was Johnny Stewart, from Albany, New York, in late 1965! *Holy shit,* Carl!"

"So all these kids would have taken this test?"

"You bet! Every public school in the *country* has to administer these tests."

"Wow. I'm afraid to ask, but . . . what organization runs it?"

"Shit, Carl. *Shit!* Federal government. Department of Education."

There was a long silence on the other end of the line, and Josh half expected Carl to simply hang up and from that moment forward pretend Josh Metcalf didn't exist. After all, who wanted to go up against the Feds? Even when you *were* the Feds. Hell, *especially* when you were the Feds.

"I hope you're wrong, Josh. Because if this is true, it's going to get us killed."

CHAPTER NINE

"I don't get it. You're remembering new things about your childhood?" Dan asked. He looked strangely out of place on my living-room couch in his cargo pants and faded blue sweatshirt. It came as a shock to realize no man had ever sat on my couch, let alone a rugged science geek drinking Coors at nine in the morning.

"Maybe. I don't know." I was too agitated to sit and instead moved back and forth through the living room, flapping my arms like a flightless bird.

"Red, sit down and have a beer. You're making me nervous, and you're burning a hole in the carpet over there."

I sat, wrapping my arms around myself and ignoring the proffered can.

"It's not really like remembering. It's more like *remembering* I *forgot*. Does that make any sense?"

"Uh, not really, no."

"My whole childhood, where I grew up, where I went to school, my dad . . . I don't know. It's all gone foggy somehow. Like the sharp corners have gone soft and spongy. Does *that* make sense?"

"Once again, I'm going to go with no."

"Do I sound totally insane?"

"Is that a trick question?"

I flopped back against the velvet cushions. "I don't know what to do!"

"Once again, I think you should have a beer."

"I don't drink."

"Seriously? Sugar is your only vice?" He tossed a can in my direction. It landed with a cold thump in my lap.

"Seems like now might be the perfect time to start," Dan said.

Popping the top on the can, I asked, "What have I told you about my childhood? Eeeew, that tastes terrible!" Dan rolled his eyes, then sat forward and plucked the Coors out of my hand.

"Well, I know all about your life at MIT, from what you studied to that chick you banged sophomore year—"

"I never!"

He laughed, ducking just in time. My pillow missile missed his head by an inch.

"Well, one can dream, and it got you smiling. But seriously, you've told me a lot about your college life, and about working at Westford, but before that?" He shook his head. "Not much. I know your dad died when you were eighteen. Heart attack, wasn't it?"

I nodded, but uncertainly. Closing my eyes, I tried to recall the hospital where I had said good-bye to the only parent I'd ever known. The beeping of the machinery, the astringent smell of cleaning fluid mixed with vomit. These memories had been permanently etched in my mind. They were trauma memories, infused with sharp grief and the prolonged loneliness that came after.

But they were no longer clear.

With my mind's eye, I looked down at the still form on the bed, trying to recall the man who had raised me, then left me to face adulthood alone.

There was a cloud of gray hair, matted against the pillow. But the face was a blur. Was his nose straight or hooked, big or small? Did he have a strong chin, or did it recede into the folds of his neck? Did he have my pale skin, or was he more tanned?

Why couldn't I remember?

The panic crested inside me like a wave filled with malevolent, biting sharks. I launched myself off the couch, startling Dan into spilling beer on his pants. "Oh my God, Dan. I can't remember my dad!"

"What?"

"I can't . . . remember . . . my *dad*!"

"What are you doing?"

"Looking for a picture!" I yelled, continuing to pull books off the built-in shelves surrounding the flat-screen TV and throwing them behind me like a dog digging for a bone.

"Whoa! Watch out!" Dan ducked aside as an Astronomy 305 textbook flew toward him.

"Where are my photo albums? I can't . . . aha!" I pulled a thick album out from the bottom shelf, sat down on the floor, and opened it over my crossed legs.

"Here we go, let's see . . . no, this is at MIT." Shoving the album aside, I turned back to the shelves. Dan picked it up and flipped through it.

"Ooh, sexy." He held up the album, and I glanced back. It was a group shot taken at Carson Beach during the summer of 2005. While the others around me looked tanned and fit, my skin was albino white, my hair a lit candle in the summer sun. I grabbed the album away from him.

"Yeah, I was twenty-three. I haven't worn a bikini since."

"You should. Maybe you'd get a boyfriend."

"Ha-ha," I murmured as I continued to yank books and toss them aside. Finally I sat back on my haunches.

"What the hell?"

"No more photo albums?" Dan asked, although the answer was obvious.

"What did I do with them?"

"I don't have any albums, either. All my pictures are digital ones on my computer and phone."

"Sure, me too, for my recent photos. But where are the albums from my childhood? I used to . . . I mean, I could have sworn . . ."

"Could they be in a box somewhere? Maybe in your garage?"

"There's nothing in the garage but my car. I unpacked everything when I moved in."

"Maybe you lost them in the move from Westford, but you didn't notice until now?"

"Maybe."

"Okay, try this. When was the last time you remember seeing them?"

Closing my eyes, I tried to picture the albums. But just like my dad's face, they were hazy. I shook my head and looked up at Dan from the pile of books, a drowning woman looking to be saved.

"I don't know."

Dan's brow was furrowed. He grabbed my hands and pulled me back onto the couch.

"Listen, maybe I should take you to your doctor?"

"Jesus, Dan. I don't have a brain tumor or anything."

"I'm sure you don't, but it couldn't hurt to get checked out, right?"

"Dan, come on. You saw that note; you probably still have it in your pocket! Something in that note has *triggered* something inside me."

He opened his mouth to argue, and then shut it and handed me another beer. This time I drank the whole thing.

***

"Let's be scientific about this," Dan said three beers later. He pulled a notepad off the kitchen counter and found a pen. Sitting at the table across from me, he ripped my grocery list off the top of the pad.

"Sounds good," I said through a mouthful of rocky road.

"I'm going to write down everything you remember, okay?"

I nodded, pouring more caramel sauce into the bucket.

"Where were you born?"

"Well, I don't exactly *remember* that, but I was born in Chicago on May 24, 1981."

"And your mom?"

"She died during childbirth."

"That still happens?"

I shrugged. "Apparently."

"So your dad raised you?"

"Yup."

"Okay." He was writing as he spoke. "So you grew up in Chicago?"

Chicago?

"Rowan? You grew up in Chicago?"

"Sorry, yes. That sounds right."

He looked up from the notepad, eyebrows raised.

"I . . . yes, I grew up in Chicago."

"And where did you go to school?"

"Uh . . ."

"Rowan?"

"There were horses . . ."

"What? In Chicago?"

"Sorry, what did you say?" I blinked, bringing Dan's face back into focus.

"You went to a school with horses? In Chicago?"

"No, of course not. That doesn't make any sense."

"Rowan. Can you remember where you went to school?"

After a moment, I shook my head. "No."

His hand was shaking as he put down the pen. "Maybe we should work backward instead. Do you remember moving to New Mexico? Meeting me?"

"You tried to bring me to a *Star Trek* convention that weekend."

"And you missed out; it was epic. Do you have any blanks about working at Westford? What did you do there?"

"I was working on Haystack under Kenneth Barnes. That all seems pretty clear."

"Good. So before that?"

"I got my master's at MIT. I interned at Lincoln Labs in the ISR program."

"What's that?"

"Come on, you know what that is."

"Do you?"

I sighed. "ISR stands for the Intelligence, Surveillance, and Reconnaissance Systems and Technology Mission. I worked on airborne targeting and moving-target-detection radar. Do you want me to go on?"

"Don't get snarky, Red. I'm trying to help."

"Sorry, I know. I'm just . . ."

"Freaked out?"

"Yeah."

"Before you got your master's and worked at ISR?"

"I was at MIT doing an undergraduate. I did a double major in aeronautic engineering and astronomy."

"Anything about that time in your life seem fuzzy?"

I shook my head. "No, it all seems pretty clear."

"All right, we're getting somewhere. So before you started at MIT you would have graduated high school. Where was that?"

There were horses.

"I . . . I need more ice cream."

"Can you remember high school? Prom? Graduation? Anything?"

"That's all a blank," I admitted, and swallowed past the cold lump in my throat. "Dan, what the hell is happening to me?"

CHAPTER TEN

Within hours of Sumner's deposit at the UPS drop box in the Cheyenne Regional Airport, Ora was sitting in Phoenix's downtown Houston apartment with the envelope in hand. It had taken all her willpower not to open it, but she knew Phoenix would want to see it first, and she didn't want to deal with one of his rages.

In bed with Ora one time, Lexy had joked that Phoenix had small-dick syndrome. They had giggled like naughty schoolgirls afraid of getting caught by a cruel headmaster. Of course, not many headmasters could set you on fire without so much as striking a match. Phoenix could.

Phoenix was taking his damn time on the phone in the study, and she was getting jittery. The leather couch creaked against her bare thighs as she shifted. She knew better than to touch anything; Phoenix was totally OCD about his pad. He went mental if something was out of place.

The penthouse suite was on the thirty-first floor of one of those ultramodern glass high-rises in downtown Houston. The inside was all glass and white; the walls were a stark snowy white, the floors were white Italian tile, and the furniture was white leather. The kitchen was white granite upon white cabinets with shiny white appliances. Ora doubted Phoenix ever cooked in there; the kitchen was just for show.

There wasn't a speck of dust or an ounce of color anywhere. Lexy, who had an unruly mop of dark curls, once admitted she was terrified of shedding hair in the apartment. Ora knew what she meant. She had carefully removed her boots and left them on the white rug by the door, hoping they wouldn't leave dirt on the pristine shag.

Phoenix emerged from the study wearing white silk pajamas and a robe, like some kind of KKK version of Hugh Hefner. Ora stifled an eye-roll and tried her best to look respectful. Respect was key when dealing with a human version of a blowtorch, even if she still remembered the spazzy kid who had picked his nose while hiding behind his dad's robes.

He was movie-star hot, but in an albino kind of way. His white-blond hair was cut in what Ora thought of as Euro-douche style: short everywhere with a fauxhawk gelled up at the front. His body was roped with thick muscles, his jaw was strong, and his features were chiseled. He had a dimple in one cheek, and his eyes were the pale ice-blue of a glacier.

Dumb chicks swooned over him, missing the coldness in his eyes and the way he calculated every move to suit his own needs.

"There go three more shipments, on their way to The Ranch." He bent down and kissed her cheek. He smelled like man-sweat and Axe body spray—the one that was supposed to turn women into slobbering fools.

"What is it this time?"

"Metal fencing. Our agents are loading it onto rental trucks as we speak. Lexy's been on the phone with New York cashing out IPOs all day. She's been ordered to liquidate everything that's left. And I've got a purchase list as long as my arm."

"What kind of stuff?"

"The usual. Arms and ammo, clothes, generators, tools. Livestock, too. They're converting all their money into supplies. You know what that means."

"Cash isn't going to be useful much longer."

"You got it. So did you have any success?"

She nodded at the envelope on the glass table in front of her.

"Sumner was trying to send that to the National Center for Missing & Exploited Children." It had the anticipated effect; Phoenix's fair eyebrows sprang up with surprise.

"No shit." Phoenix slid a nail under the flap and opened the envelope. He pulled out a one-page typed letter and read it slowly.

"Well? What does it say?"

He handed it over with a satisfied smile. There was a small metal key taped to the top of the letter.

To Whom It May Concern:

Re: Missing Child Case # 1249058, James Alexander Keightley, D.O.B. September 19, 1971, who went missing from Van Nuys, California on Dec 5, 1977.

You will find urgent information about this case, as well as hundreds of other missing child cases throughout the US, in PO Box 978, 600 Q Street NW, Washington, DC 20001.

"Well," Ora said after a moment. "I guess you were right."

Phoenix nodded. "If he survives The Ranch, he could make a powerful ally."

This time she couldn't help the eye-roll. He sounded just like that emperor in *Star Wars*. "Yes, the force is strong with this one. What do you want me to do with the letter?"

"Keep it. But give me the key. I'll check out this mailbox if I have the chance."

"Do you think he's telling the truth? About all the missing kids?"

Now it was Phoenix's turn to roll his eyes. "You are so fucking naive, Ora. Where do you think all the kids have been coming from? Don't you think your precious papa is capable of this?"

"I'm not an idiot. I know my dad is a first-class dick. If he had his way—"

"You'd be fucking me instead of Lexy, making *I Fidele* some psycho babies for their Generation Zero."

Ora's cheeks warmed. "Right. But you don't want that any more than I do?" She bit down on her lip. She had meant for it to be a firm statement, not a question. The last thing she wanted was to leave the topic open for discussion. Again.

Phoenix moved in on her. The heat was radiating off him in waves, and Ora froze in panic. If he got angry, the fires would start.

"The babies, no. The *rest* . . ." One searing-hot finger burned a trail from her collarbone to the *V* of her cleavage. She opened her mouth, but no words came out. Encouraged by her silence, he drew a circle around her nipple. When it poked up its traitorous head, he grinned and gave her breast a hard squeeze. His hand was as hot as an iron. She half expected the fabric of her top to blacken and start smoking.

"Phoenix." She inched away from him. "You know if I were ever going to be with a man, it would be you. But I don't want to hurt Lexy."

Mentioning his sister was the only card she could play under the circumstances. There was a long, hot silence.

"You mean it?"

"Of course I do," she croaked. One thing she couldn't do was lie to him. She could misdirect, perhaps. But never lie.

"Prove it. Kiss me."

"Phoenix . . ."

"Ora."

Beads of sweat were forming on her upper lip and brow. She leaned forward.

The kiss was surprisingly deep and passionate. Consuming. Eventually she pulled back. The air was cooling, and she let out a shaky breath.

"If I ever decide to play for the other team, you are the *only* man I can imagine being with." It was the truth. It was insane, but it was the truth.

If you grew up on The Ranch, you just couldn't do normal. You were too broken. Which was just what the Fathers wanted, anyway. Phoenix was right; he and Ora were no better than a couple of prized thoroughbreds. They were *expected* to breed, to contribute to Generation Zero by combining the strengths of their DNA into a new person.

After all, they had been bred themselves. They were the Chosen. The elite of *I Fidele*. The product of a horny Priest and a female Disciple.

Any seventeen-year-old Disciple was at risk. If she caught the eye of one of the Priests, her departure from The Ranch might be delayed so she could become his *Amante*. A fancy Italian way of saying she became his baby-mama.

The Priest would have to make a formal petition to the Founding Fathers for permission, citing the potential abilities of the baby they would create, and how that would benefit *I Fidele*.

In Ora's opinion, it was pure bullshit. The way she saw it, a Priest got a hard-on for a girl and used the legalese of *I Fidele* to take her to bed for however long it took for her to get knocked up.

Her obligation during this time was complete servitude to her Priest, and Ora could only imagine what went on behind those closed doors.

The only bit of good news was there was a time limit of one year. If she didn't get pregnant by her eighteenth birthday, she was released from her obligations as an *Amante* and sent to the Cocoon in preparation for Outside.

If she did have a baby, she was allowed to care for it for the first year of its life. But around the child's first birthday, the baby was taken away from its mother and indoctrinated into *I Fidele*.

Ora had witnessed several of these indoctrinations, and found them excruciating and fascinating all at the same time. She'd seen grief-stricken mothers screaming for the children ripped from their arms. She'd seen them fight and beg and sob.

It always made Ora wonder about her own mom. Had she fought? Had she howled like she was being gutted? Most of them did, and Ora hoped her mother had loved her that much, too.

Once the baby was removed, the mother was dragged to the Cocoon for mind-washing, and if that was successful she was trained for her mission Outside. But on several occasions, the mind-washing hadn't worked. Those women had simply vanished, never to be spoken of again.

Ora was haunted by questions about her mom. Had she survived the mind-wash? Would Ora ever meet her? And if they met, would she recognize her daughter?

"Ora, did you hear me?"

She blinked, and Phoenix's pale face swam back into focus. "Sorry, what did you say?"

"I said you better get going."

"Right. I mean . . . where am I going?"

"Did that kiss scramble your brains? Back to Wyoming. Someone should be waiting there. You know, in case Sumner survives The Ranch."

CHAPTER ELEVEN

"I think I'm heading back to Washington," Josh said, taking a sip of his tepid coffee. "I have a contact at the Department of Education who owes me a favor."

They were sitting on a bench overlooking the wide expanse of sandy beach a couple of blocks from where Mr. Barbetti sat, drunk and miserable, in his empty yellow house. The day was overcast, threatening rain. The fall wind that cut through Josh's light parka was cold and damp.

"Sounds good." Carl nodded. "I spoke to the principal at Jack's school, and he says the last PSST was done in May, when he was in the third grade."

"And Jack participated in the testing?"

"As far as he knows. The testing is funded by the Department of Education, but orchestrated by the National Center for Education Statistics. They send their own people out to run it, so the school administration doesn't have much involvement."

"Really? That seems odd. Does NCES send its own people out to administer other standardized tests as well?"

"I was wondering the same thing. It seems like a big expense." Carl paused to take a sip of his coffee and wait for a woman walking two poodles to pass them. She was wearing tight yoga pants that left little to the imagination, and both men took a moment to admire the view before returning to the business at hand.

"The other standardized test is the NAEP, or National Assessment of Educational Progress." Carl pulled a notepad out of his breast pocket and flipped it open. Josh could see Carl's untidy scrawl covering every inch of the page.

"That one is done in fourth, eighth, and twelfth grades, and covers a broad range of topics from math to science, reading, writing, the whole shebang. That test is administered by school staff."

"Huh."

"Also, the NAEP is focused on averages; the information goes toward the National Report Card. So individual children remain anonymous.

"The other thing the principal said? Apparently the PSST is hands-on in its testing. NAEP only starts their testing in fourth grade, so the kids are old enough to sit for a test. They can read, write, et cetera."

"Right, that makes sense."

"But the PSST starts in *kindergarten*. These kids can't read yet; they're just starting to learn their ABCs. So the test is verbal. The testers get one-on-one time with all the kids from kindergarten through third grade. It's only from fourth grade on that the test is written."

"Holy crap. What are they testing them for?"

"I asked that. The principal spouted off some stuff about fine motor skills, social development, language skills, yada, yada. He acted surprised when I asked, like he'd never really thought about it. And you know what? I don't think he knows *what* they're testing, at least not the specifics. Seriously, Josh, how can that be going on in classrooms around the nation and no one ever questions it?"

Josh shrugged. "This test has been around since 1965. It's become a permanent structure. It's the way things are done because they've always been done that way."

"I guess so. Who's going to question a test administered by the National Center for Education Statistics, and funded by the US Department of Education? How much more official can it get? To tell you the truth, I'm having trouble believing our government is involved in some kind of child-kidnapping scheme. It seems ridiculous."

"I hear you. We're a part of that institution; we took oaths to protect it. But that doesn't mean there aren't bad apples in the basket. We've both been around long enough to know that."

"That's true," Carl said, nodding.

"For what it's worth, I doubt this thing is government-wide."

"Maybe not, but it would have to go pretty far up the chain of command, and be pretty widespread, too."

Josh sighed. "Yeah. Maybe that's why it never occurred to me before."

The two agents sat in silence for several minutes, each lost in their private thoughts. Finally, Carl asked, "Have you seen Mr. Barbetti today?"

"I have. He's not looking so good."

"He's drinking a lot."

"He's given up hope of us ever finding his son. Nothing left to do but drink himself to death."

Just like Sherry Jervis, now seventeen years in her grave. Yet her decision to give up had spurred him to do just the opposite. Her suicide pushed Josh's interest in finding Ryanne into an obsession that had eaten almost two decades of his life, and snowballed to include hundreds of missing children.

"And you?" Carl turned to Josh, eyebrows raised.

"I think I've got hope for the first time in over a decade."

Carl stood and stretched. "What time's your flight?"

"Not until three."

"Want a ride? I'm heading back to the Portland office now, anyway."

"I've got the rental to return, but thanks."

He had spent the last few days in Seaside and Astoria going over the crime scene, questioning Jack's teachers, friends, and acquaintances, and following up on any other potential leads. The only person who had been difficult to track down was the principal of Seaside Heights Elementary. They had finally located him on his way back from a symposium in Seattle.

After three days on the West Coast, there was no longer a doubt in Josh's mind that Jack Barbetti was missing child number 779. There was nothing more to be done in Oregon. He doubted Jack Barbetti was even in Oregon any longer.

For the first time in a long while, Josh felt the nervous anticipation of having an actual lead to follow. And he was heading back to his own neighborhood. It was time to pay his friend at the Department of Education a friendly visit.

The two agents shook hands, and Josh watched Carl climb into his Chevy Suburban and pull away. Carl hadn't offered his continued help, or asked to remain in the loop.

That's what it looks like when you start doubting the institution you've spent your life serving, Josh thought grimly. He felt a momentary stab of guilt at being an instrument in the older man's loss of faith.

***

"Hello? Helloooo? Ahem. Well. Please tell Joshua it's his mother calling. *Again.* Is he there? Hello?"

Josh yanked his tie loose, listening to his mother's raspy breath on voice mail as she waited for him to pick up. "Well, I don't know where he might be at nine o'clock at night. Joshua!" She was yelling now, reminding him of the way she had called him in for supper as a child. "Hello?"

Josh grabbed a beer out of the fridge and popped the tab, taking a long and much-needed swallow.

Her voice became a low, raspy whisper. "Listen, tell Joshua the head nurse is stealing from me. My silver brooch is missing this time, and I just *know* . . ."

He hit the "Stop" button on his phone. He had eight more messages, and he was certain they were all from his mother. He pressed "Delete," and then jumped guiltily when the phone jangled. "Hi, Mom. I was just listening to your messages."

"Joshua, where have you been? I've been worried sick!"

"Working. Remember, I told you I was going to Oregon for that missing child case?"

"You told me no such thing, Joshua." There was no point in arguing.

"You have my cell number. Call me on that; I always have it with me."

"Oh, I don't want to bother you while you're at work. I know how *busy* you are."

Josh took another long swallow of beer. "It's no trouble, Mom. And by the way, when you call my house, you're leaving a message on a *machine*, remember?"

"What are you drinking, Joshua?"

"Just water. Listen, I just got in and I'm exhausted. Can I call you tomorrow?"

"Look into that head nurse; she knows I'm on to her. I think she's trying to get rid of me. I keep warning her my son works for the FBI, but that doesn't stop her from stealing from me. And I think she slipped some pills into my drink at lunch today. I slept all afternoon."

"I'm sure that's not true. And your silver brooch is in the safe-deposit box. Remember?"

"Who said anything about my brooch? She's taking *money* from my *purse*, Joshua."

"I'll look into it tomorrow." There was no point in reminding her she didn't have any money in her purse. It was an argument he couldn't win.

"Good. Have you called Gloria yet?"

"Who?"

"For heaven's sake, Joshua. Gloria! The nurse's aide."

"*Geez*, Mom. I'm not calling *her*."

"Why not? She's a lovely girl. She even gave me a pedicure the other day. You could do much worse."

Josh stifled a groan. "I'm not interested."

"Why not? I know she's not the prettiest girl, but I hear they're doing wonders with laser treatment these days. Those pockmarks could be fixed, if that's your problem."

"She's *twenty-two*."

"Joshua, you keep letting these opportunities pass you by. I want to see you settle down. I'd like to hold grandbabies in my arms before God sees fit to take me home."

"I know."

"Are you dating anyone?"

"Listen, I'll come by tomorrow. We'll have dinner together, all right?"

"You're married to your job, Joshua. But the job won't take care of you when you're sick, or—"

"Let's talk tomorrow, okay? Love you, good night." He dropped the phone back in its cradle. Then he got another beer out of the fridge and carried it upstairs to the bedroom.

***

"Hi Frieda, thanks for meeting with me."

Her hand was warm and damp. Frieda Sutcliffe weighed nearly three hundred pounds. She was dressed impeccably in a black suit, gold blouse, and black flats. Her legs bulged like sausages inside her support hose.

She sat down behind her desk, for which he was grateful. He preferred to avoid the distraction of being able to look up her skirt. From past experience, he knew she preferred those shiny beige support panties favored by grandmothers the world over.

She pulled the tab on the Diet Coke he passed across the desk, and took a long swallow. Her only availability was over the lunch hour, so he had offered to bring sandwiches from Schwartz's Deli. He handed her a pastrami on rye and unwrapped his turkey with hot mustard on the corner of her desk.

"No problem. How goes it over on Pennsylvania Avenue? I hear you got a promotion."

"That's Senior Special Agent Joshua Metcalf to you." He winked over his bottled water and took a sip.

"Oh my." She pretended to fan herself with a napkin, and then smiled. "Congratulations, Josh."

"Thanks. How are things at ED?"

"Same old, same old. I'm counting down to retirement. Only two years, three months, and seventeen days left."

"So you're taking early retirement?"

"You flatterer." She waved off the compliment and took a hefty bite of her sandwich.

"How is Todd doing these days?"

She swallowed and shrugged. "Better, I think. He's alive, at least. Thanks to you."

Frieda's son had been a member of the Metropolitan Police Department. Josh met him while working a joint investigation into a series of bank robberies involving a Colombian drug cartel. During the investigation, information surfaced about a storage facility where the cartel was believed to be hiding the stolen goods as well as a large shipment of crack.

The SWAT team penetrated the facility, but either the information was bad or the cartel had a snitch inside the department. Whatever the reason, they found nothing except used furniture and a whole bunch of gun-wielding Colombians. Six officers were wounded that night: two from the FBI and the rest from the police department. One of them died in the hospital the next day.

Todd Sutcliffe took a bullet to the head, and the shot was both lucky and unlucky. The bullet ricocheted off his skull, never penetrating the brain. However, it severed his spinal cord between the C3 and C4 vertebrae, rendering him a quadriplegic.

Josh had pulled an old sofa down over the top of him, cocooning Officer Sutcliffe in the triangle created by the seat and backrest of the sofa. It protected him from detection and from further injury by stray bullets, and had possibly saved his life.

Under the same circumstances, Josh would have preferred to die, and he suspected Todd felt the same. Nevertheless, Frieda Sutcliffe was eternally grateful to Josh for saving her only child's life.

"All right, Josh. I know you didn't come here for a social visit. What can I do for you?"

"Know anything about the PSST?"

"We fund the test, although it's not my department. Why?"

"What can you tell me about it?"

She shrugged her meaty shoulders. "It's run by NCES. Testing is done in all public schools from kindergarten through seventh grade. We've been funding it since sometime in the sixties, I think."

"Do you know what kind of questions are on the test?"

"I don't. Why?"

Josh hesitated. "I need to keep things confidential, Frieda."

She eyed him carefully. "Of course."

"Do you know anyone in NCES I could talk to? Is there anyone you trust?"

Frieda leaned back in her chair, mulling it over. "I know a couple of data-entry clerks, but I doubt they'll be much help. I think you want to talk to Connie Fisher. She's an acquaintance, but I've known her for fifteen years. We go for lunch every few months. She's in the Post-Secondary Division, so not quite what you're looking for, but perhaps she'll be able to guide you in the right direction. Let me give her a call." She picked up the handset and started pressing numbers.

"Thanks. And Frieda . . ."

She waved a hand full of gold rings at him. "Yeah, yeah. Top secret, I know. Connie! It's Frieda. How are you, darling?"

Josh waited while Frieda exchanged the necessary pleasantries before getting down to business.

"Do you remember the FBI agent who saved Todd's life? Can I send him over to you? He's got some questions . . . No, nothing to do with you, it's about the PSST. Right. I know. But listen." She held up a hand as Josh opened his mouth. "This needs to be kept quiet. Great, that's perfect. When? Okay. I'll tell him. Thanks Connie, I owe you one." She laughed at something Connie said. "Right, you got it. See you next week, then." Frieda hung up and scribbled on a pink Post-it note. She peeled it off the pad and handed it across the desk.

"You're taking her for dinner tonight at Filomena's. Don't look at me like that; you can afford it after that nice promotion."

Swallowing hard, he nodded. What he really feared was canceling another dinner with his mother. He'd never hear the end of it.

"Thanks, Frieda, I really appreciate it." He stood and shoved the pink note into the breast pocket of his suit. "How will I know her?"

"Oh, that's easy. Just look for the classiest woman at the bar. And then find her polar opposite. That will be Connie."

"Right. Well, thanks again."

"Oh, and Josh? Watch out. She gets a bit flirty when she's had a few martinis." She laughed at him. "Don't look so worried. I'm sure you can handle it."

CHAPTER TWELVE

When I awoke, the dream-woman was standing in the corner of my bedroom, by the dresser. I closed and opened my eyes several times, but there she stood.

She was watching me with those sad brown eyes, her red hair like embers against the white wall behind her. There was a dusting of freckles across the bridge of her nose. Her skin was creamy, like expensive silk, and became rosy as it approached the plunging neckline of her blouse.

I closed my eyes again, trying to shake the dream that was not a dream, and when I opened them this time she was gone. Shuddering, I rolled over, only to come face to face with her lying next to me, smiling. Her teeth were white and straight, save for one in the front that was enchantingly crooked. She reached out to touch my cheek.

The screaming woke Dan and he charged into my bedroom wielding a frying pan. He had passed out on my couch in the afternoon, and I had left him there.

"What the hell, Rowan?" Some of Dan's hair was standing up, while other parts were mashed flat to his head. His clothes were wrinkled and twisted around, as though he'd spent the last few hours in the middle of a tornado.

His eyes were red and wild as he scanned the room. He held the frying pan above his head, ready to bash in somebody's skull. It was part of a set from Le Creuset, so heavy I needed both hands to lift it, and could have done some serious damage if the intruder were flesh and bone. In this case, I doubted it would do much good.

"Stop screaming!" Dan yelled.

I hadn't realized I still was, and closed my mouth. The silence that followed was abrupt.

"What the hell happened? I thought you were being *murdered* in here or something!"

"Sorry. Just a bad dream, I guess." Without looking, I knew the woman was gone. Not that Dan would have been able to see her, anyway.

"What's that smell?" he asked.

"Violets."

He dropped the pan to the floor and rubbed his temples, moaning. "Do you have any Advil?"

***

Dan insisted on taking the shift at work by himself, leaving me alone in the pooling shadows. I moved through the house, turning on lights and tightening the slats of the blinds against the darkness.

As a balm for the solitude, I found a comedy on HBO and turned up the volume. A frozen pizza went in the oven, and I opened a can of Coke and poured it over ice.

I ate the pizza off a napkin on my lap, focusing on the TV in an attempt to dam up the river of questions threatening to drown me in fear and confusion.

When every last crumb was devoured, I turned to the task at hand. Starting in the office, I systematically tore the place apart. Although I found every textbook and notebook from every course I had ever taken, there was nothing from my childhood. It was like I hadn't existed before nineteen. There were no photo albums, no old greeting cards, nothing.

A large manila envelope in the bottom desk drawer contained all my vital documents, such as they were. My university degrees got tossed on top of the desk, along with my passport, while I focused on the remaining two documents: my birth certificate and high school diploma.

The birth certificate looked legit to me, but what did I know? It had an embossed seal that said "State of Illinois, Certificate of Live Birth." Underneath were the particulars, including my name, Rowan Jane Wilson, and my date of birth, May 24, 1981, at 3:18 a.m. The place of birth was listed as Saint Anthony Hospital, Chicago, Illinois. My father was listed as Thomas John Wilson; his date of birth was September 28, 1949. My mother was listed as Jillian Mavis Wilson. Her maiden name was O'Connor, and her date of birth was July 12, 1953.

My high school diploma was less informative. It was from Jones College Prep in Chicago, and said I had graduated with honors in June of 1999. Closing my eyes, I tried to picture anything about my high school years, about graduation, anything.

It reminded me of having a word on the tip of my tongue, but being unable to pull it forward. My early life was shrouded in darkness. The first thing I could clearly remember was moving into my dorm room at MIT that fall.

I carried both documents back to the living room and opened my laptop. Jones College Prep's website was full of pictures of happy and well-adjusted-looking teens, all engaged in wholesome school activities. The building and grounds in the background didn't spark any memories. I had no recollection of spending four years of my life there.

There was a transcript request form on the Student Record Services page, so I filled it out. Not surprisingly, there were no Google hits for either of my parents. All the links for myself were university- or job-related.

On the Illinois Department of Public Health and Illinois Vital Records websites, I filled out requests for another birth certificate for myself, as well as my parents' marriage and death certificates. Since I had no idea where either of them was born, I didn't bother requesting their birth certificates. I paid extra for the documents to be shipped by UPS next-day delivery, although it would still take over a week to process.

Once that was done, I grabbed another Coke out of the fridge, poured it over fresh ice, and stood at the counter taking big gulps and debating what else to do.

It was beyond disconcerting to have my solid foundation ripped away. I wondered if this was how people with head injuries felt, like something that had always been in their grasp had turned to vapor. No matter how hard I tried to grab at them, the memories were dissipating before my eyes, leaving nothing but a gaping black hole.

Even worse than the loss was the suspicion that new memories were waiting just beyond my view, ready to fill the empty space with something far different from what had been removed. It was terrifying, and more than anything I wanted to bury my head in the sand.

But wasn't that what I always did? How many years of my life had I believed in a childhood for which I apparently had no documentation, no photos, and no proof? And before now, it had never even occurred to me to look.

I had created blinders with which to shield myself, focusing on the narrow path directly in front of me, and pretending what I glimpsed out of the corners of my eyes didn't exist.

My avoidance of mirrors was a perfect example, but there were many others. How often did I turn on the TV or radio to drown out the voices that wanted my attention? How often did I turn on every light in the house so there would be no shadowy corners in which someone might hide? How often did I walk past people I knew no one else could see, and pretend I couldn't see them, either? And when they reached out for me, I quickened my pace just the way city folk did when passing a homeless person begging on a street corner.

And though I knew it was time, *long past time*, to take off the blinders and see what I had been ignoring, the idea was terrifying. I dumped the Coke into the sink, ice and all, and popped the tab on one of Dan's beers.

"Bottoms up!"

It went down in five disgusting swallows, and I belched like a frat boy. Down went a second beer, and then a third. I stood by the sink, belching and willing it all to stay down.

Within minutes, there was a warm rush of booze-induced relaxation. I headed for the bathroom, staggering a little and bumping into the doorframe as I passed.

Taking a deep breath, I positioned myself in front of the mirror. Ignoring the thunder of my heart against my rib cage, I forced my gaze up to the mirror.

The dream-woman wasn't peering over my shoulder, as I had expected. All I saw was my own pale face. My eyes were wide and bright with fear, my mouth drawn into a pinched line. There were faint lines crinkling the corners of my eyes, and a dusting of freckles dancing across my nose and along my cheekbones. My red hair, pulled back from my face in a messy ponytail, had yet to show any signs of gray.

The contours of my face were fascinating, as were my green eyes. How strange were a human's eyes, with their black pinpoints in the center, a pathway that could be followed inward to the very beginning, to the creation spark, an eye corridor right to the center of I.

As I watched, the small wrinkles around my eyes smoothed away, and my face rounded out. My nose grew rounder, too, and freckles disappeared from my cheeks. My lips plumped up, rosy and fresh with youth.

Younger and younger.

To the graceful perfection of the early twenties, and then younger, to eighteen, and younger still, into my early teens with the buds of womanhood beginning to blossom, and then that roundness disappeared into twelve, eleven, and I was full of awkward bony angles, and younger still, nine, eight, seven.

The child in the mirror looked back at me with awe. Her green eyes overpowered her pale face. Her red hair, *my* hair, flamed in soft clouds around a face that still held the last traces of babyhood.

She was full of fledgling promise. I felt an overwhelming desire, a *mother need*, to reach out and wrap her in my arms. The girl in the mirror. The me/not me.

"Find him. You need to find him." Her voice was a clear ringing bell, so sweet and so familiar.

"Find who?" I managed to croak.

"The truth-seeker."

"Who? What do you mean?"

"Find the one who searches for you. You need his help, if you're going to stop them."

"Stop who? I don't understand."

For a moment I thought she would say more. But then she looked over my shoulder and her eyes widened in horror. She screamed, and her voice rose octave after octave until the scream became silent. She was frozen in a rictus of terror.

I wanted to turn, to see what had caused her fright, but I, too, was frozen. I stared helplessly into her open mouth, her enormous green eyes. A fireball streaked across her eye-sky, trailing a tail of blue-white light. I fell back, landing hard against the tile floor.

"Find him!" she screamed, and then the world exploded.

CHAPTER THIRTEEN

"My name is Jack Elias Barbetti. I was born May 9, 2004. I live in Seaside, Oregon. My parents are Emma and Keaton Barbetti. My dad works at a sawmill. My mom died because—"

No, don't go there!

"I'm in fourth grade at Seaside Heights Elementary. My teacher is Mrs. Sutherland. My favorite subjects are math and science. My best friends are David McGregor and Mikey Parsons."

Jack's head was splitting open. The shots they injected every morning not only made him feel slow and far away, but the headache lingered until dark, when the sleepy-time injection took away all pain and consciousness.

He began the mantra again. "My name is Jack Elias Barbetti . . ."

It had been repeated so many times the words had lost their meaning. They were the strings that tethered him to a bunch of balloon-memories. But they kept trying to float off into the ether, while he clung desperately to the strings, knowing that to let go was to lose the Jack that was.

He didn't know where they had taken him, or how long he'd been there. His old life ended when the bee stung the back of his neck. He'd had just enough time to lift his hand to swat the bee away, hot dogs dropping unnoticed to the dirt, and then the whole world went black.

Some time later, he'd been swaddled in blankets in the backseat of a moving car. There was the sensation of speed, and he understood they were on a freeway.

The next time he regained consciousness, he was in a soft bed, covered with quilts that were scratchy against his cheek. When he rolled over, searing pain ripped through his skull, making him want to vomit. His eyes closed as he fought the wave of nausea. Eventually, he was able to crack open an eyelid and inspect his surroundings.

The walls were made of logs, rough and splintery. There was a wicker dresser in the corner. Slowly, he sat up. The room around him throbbed in time with the pounding in his temples, and he moaned and closed his eyes, swaying.

That first morning of his new life, a man in dark robes entered the small bedroom. Jack had learned about predators, about what men like this wanted to do with boys like him, and he gritted his teeth and vowed he wouldn't cry.

"Remember, Jack. Remember everything you see, and look for your chance to escape. When he does those things to you, you must go to the White."

Was that his voice, or his mom's? It didn't matter. He would obey.

Flattening his hands against his thighs, he pressed until the tips of his fingers were white. It took all his willpower, but he looked the man straight in the eye, taking a mental tally of his features and committing them to memory. Old and skinny, with narrow shoulders. Gray beard and bushy eyebrows. Soft brown eyes, with lots of wrinkles around the edges. Red cheekbones and nose, like he needed to use sunscreen.

He was dressed like a priest, and Jack found this very unnerving. The last priest he had met thought Jack was infested with demons.

But Jack knew where the demons lived, and it wasn't inside him. What a ridiculous idea! Father Santos hadn't understood Jack was of the White; no demons could enter his soul. They were all around him though, oh yes, they were. Jack knew them well, as they knew him.

"Are you going to molest me?"

The man seemed startled by the abruptness of Jack's question, and then somewhat horrified.

"No!" He sat on the edge of the bed, as far away from Jack as he could manage. "I am Father Gabriel, of the Holy Order of *I Fidele*. I am not here to violate you, or to harm you in any way. I am here to be your guide, your advisor, as you begin your new life here among your brethren."

"I want to go home."

"Of course you do. This time of transition is difficult, full of pain as one sheds the skin of the past. But like a snake, one must shed that skin to become new again. A wonderful life awaits you, my child—"

"I am *not* your child," Jack cut in.

"Nevertheless, in time you will, I hope, look to me as a father of sorts. Today—"

"My father is Keaton Barbetti, and I want to *go home* to *him*!" Jack stood on the bed and screamed directly into the man's face.

Father Gabriel wiped spittle off his cheek with the sleeve of his robe. "I'm sorry to tell you Keaton Barbetti is no longer your father. Soon, you will forget he ever existed, as you immerse yourself in your new life."

"I *won't* forget him, and I *won't* stay here!" And then Jack did the only thing he could think of to do. He filled his lungs and screamed. And screamed. And screamed.

Eventually Father Gabriel got mad. He leapt across the bed and clamped a large paw over Jack's mouth and nose, sealing his airway and stifling the scream, which lodged in his throat.

Up close, his eyes were pinwheeled with orange. His mask fell away, and Jack saw the demon that lurked behind it. He saw the forked tongue and the leathered gray face. He knew the demon for who it was. Jack's angels sprung to life, swarming around him with buzzing alarm.

"Shut up! Your father will soon be *dead*, along with the rest of the cockroaches who walk this earth. So shut . . . the hell . . . *up!*"

His hand tasted like roast beef. Jack bit down.

***

After biting Father Gabriel's hand, he was left alone for the better part of the day. The buzz of his angels swelled and receded as he lay, wide-eyed, on the scratchy quilt. Eventually, hunger and the need to use the toilet forced him to emerge from the bedroom. He found the tiny bathroom off the combined living room and kitchen area.

He peed, washed his hands in the bitingly cold water that emerged from the tap, and dried them on a purple towel.

He was alone in the small log cabin. The kitchen held a sink, a small ice chest, and a propane stove. Beside the kitchen was a scratched wood table with two mismatched chairs. A couch sat in the main living space, covered in a fraying red plaid quilt. Across from the couch was a dull gray chair with yellowed lace doilies covering the arms.

The floor was made of rough wooden planks, sanded but unstained. Jack pulled at the door, but it was locked from the outside. He wasn't surprised.

A red pillowcase covered the one small window. He pulled it to the side and stood on his tiptoes to look out. The window was only two feet across by one foot high, and it provided a view of trees, trees, and more trees. They were different from the ones he was used to, with thinner trunks and lots of needles.

In the ice chest he found bread, cheese, and milk. There were also apples, the Red Delicious kind. Jack made himself a meal and sat at the table, munching. His headache eased with the food and drink.

By the time Father Gabriel returned, right hand in a bandage, Jack was clearheaded enough to feel the full extent of his fear. He sat at the table, watching as Father Gabriel took the seat across from him.

"Well, then," he said. "Perhaps we should start again?" He waited a moment, but Jack remained still and watchful.

"As I said before, I am Father Gabriel. I will be your spiritual advisor here at *I Fidele*. This is a large place, with many children I'm sure you will befriend." He smiled, as though he expected Jack to get excited. Jack gave no response.

"In the beginning, we keep new children separated from the group, but it's only temporary. Think of it as a sort of cocooning; you come in here as a caterpillar and will emerge, in time, as a beautiful butterfly. But that will only be the beginning of your life here. You will join the *I Fidele* family, and your life will be given a purpose beyond your wildest imaginings."

He smiled again at Jack, and the smile was so sweet, so gentle, Jack could almost forget the demon he had seen lurking in the underworld of his soul. Almost.

"In fact, what we do here is very much like superhero training. Do you like superheroes, Jack?"

Despite himself, Jack nodded. Encouraged, Father Gabriel continued.

"Of course you do! Have you ever wished to be a superhero? I know I did when I was a boy, way back in the dark ages." He laughed, and Jack felt his lips curl up into the beginning of a smile.

"Well, I have a secret for you. Do you want to know what it is?" Father Gabriel leaned across the table, whispering. "The secret, Jack, is you actually *are* a superhero. But you already know that, don't you?"

Jack watched him, eyes wide.

"Of course you do! You've always been different than the rest of your friends, right? You've had secret powers no one else could understand, powers you've had to hide from *everybody*, even your *dad*. Isn't that right?"

Jack found himself nodding.

"Have you ever wondered *why*? Why you have these special powers no one else has? What their purpose is?"

Jack did wonder. He wondered all the time.

"Well, I have the answers to all those questions. Right here, at *I Fidele*, you are finally where you *belong*. Because we are all special here. We are all superheroes, and you are going to be joining an elite team of *superheroes in training*."

"There's no such thing as a superhero."

"Oh, but there is, Jack, there *is*!" Father Gabriel smiled. "Of course, you're right. Superman doesn't exist. Or Batman, or Spider-Man, or any of those other silly made-up superheroes. Their stories are fictional. But the *idea* of them? That had to come from somewhere real, don't you think?"

Jack shrugged.

"Let me ask you this. Are demons real?"

He stared at Father Gabriel, waiting for the mask to disappear again. When it didn't, he gave a small nod.

"And the White? Is that real?"

Jack was stunned. "You know about that?"

Father Gabriel laughed. "Of course! Who do you think we serve? The *I Fidele* family *serves* the White!"

"But you . . ." Jack stopped, confused. His angels had quieted to a low hiss. What did that mean?

"I know it's a lot to take in. Don't worry. For now, all you need to understand is we're your friends. You're *safe* here, Jack. Safe to be yourself, for the first time in your life."

There was a quiet knock, and then the door to the cabin opened. A woman in a red robe entered, smiling at him. Jack was stunned into stillness at the sight of her. He had never seen a woman so beautiful in all his life. She was like a golden princess. Her hair was long and silky, and it floated around a face so perfect it reminded him of the angels who had visited that time he ran a fever of 105.

"Hi, Jack." Her voice was like the tinkling of a wind chime, sweet and enticing. "I'm Maya. I'm here to give you some vitamins."

CHAPTER FOURTEEN

Everything returned to normal so quickly, it was like waking from a dream. My right hip was throbbing. I pulled myself up using the frame of the bathroom door, and stood there like a palm tree swaying in the breeze. The mirror girl was gone.

From the living room, my computer beeped to signal a new message in my in-box. It spurred me to action, and I staggered away from the bathroom. My laptop was open on the coffee table. The in-box was open, and the new message was highlighted at the top of the list. It was sent from my own e-mail address, rwilson@linear.com, and the subject line said "FIND HIM!"

Heart throbbing painfully against my rib cage, I clicked to open the message. It was blank. I leaned back against the cool leather, rubbing my temples. Had the girl in the mirror really been a younger version of me? And who was this truth-seeker she wanted me to find? And how in the world had I sent an email to myself while passed out on the bathroom floor?

"Maybe it's time to check yourself into the psych ward," I muttered to myself.

While that certainly seemed like the right place for me to be, instead I grabbed the notepad and pen Dan had used earlier. Perhaps if I put everything down on paper, it would all begin to make sense. At the very least, I could document my trip into insanity for any future psychiatrists, so they could dial up the dosage on my meds from "calm and complacent" to "comatose."

It took ten minutes to write down everything I could remember, from the *"Ricordare, Ritornare"* note to this latest vision. Then I started digging for any recollections of my childhood. My temples began to throb as I searched the blackness of my mind for some spark of memory.

The most important missing piece was my dad. I couldn't remember anything about him. Not his life, not his death. Shouldn't I have some kind of emotional response? Residual feelings of love? Grief? Had I felt those things yesterday, before that note had turned my life on its head? My tongue rolled over the ridges of the roof of my mouth as I thought back.

Yes, I was certain I had. That loss had been my traveling companion through the solitary journey of my twenties and early thirties. It had laid its head on the empty pillow beside mine. It had been the empty seat in the auditorium when I crossed the stage for first my BS and then my master's. It had stood sentry over my desk through endless hours of study. It had been my silent dinner companion at restaurant tables set for two, while I buried my nose in a book to avoid the questioning gaze of other restaurantgoers, and pretended I dined alone by choice.

Not twenty-four hours before, that grief was a part of my daily routine. Mine was a solitary existence that occasionally crossed over into loneliness, but more often than not was filled with the busyness of academia.

The Spaceguard Program had always been so much more than just a job. It was an obsession that had pushed me through each grueling course, from Astronomy 101 to the recent completion of my doctorate.

Relentless in my pursuit of scholastic achievement, I had never vacillated between different academic pathways. My goal of joining MIT's Linear program had been completely single-minded. Every academic step brought me closer to being a meteorite hunter with Spaceguard.

When they had posted the Space Data Analyst job three years before, I had jumped at the chance to move to New Mexico, eager to get my hands on those GEODSS telescopes.

It was thrilling to be on the front line in the hunt for dangerous meteorites. To be the first to find new threats, the first to study the telescopes results, the first to *know*.

Since moving to New Mexico, I felt a sense of peace for the first time in my adult life. I was exactly where I was supposed to be, and doing exactly what I was supposed to be doing. I was home.

Besides Dan, I had made no friends, and hadn't dated anyone, either. I had chalked it up to the lack of free time that came with working nights at Linear and completing a doctorate during the day.

But the truth was, I had rarely dated in Massachusetts, either, and any friends were more like acquaintances; I kept people at a safe distance. The more I liked someone, the more I distanced myself.

Dan was the exception, and although I had not analyzed the reason why, if asked I would have said Dan was closer to me than anyone else because I was so happy in my current situation.

With a shake of my head, I turned back to my notes. To the words "truth-seeker," circled over and over. Who could be considered a truth-seeker? I chewed on the pen while I pondered, letting the plastic bitterness tickle my tongue. Some kind of spiritual leader, like a rabbi or a priest? Or a scientist? Or maybe a journalist?

Pulling the computer back onto my lap, I typed "truth-seeker" into the Google bar. The first two hits were a news site out of the UK and a "freethinker" site in the US.

The UK site dealt in conspiracy theories and stuff the mainstream media wouldn't touch. I skimmed articles on militant rebels in Syria merging with Al-Qaeda, North Korea's latest crazy antics, and how the US Navy was apparently deploying a laser-prototype weapon near Iran.

Focusing solely on the men, I searched through their list of columnists. Several were listed as ex–Israeli army, or Middle East correspondents. None of the names jumped out at me, so I focused on the Americans for lack of a better idea.

One of them seemed to favor political rants aimed at the current president as well as 9/11 conspiracy theories. The other was an anti-Semitic propagandist who seemed to be blaming Jews for the paltry state of his life. It didn't seem like truth was high on his priority list. I closed the site and moved on to the next.

This one advertised as "Free Thought Publishers since 1873." The founder was listed as D. M. Bennett, the original "truth-seeker." This might have caused excitement, but he had died in 1882.

I refused to entertain the idea that someone who had died more than a century before was the person I needed to find, the person who was searching for me in return. A woman named Bonnie Lange, who spouted some gobbledygook about a magic community and getting in touch with the cosmos, was currently running the publishing company. Somehow I just didn't think I was on the right track there, either.

There was a site for a band called the TruthSeekers, who made some interesting music, but I couldn't find a tie to my current situation. There were numerous weird mystical or religious sites I was afraid to open for fear of infecting my computer with a virus.

The only other site that popped out at me was for a parapsychologist in the Las Cruces area. Despite a hefty dose of skepticism, I clicked on the link. It opened with some New Age music and I quickly hit the mute button on my keyboard.

At the top of the page was the slogan "Kahina Dokubo-Asari, Seeker of Truth." Underneath, there was a picture of a woman who was probably in her early fifties. She had a cloud of soft black curls that surrounded her head like a halo. Her skin was the rich color of coffee with a dash of cream; her brown eyes were wide set and gazed off into the distance. A small smile curled her lips as though whatever she saw out there was all right with her. I wasn't so sure.

She advertised as a medium and parapsychologist who specialized in helping people with post-traumatic stress disorder, those who had been the victims of violence, and people with unexplained phobias. She purported to help people cure themselves using "Hypnotism, Past-Life Regression Therapy, and Memory Repression Therapy."

My eyes wanted to roll up into my head, but I wrote down her number and vowed to call her at a reasonable hour in the morning. Her office was listed with an address on Alameda Boulevard, near Lohman Avenue. By car it was perhaps ten minutes from where I sat.

With a course of action set for tomorrow, I curled up on the couch and touched the power button on the remote. The TV sparked to life and I found a mindless comedy with which to pass the time, hoping sleep would overtake me. I had done enough truth-seeking of my own for one evening.

CHAPTER FIFTEEN

"I never drink water, fish get busy in it." Connie Fisher winked slyly as she slurped at her second martini. She pulled out the plastic stick and flicked her tongue indelicately over the blue cheese–stuffed olive. Her lips were coated in a glossy cotton-candy color with metallic sparkles.

"That's W. C. Fields. But I cleaned it up a bit for you." Some of her lipstick had made a home on her snowy-white front teeth. Josh guessed she had invested in caps; her teeth were too perfect. And was that a minuscule diamond embedded in one of her upper incisors? He thought it might be, and tried hard not to stare.

The problem was, Josh was at a loss as to where else to look. Connie had stuffed her ample frame into a purple pleather dress meant for a heroin-chic streetwalker one-quarter her size. Her breasts were plump globes that had been pushed up to her neck and then dusted in some kind of gold powder. Every time she leaned forward, he felt a flash of anxiety that they were going to pop right out of their casing and land on her lap. When the host approached to tell them their table was ready, Josh leapt off his stool.

Connie sashayed in her three-inch stiletto boots as they wound their way through the restaurant toward a two-person table near the fireplace, causing all eyes to focus on her as she passed. Josh studiously avoided the raised eyebrows of the other patrons in Filomena's, but he could feel his cheeks flushing with heat. He probably looked like a john with a shallow pocketbook and a fetish for forty-year veterans of the sex trade.

Once they were seated, Connie ordered another martini, and Josh, feeling the need for some liquid fortitude, switched from Perrier to a gin and tonic. Before he could even open his menu, Connie had scanned the appetizers and ordered the oysters Rockefeller and a steak tartare. She trailed a fingernail shaped like a red dagger down his arm, causing him to splash some of his drink on his shirt.

"To share," she said to the waiter, smiling coyly. The waiter nodded and made a slow retreat, seeming more interested in the view down the front of Connie's dress than in bringing their order to the kitchen.

"So, Josh," she purred, placing her chin in one hand and looking up at him through a thick rim of false lashes. "What's it like working at the FBI?"

He cleared his throat, hating how much this seemed like a date. "It's exciting work. I get to meet a lot of interesting people."

She laughed as though he'd said something witty, and fluffed her platinum-blond hair. "I'm sure you do. But it must get lonely at times, no?"

"Not really, no," he mumbled, pulling his legs away as she brushed them with hers under the table.

"So, listen, Ms. Fisher—"

"Connie, please."

"Frieda tells me you work in the Post-Secondary Division of NCES?"

"That's right."

"Do you know much about the PSST?"

"Straight down to business, huh? Can't a girl enjoy her meal first?" As if on cue, the waiter brought out the appetizers. Her eyes bulged in anticipation as the plates were set down in front of them.

"Oooh, that looks *good*," she breathed.

The waiter, who still had the last vestiges of teenage acne on his cheeks, solicitously unfolded her napkin and placed it in her lap. Josh could have sworn he brushed an arm against her breasts as he did it, and a look passed between them that was full of promise. Josh squirmed in his seat, and took a big gulp of his gin and tonic.

He stared at the ice cubes in his glass as Connie and the waiter discussed the menu, nodding in vague agreement to the steak and lobster dinner for two.

"Have an oyster, Josh." Apparently she wanted him to lean in and slurp it out of her hand. Instead, he grabbed one off the plate and downed it so quickly he barely tasted the brine and garlic. He dropped the shell on his side plate with a clatter.

"Very good," he muttered, because he felt he needed to say something. She shrugged and took the proffered oyster for herself.

Josh watched in discomfort as she licked the sides of the shell, her tongue making obscene flicking motions until it eventually teased the tender morsel of meat into her mouth. She closed her eyes and moaned in pleasure, causing an elderly couple at the next table to look over and smirk.

Josh could feel the sweat breaking out on his forehead. In self-defense, he began to stuff oysters into his mouth, eager to empty the plate as quickly as possible. She finished the last one and licked her fingers like a porn star.

Then she started on the tartare. A pile of raw beef had never been so sexualized. Josh was drenched in sweat and feeling woozy. She finally cleaned the plate and signaled the waiter for another martini, then caught Josh's eye.

"Are you all right?" she asked, dabbing at her mouth with the napkin.

"I'll never be able to look at a cow the same way again."

Her laugh was deep and sultry.

"You're funny," she cooed, and took the opportunity to trail a fingernail down his forearm, causing him to jump as if she'd given him an electric shock. "Tell me, Agent Metcalf, are you as innocent as you seem?"

"I suppose that depends on your point of view, ma'am."

"Oh, *ma'am*. That's *hawt*," she drawled, fanning herself.

"Listen, Ms. Fisher. *Connie*. I'd really like to speak with you about the PSST. Please."

"I used to be just like you, you know. Inhibited, shy. If someone said the word 'penis,' I practically passed out." She laughed, shaking her head. "I was married for twenty years to a professor from Georgetown, and he wanted a perfect little Stepford wife. I did the whole stay-at-home-mom thing. I baked pies. I served three-course dinners I barely touched for fear of losing my figure. I wore these buttoned-up dresses like Jackie Kennedy. I even ironed my husband's *boxers*, for heaven's sake.

"I was totally miserable. I mean, like, practically *suicidal*. The effort to keep up that ideal of perfection was sucking me dry. There was a Connie inside just dying to be set free. A beautiful, sexual being. And every year that Connie died just a little bit more. Finally, I just *snapped*. If you can believe it, I screwed the pool boy. I mean, can you get any more clichéd?" She laughed and took a big gulp of her martini.

"That was a transformative moment, though. I realized I was wasting my life being something someone else wanted me to be. I wasn't *me*, you know?

"So I left my husband. I started eating again. I got into yoga, and met this man who introduced me to tantric sex. It was like an awakening. I could feel my womanhood blossoming into . . . Josh? Agent Metcalf? Are you all right?"

"Yes ma'am. Oh, look! There's our food."

"How do you manage to stay so pure, working at the FBI? I'm sure you've seen things that would shock even me."

"That's probably true." But blood and guts were things Josh could handle. "I'd really like to ask you about the PSST. *Please.*"

"All right, all right." She plucked a piece of lobster meat off the tray and dipped it in butter. "What do you want to know?"

He got right to the point. "Any chance I could get my hands on a test?"

"Well, now, that depends."

"On what?"

"On what you're willing to do for me, of course." She grinned suggestively at him.

"Ms. Fisher—"

"Don't go getting your knickers in a twist; I'm just joking. I'll see what I can do, but I can't promise anything. They play it pretty close to the vest in that department."

"Why do you think that is?"

She shrugged. "I never gave it much thought."

"Any idea what kind of questions they ask on the test?"

"Well, I've never seen one for myself. I gather it's more psychological than the NAEP, which is focused on educational trends."

"What do you mean by psychological?"

She shrugged again. "Like I said, I haven't seen the test. I've just heard talk over the years. And they're mainly psychologists in that department."

"Really? That's interesting. Is that a requirement?"

"I don't know. As long as I've been there, which is fifteen years by the way, I've never seen them hire internally."

"They only hire people from outside the NCES family?"

"That's right."

"Huh." Josh didn't know what to make of that. "So would you say the PSST is more focused on learning about each individual child?"

"Definitely."

"And they test kids from kindergarten up?"

"Sure."

"Is it true they do oral exams with the younger kids, rather than written?"

"That's right. There's a team that travels the country administering the test. They begin on the East Coast every fall and finish on the West Coast by the late spring. The summer months are about data compilation, and then they start all over again the next fall."

"How many people are on this team?"

"Eight in total."

"Do you know them?"

"Not really. I've seen them around the office, mainly during the summer. They're an odd group though, and they stick to themselves. I guess that goes along with the territory, all those months on the road with just each other for company."

"So all the data gets entered into a computer program?"

She eyed him. "Now, Agent Metcalf. I've been a good girl so far. I've given you a lot of information without asking questions. But I know how you FBI people work, and it's usually all very official. Why do I get the feeling you're off the books on this one?"

He sighed and leaned back in his chair. "Because I am. This is a very sensitive investigation, Connie. The fewer people involved, the better."

"You over your head, darling?"

"I just might be. I'm not sure who can be trusted, and it's better if you don't know much about it."

"Am I in danger?" The idea seemed to excite her.

He shook his head. "I don't think so. But I'd appreciate it if you kept this conversation to yourself."

"Of course."

"Could you give me the names of the people who do the testing? And anyone else in that department?"

"I'll have to get back to you. They're around so seldom, I've never gotten to know them. But there's one guy in the office full-time, the program director of the PSST Division. He's a quiet guy, but really funny. Mainly keeps to himself, stays out of office politics. He's pretty hot. I've tried flirting with him a few times, but no luck. Maybe he's gay, I don't know."

"What's his name?"

"Sumner Macey."

Josh made a note. "Thanks, Connie, I really appreciate your help."

"Well, Agent Metcalf, you can pay me back anytime." She winked at him, sucking suggestively on a lobster claw.

They finished dinner, and Josh paid the bill. He gave Connie his cell-phone number, and she promised to call him with more information as soon as she could. He left Filomena's alone, politely declining her last-ditch effort to take him home. Connie shrugged off his rejection and swaggered back to the bar to wait for their waiter to finish his shift.

As soon as he was outside, he pulled his phone out of the breast pocket of his suit jacket and called. She was already laughing when she picked up on the other end.

"Frieda. I don't know whether to hug you or kill you."

"I take it she ordered the oysters?"

CHAPTER SIXTEEN

"You must be hungry. Join us for a meal." It wasn't a question, and Father Narda didn't wait for a response.

Sumner stepped through the doorway and into the intoxicating smell of garlic-roasted chicken, freshly baked bread, and the sweet cinnamon-nutmeg blend of apple pie.

He followed Father Narda's black robes toward the din coming from the dining hall. They passed the stone bust of Father Barnabas, standing sentry outside the library like a benevolent king. Out of habit, he kissed the tips of his fingers and touched them gently to the cold stone cheek. How quickly it all came back, like putting on an old coat and finding it was still a perfect fit.

As they approached the rear of the building, the dinner-orchestra separated into individual notes: the percussive clatter and clang of cutlery against porcelain, the lower staccato rumble of the Fathers involved in their nightly philosophical discussions, and the high-pitched purity of young voices engaged in excited chatter.

"Attention, my darlings!" Father Narda's voice boomed, and all eyes turned in his direction. Silence descended immediately. Within seconds, it was so quiet all Sumner could hear was the rapid thud-thump of his heart.

Taking a deep breath, he arranged his features into as neutral an expression as he could manage. He focused on a spot above the kitchen door, fearful of meeting the curious and probing eyes that turned toward him.

Keep your mind blank, he told himself. Focus on the good. Doesn't dinner smell delicious?

"We are blessed to be joined this evening by one of our returning Disciples. He has nobly sacrificed the last twenty-four years of his life for our mission on the Outside. Please join me in greeting Sumner, *Summoner of Spirits.*"

As one, the children stood. There must have been eighty in total. The youngest was perhaps three years old (one of the Chosen, of course) and the eldest, seated together at a far table, were in their midteens. In unison, their voices rose in the familiar chant.

From the ever-present light of the Righteous,
And the gloved strength of the Mighty,
And with Faith in the world to be,
And love to you from we,
We hail thee, Summoner of Spirits.
Welcome home, where you belong!

It was the same chant he had first heard upon his indoctrination into *I Fidele.* Despite all the years that stretched between the two moments, like half-forgotten tomes stacked between bookends on a dusty shelf, he felt just as small and scared.

He managed to nod at them, and Father Narda placed a hand on his back and guided him to a table where several young girls were eyeing him with awe.

"Watch your tongue," Father Narda said, and before Sumner could think of a snappy retort, he left to join the other Priests at their appointed table, which was at the head of the room nearest the kitchen door.

"Hello," he mumbled contritely, purposely taking a seat with his back to the Priests' table. Next to him was a petite Filipino girl, who scooted over to give him more room. He reached for the platter of chicken and potatoes and began scooping food onto his plate.

"Aren't you going to have any vegetables?" asked the girl seated across from him. She had shiny brown hair that she'd twisted into a long coiling bun on the top of her head. Her brown eyes were sharp with speculation. "Father Cassiel says you need to eat a lot of vegetables to keep your mind and body strong."

He scooped more potatoes onto his plate. "I once caught Father Cassiel eating a whole plate of doughnuts." The brunette looked scandalized, although the girl seated next to her, a blonde with pretty blue eyes, giggled.

"What's your name?" he asked. The brunette pursed her lips and looked down at her plate. After a moment, the blonde rolled her eyes and answered for her.

"That's Disa. Just ignore her; she's always like that. I'm Talia."

"I'm Bayani," the girl on the other side of him said quietly. "Is it true you've been Outside for twenty-four years?"

"That's right."

"You must be really old," Talia remarked, and Disa nudged her with an elbow. "What? I'm just saying!"

"I'm forty-two."

"Wow. You're older than my dad," Disa chimed in, and Sumner realized she was one of the Chosen. It explained her attitude.

"Who's your dad?"

Her lips clamped shut. This time Bayani answered for her. "Father Zaniel."

Sumner felt the shock ripple through him. Zaniel had been a good friend, once upon a time. He hadn't realized Zaniel was called to the Priesthood. Now that he knew, he could see Zaniel in the shape of her jaw, and in her brown eyes.

"Speaking of doughnuts, I could tell you all sorts of stories about your father, Disa."

Her mouth dropped open. "Really?"

He nodded, and waited for her to start asking questions. Instead she gave him another speculative look, and then closed up like a dandelion at nightfall.

Talia waited a breath before asking, "What's it like Outside?" All three girls leaned in, eager for his answer.

But he could feel Father Narda's gaze on him, a barely veiled threat. Sumner sent his mentor a curt response. *"Chill. I get it."*

He focused on Talia. "Not half as exciting as life on The Ranch. There aren't as many horses." Talia nodded, looking disappointed but resigned. They resumed eating in silence.

The food was delicious. The potatoes were fluffy. The chicken was redolent with garlic and fresh rosemary, and so succulent Sumner used a pillowy piece of bread to mop the juice off his plate. Over warm apple pie and vanilla ice cream, Sumner asked Talia how old she was.

"I'm nine," she responded, and he picked up the slightest hint of Boston twang.

They could mind-wash all they wanted, but there were some things they couldn't get rid of.

"Disa is ten, and Bayani is twelve."

He was surprised Bayani was the eldest of the three, since she was the smallest. His mind alighted on that briefly, but something bigger was cresting within him.

It was something he should have realized before, and might have if he hadn't been so overwhelmed by returning to The Ranch. Like the ultimate self-centered prodigal son, he had completely missed the obvious: he was responsible for them being here.

Well, not Disa, of course. But he was responsible for Talia, and Bayani, and the rest of the Disciples in the room. He felt a flush of heat prickle his scalp, and the room began to spin. The edges of his vision dimmed.

"Are you all right?" Bayani asked, and before he could pull away, she placed a small brown hand on his forearm. "You are unwell."

"Bayani is a healer," Talia said.

Sumner pulled away from her, trying to quell the shaking. "I'm fine; it's just been a long trip. I must be tired."

Bayani frowned at him. "Are you sure?"

A girl from Boston.

Nine years old.

They were all looking at him. The whole room had gone quiet. He could feel the tension at the Priests' table.

Careful. Careful, he thought.

But he couldn't stop his mind. It was flipping through a catalog of kids' profiles, searching out the match. And then he had it.

Four years ago. Mary-Beth Hammond. Five years old. She had displayed strong telepathic tendencies.

He gritted his teeth, desperate to clamp down on his racing mind. But it was too late. Disa picked up his thoughts.

"Who is Mary-Beth Hammond?" she asked, wide-eyed.

He couldn't help it; his eyes found Talia's across the table. Her mouth was open. Her skin was gray. Her blue eyes were glassy. He could almost hear the snap as her mind broke.

And then she started screaming.

***

"That was *most* unfortunate."

"I'm so sorry, Father. I don't know what came over me."

"Your level of control is not what it once was."

Sumner was slumped in the chair in Father Narda's study. "According to you, I never had much control."

"Yes, well . . ."

Beyond the study was the Priest's private bedroom. The door was slightly ajar and there was a pair of white lace panties hanging from the bedpost. Father Narda clearly had an *Amante*, although she wasn't present at the moment.

And speaking of lack of control, Sumner thought. He shook his head and returned to the subject at hand. "Will she be all right? Talia?"

Father Narda was removing his robe. He hung it from a hook behind his desk chair and sat on the recliner opposite Sumner. His beige pants were threadbare, his shirt dingy and gray.

"It's hard to say. She's Father Palidor's pupil. He'll work hard to repair the damage that was done. It would be a great loss to him if she were to require termination."

"Termination!" Sumner choked. "You're joking, right?"

"You know this is the way of things. Nothing can harm our mission. If she becomes a hindrance . . ." Father Narda raised his shoulders in a shrug.

"But . . ." Sumner sputtered. "She's only *nine*!"

"And a valuable asset. But what must be done *will* be done. Don't blame yourself, Sumner." The Priest caught him with his gentle brown eyes. The creases around them were much deeper, and his hair had gone gray. Otherwise, he looked exactly the same.

"It wasn't your intention to hurt the girl, but may it serve as a lesson. Everything you do has a potentially disastrous consequence, if you do not follow the straight path. Do you understand?"

Sumner nodded.

"Good." He rose with a grin. "My beloved Angeni is approaching. Let's speak more when she's out of hearing."

Sumner rose from his chair. He hadn't heard anyone approaching and doubted Father Narda had either—at least not with his ears.

"You'll stay the night. I'll have breakfast brought to your suite so we can avoid any more unfortunate occurrences."

"All right." He knew he had no choice.

"Angeni, there you are, my darling!" he said as the girl hesitated in the doorway.

"I'm sorry, Father. I didn't realize you had company." Her voice was as soft as silk. She was petite and doe-eyed, clearly of Native American origin. Her black hair was straight and hung down her back in a thick curtain. She was dressed in the red silk robe that befitted her status as an *Amante*.

"Nonsense, my dear. Please, come in." Father Narda eyed her with the greedy hunger of a ravenous teenager. "Let me introduce you to one of my dearest pupils. This is Sumner. Sumner, this is Angeni." The Priest wrapped a possessive arm around the girl's waist and pulled her forward.

Sumner nodded awkwardly and mumbled hello. Of course, he knew this was the way of things on The Ranch, but the years Outside had sharpened his vision.

"Angeni, why don't you prepare for me while I show Sumner to the guest suite."

She bowed her head and moved toward the bedroom. Father Narda grabbed her arm as she passed. She looked up at the Priest with dead eyes, and Sumner's heart squeezed painfully. Although they were brown, they reminded him of the blue eyes of the girl from long ago. His love. His heartache.

"The black lace, tonight, my dear."

"Of course, Father." She nodded at Sumner and disappeared into the prison of Father Narda's bedroom.

***

"It's a beautiful morning. Shall we take a walk?" Father Narda poked his head into the guest suite.

Sumner had slept fitfully, haunted by dreams that were likely twisted memories of his childhood. He had only picked at his breakfast of eggs, toast, and strawberries. He had finished the whole carafe of coffee, however, so he made a side trip to the toilet before joining Father Narda on the front porch.

The fall air was crisp and thin. He closed his eyes and took a deep breath. He could smell horses and cows and dying leaves, pine trees and pig slop and pancakes. It all mixed together to tug on the bitter roots that were intertwined around his heart.

"I'm glad to have you back, my son." Father Narda was smiling at him.

How many miles had passed beneath their rugged shoes as he and Father Narda walked, side by side, across the barely tamed wilderness of The Ranch? They had spent hours in such fashion, discussing *I Fidele* philosophy, or Sumner's burgeoning skills, or, during his teen years, the need to control his deepening interest in all things female.

For a time he was consumed with desire for Adelia, a dark-skinned beauty whose shocking blue eyes had captivated his young heart. She was quick-witted and joyful, full of laughter.

Adelia laughing. It was an image he still nurtured within his heart, her fragile glory forever captured in vibrant colors, untarnished by the heartbreak that came after. It was no wonder that he was in love with her, but he wasn't alone in his desire for her.

She was two years his elder, and though they had never shared more than a few stolen kisses, he was crushed when Father Narda took her as his *Amante*.

The jealousy drove him to the brink of insanity. For months he refused to so much as look in his mentor's direction, and he even made a formal request to the Priests that Father Cassiel take over his mentorship. That request was denied.

He could remember the torment of seeing her in the red robe, sitting in subservient silence at Father Narda's side. The first time he noticed her belly rounding out with the evidence of what the Priest was doing to her in private, Sumner went stark raving mad. With the classic stupidity of a fifteen-year-old boy, he hunted her down, certain he could make all things right.

Cornering her in the stables, he kissed her fervently and pushed her up against the paddock door amid the earthy scent of hay and manure. He felt the small swelling of her belly pressing up against him, and placed a possessive hand over it, trying in some desperate way to claim the baby as his own.

She kissed him back, and wept when he swore his undying love for her. He vowed to take her and the child away, promised her a new life on the Outside, far from the prison of *I Fidele*.

But she was older than him, wiser, and knew it was impossible. Just as hopelessly as a rabbit in a snare, she was trapped. She kissed him one last time. He felt the damp warmth of her breath on his cheek. As they parted, she did not say a word; she simply turned her back and walked away. Adelia leaving.

Never again did she speak to him. He watched from a distance as her belly swelled to an alarming size, and he heard quiet speculation about twins. Her skin grew wan, her hair and eyes dull.

On a bitter winter night she gave birth to twin girls. The babies were small, but viable. Adelia hemorrhaged, bleeding out to the sound of her newborns' first cries.

That night, Sumner awoke from a troubled sleep to find her sitting at his bedside, watching him. She smiled, and bent as though to kiss his lips. He felt her heated whisper on his skin. A moment later she was gone, a wisp of smoke curling toward the ceiling.

Adelia leaving.

***

"For what it's worth, I cared for her, too." Father Narda brought him back to the present. Sumner bowed his head, wounded by the Priest's words even as he doubted the truth of them. The last person with whom he wanted to share Adelia's memory was the man he blamed for her death.

Of course, Father Narda read this from him as well. He shrugged his shoulders, and they continued on in silence.

"Her daughters?" Sumner finally managed to ask.

The Priest smiled. "They are well. Beautiful girls. They look just like their mother."

"Are they—"

"On The Ranch? No. They are Outside," Father Narda said. Sumner was reminded of their habit of cutting each other off midsentence, already aware of what the other would say.

"Should we visit the stables?" suggested the Priest.

That long-ago moment of stolen passion was at the forefront of his mind, so Sumner shook his head.

"Very well—let's walk to the cliff."

"All right."

They made their way past the stables and riding ring, past the chicken coop, and into the shadows of the trees. Sumner was only half listening to Father Narda's discussion of the summer crops, what had fared well and what was a disappointment. He nodded in the right places and watched his feet, only coming back to the present when they neared The Hut.

Through a break in the trees, he caught a quick glimpse of the front of the cabin. The red fabric that hung across the small window twitched, and Sumner locked eyes with a boy on the other side.

"My name is Jack Elias Barbetti. I was born May 9, 2004. I live in Seaside—"

With all his force, Sumner sent his thoughts flying back at the boy. *"Oregon. I know you, Jack. Keep your mind shielded, and don't forget yourself."*

He broke contact and continued past the cabin beside Father Narda. Out of the corner of his eye, he saw the red fabric twitch back into place.

"Yes, we are well prepared." Father Narda nodded, stepping over a tree root that bumped out across the path. His brow was furrowed in thought, and Sumner released a breath. Perhaps the Priest was too distracted by his own thoughts to notice the brief communication between him and the boy.

"Our store of wheat, dried corn, and potatoes is enormous. Oh, you should see it; it's a thing of beauty! We also have enough dried fruit, meat, and fish to keep us going for decades to come if necessary. I wish I could show you the underground facilities, but they're off limits."

In shock, Sumner stumbled and caught himself against a low-hanging branch. "It's . . . *real?* The Underground?"

Like most children raised on The Ranch, Sumner had dreamed about The Underground. He'd dreamed of a giant shadowy labyrinth. Of row upon row of generators, fueled by the black water of a subterranean river. He had dreamed about plants and flowers and fruit trees happily flourishing under artificial lights, about bee colonies and animal runs and giant fish tanks. And air purifiers. Oh, yes. Hundreds upon hundreds of air purifiers.

Father Narda chuckled. "Of course. We're walking above it now."

Holy hell, Sumner thought. He looked down, but there was nothing unusual to see.

The trees gave way and they stopped near the cliff's edge. Hundreds of feet below them, the farm stretched away in neat rows. They watched the antlike figures harvesting the last crops of the season. Squash, broccoli, and beans were directly below them, and farther away the old green combine was moving along the rows of dried field corn.

"The time is fast approaching, Sumner. We are in the endgame now." Father Narda turned into the brisk wind and took a deep and satisfied breath.

"We are making our final preparations, and *you* have an important job to do."

"What is it?" Sumner was shivering. The wind was biting at him through the thin fabric of his fall jacket.

Father Narda turned to face him, and Sumner felt the probing at his mind, like a fingernail digging a trench into his forehead. He resisted as best he could.

"You are struggling with your faith." It was a statement.

"I'm all right."

"Are you?" Father Narda tipped his head to the side, studying the younger man thoughtfully. "You seem confused, lost. Am I right?"

Sumner shrugged. "I have my moments."

"Yes, I can see that. Always best to be honest, hmm? After all, *I Fidele* does not require absolute blind faith. It's acceptable to question our Doctrine. From time to time."

"It is?"

"Oh, most certainly! Even I have had occasion to question." The Priest's hands on his shoulders were warm, soothing. But his eyes were cold. "But time is too short to waste in such a way. If you hesitate, young ones will die."

"I . . ."

"The time of gathering is upon us. Our family is being awakened and called home. One by one they are mobilizing. Within the week we expect most of them to return to The Ranch. But the younglings who have not yet been taken, their lives are now in peril. We need to gather them in."

"All of them?"

"If you wish them to live."

"What . . . what's going to happen, Father?"

Father Narda's jaw tightened. "The details of Day Zero are not your concern, *Disciple*." The last word hissed through his teeth.

Sumner swallowed hard, knowing he'd crossed a dangerous line. More tentatively, he asked, "What's the time frame?"

"This must be done immediately; there is no time for delay. Do you understand?"

"Yes. Yes, of course."

"I do not need to remind you we are watching."

"No, Father."

"Good." He clutched Sumner's face between his bony hands. Despite the chill, his hands were hot. They seared Sumner's cheeks, and he tried not to wince.

"Sumner, I love you as my own flesh and blood. Follow the straight path. Don't force me to end your life."

CHAPTER SEVENTEEN

I was dreaming about horses. Huge, glorious creatures whose legs were as tall as I was. They had softly rounded bellies and thick coats, rich with their musky scent.

Broad hands encircled my waist and lifted me, up and up, as though I were no more substantial than a puff of cloud. My legs kicked out at just the right moment and came down upon the bare back of a pure white mare. A thrill of exhilaration rippled through my stomach. The mare's flesh was tense beneath my thighs, ready to take flight at my bidding. Tighten my legs against her flanks, and I would become the wind.

Curling my fingers into her coarse white mane, I leaned in. My hands were not my own. They were small, the color of coffee.

Go! Go fast! Fast! I want to fly!

The horse complied, galloping out of the darkness and into the open fields beyond, into glorious sunshine that blinded me with its beauty. Peals of laughter escaped my lips and were sucked back into the wind behind me, like tumbleweeds.

Free!

For those few precious moments, my body became one with the horse.

We were united, flesh upon flesh. And then we weren't.

The horse shied left, and I took flight, spinning free. But I didn't fall. Instead I flew. Up and up to the trees and beyond them to the watchful mountains. They were darkly beautiful and full of secrets, and I flew toward them, arms outstretched on the wind. They reached to embrace me with their shadows, but at that moment, ropy arms wrapped around my waist with urgent strength. They were demanding of me and loving me at the same time. My eyes closed over hot tears and I succumbed to the kiss. It was fervent, passionate, and desperate for more.

Although no longer a child, I was barely a woman. He tasted of salt and fear. I could smell hay and horse and sweet oats. His hand was hot against the firm swell of my abdomen, trying to possess what lay within. In response I felt the first butterfly tickle from inside, as though his touch had brought forth life and promise within me.

We were united, flesh upon flesh. And then we weren't.

He was demanding what could never be. I was weeping, grieving for the death of desire. Mourning for the life that was ending at the beginning.

I pulled away, and then I was floating, small and weightless on the breeze. The boy had sorrowful blue eyes. He was blond and beautiful, like an angel without wings. But I had wings, and it was time to fly. I tried to smile, to reassure him all would be well, but it seemed I could not lie.

So instead I turned to the shadow of the mountains, and let the wind blow me in their direction. The heat of the sun baked my shoulders and the top of my head. I closed my eyes and whispered my good-bye.

"Sumner . . ."

***

Her voice woke me. It was honeyed, sad, and peaceful at the same time. She touched my cheek in farewell, and was gone.

What had she said? That it was summer?

With bleary eyes, I focused on the ceiling. She had faded back into the ether along with her dream, but had left behind a tidal wave of sorrow that threatened to drown me if not released.

Hot rivers of tears coursed down my cheeks, and my nose clogged. Rolling onto my side, I curled into a ball, trying to protect what was inside me. But my abdomen was flat and empty. I could still feel that butterfly promise, but there was no swelling of life there.

My body shook with sobs and I succumbed, unable to control this grief that was not my own. It had to run its course. Eventually it did, and I lay on the couch, wounded and wiped clean.

On the TV, the morning news anchor was telling the latest tale of tragedy and woe through her plastic smile. The empty tub of rocky road was lying under the coffee table, leaking brown sludge onto the floor. The harsh morning light wedged daggers through the gaps in the blinds.

My head pounded, and my sinuses felt clogged with tears. Groaning, I eased myself upright. My right hip was still throbbing from my fall in the bathroom, and I added that to the list of gripes, along with a stiff neck from sleeping on the couch.

I rose unsteadily and stumbled to the bathroom. The coolness of the damp cloth brought instant relief to my puffy eyes, but I made sure to step away from the mirror before removing it.

While a double-strength pot of coffee brewed, I cleaned up the ice-cream mess in the living room. I filled my MIT mug with coffee and popped two Advil.

There were two new e-mails in my in-box. One was from the Illinois Department of Public Health, confirming that my request for new documents was being processed. The other was from Dan, asking how I was doing. I told him I was feeling better and would see him at work that evening. There was no point in dragging him further into my mess.

It was almost nine in the morning, which was the time I would normally be hitting the pillow. My sleep schedule had been turned on its head, for which I would pay the price later. In the meantime, I would take advantage of being awake during daylight hours, and hope to catch a nap before work.

I showered and dressed in a pair of jeans and a black T-shirt, tying my wet hair into a ponytail before I grabbed my purse and headed out into the stark daylight. The glare made me squint, and my temples pounded. I hoped the Advil would kick in quickly.

The address corresponded to a small office building near St. Paul's Methodist Church. It was surrounded by a dusty, half-empty parking lot.

If the directory was up to date, at least half of the offices were vacant. There was a small sign with a phone number to call if I was interested in renting office space. Several doctors were listed, as well as a few dentists and small law firms and a private detective agency.

Kahina Dokubo-Asari had an office on the second floor. I took the stairs, which smelled of someone else's breakfast. The second floor was dim. Half the fluorescent lights were burned out, leaving the others buzzing in indignation.

I expected a reception area, so instead of knocking, I simply opened the door and walked in.

"Oh! I'm so sorry!" I sputtered, retreating from the enormous denim backside protruding from underneath the coffee table. I had practically kicked her in the rear.

She wiggled out, exposing a broad back and then a head of black curls. The woman turned and plopped down with an indelicate grunt.

"Oh! I wasn't expecting anyone!" She placed her hands on the floor and pushed herself up, then dusted off her meaty thighs. She was almost six feet tall, towering over my five-foot-two frame. She was older than in her website picture, her dark curls laced with gray. "Do we have an appointment?"

"I'm sorry, I didn't think to book one. I thought I'd just stop by . . . I can come back later."

"Oh, not to worry! I'm not doing anything other than searching for my darn glasses. Again!" She fanned herself with one hand. "Getting old is such a bitch!"

"Um, are those your glasses?" I asked, pointing to the top of her head.

"Oh, for heaven's sake!" She pulled them out of the tangle of hair. "How embarrassing! You must be wondering what kind of psychic I am!"

"Not at all," I said politely, although that was exactly what I was thinking.

"Well, thankfully one can be a psychic and a complete scatterbrain at the same time. I'm living proof!" She laughed, and I had to smile. She was charming and self-deprecating, and instinctively I liked her.

"I'm Kahina. What's your name, dear?"

"Rowan Wilson."

"Rowan, as in witchwood? Interesting. Did you know the wood from a rowan tree was used to ward off witches? Why don't you have a seat?"

I waited while she cleared a pile of papers from a red vinyl recliner, and then did as she suggested. She pulled the lid off one of the tins on the coffee table and took out a pinch of fragrant tea leaves, which she sprinkled into a pink mug. She poured steaming water on top and handed it to me.

"It's good for headaches." She sat across from me in one of those fake-leather desk chairs on wheels, and waved off my look of surprise.

"Anyone with moderate observational skills could see you have a headache. Your eyes are pinched and puffy-looking. You've either been crying a lot, or you have a hangover. Or maybe both."

"Thanks," I said, and took a sip. It was hot and tasted of mint, ginger, and something bitter I couldn't place. I set the mug on the coffee table to wait for it to cool.

"So, what can I do for you?"

"Well, I saw on your website you work with people to retrieve their repressed memories?"

"That's right. It's called recovered memory therapy. It's controversial, not considered part of mainstream practice. Most of the concern in the medical community is about false memory syndrome. There have been a number of cases where people reported childhood sexual abuse that was later disproved. I'm very careful when using this therapy, of course. It does no good for my clients to come up with memories that are untrue."

"How do you avoid that?"

"Studies have shown false memories can be implanted by a therapist using a technique called familial informant false narrative procedure. In other words, the therapist enforces a memory by explaining that a family member or some other trusted person has confirmed the false memory is true.

"So it's pretty simple, really. I don't overstep my boundaries. While I have a subject under hypnosis, I make sure they take the lead. Any questions I pose will be to help clarify, and I never push a subject in any direction. I let them tell the story."

"Are you a psychologist?"

She nodded. "I got my degree from Stanford. Most of my colleagues wouldn't be quite so generous as to call me that, though. They're more likely to call me a New Age nutbar." She grinned, and I smiled in return.

"It's true that most of what I practice is outside the mainstream of psychology, but I went into the field with hopes of answering questions about myself I couldn't seem to find answers to."

"Like what?"

"Like why I knew things others didn't. Why I saw things no one else could see. Why my dreams often predicted future events.

"Unfortunately, a doctorate in psychology didn't help answer those questions. For a long time, I was very disappointed. Eventually I realized that to truly help people, to practice therapy that would be genuinely effective, I needed to combine my book knowledge with my God-given talents." She shrugged. "And so here I am."

"So, do *you* believe false memories can be implanted?"

"Most certainly. I've helped numerous patients overcome false memory syndrome and get to the truth."

"Do you think it's also possible to erase real memories?"

She pursed her lips in thought. "I'd imagine so. The brain has an amazing capacity to forget. Under the right circumstances and with a patient in a suggestible state, I'd say that would absolutely be possible."

There was a moment of silence while I digested this information, and then she asked, "So, what does this have to do with you?"

I shrugged. "I'm not sure. Some strange things have been happening, and I don't know what it all means."

"Do you want to tell me about it?"

"It's hard to put into words. But I think I might have been implanted with false memories of my childhood."

"Are you talking about abuse? Or traumatic events?"

"No, not like that. I, um, think my whole childhood might have been a false memory."

"What?" she blinked at me. "Your *whole* childhood?"

I nodded.

"Can you give me an example?"

"Well, I don't really remember anymore."

She leaned back in her chair and looked at me. After a long moment of contemplation, she said, "I don't understand what you're saying."

"It's a long story, and very confusing."

"I have time."

"All right." I took a long swallow of tea. "Until yesterday, I remembered being raised in Chicago by my dad, who died of congestive heart failure when I was eighteen. I had millions of memories of a normal childhood. A couple of nights ago I was at work, which is out on the White Sands Missile Range, and I received a card. It said '*Ricordare, Ritornare,*' which means 'Remember, Return' in Italian. I understood it, even though I've never studied Italian."

"That's odd," she said, and I nodded.

"Right. It scared me. I actually passed out, which I've never done before . . . I don't think." I shook my head. "Anyway, at that moment, it's like some kind of switch got flipped inside me."

"What do you mean?"

"My life before college has become a big black hole. I remember that my dad died when I was eighteen. But it's just a piece of information, like if I told you two plus two was four. I don't have any real memory of him, or of his death. I don't have any emotion about it, although I'm sure I once did."

"Do you remember anything about your childhood?"

I shook my head. "It's like I was born the day I began college. Everything after that point in my life is clear and normal."

"Well, how fascinating!" she exclaimed.

"I guess you could say that. There's more, though." I hesitated, caught by the same reticence that always took hold of me. But she claimed to have the same ability. And maybe she even did.

"Yes?"

"I'm also able to see things, and know things, others can't. I've had that ability as long as I can remember—" That stopped me, and I had to laugh. "Well, that means less today than it did a couple of days ago, but still."

"You're psychic?"

"I've never categorized myself that way."

"Ah. A closet psychic."

I smiled. "I've never been very comfortable with it."

"In my experience, none of us are. Very few psychics find the will to turn it to their advantage. And even for those of us who do, it's still more nightmare than gift most of the time." She rolled toward me, wheels squeaking across the carpet.

"It might help me gain some insight if I do a reading. Would you mind?" She held her hands out to me. Her palms were pink and callused, and after a moment of hesitation, I placed my hands in hers.

"Great. Now, close your eyes and take some deep breaths. Don't worry!" she said as I looked at her with alarm. "I'm not hypnotizing you. I just want to see what I can pick up. The more you relax, the better."

At her bidding, I closed my eyes. All I could hear was her breathing. Eventually she pulled back, wheels squeaking, and I opened my eyes.

She had pulled as far away from me as she could manage, and was looking at me with horror.

My heart lurched. "What's wrong?"

"Everything is dead!" She leapt up. The chair spun away and crashed against the far wall.

"What?"

"You need to leave!"

"What? I don't understand! What did you see?"

"You walk with death. No, not just death. Annihilation! Extinction!"

"What! Please, I don't . . . what do you mean?"

"You must leave! Please, *please* you *must* leave!"

Tears stung my eyes and burned the back of my throat. I stood up on trembling legs and reached out for her. She shrank away from me as though I were a demon.

"Please help me! I don't understand what's happening to me! I'm so scared . . ."

"Get out! You have brought evil to my doorstep!"

"How? I don't understand! Please, help me to understand?"

She was shaking her head, hands over her mouth as though she had just witnessed the murder of her entire family, or something equally horrific.

"You must go! There's nothing I can do for you."

"Kahina, *please* . . ."

"Just go!"

Sobbing, blinded with tears, I turned to the door. Just before I left, I turned back to her. She was on her knees, weeping, her head bowed to her chest.

"Who is the truth-seeker? Do you know?" I asked.

She raised her head, piercing me with her red, streaming eyes. She looked like a ghost.

"What does it matter? He'll be dead soon, too."

CHAPTER EIGHTEEN

"I've got that information. Where can we meet?" Connie whispered seductively, and Josh rolled his eyes.

Still, he was eager to get those names, and equally eager to get out of the office. He had spent the last two days at his computer. Getting some fresh air sounded good. He stretched, feeling the satisfying pop of his vertebrae as they realigned.

"Is it still sunny out there in the real world?"

She chuckled. "It is."

They agreed to meet in front of the Vietnam Veterans Memorial at 12:15. She offered to bring lunch, and he agreed. Hanging up, he checked his watch. It was 11:00 a.m.; he had plenty of time to get some exercise.

After locking the door to his office, he changed into sweatpants and a Georgetown sweatshirt. He pulled on his Reeboks, thundered down the stairs, and exploded out into the sunshine with the glee of an escaped convict. He headed west on F Street at a fast clip, relishing the mindless rhythm of his shoes slapping the pavement as his body adjusted to the inertia of forward motion.

He'd spent the morning submitting the latest DNA samples to the Evidence Control Unit, or ECU. In 2000, the FBI began the National Missing Persons DNA Database, or NMPDD, to assist in the identification of missing persons. The DNA was gathered from hair samples, toothbrushes, or other sources such as saved baby teeth, and sent to the ECU for analysis. The information was then uploaded to CODIS, the Combined DNA Index System.

Over the past decade, Josh had been gathering DNA samples for the children who had gone missing prior to the inception of the NMPDD. This required tracking down scattered family members to get familial samples, which could be obtained by a cheek swab.

It sounded simple enough, but since the cases spanned the last five decades, the task was extremely tedious. For accuracy, DNA samples were required from more than one relative. Ideally, a sample could be obtained from the mother and father of the missing child. Samples obtained from siblings were less useful, and as a last resort, a sample from a maternal relative could be used. A sample from a paternal relative was useful only if the missing child was a boy.

It was a sad fact that many marriages didn't withstand the grief of losing a child, and divorce was common. This presented a challenge when searching for the biological mother, who had often remarried and changed her name. Finding female siblings presented the same problem.

With the older cases, the search for the parents often ended in death certificates, and surviving family members were hard to find. Josh had a stack of cases awaiting a second DNA sample so they could be submitted to the ECU.

Just to add to the challenge, the ECU allowed only five submissions per month. Josh often had to sit on DNA samples for several months before he was able to submit them.

To date, he'd managed to collect DNA samples for almost half of the children who had gone missing prior to implementation of the NMPDD.

Josh turned on 15th Street and jogged along the south lawn of the White House. He crossed Pennsylvania Avenue and continued past the oval drive of the Ellipse. It was a large grassy area that had been used as a trash dump and a slaughterhouse, and, for a time during the Civil War, it had even housed soldiers. Currently the Ellipse was the location of choice for everything from protest demonstrations to rock concerts.

At Constitution Avenue he turned west, jogging alongside the greenery of Constitution Gardens. He still had forty minutes until his meeting with Connie, so he cut down to the Reflecting Pool and ran the length of it between the Lincoln and World War II Memorials. He entertained himself by watching the camera-wielding tourists, picnickers, and locals out for some lunch-hour exercise.

On his second round he slowed to a brisk walk, stretched, and plunked down on the grass beside the Vietnam Veterans Memorial.

Connie arrived five minutes later, tottering along the grass in snakeskin heels. She was dressed like an eighties heavy-metal groupie, in an acid-washed denim miniskirt and skintight Mötley Crüe T-shirt, her blond hair teased into a hair-sprayed cloud Josh just knew would feel crunchy.

He tried not to goggle at her, wondering what on earth her coworkers thought. He was used to the strict dress protocol of the FBI, where even the women dressed in boxy suits.

Smiling, she dropped a takeout bag onto his lap. "Well, my oh my. There's nothing sexier than a man all sweaty and hopped up on endorphins. Howdy, Agent Metcalf."

Her lipstick was bright purple, and the diamond in her incisor twinkled in the sunlight. She sank down beside him on the grass, her skirt sliding up her generous thighs toward her hip bones. He caught himself staring and hastily averted his gaze, only to see her smiling devilishly at him.

"Hello, Ms. Fisher. It's nice to see you again."

"Come on, now, only my kids' teachers call me that. *You* can call me Connie." She had changed her nail polish to match her lipstick.

Desperate for a change of focus, he turned to the paper bag she had dropped into his lap. It was radiating warmth onto his legs.

"Thanks for lunch. So, what did you bring us?" Unrolling the top, he peered in and groaned.

"What's the matter?" Connie asked with feigned innocence. "Don't you like corn dogs?"

***

Josh got back to the office at 1:30 and tucked the envelope Connie had given him into a locking file cabinet. He grabbed his suit and toiletry kit, locked the office door behind him, and headed for the nearest shower, which was adjacent to one of the gym facilities on the third floor.

Back in his office fifteen minutes later, he pulled out the envelope and grabbed a bottle of water from the minifridge. He ripped open the envelope and pulled out the single piece of paper.

Connie had come up with the names of four of the PSST testing agents, and noted the name of Mr. Macey's personal assistant as well.

The information had been gathered from Mr. Macey's assistant, a man on the prowl after a recent bitter divorce. She had promised to get more, explaining slyly that they had made after-hours plans. She was clearly enjoying playing secret agent, and Josh reminded her to be discreet.

"Don't worry. Sumner Macey is out sick right now. He'll never know I've been poking my nose into his business." She seemed confident, and he decided it was worth the risk. He would risk quite a bit to get his hands on one of those PSST tests.

In the meantime, he turned his attention to the information she had given him. He ran each of the names through NCIC, the National

Crime Information Center. There were no outstanding warrants and no criminal records. None of them were suspected terrorists, sex offenders, foreign fugitives, or missing persons. He grunted in frustration and rubbed his neck, taking a giant gulp of water.

He logged onto the newest tool at his disposal, the Data Integration and Visualization System. The DIVS was a new database search tool with the ultimate goal of gathering data from different sources and compiling it in one place. There were still plenty of kinks to be worked out, but it would eventually provide the ability to search hundreds of millions of documents gathered from different sources, saving agents time, resources, and plenty of gray hairs.

"Curiouser and curiouser," Josh muttered, fingers clacking over the keyboard. There was nothing. Not even a speeding ticket. No bad credit. *Nothing.*

This would require legwork. Josh decided to start with Sumner Macey. He made note of his address in Temple Hills, grabbed his suit jacket off the back of the chair, and left the office. It was time to pay some of Mr. Macey's neighbors a friendly visit.

CHAPTER NINETEEN

"What is it, Evelyn?" Executive Administrative Director Dean Forster barked into the phone, running a sweaty hand over the stubble on the top of his head. Large wet patches had seeped through the armpits of his creased white dress shirt, and the ugly pink tie his wife had given him for his last birthday was hanging like a limp penis over the edge of the file cabinet.

He was having a bad day. A very bad day indeed.

First, the director, Roger Whitehorne, had raked him over the coals for that Abousamra mess, blaming Dean for those incompetent idiots who had lost Abousamra just before he killed that family in Silver Spring.

Then that dumb-ass jury had failed to indict Xian Lim in that human trafficking operation. The evil bastard was going to walk, flushing thousands of man-hours down the toilet. They would have to start all over again.

And for the icing on the cake, he was in the midst of staff evaluations, under orders to cut back on much-needed agents due to budgetary concerns. These days, all the money was being funneled into the Counterterrorism Division, and where the money went, the agents had to follow. This meant more cuts to the already-taxed Criminal Investigations Division, and he was seething as he flipped through the personnel files.

"Agent Spring is here to see you. He says it's important."

Oh, hell. Agent Lewis Spring's presence could mean only one thing.

"All right," he grumbled. "Send him in."

Agent Spring was young, still brimming with the internal fire that made him choose the FBI as a career. His brown hair was cut with military precision, his clothes so neatly pressed it was hard to imagine a drop of sweat daring to make its way onto the pristine fabric. He was green, eager, and a quintessential rule follower, which was why Dean had chosen him for the task. He was also an IT genius.

Agent Spring was honored to the point of apoplexy to receive direct orders from the executive administrative director. He never paused to question the validity of Dean's request.

"I take it you have some news for me, Agent Spring?"

"Yes, sir. I set up the net exactly as we discussed. It's been operational for eight months now, and I test it once a week to make sure it's working."

"Yes, yes." Dean Forster waved a hand in the universal signal for "hurry it up, already." "And?"

"Well, it's never picked up a single hit. But today it started pinging all over the place. I thought maybe something had gone wrong with the programming, but I double-checked everything and it's all good."

"Agent Metcalf?"

"Yes, sir." Agent Spring bobbed his head excitedly. "He's been searching both the NCIC and DIVS today, and six of the names you gave me pinged."

"I'm sorry, did you say *six?*"

"Yes, sir. Here's a printout." Agent Spring pulled a folded sheet out of his breast pocket and handed it over.

Although his legs were trembling, Dean forced himself to stand. As calmly as he could, he shook Agent Spring's hand. He ignored the quick grimace of distaste that flitted across the young agent's face at the feel of his sweaty palm.

"Good job, Agent Spring. Let me know if you get any more pings." Agent Spring left smiling, and Dean sat down behind his desk and unfolded the piece of paper.

Jessica Halliwell
Rupert Vargas
John Easton
Penelope Divisario
Mary-Ellen Litchfield
Sumner Macey

"Shit." He picked up the phone. "Evelyn, get Deputy Director Warner for me."

As he waited to be connected to the Office of Congressional Affairs, he sorted through the pile of staff folders on his desk until he found Agent Spring's file. He pushed it to the side of his desk.

Agent Spring was about to receive a transfer to the Counterterrorism Division, along with a nice jump up the pay scale.

CHAPTER TWENTY

The cowgirl was sitting at the same table at the Peaks Cafe in the Cheyenne Regional Airport, newspaper propped in front of her as she sipped from a takeout coffee cup.

Well, shit. Sumner blinked, unnerved.

If not for the fact that she was wearing different clothes—snug jeans and a tight black T-shirt—he would have wondered if she'd ever left.

Although he'd been warned he would be watched, the notion of having to ignore her bumbling surveillance was daunting.

And weren't they a bunch of psychics? Was having this chick follow him around like a well-trained puppy really the best they could do?

Quickening his pace, he shook off his annoyance. There were way more important things to worry about. Joining the long lineup at the ticket counter, he obediently shuffled forward, chewing on his lip as he worried the problem.

What the hell was he going to do?

Sumner had been turning this over in his mind since the moment the gates of The Ranch miraculously opened, allowing him to live another day. The brief exultation that flooded through him at this unexpected gift of life was quickly doused by the stark reality of the situation.

Walk the straight path or die.

It should have been a pretty simple choice, really. And technically, it wasn't a hard job to do. A few minutes at the computer and all the information would be transferred to the right people. Agents around the country would swarm upon unsuspecting children, ripping them from their families.

It was a job he had been doing for over a decade, albeit in blissful ignorance for most of that time. But that all changed six months ago, when the note in his mailbox started his awakening.

Since then, he'd learned some tricks to try to quell his conscience. He'd drink until he forgot he had just pointed his electronic finger and destroyed another life, filling the empty hours of the night with booze and whatever Western was on TV.

But now he was stone-cold sober. And he couldn't deny his culpability anymore.

From the safety of his office, just how many kids had he kidnapped? How much heartache had he caused? How many families had he destroyed?

Anguish twisted a knot in his gut. He couldn't ignore the truth any longer. He knew what happened to the kids he selected, so how could he continue? And yet, if Day Zero was approaching, how could he not?

In the end of days, could an evil act be turned on its head? Could it become the honorable thing to do? If gathering them in meant saving their lives, he thought it was possible. How ironic to continue to do the wrong thing, but this time for the right reasons.

He reached the front of the line and bought his tickets. Cheyenne to Denver to Washington, DC. As he passed the cowgirl, his frustration boiled over, and he blasted her.

"Ora, go back to your girlfriend. And unless you're willing to let me watch, stay the hell away from me. Tell the old bastard I'll follow the straight path."

She gave no response save the irritated flutter of her newspaper, and he continued past her to his gate.

***

The next time he saw her was during his layover at Denver International Airport. He had two hours to kill until boarding. He grabbed a *Denver Post* and a beer and settled into a deep booth at the Boulder Beer Tap House. To hell with not drinking.

When she sat down across the table from him, he was engrossed in an opinion piece about the Denver Broncos' aging quarterback. He looked up, startled. She was smiling and casually sipping beer from a bottle.

From a distance, she had seemed Barbie-doll perfect, but up close her bottom teeth were crooked and her upper lip was plumper than the bottom one, making her mouth into a bow. Her nose was a bit too big for her face and covered in freckles, and her blue eyes were wide-set and slanted down at the outer edge. She was young and perky and he did his best not to stare at her cleavage.

"Are you sure you're old enough to be drinking that?" he managed, and she rolled her eyes in response.

"Do you want to see my ID?"

Leaning back in his chair, he took a sip of beer as he appraised her. "What do you want?"

"Are you really going to continue to be one of their sheep?"

Taken aback by her directness and the obvious disdain in her voice, he shrugged noncommittally. "I said I would follow the straight path."

"The one that's paved with ill intentions?" She was probing at his mind, looking for the key to unlock the dead bolt and let herself in. He clamped down, staring back at her stubbornly.

"You're pretty strong. But I'm stronger," she said.

"Oh really?"

Tipping her head back, she drained the bottle. Against his will, his gaze traced the length of her neck. Down and down.

"Yup. You'll see."

"You're pretty confident for someone so newly out of diapers," he said gruffly.

She laughed, flipping her blond hair over her shoulder. "Go on, try to read me," she dared.

Not one to resist a challenge, he set down his glass and focused on her. She was closed. Completely closed, impossible to read. He tried nudging at her from one direction, and then another. While beads of sweat popped out on his forehead she sat there smiling, completely at ease. With a loud exhale he gave up and leaned back against the chair.

"Impressive," he admitted.

"That's not the half of it." She waved a hand in casual dismissal.

"At least you're modest about it."

They paused while the waiter slapped a basket of fries down in front of him, along with a couple of napkins. She wiggled her empty bottle, indicating she wanted another, and then eyed his fries.

"Ooh, those look good. Mind if I share? I'm starved."

The basket slid across the table as if magnetized and stopped right in front of her. She popped a fry into her mouth and chewed vigorously.

"Do you like ketchup?" she asked, and before he could answer the bottle lifted off the table. It hung suspended in the air in front of his nose. The cap turned once, twice, three times, and fell to the table with a clatter. The bottle upturned and a glob of red sauce plopped onto the fries.

He grabbed the bottle and twisted the cap back on. "I don't like ketchup, and I don't like show-offs."

Before he could pull the basket away, she snatched a handful of fries and stuffed them into her mouth, smiling cheekily at him.

"Why didn't they ship you off to The Command with the rest of the Telekinetics?"

"Because I'm one of the Chosen. *Duh.*"

Her teenage attitude was tiresome, but that did explain her strength. And speaking of which . . .

"So you *allowed* me to read you in Cheyenne?"

"Of course. If I didn't want you to see me, you wouldn't have." She wiped the grease off her fingers and slid an e-ticket across the table to him. "That's for you."

He glanced down. It was a Southwest flight to Houston, leaving in an hour and a half.

"What's in Houston?"

"Maybe nothing. Maybe a chance to redeem yourself."

"What do you mean?"

"'Just how many kids have I kidnapped?'" she imitated in an insulting falsetto. "'How much heartache have I caused? How many families have I destroyed?'"

"Okay, I get it."

"You have a choice to make, *Summoner of Spirits.* Fly back to DC and continue to walk the straight path, or fly to Houston and fight back."

"And what makes you think I'd go with you?"

"This," she said, and shoved an envelope toward him. Apparently she had fished his letter out of the UPS drop box. He picked it up and stuffed it into the inside pocket of his jacket.

"They'll know if I go to Houston. I'll be dead within hours."

She shook her head. "I can shield you from them. They won't know where you are, just that you're not in DC."

His stomach clenched with anxiety. "But . . ."

"There's no 'but.' It's time to choose. Are you going to be an *I Fidele* patsy and contribute to the destruction of the world, or are you going to go down with your guns blazing? It's your choice, Sumner. And for the first time in your sorry life, you actually have the freedom to choose. We won't force you. We're not like *them*."

"We?"

She nodded. "Come see for yourself."

"Wait!" he said as she stood up. "Why should I trust you? Who are you?"

Her smile was tight, and it didn't reach her eyes. "Even *I Fidele* has black sheep. Kids who will never meet their parents' expectations." Placing her empty beer bottle on the table, she said, "I hope to see you again."

She left him in the Boulder Beer Tap House with trembling hands and a stomach that churned with anxiety.

***

"Sir, are you all right?"

"Huh? Oh, sorry. What did you say?"

"I asked if you were done with that newspaper."

"Oh. No. I mean yes; go ahead." He folded the paper and handed it over to her.

"Are you all right? You look a little pale." She was a grandmotherly sort, and he sensed her desire to reach out and feel his forehead.

"I'm all right. Thanks."

"Nervous flyer?" she asked sympathetically, and he nodded.

"Well, don't worry." She patted his shoulder. "I've got good instincts when it comes to these things. Everything is going to be just fine, you'll see."

His smile was halfhearted. With another pat on the shoulder, she moved away.

For what must have been the thousandth time, he checked his watch, counting the minutes until it would be too late. There were forty until the flight to Houston departed, and here he was sitting at the United gate in Terminal B, one train ride away from the Southwest gate in Terminal C.

Follow the straight path and save some kids' lives. Follow the cowgirl and maybe save the world.

But what if it was a trap? What if Father Narda was using her to test his loyalty?

Groaning, he folded in on himself, rocking from side to side in an agony of indecision.

"Are you sure I can't help you?" It was the grandmother again. Her boxy black shoes were visible from the space between his knees. He sat back up.

"I'm all right."

She sat down beside him, folding her hands primly in her lap. "I don't think you are, dear. Would you like to talk about it?"

"No, thanks."

"Hmm. It seems to me you're running out of time to do the right thing."

"What?" His eyes sprang open. She was watching him, not unkindly, with her rheumy blue eyes. Her skin was pale and wrinkled, her white hair a cloud of tight curls.

"It's time to find your moxie, Sumner. There's a lot of work to be done, and there's no room for cowards."

"How . . . ?"

When she leaned toward him, he saw the slightest hint of transparency in her features. He could almost make out the chair behind her and the woman reading a romance novel three seats down. She wasn't sitting on the seat, but floating just above it in a parody of sitting. If he tried to touch her, his hand would pass through with no resistance save a puff of cold air.

"Wow. You're good. I thought you were real."

"I am real. And I'll kick you right in the buttocks if you don't get going. It might not be too late to save the world, dear." She was fading by the moment, running out of strength from the effort of having made herself known to him. A few more seconds and she would be invisible, but it didn't matter. The message had been delivered. He pulled himself to his feet and started to run.

In his eternally helpful way, the bogey he'd dubbed *Coach* chose that moment to show up. Sumner groaned.

"Faster, you maggot!" Coach bellowed. Bellowing was all that particular bogey knew how to do.

"Sir yes sir!"

Sumner's lungs were burning. He hurled himself onto the train just as the doors were closing. He bounced on the balls of his feet as he watched the airport pass by outside the window, trying to ignore the bogey's brash insults. He was first off the train at Terminal C.

"Come on, candy-ass! You run like a little girl!"

"Keep it up, Coach! You're giving my middle finger a boner."

Ora was waiting for him at the Southwest gate. He stopped in front of her, sweating and out of breath.

"It's about time! They're about to close the door!"

"I ran as fast as I could," he wheezed.

"Yeah. He almost busted his hymen getting here." And before Sumner could think of a comeback, *Coach* was gone.

"Never mind, you're here. Come on!" She pulled him toward the door, where a woman in a Southwest uniform stood waving them forward impatiently. He produced his boarding pass, then ducked through the doorway and ran down the ramp.

Settling into the seat beside her, he said, "I'm giving you one week. If we haven't figured out how to stop whatever is going to happen by then, I'm going to follow Father Narda's orders to gather in the children."

She shrugged. "Fair enough."

CHAPTER TWENTY-ONE

Her back was small and fragile. Her shoulder blades poked out at the pink fabric of her sweatshirt. Her skirt was also pink, and had a band of neon-green ribbon stitched along the bottom hem. Her hair rose in a mass of uncontrolled knots and curls, a piece of leaf and a small stick poking out like captured prisoners.

I followed behind her, unseen. My legs were trembling with exertion, my lungs on fire. Flying down the path, I plunged through flickering sunlight and shadow, desperate to reach her.

"Leora! Leora!"

She ducked low each time her name was shouted, but continued running.

"Leora! Get back here . . . this instant!"

On she ran, peals of laughter trailing behind her. It was a game to her. The woman calling her sounded tired and shrill the way only a mother of young children could. In the distance, I could hear the sound of children at play and the quacking of ducks.

"Leora! If you don't get back here . . . RIGHT NOW . . . there is going to be a CONSEQUENCE!"

One of the girl's neon-green Crocs flew off and landed on the red earth. She kicked off the other and pressed on barefoot.

Picking up speed, I passed her shoes. Something was about to happen. Something was about to go very, very *wrong*. I tried to scream, to warn her, but managed nothing more than a thin burst of air, ineffective and unheard.

There was a parking lot at the end of the path. As she raced forward, the shadow-figure of a man stepped into view, directly in front of her. She skidded, trying to slow down, but he was too close and she went careening into him. I saw the flash of sunlight dancing across a needle, and then she went limp.

He scooped her up and ran toward the parking lot.

"No!" Too late my voice came unstuck, and he turned to me. His face was a black hole. He hoisted the girl over one shoulder and pointed a finger directly at me, as though marking me.

"Rowan." His voice was the hiss of a snake, both acknowledgment and warning. As he turned away, the small girl hanging limply over his shoulder, the world went black.

***

The dim lamplight of my living room swam into focus. The news was on. I had fallen asleep on the couch. Was it morning or night? I eased myself up, groaning. An empty Doritos bag slid off my lap and landed on the carpet, scattering a bright-orange spray of crumbs over the pile of crumpled tissues on the floor.

Ah, yes. Evidence of the grand old pity party I'd been having since my terrible encounter with Kahina. I had called in sick to work, and Dan had dropped a huge bag of junk food on my doorstep on his way to WSMR.

I grabbed a chocolate out of the box on the coffee table and sucked on its sweetness. It cut nicely through the fuzz in my mouth.

So, was it a dream or a premonition or . . . what?

Perhaps a news story about a missing girl had transferred into my dream? I grabbed the remote and rewound the DVR to the beginning of the news hour. They made it through the morning headlines in ten minutes. When they turned to the weather, I turned off the TV. If a girl had gone missing in Las Cruces, it would have been a lead story. A Google search for any missing girls by the name of Leora came up with nothing pertinent.

It was tempting to dismiss it as a dream, but what if it was a premonition? What if a little girl was about to be kidnapped?

On Google Maps, I searched parks in the Las Cruces area. There were quite a few, of course, but only one with red dirt pathways *and* a duck pond.

Dripping Springs National Park was in a secluded area halfway between Las Cruces and the peaks of the Organ Mountains, probably a thirty-minute drive from my home. It had a large playground that boasted a water park, tennis courts, trails, and a duck pond. There was a snack bar from which one could buy refreshments and bread crumbs for the ducks. The few pictures I found online were focused on the playground and duck pond, but in the background were red, tree-lined trails.

So now what?

Sitting back against the couch, I tried to work it through. I could call the cops, of course, but didn't like the idea of facing their eye rolling and sarcasm. I might have been cuckoo for Cocoa Puffs, but no one else needed to know it.

Well, it looked like a nice day for a stroll around a duck pond.

And if it all turned out to be for naught, no one would have to know about it but me. And just maybe I would save a girl's life.

"Yeah, you and all your kung fu moves." I hauled myself off the couch with a newfound sense of urgency. After a quick shower, I dressed in sweatpants and a yellow T-shirt. I unearthed my Nikes from the closet and slipped them on over athletic socks. I grabbed a bottle of water from the fridge and stuffed it into a backpack along with my wallet, cell phone, sunscreen, and a novel by Jodi Picoult.

With purpose, I peeled out of the garage. The traffic on I-25 South was light, the morning rush hour already finished. I took the exit for University Avenue eastbound, which eventually became Dripping Springs Road. It wound through empty scrubland dotted by the occasional farm, and traffic thinned. The road climbed gently into the red rocks and majestic canyons of the Organ Mountains. I caught sight of the sign for Dripping Springs National Park, and slowed to make the turn into the parking lot.

There were a handful of cars, and I circled, eyeing each of them in turn. None seemed suspicious, and there was no gray-hooded man conveniently lurking in the lot. I parked near the south edge and set out, taking a moment to adjust the straps of the backpack onto my shoulders.

Three trails led from the parking lot into different areas of the park, and I walked them one at a time. The first two led to different sides of the large playground, and the third looped around the duck pond.

Parents chased their children on the playground, or policed them from the comfort of blankets spread out in the shade. They occasionally called reminders to share, play nice, or not throw dirt, before turning back to their adult conversations.

There was no sign of the little girl from my dream. I made another casual circuit of the duck pond before buying a basket of fries and a Coke from the snack bar, and a bag of bread crumbs for the ducks. I munched my midmorning snack from a bench on the edge of the playground.

Once finished, I tossed my trash and strolled back to the duck pond. The ducks waddled around, quacking and fighting over the tiny morsels. When the bag was empty, I wandered back to the playground.

Grateful for the shade, I sat on the grass under a large sycamore tree. I spent the next couple of hours watching families come and go above the rim of my book. I wished I had brought a blanket.

Lunch was two hamburgers, another basket of fries, and a Coke, all devoured from my spot under the tree. I dumped my garbage, made a trip to the ladies' room, and then settled under the tree to continue my surveillance.

The carbs hit my system, making me drowsy. Some unknown time later, I awoke with a start, heart pounding with a jolting burst of adrenaline.

"Leora!"

It wasn't part of a dream. I *had* heard it. Jumping to my feet, I frantically searched the area for the little girl.

"Leora!"

The woman was pushing one of those hefty double strollers wearily around the duck pond. She was African American, her hair pulled tight against her scalp, and wearing a red dress and sneakers. One tiny baby foot poked out of the front of the carriage, and a small boy was drinking from a juice box in the rear seat.

The girl must have been somewhere along the third path, the one that meandered from the duck pond to the parking lot. It was the farthest away from me. That was bad, but it was also the longest of the three paths. Maybe that would give me an advantage.

I took off at a dead run, flying down the path nearest to me. My lungs were burning within thirty feet. I really was in terrible shape, and the hamburgers had formed a big greasy lump in the pit of my stomach. I careened down the path toward the parking lot, weaving around a lumbering family of five with a speed induced by pure panic.

Skidding into the parking lot, I almost fell on my side, but rallied and pushed toward the mouth of the third trail. It did a long, lazy loop toward the duck pond, which made it impossible to see more than twenty feet ahead.

"Leora! If you don't get back here . . . RIGHT NOW . . . there is going to be a CONSEQUENCE!"

I surged forward with renewed energy. She had to be close! But where was the man in gray?

Rough arms encircled my waist like a steel trap. The air squeezed out of my lungs in a high-pitched whistle. My feet, still trying to run, left the ground. They scissored ridiculously through the air, and then I was flying.

Well, shit. I had been tossed aside as easily as a used tissue. My head cracked against the tree trunk with a bone-jarring explosion of light, and I was gone.

When the world returned, I pulled myself up and staggered drunkenly to the parking lot. My feet didn't want to stay under me, and the rest of me kept trying to detour in different directions. I overcorrected and fell, landing on my face with a grunt. Burning anger pushed me to my feet and I staggered on, furious at being so easily bested.

"Leora!" The woman was still somewhere behind me on the path. Her voice was becoming more strident. She must have realized her daughter was nearing the danger of the parking lot. But, oh, it was so much worse than that.

The man in gray was stuffing the girl into the backseat of a dark blue Ford Escape.

"No!" I managed to turn my stagger into a run. He turned and pinned me with his dark eyes. He was smiling.

Do I know you? I thought. But that was crazy. He slid into the backseat and slammed the door shut. There was a blonde woman in the driver's seat. The tires screeched as she reversed out of the parking spot, and I pushed forward with one last burst of energy.

Doing my best kamikaze dive, I slid across the hood's hot metal and grabbed onto a windshield wiper.

The woman looked quite surprised. Our eyes met, and she hit the gas. She yanked the wheel sharply to the right, and then spun to the left. Picking up speed, she raced through the parking lot in a mad attempt to dislodge me.

To give myself credit, I hung on for quite a while. But when she slammed on the brakes, I slid off the front grille and hit the concrete like a sack of melons. She didn't hesitate. She ran right over me.

CHAPTER TWENTY-TWO

Temple Hills, Maryland, was a suburb to the southeast of Washington, DC. Sumner Macey's house was a two-level, red-brick structure halfway down a dead-end street filled with similar houses. The properties were large and unfenced, and boasted patchy lawns and cracked driveways. There were no sidewalks and few streetlamps, adding to the countrified feel.

Josh was getting nowhere but frustrated. There were only ten houses on Crystal Lane, a fact that would have guaranteed neighborly camaraderie twenty years before. He interrupted mothers feeding their families, tired men in wrinkled business suits, an elderly couple watching *The Price Is Right*, and a doped-up twentysomething who, by the look of panic in his eyes when Josh flashed his badge, was the local drug dealer.

None of them knew Sumner Macey, except by sight. Most didn't even know his name—just that he lived there alone, he was quiet, kept his yard clean, and never bothered anybody. Josh refrained from mentioning that they were giving the same description the neighbors of terrorists and serial killers gave after the shit hit the fan.

He seemed like a nice guy. He was quiet and kept to himself. I had no idea he was marinating human flesh in the basement.

Josh sighed, dragging a hand through his hair as he eyed the plain facade of Mr. Macey's house. There hadn't been any movement in the residence since his arrival. No twitch of the curtains, no telltale TV flicker, no moving shadows. As dusk settled into darkness, lights flicked on in houses up and down the street. But not in the Macey residence.

Mr. Macey's 2008 silver Honda Accord was missing from the carport. Josh crossed the street and ambled up the driveway. Newspapers had piled up on the doorstep.

He rang the doorbell and waited. If Sumner Macey opened the door, he would inquire about the drug dealer down the street, but Josh wasn't holding his breath. With the tip of his car key, he pried open the mail flap and peered inside. In the dim expanse of hallway, there was a rectangular table over which a tan overcoat had been thrown, and a black umbrella was propped against the hall closet. Mail fanned out from the base of the door into the hall, a *Rolling Stone* and a *True West* magazine tucked among the bills and flyers.

Sumner Macey had called in sick to work, but Josh doubted he was laid up in bed with a box of tissues and a tub of Vicks VapoRub.

Josh worked his way along the front of the residence, hoping to see something that might allow him probable cause to enter the premises without a search warrant. All the curtains were drawn tight, and Josh could see nothing save his own frustrated reflection in the dark panes of glass. A check of his watch told him it was almost 7:00 p.m. Time to pack it in for the evening and grab some dinner. His stomach rumbled in agreement.

He climbed into his Impala 9C3 and started the engine, making a mental note to check the FAA database in the morning to see if Sumner Macey appeared on a recent passenger list.

***

Josh arrived at the office at seven-thirty the next morning, eager to get a jump on the day. As he rounded the corner, coffee and yogurt in one hand and briefcase in the other, he saw the door to his office was open a couple of inches, the lights on inside.

His heart hammered with anxiety. A quick backtrack and his breakfast was unloaded onto the empty reception desk. On his way back, he unclipped the harness over his Glock 22. His hand found its natural place on the grip, finger loose near the trigger. In deference to his location inside a secured building, the gun remained holstered. But someone had clearly broken into his office, which made him both wary and indignant.

Josh pushed the door open with his foot. There was a man lounging in the desk chair, hands steepled on his chest, feet crossed on the corner of the desk. As the door swung open, he straightened out, letting his feet fall to the floor.

"Can I *help* you?" Josh spat.

The man seemed nonplussed by the terseness of his tone. The smell of his aftershave was overpowering, a mix of pine and ginger. Josh put him in his late fifties, with a head of glossy silver hair and eyes the color of caramel. He wore a pair of gold-rimmed glasses propped on the edge of a nose as sharp as a razor blade, and a gold Patek Philippe watch. His gray suit looked custom-made, and his navy silk tie was looped in a crisp Windsor knot against his throat. All in all, he gave the impression of money, power, and political influence.

"Senior Special Agent Metcalf?" His voice was smooth, a self-satisfied drone that made Josh think of wasps bathing in honey.

"That's what it says on the door. Who are you?"

"My apologies." He managed to inflect his tone with mild surprise, as though he was used to being recognized. "Deputy Director Michael Warner, from the Office of Congressional Affairs."

"Well, Deputy Director Michael Warner, it might be okay to break into offices in the OCA, but around here it's considered poor form."

His smile didn't reach his eyes. "You must forgive me; I didn't want to wait in the public reception area."

"Uh-huh." Josh didn't attempt to hide his anger. "And what's your excuse for searching my desk and file cabinets?" Everything had been replaced with care, but it was obvious his office had been tossed.

Deputy Director Warner lifted his hands, smiling bashfully. "All right, I'm caught. Blame it on a restless mind."

Josh stood, one hand on the grip of his gun, watching him silently.

As though to appease him, Warner slithered out from behind the desk. He sat down in the brown visitor's chair, smoothing his tie and watching Josh with wide, innocent eyes. Josh wasn't buying it for a second.

"What do you want?"

"I hear you're one of the best CID investigators."

Josh remained silent.

"That your promotion to senior special agent is one of the quickest in the history of the division."

"I wouldn't know."

"Word is, you might make director one day. If you keep your nose clean."

Josh clamped his mouth shut.

"Of course, there are political issues to be aware of. Toes you don't want to step on. You get my meaning?"

"No, I don't believe I do."

"How disappointing. Perhaps you'll have a seat so I can enlighten you?"

"I'm fine right here."

Deputy Director Warner sighed. "Very well. One of your *investigations* has delved into some sensitive territory."

"Oh, really. And which one of my *investigations* would that be?"

"Let's just say there are certain cabinet members who'd like to avoid an investigation into the Department of Education."

"Which cabinet members?"

"That information can only be shared on a 'need to know' basis. I'm simply a friendly messenger."

Josh laughed. "You're kidding, right?"

"No, Agent Metcalf. I couldn't be more serious. Stop your investigation into the ED, and you'll find your rise through the FBI ranks to be swift and easy. If *not* . . ." he shrugged, implying all manner of negative ramifications.

"Look, *Deputy Director Warner*, I don't know who the hell you think you are, but you have seriously misjudged me. I don't care if I climb up the ranks, and I don't take well to being threatened. Also, the last time I checked, I don't take my orders from the OCA, *or* from crooked members of the cabinet."

"No, but you *do* take orders from me."

Josh turned to find his boss standing in the doorway.

"Ah, *shit*, Dean. You can't be serious!"

Executive Administrative Director Dean Forster was rumpled and sweaty. He was always rumpled and sweaty, so that wasn't what caused the nervous flutter of alarm in Josh's gut. It was his eyes, which were very still, determined, and . . . *sad*.

"Dean, what the hell is this about?"

"You need to do what he's saying. Shut down your investigation of the ED. Right away."

"*Why?*"

"Come on, Josh. You know better than that."

"Dean, you don't seriously expect me to stop an investigation just because some OCA guy breaks into my office and tells me to?"

"No. I expect you to do it because I've *ordered* you to. I've been your boss for six years now, Josh. I pushed for your promotion. I supported your use of man-hours on an investigation others thought was a waste of time and money. I've been your mentor, your friend, *and* your boss. You need to trust me on this. For your own good, let it go."

"Dean . . ."

"Josh, I'm serious. *Please.*"

He could feel them watching him from the mural behind his desk. Seven hundred and seventy-nine sets of eyes, pleading not to be abandoned. "Fine."

"Good."

Without another word, Josh left his office. He grabbed his briefcase and breakfast off the reception desk and headed for the stairs.

CHAPTER TWENTY-THREE

Back in Josh's office, there was a minute of silence as they listened to his clipped retreat down the hallway. Dean Forster's stomach was in knots.

"He won't give it up, will he?" Warner asked.

There was no point in lying. "No."

He knew Josh well, knew how important the case was to him. It was an obsession. Dean liked Josh. He liked him a lot. Which is why he had begged Michael Warner for this one chance to deter the agent from his current path.

"You know what needs to be done, Dean."

Dean couldn't look at him. "Do what you have to do. Just leave me out of it, please."

"Of course." Dean flinched as Deputy Director Warner clapped him on the shoulder. "It's hard to lose a good agent."

CHAPTER TWENTY-FOUR

"Is this Senior Special Agent Metcalf?" Josh muted the TV and checked his watch. It was just after nine o'clock in the evening.

"Who is this?"

"This is Agent Rosa Ortiz calling from the field office in Albuquerque. Agent Dennis Chang asked me to call you."

"All right. What's up?" Josh remembered Dennis Chang well. He had worked with Josh on a kidnapping in Santa Fe five years before.

"Well, sir, we have a kidnapping case Agent Chang says you might be interested in?"

Josh grabbed a pen and paper off his coffee table. "What can you tell me?"

"A six-year-old girl, Leora Wylie, was kidnapped from a park near Las Cruces this afternoon. Agent Chang wanted me to tell you there was blood found at the scene. They are still typing it, but they don't think it's from the victim."

"Anything else?"

"Yes sir, he told me to say 'Other factors might be similar as well.' I don't know what he means."

"That's okay, I do. Anything else, Agent Ortiz?"

"Yes, sir. This is why Agent Chang wanted me to get ahold of you so urgently. He says you'll probably want to get here as soon as possible."

"Why?" Josh leapt up and took the stairs two at a time. He flicked on the bedroom light, moving toward his closet.

"There was a witness. She tried to stop the kidnapping and got pretty banged up. She's in Mesilla Valley Hospital. Agent Chang thought you'd want to talk to her."

He was already throwing clothes into his duffel bag.

"I sure do. I'll be there as soon as I can."

CHAPTER TWENTY-FIVE

"A flower cannot bloom without the kiss of the sun, and a child cannot flourish without the nourishment of food. You must eat, my dear."

Through the curtain of her red hair, she watched him place the bowl of soup on the bedside table. Turning her back, she curled in on herself and pulled the quilt over her face. Blessed darkness. It was a soothing balm against her puffy eyelids. Inside the quilt cocoon, she cupped her hands over her ears, blocking out the man's voice. Just before she was taken, she had been reading a library book about wormholes. The idea of a tunnel through time captured her imagination.

Now she pictured her mind as a wormhole, and she used it to swim away from the man who was trying to make her forget. She swam and swam, letting his voice recede behind her as she moved back toward home, toward her mother and a sweet-smelling Sunday in the spring.

***

None of the girls at Penny Marsh's birthday party wanted to play with her, and she was sitting on the front steps, watching as they bounced on the trampoline that was set up in the yard. She had just decided to leave—her house was only five blocks away and no one would miss her—when Penny's grandma sat down beside her.

"Don't you feel like going on the trampoline, dear?"

"I guess not."

"It's just not right for a young girl to be sitting all by herself on such a beautiful spring day. Why don't you go join your friends for a bounce?"

"They're not my friends."

"Nonsense. You were invited to the party, weren't you?"

"Penny's mom probably made her invite me. Every girl in the class is here."

"Hmm. Like that, is it?"

"Yeah."

The woman leaned back against the steps. "I'd place a bet everyone feels like you're feeling right now, on occasion. Like you just don't fit in with the rest of the world around you. Like you wish you had just one good friend. Does that about sum it up?"

She nodded. "How did you know?"

The woman chuckled, but her eyes looked kind of sad. "Might be I've felt that way myself a time or two."

"Really?"

"Well, sure. It happens more as you get older, you know. Young folk start to think they know better than you, that all your understanding of the world is outdated.

"Comes a time you start to believe they might be right. And then even your own kin don't acknowledge you anymore. You're sitting right there in the armchair, but the conversation just keeps passing back and forth right over the top of your head. You might as well be a houseplant, sitting neglected in the corner of the room."

"That's really sad."

Penny's grandma patted her chest, chuckling. "Oh, look at me going on like an old fool. A young girl doesn't need to be listening to this kind of drivel. The point I was trying to make is you're young. I know you sometimes feel afraid, or like you don't quite belong. But never mind that; it's just the 'scaredies' trying to get you down. You've got to pick yourself up and get back into the thick of it. You get my meaning?"

"Yeah."

"Well, then. What are you waiting for?"

She hesitated for another moment and Penny's grandma shooed her forward. "Go on with you, already!"

Nervously, she approached the trampoline. When no one yelled at her to leave, she clumsily pulled herself up and over the blue lip and rolled onto the wildly bouncing surface.

The next forty minutes turned out to be some of the best of her young life. She bounced and laughed and spun and danced. Just like any normal girl.

Every once in a while, she looked out toward the stairs. The older lady would smile and wave in response, and once she even gave her a thumbs-up.

"Who are you waving at?" Deborah Matheson asked. She was bouncing in front of her, blond pigtails flying. Penny Marsh was bouncing and spinning in circles beside Deborah, giggling madly.

"Penny's grandma," she answered absently, focused on a jump where she did the splits in midair. The goal was to grab her ankles at the top, and then come back down on her feet without falling over.

She came down from a split-jump, proud of the perfect execution of her move, and noticed the two girls staring at her.

"That's not funny," Deborah said. Penny's eyes were wet, her lower lip trembling.

"You should apologize to Penny."

"For what?" she asked, perplexed.

"For what you just said, you freak." Teresa Hernandez sidled up on Penny's other side and held her elbow in support.

"What did I say?" The trampoline was suddenly still. Silent. All eyes were focused on her, and she could feel the heat beginning to creep up her neck.

"That you were waving at my grandma." Penny's voice was soft.

"What's wrong with that?"

"Penny's grandma died last month, freak show," Jennifer Morrow said, her eyes angry and cold.

"What . . . ?"

"I think you should apologize," Deborah said again.

"I . . . Penny, I didn't know." She looked over at the stairs, but they were empty.

"You should go," Penny said.

"I'm sorry! Penny, I'm sorry!"

Penny turned on her, screaming. "Just get the hell out of here, you . . . freak!"

In her haste, she fell getting off the trampoline. A few girls snickered. She grabbed her shoes and ran home, sobbing.

Her mom was on the phone, but she quickly hung up when she saw the state of her daughter.

"What happened, Boo?" her mother asked, coming toward her.

She inhaled the soothing smell of her mother's lotion, which always reminded her of violets baking in the sun. Between sobs and hiccups, she managed to get the story out. Her mom listened with that same sad look on her face she got every time her daughter came home this way. When she was done, her mom mopped up her face, kissed her raw cheeks, and pulled her up off the couch.

"Who needs them and their stupid trampoline, anyway? Not when we've got the coolest trampoline in town, right here." Her mom pulled her toward the back of the house, to the master bedroom.

"Come on!" She pressed the power button on the ghetto blaster, turning the volume all the way up. It played the same song it always did: Katrina and the Waves' "Walking on Sunshine." It was their theme song.

Her mom jumped up on the bed and started singing and bouncing. She had a terrible singing voice and it always made her daughter laugh. "Come on, get up here!"

But she was too busy giggling. The sight of her mother bouncing on the bed like a kid was too funny. And the more she laughed, the louder and more off-key her mom's singing became.

"Come on, Ryanne! Don't be a party pooper!"

She climbed onto the bed and joined in, holding hands with her mom as they bounced crazily around the bed.

They sang together, daughter as off-key as her mother, giggling and bouncing like two little girls.

***

Through the wormhole and a million light years away, she sang softly to herself under the quilt, pretending she was back there, in that bedroom with her mom on a sweet-smelling Sunday in the spring. Remember, she thought. Remember the sunshine.

***

"I'm Dr. Sanchez, the doctor on call this evening. You're at Mesilla Valley Hospital. Do you remember what happened to you?"

I licked my lips. They were so dry. "Yeah. I decided to wrestle with a Ford Escape and lost."

His smile was tight. "That sums it up, but you put up a better fight than one might expect."

"Can I have some water, please?"

"Of course." I waited while he filled a Styrofoam cup and stuck a straw into it. He bent the straw to my lips and held it while I sipped. Once the cup was empty, he placed it on the side table.

"Thanks."

"You're welcome. How are you feeling?"

"Sore. My head is pounding. My right leg feels numb."

"The car ran over the lower portion of your right leg. Your X-rays show no broken bones, but your leg is swollen and bruised. It's wrapped in ice; that's probably why it feels numb. Expect to have pain and swelling for the next five to seven days, and some difficulty putting weight down on the leg while it's healing. There is a small chance of a blood clot forming, so we will be keeping an eye on that."

"Okay."

"Your left shoulder was partially dislocated, and we've put it back into place. Your arm will need to be in a sling for the next week, and it's also going to be sore for a while. Pretty much every other part of you has been cut or scraped in some way, but nothing serious. The worst of your injuries is a concussion."

"I got thrown headfirst into a tree."

He blinked several times. "I see; well, the tree did more damage to you than the car did. We're going to keep you overnight for observation. I'm going to give you acetaminophen to help with the headache and other body pains. Are you experiencing any nausea or sensitivity to light?"

"No nausea, but yes to the light."

"How about your vision?" he asked. "Is it blurry, or are you seeing double of anything?"

"No, I don't think so."

"Good. I think it's a mild concussion. I'm not too concerned. But please let us know right away if you experience any vomiting, or seizures, or difficulty with your balance and motor skills."

"Okay."

"Now, cognitive symptoms of a concussion can include confusion, irritability, and difficulty focusing your attention. Also, on occasion, there can be issues with amnesia."

I couldn't help it. I giggled.

Dr. Sanchez sat watching me, perplexed. With some effort, I managed to control myself and apologize.

"Do you have any family around? Anyone who can drive you home from the hospital and help you out?"

In deference to the hammer trying to break its way out of my skull, I shook my head slowly. "Just a coworker, Dan."

"Is that the Dan Parks listed as the 'In Case of Emergency' in your cell phone?"

"Yes, that's right."

"I believe he's been called, but I'll double-check. Your backpack was given to the paramedics. It's over there on the counter. Would you like anything from it before I leave?"

"My phone, please."

Dr. Sanchez rummaged around in the bag and handed it over. "Nurses will be checking on you throughout the night, and I'll be back in the morning. In the meantime, get some rest. Press the call button if you need anything; a nurse will be in shortly with some pain meds." He turned back at the doorway. "No web surfing, okay? It's a bad idea after a concussion."

"I promise," I lied.

"Also, there's an FBI agent waiting to speak to you. Do you feel up to it?"

"All right."

"I'll send him in." He gave me another tight smile and departed, the staccato sound of his footsteps receding down the hall.

The moment he left, I opened the Safari browser. It was awkward with my left arm in a sling, but by holding the phone in my left hand I was able to use the fingers on my right to type into the search bar "Ryanne, missing child."

The wheel spun and spun, trying to get enough of a signal to perform the search. A list of websites had just popped up when an Asian man in a black suit entered the room.

"Ms. Wilson? I'm Special Agent Dennis Chang, of the FBI."

I barely glanced at his badge.

"How are you feeling?" he asked, taking a seat on the plastic chair beside the bed.

"I'll live."

"It was a very brave thing you did, ma'am."

I shrugged as best I could with only one working shoulder. "I would have wanted someone to do the same for me." My fingers gave an involuntary twitch over the phone.

"Do you mind if I ask you a few questions?"

"Go ahead."

"Please let me know if it gets to be too much for you; I understand you suffered a concussion?"

"I'm all right."

"Great. First, can I get your full name?"

"Rowan Jane Wilson." He took me through a few more standard questions such as my date of birth, address, phone number, and occupation.

"I'm sorry, I didn't realize I should be calling you Dr. Wilson."

"Rowan is fine."

"All right, Rowan. Do you mind if I tape this? Great, thanks. We can go through all the other details later; for now, let's focus on the most important things. Can you give me a description of the suspect?"

"Suspects—there were two. A man and a woman."

"And the man grabbed Leora Wylie?"

"That's right. The woman was waiting in the driver's seat of the car. She's the one who ran over me."

"Let's start with him. Can you describe him for me?"

"He was tall, maybe six feet or more. Caucasian, with brown hair. He was wearing blue jeans and a gray hooded sweatshirt."

"How old would you say he was?"

"I don't know, maybe in his thirties."

"Did you get anything else? Eye color?"

"I think they were brown."

"Anything else you can remember?"

I shook my head.

"What about the woman? Did you get a good look at her?"

"Yeah, we locked eyes through the windshield."

"Can you describe her?"

"Blond hair, blue eyes. Maybe in her twenties? I don't know about her height or anything."

"Of course. If I send over a sketch artist, do you think you could help us with a couple of composites?"

"I'll do my best."

"Thanks, that would be a big help. So, on to the vehicle. Other witnesses at the scene described it as a blue Ford Escape, is that correct?"

"Yeah."

"Any chance you saw the license plate?"

I slumped back into the bed. "No, sorry. How dumb!"

"Don't worry about it. We've issued the Amber Alert with a partial plate of the vehicle. But this has been a big help. No one actually saw the suspects. It might help us to track them down."

"I hope so."

"So, can you tell me what happened? Leora's mom told us her daughter ran down the path to the parking lot."

"That's right. I heard her mom calling for her."

"And then what happened?"

"I guess the guy came up behind me. He lifted me up and threw me headfirst into a tree. I blacked out. When I came around, I ran to the parking lot. I saw him shove her into the backseat of the car, and then climb in beside her. So I jumped on the hood."

"Was Leora fighting him? Screaming, crying?"

"No, she was limp. He'd injected her with something."

His eyes sharpened on me, and I realized my mistake. I'd only seen that part in the dream.

"He drugged her?"

I nodded mutely.

"Witnesses say you were lying down near the playground. That you suddenly jumped up and ran, leaving your possessions behind. Is that true?"

Well, damn.

"Agent Chang?" A woman with skin the color of caramel and spiky black hair poked her head through the door.

"Yes, Agent Ortiz?" he turned his penetrating gaze away from me, and I tried not to let my sigh of relief be audible.

"I just got a call from Agent Metcalf. He says he missed the eleven o'clock flight into Albuquerque tonight. He wanted you to know he's catching the next flight out, but it's not until the morning. He's flying into El Paso instead and should be here just before lunchtime."

"How did he miss his flight?"

She smiled. "Apparently he caught some guy trying to break into his townhouse, and had to subdue him until the cops arrived."

"No kidding?"

She nodded. "The guy was armed to the teeth. Agent Metcalf said he didn't know who was more surprised, him or the perp, when he opened the door and they came face to face."

"I'll bet. Is Metcalf all right?"

"He's fine. Can't say the same for the perp, though."

"Good."

"Hey, listen. Leora Wylie's grandmother is here. She asked if she could have a moment with Ms. Wilson, to thank her for what she did."

Agent Chang looked at me for consent, and I managed my one-shouldered shrug. Agent Ortiz disappeared.

"So, where were we? Oh, right. Can you tell me what you were doing in the park in the first place? And why you suddenly jumped up and ran down the path? Did you know Leora was in danger?"

"Excuse me, sorry to interrupt," a woman said from the doorway. Agent Chang and I both turned toward her. My heart sank.

She was Leora's grandmother?

Kahina recognized me at the same moment. "You!" she screamed, barreling forward. Startled, Agent Chang jumped up.

"*You* were at the park today? *What did you do to my grandbaby?*"

Agent Chang stepped in front of her, trying to protect me.

"What did you do to Leora, you devil's spawn!"

"Ma'am, I'm going to have to ask you to leave." Agent Chang was trying to push her back to the door.

"I won't! I won't! Not until she tells me where my grandbaby is! *She knows.*" She stabbed her finger at me, spittle flying from her mouth. "She's a part of it! *She knows who took my Leora!*"

"No . . ." I finally managed, shaking my head. Nausea swelled inside me, and I began to retch.

Agent Chang turned to look at me, his eyes full of speculation.

"No, I swear! I had nothing to do with it!" I said between heaves.

He pushed Kahina out the door, still screaming and slobbering. I could hear Agent Ortiz arguing with her out in the hallway, trying to get her to calm down. Agent Chang gave me one last hard look as he left the room.

"I'll be right back."

CHAPTER TWENTY-SIX

Although hurling up the contents of your stomach while your head is splitting open is nothing I would recommend, there was an upside: Dr. Sanchez refused to allow Agent Chang to continue the interview. Through bouts of retching, I heard them arguing in the hall outside my room. Agent Chang was desperate to question me further, but the doctor stood his ground.

"She's given you as much information as you're going to get right now. You can talk to her in the morning, *if* I think she can handle it."

"She has vital information about this case, and I'm sure you're aware that every second counts in a kidnapping."

"I understand your predicament, Agent Chang. But my job is to protect my patients, and I do not believe further questioning is in her best interest at this time. Concussions can have very serious long-term effects, if not handled with diligence and care. Dr. Wilson needs to rest. She needs time to recover from her injuries. I'm off shift for the evening, but I will re-evaluate her tomorrow—"

"She's agreed to speak to a sketch artist—"

"In the *morning*, Agent Chang. She's not to have any more visitors until the morning, and only *after* I've examined her and given the okay. Understood?"

Silence descended. I felt vaguely queasy, but doubted there was much left in my stomach. The nurse shuffled around, cleaning up the mess. I kept my eyes closed and my hand over my phone, hoping she wouldn't take it away. She placed a damp cloth on my forehead and dimmed the lights; I sighed gratefully.

"I'm hooking up the acetaminophen drip to the IV now. Do you need anything else?"

"No. Thank you."

"The call bell is by your right hand. I'll check on you in a bit."

"Okay."

"Get some rest." She squelched away, her shoes wet from the postvomit mopping.

I lay there until the pain medication kicked in, and then pulled the cloth off my forehead and used the button on the side of the bed to raise myself to a sitting position. I stayed that way for a while, eyes closed, waiting for my stomach to settle, and then pulled my phone out of the nest of covers.

I read through the list of hits, scrolling past links for the National Center for Missing & Exploited Children, several articles for missing boys with the first name Ryan, and a Wikipedia link to a martial artist named Ryan Bader.

On the second page, there was a link to a news article from the *Omaha World-Herald*, dated Sunday, June 22, 2008. My heart fluttered, and I noticed my hand was trembling as I touched the link to open it. After what felt like an eternity, the article appeared. I had to squint to make out the small print.

KIDNAPPING OF LOCAL GIRL STILL A
MYSTERY TWENTY YEARS LATER

By Samantha J. Mathis

This Tuesday will mark the twenty-year
anniversary of the disappearance of seven-
year-old Ryanne Elizabeth Jervis, and police
say they haven't given up hope of finding her.

Ryanne was last seen biking home from
Elkhorn's Westridge Elementary School on the
last day of school before summer vacation,
on June 24, 1988. Her disappearance rocked
the small community of Elkhorn, and led to
the implementation of new laws regarding
police procedure in the first twenty-four hours
following the disappearance of a minor.

Ryanne's bicycle was found just off Main
Street, in the bushes near Papillion Creek, a
small tributary bordering the train tracks that
run through downtown Elkhorn.

Despite receiving hundreds of tips, the Elkhorn
Sheriff's Department ran out of plausible leads
within days of her disappearance, and the
case quickly went cold.

Joshua Metcalf had just joined the Elkhorn
Sheriff's Department as a junior officer

when Ryanne Jervis went missing, and her disappearance had a lasting effect on him.

"Finding Ryanne became an obsession for me," said Metcalf, now a special agent for the FBI. In the years since her kidnapping, he has dedicated time and personal resources toward finding her.

In 1992 he started the "Run-4-Ryanne," a ten-mile walk/run that takes place every June, and raises funds for the National Center for Missing & Exploited Children.

"Ryanne would be twenty-seven now," Agent Metcalf said. "Her disappearance destroyed her family and shocked the citizens of Elkhorn. I'm committed to finding out the truth."

Asked what he thought happened to her, Agent Metcalf responded, "I don't know. But I still think she's alive out there. Call it intuition. Or maybe it's just blind hope. Maybe I just want to believe she's still alive."

Over the years, the FBI has released composite sketches to show what Ryanne Jervis would look like as a teen or an adult.

"It's been twenty years," Metcalf said. "For the

sake of those she left behind, those who loved her, it's time to bring Ryanne home."

The Run-4-Ryanne will take place this Saturday at 9:00 a.m., beginning in the lot of Enfield's Tree Services on North Main Street in Elkhorn.

Anyone with information about Ryanne's disappearance is asked to contact Special Agent Joshua Metcalf of the FBI Criminal Investigation Division at (202) 555-6311 extension 332, or the National Center for Missing & Exploited Children at 1-800-555-5678.

At the bottom of the article were two pictures: a school photo of Ryanne Jervis from first grade, and a composite of what she might have looked like at twenty-seven.

I had come face to face with the girl in the school photo. From the other side of a bathroom mirror, she had begged me to find the truth-seeker.

The composite wasn't an exact match. The shape of the chin was wrong and the nose was bigger than my own. Nevertheless, the woman in the composite looked enough like the face I saw in the mirror every day to leave me no doubt.

I was Ryanne Jervis.

CHAPTER TWENTY-SEVEN

He saw Dennis Chang the moment he entered the second-floor lobby. The agent was sitting on one of those uncomfortable plastic chairs, a cup of coffee in his hands.

"There you are!" He smiled and stood up as Josh approached. His eyes were bloodshot and his hair was matted on one side of his head, as though he had spent a restless night sleeping on a hospital chair. Come to think of it, he probably had.

"Agent Metcalf, how the heck are you? I hear you had a little run-in?"

"Nothing I couldn't handle; I'm just frustrated it slowed me down. So, fill me in."

"We've still got the Amber Alert going, with the suspects and vehicle description. Lots of tips are being phoned in but nothing's panned out yet. We do have a partial plate, so I'm hopeful. If they haven't dumped the vehicle by now, that is."

"And the blood?"

"Lamb's blood, just like I expected."

"Have you spoken to the family at all? Any idea if Leora has psychic abilities?"

"Let's put it this way. Her grandma, who is quite the character by the way, is a local medium and spiritual counselor. When I heard that, I had Agent Ortiz call you."

"Great. I can speak to the family later. Any chance I can get in to talk to the witness? Who is she?"

"Dr. Rowan Wilson. She works at LINEAR."

"What's that?"

"It's part of the space program, searching the skies for objects that might crash into the earth and kill us all. NASA has some telescopes out on the White Sands Missile Range. She works there."

"What's your impression of her?"

"Well, at first I thought she was one of those heroic citizens—spots a girl in trouble and risks her life trying to save her. She got a concussion for her trouble, as well as a dislocated shoulder and a banged-up leg. The kidnappers drove right over it."

"Ouch. You said 'at first'?"

Josh listened as Agent Chang filled him in on the previous evening's altercation.

"Grandma calmed down after a while, but she's adamant Dr. Wilson isn't what she seems. Apparently she came to see her the day before, looking for help with some memory problems. Grandma says as soon as she touched her hands, she got a sense of evil surrounding her. Says she kicked her out of her office. Now, I'm not much of a believer in all this psychic stuff, but it's quite the coincidence that Dr. Wilson visited her, and then popped up at her granddaughter's kidnapping the next day. And I don't believe in coincidences."

"No, neither do I." Josh pondered this for a moment. "So what's Dr. Wilson's story? What does she say happened?"

"She's pretty vague, actually. There are some discrepancies."

"Such as?"

"First off, witnesses at the scene say she was sleeping under a tree near the playground. That all of a sudden she jumped up and ran like her ass was on fire, leaving behind her bag, which had her wallet and phone inside it. *Her* story starts with the male kidnapper coming up behind her and throwing her into a tree. I have no doubt that happened, but she's pretty vague about what she was doing there in the first place. Secondly, she said they drugged the girl, injected her with a needle."

"Really? That's interesting." Josh's heart kicked into high gear. What if all the kids had been drugged? That would explain the ease with which they were taken.

"Yeah, I thought so, too, but as soon as she said it she got kind of squirrelly. Which made me think: If the male suspect threw her into a tree and she blacked out, how did she see that?"

"Hmm. Is there any chance I can talk to her?"

"Definitely. The doctor has given us permission to continue the interview, but she's not talking to me anymore. She'll talk to you, though."

"Why is that?"

"Because she told me she would."

"What?"

"In fact, she told me very specifically you were the only person she *would* talk to."

"Me? But I don't know her."

"Well, that may be so, but she seems to know you."

"Are you sure?"

"Her exact words were 'I will only speak to Agent Joshua Metcalf.' I thought that was pretty specific."

"All right, where is she?"

"Room 240. On the left, at the end of the hall."

Heart trip-hammering against his ribs, Josh made his way to the room Agent Chang had indicated. The door was open, but he gave a polite knock on the doorframe before entering.

She was asleep, her lashes a dark fan against the purple moons underneath her eyes.

Josh froze in the doorway. The red hair. The high cheekbones. The pale skin, with just a dusting of freckles.

"Sherry?" he gasped.

She opened her eyes. They weren't brown. They were green. Coke-bottle green.

And of course it wasn't Sherry. Sherry Jervis was almost twenty years in her grave.

This was Ryanne.

CHAPTER TWENTY-EIGHT

No one had ever stared at me the way the man in the rumpled suit did, as though I were a ghost and just didn't know it yet.

I pinched my left arm under the covers, hard enough to feel pain. It felt solid enough, but maybe all ghosts imagined themselves to be stitched of blood and bone, unaware they were no more substantial than a wisp of shadow.

Time seemed to stretch like taffy. Even the dust motes dancing in the light coming through the curtains stilled in deference to the man who stood frozen in the doorway.

When his jaw wasn't slack, he was probably quite handsome. He had a thick shock of black hair that was dusted with silver at the temples, wide blue eyes, and a rounded face covered in black stubble. His nose might once have been straight but it had clearly been broken. Perhaps more than once.

He was tall and slender, and looked like he worked out a lot more than I did, which always made me wary. I knew there were people for whom exercise and healthy eating were as vital as breathing. To me they were part of an alien race who spoke a language I found vaguely threatening. After all, who in their right mind would choose to eat tofu over a nice, juicy steak?

Maybe he was a new father, lost on his way to the maternity ward. He did have the look of a man who was taking a header off the cliff into fatherhood.

"I think the maternity ward is on the third floor," I told him helpfully. At the sound of my voice, his eyes widened even more.

Okay. Was he an escapee from the fifth-floor psych ward?

He shuffled forward like a drunk and collapsed onto the hard plastic seat beside the bed. My right hand moved toward the call bell.

Like a drowning man, he reached for me. His hand clamped down on mine in the folds of covers. The blood was rocketing through the veins of his inner wrist, like a secret we shared.

"I can't believe it . . ." The dam broke in a flood of laughter and tears.

I watched him fall to pieces with the detachment of a scientist examining an odd specimen under a microscope. He wept with the openness of a child. There was none of the adult shame that made people hide their faces. I'd never seen a man come so completely unhinged, and apparently this was over *me*. The intensity of his emotion was frightening.

"Are you all right?" I finally asked.

He snuffled unbecomingly and wiped a sleeve across his damp face. "I'm sorry, I'm sorry. It's just such a shock! I never really thought . . ." He took a deep, trembling breath. "I mean, I always hoped you were *alive*, but I never really thought I would find you."

"Um, who? I mean, who do you think I am?"

"You're Ryanne Jervis. Aren't you?"

Was this Agent Metcalf? The rumpled suit and scruffy face didn't scream "FBI agent" to me.

"I guess I am."

He pulled a handkerchief out of his pocket, mopped his face, and honked his nose. I bit my lip; he sounded like a goose. And who carried handkerchiefs anymore?

"I understand you've been using the name Rowan Wilson?"

"That *is* my name." I shook my head. "Or . . . I thought it was."

"You were raised as Rowan?"

"Yeah. Kind of. It's a long story."

"We'll have plenty of time for that later. For now, do you know where they took Leora Wylie?"

The look of disappointment on his face when I shook my head caused my heart to drop.

"I really don't, I'm sorry. If I knew I would tell you, I *swear*."

He searched my face, and finally nodded. "Okay. But I want to hear everything you *do* know. I mean *everything*. We need to find her."

"My friend Dan should be here soon to drive me home. They're just filling out the paperwork for my release."

"I'll take you home."

"But Dan—"

"Ryanne, I've been searching for you for over *two decades*. There's no way I'm letting you out of my sight."

"All right, I'll call him. But first, could you show me some ID?"

"Oh, hell. Sorry." He pulled his badge out of his breast pocket and held it up for my examination. It said "FBI" at the top and "Senior Special Agent Joshua Metcalf" beside his photo. It looked legit, but what did I know?

"You're not very photogenic, are you?"

He snapped the leather case closed and the corner of his mouth twitched up in the hint of a smile. "They like to keep us humble."

At that moment, a nurse came in to take me through another round of questions. I guess the concussion wasn't getting worse because she seemed satisfied with my answers. She took my blood pressure and temperature, and then wrote the results in my chart. She promised I'd be on my way home in the next half hour, smiled flirtatiously at Agent Metcalf, and left with a squeak of her soft-soled shoes.

The interruption gave me a chance to collect my thoughts, and I had my questions ready for him. "I read a news article last night that said you were a junior officer when I went missing?"

"That's right, I was."

"So I'm from Nebraska?"

He nodded. "Elkhorn."

"I've never heard of it. I mean, well, I guess I *have*, but I don't remember."

"It's now a suburb of Omaha, but back then it was its own separate town. Do you remember anything about your childhood?"

I thought about the dream I'd had the night before, about the woman jumping on the bed. "Not really. Did you know me? I mean, before . . ."

He shook his head, suddenly looking wary. I could guess why, but I plunged ahead anyway.

"Did you know my mom?"

This time he nodded. Even if I hadn't already known, it was written all over his face. He would have made a bad poker player, and I wondered how he managed as an FBI agent.

The newspaper article had made no mention of Ryanne's family, other than the vague reference by the man who now sat beside me. I found that odd. "She's dead, isn't she? Did she kill herself?"

"How do you know that?"

"I think it was the only way she could find me." I glanced at the woman standing in the doorway, finally ready to acknowledge her. Her red hair floated free around her head. Her brown eyes were soft. She seemed pleased, perhaps even relieved. "And she's been with me a long time."

She blew a kiss in our direction. It ruffled Agent Metcalf's hair and tickled my cheek. And then she was gone.

CHAPTER TWENTY-NINE

The sketch artist worked on the composites with her for forty-five minutes, and then the next hour was spent engrossed in the red tape and awkwardness of getting Ryanne (*Rowan*, he corrected himself) out of the hospital. First came the long list of instructions on how to recover from her injuries. Dr. Sanchez directed all of his instructions toward Josh, mistaking him for her boyfriend.

Neither of them jumped in to correct the doctor, and once they passed that brief moment at the beginning of the conversation when it would have been easy to do, they got stuck listening with increasing discomfort.

When Dr. Sanchez explained how, because of her leg, Josh might have to help her bathe, Josh jumped up and vigorously shook the doctor's hand, thanking him for his time.

Dr. Sanchez looked surprised, and glanced at Rowan for guidance. Her eyes were downcast, her cheeks aflame. Josh guessed his were equally red. Dr. Sanchez coughed awkwardly, shoved some leaflets about concussions into Josh's hands, and retreated.

The nurse returned and shooed Josh out so she could help Rowan dress, and then an orderly appeared with a wheelchair. Rowan's leg was obviously painful. She fell awkwardly into the wheelchair, avoiding Josh's eyes out of embarrassment.

Her sweatpants and yellow top were torn and smeared with dirt and blood. Her pants were pulled up to the knee, exposing the swelling and bruising along her right leg. Her left arm was in a sling, and every inch of exposed skin was marked with scratches and bruises.

But it wasn't the injuries that affected him. What caused his throat to swell with emotion was how small and vulnerable she looked in her ruined clothes. No one had cared enough to bring her fresh clothing.

He turned away, feigning interest in a chart on the wall that listed the warning signs of a stroke, until he had himself back under control.

Josh carried her backpack as the orderly wheeled her through the hospital, into the elevator, and out the sliding glass doors into the late-afternoon sunshine. He left her by the doors and ran to get his rental car, afraid to let her out of his sight for even a moment. He half expected her to disappear as though she were nothing more than a dream.

But she was still there, sitting in the wheelchair with her hands folded in her lap. The sun caught her hair and made it flame. His stomach did a slow roll of wonder.

Ryanne. He couldn't believe it.

He felt a desperate need to attack her with questions. After all, she held the key that would unlock decades of mystery. At war with that was the simple desire to take care of her, the way her mother would have wanted him to. For the moment, he would let that win out.

"Sherry." He sent his thoughts up to her, wherever she might be. "Don't worry, I've found her. Just like I promised. And now that I've found her, I promise I'll keep her safe."

***

"I'm starving," she said as they pulled out of the parking lot. She wrestled, one-handed, through her bag until she found her sunglasses, and put them on with a sigh of relief. "I guess I shouldn't be seen in public, though. Would you mind taking me home so I can get changed?"

"Of course." He followed her directions, weaving through Las Cruces northbound. Ten minutes later, he pulled into her driveway and cut the engine. Her house was interesting, a bunch of white blocks that were stacked together. The effect was whimsical and childlike.

He helped her out of the car and supported her as she hobbled to the front door. The interior was cool and dark, and she limped around flipping on lights.

"You have a beautiful home," he said, following her inside and pausing in the doorway to remove his shoes.

"Thanks," she said absently, moving as quickly as possible to the living room, where she bent down with a wince and picked up a Doritos bag and some tissues.

"Sorry about the mess; I wasn't expecting anyone. Obviously." She dumped it all into the kitchen garbage, her cheeks red.

He looked around with appreciation. The furnishings were sleek and simple, offset by special touches: a plum-colored cushion, an interesting vase, a bright piece of artwork. It all came together with warm elegance, and it made his sparse townhouse seem as well appointed as a cardboard box.

"I'm going to take a shower. I *won't* be needing your help."

He grinned, watching as she limped toward what he guessed was the master bedroom.

"Make yourself at home!" she called back over her shoulder, and then closed the bedroom door with a solid thud.

She emerged twenty minutes later in gray sweatpants and a Blondie T-shirt, her hair hanging in a wet sheet almost to her waist. Her face was scrubbed clean and shiny, without a stitch of makeup, and she looked about fifteen years old.

"Mmm. Something smells good!" she exclaimed, and he helped her to the table.

"It's just pasta. Do you realize you have almost nothing that constitutes actual food in this house? How do you survive?"

"Coffee and chocolate."

"Well, after we eat, I'll go get your prescriptions filled and stop by the grocery store."

"You don't have to do that," she protested.

"You can't drive with that leg. How long do you think you can survive on Pop-Tarts and Coke?"

"Longer than you might think," she muttered.

He shook his head. "Eating healthy foods will help speed your healing."

"Oh God. You're going to make me eat tofu, aren't you?"

She looked so much like a petulant teenager he had to laugh. "I promise, I won't. Recent studies show soy products can be bad for your reproductive health." As soon as he said it, he could feel the blush creeping up his cheeks. She started giggling.

He set a dish down in front of her and she dug in with enthusiasm.

"Wow!" she said after the first few bites. "This is really good!"

"It's the best I could do with egg noodles and canned tuna, but thanks."

The food won her undivided attention, and she shoveled in her entire meal before he'd made a dent in his. He refilled it and poured her some water from the Brita he'd found in the fridge.

She slowed down halfway through her third serving. Her eyes looked pinched. He guessed her pain meds were wearing off. He'd once had a concussion, and remembered well enough the killer headache that had accompanied it.

He loaded the dishes in the dishwasher and insisted she go lie down while he went to the store. Before limping off to bed, she handed him a spare key. He wiped down the counter, made a quick call to Agent

Chang for an update, and arranged for an officer to pick up Rowan's car and drive it home for her. He found a Toyota key on her keychain and pulled it off the ring, making plans to meet the officer in the Albertsons parking lot in half an hour.

Before leaving, he did a quick walk-through of the house, making sure all windows and doors were secured. The rooms were spacious and airy, and every flat surface held a lamp. Her electric bills must have been through the roof.

He locked the door behind him and headed out into the New Mexico dusk, ignoring the churn of anxiety leaving her caused in the pit of his stomach.

***

Around ten that night, she emerged from her bedroom, clutching her head and moaning. Josh closed his laptop and helped her to the couch. He propped her up against the cushions and then handed her a couple of prescription pain pills, along with a glass of water. She swallowed them gratefully and then lay back against the pillows and closed her eyes.

Josh pulled the ice bags he had bought out of the freezer, wrapped them in a kitchen towel, and placed them gently over her injured leg.

"Thanks," she murmured.

They sat in silence for several minutes. She looked tired and frail.

"Thanks for taking care of me; you really don't have to."

He shrugged. "It's no trouble."

"You're an FBI agent, not a nurse. I'm sure buying groceries and cooking dinner aren't in your job description."

"I was also a friend of your mom's. She would have wanted me to help you."

"What was she like?"

"Sherry?" he said, smiling. "She was something else. I was six years younger than her, but growing up, all the boys wanted to get, um, close to her. She was very loud, brash. Wildly funny, maybe a little bit crazy. She was like a woman on fire. And everybody wanted to feed off her heat."

"What do you mean?"

"Well, she was very beautiful, but she seemed vulnerable somehow, broken." He shrugged uncomfortably. "She didn't grow up in the best home, and she sought attention anywhere she could get it. A lot of people took advantage of that."

"Men?"

He nodded. "She had you when she was nineteen. She was too young to be the most responsible mom, but I know without a doubt you were the most important person in the world to her, and she tried her best to do right by you."

"Was my father . . . ?"

He shook his head, hating the tears that welled up in her eyes. "I'm sorry, I don't know who he was. She never would say."

She swallowed that piece of information like the bitter pill it was. "Is there any other family? My mom's parents? Aunts or uncles?"

"Not as far as I know. Your grandpa was, well, not the nicest man. He was heavy into the drink and generous with his fists, from what she told me. He left her and your grandma many years before you were born, and your grandma died the year after you disappeared."

She was looking down at her lap, red hair hanging across her face. He reached out and took her right hand gently in his own.

"I'm really sorry."

"Were you friends with my mom before I . . . disappeared?"

"No, I only knew her in passing. But after . . ."

"What?"

"Well, you might say I became obsessed with finding you. I kept in contact with her, and over the years I guess you'd say we became friends."

"Did you . . . love her?"

"Not in *that* way, if that's what you're implying. But yes, I cared about her a great deal."

"She trusted you." She said it with a certainty that surprised him. It was a statement of fact, not a question. His cheeks warmed under her gaze.

"I guess she did. I did my best to be a good friend to her, to help her. But it wasn't enough to keep her . . ."

"To keep her from killing herself?"

He sighed. "Yeah, from self-destructing. I tried so hard to find you, to bring you back to her. I knew it was the only thing that could heal her. Without you, she had no reason to get up in the morning. She held out hope for a long time, but I guess eventually she lost faith in me. Lost faith in ever seeing you again."

"It's not your fault." Her voice was quiet, gentle.

"I just wish I could have found you while she was still alive."

"I would have liked that, too." When she smiled she looked just like her mom. "But you've found me now."

He smiled in return. "I have. And I have to say, I'm still in shock. I keep expecting you to disappear the moment I turn my back. I don't want to let you out of my sight."

"Would it . . . I have a spare bedroom. It's got its own bathroom and everything, so it's totally private. Would you stay?"

He thought about it for a moment. "Well, I think we have a lot of talking to do tonight. And you're going to need help with the cooking and stuff. So, yes, I'll stay. At least for tonight."

She talked until her voice was hoarse, filling him in on every detail of the past few days, stopping only to sip at her water. At one point she made a pot of coffee. She drank three cups of it, and he wondered how she wasn't buzzing around on the ceiling. The caffeine from the single cup he had consumed was thundering through his body like stray voltage.

By the end of her strange tale, he had more questions than he did answers, and he wasn't any closer to figuring out where the lost children were than he had been the day before. And yet he felt excited, almost euphoric.

Behind the vault doors of her mind lay the answers to everything—of that he was certain. He just needed to find the right combination: the one that would turn those tumblers and expose what hid within to the light of day.

CHAPTER THIRTY

His lungs were burning. Each exhale seared the inside of his throat before escaping in a puff of fear-vapor. He couldn't hear anything above the thundering of his heart or his ragged breath, but he knew they were following. He could feel them closing in.

Days—or was it weeks?—of confinement had made him weak and tired. But he pressed forward, tripping over exposed roots and dodging away from the branches that tried to grab him with their sharp claws.

How far? How long until he was away? Until he was safe?

Jack didn't know where he was or where he was going. But that didn't matter; he went anyway. He had to.

He'd been dreaming. Again. Dreaming of the girl with the red hair. Dreaming of the blond boy in the stable. And was that boy a young version of the man he'd seen out the window? The man who had told him to hold on to himself? Jack thought so.

He was trying to hold on to the Jack that was. But it was so hard to do. *So hard.*

Their drugs and their words were tearing his mind apart.

Jack had to get to them, to the blond boy and the red-haired girl. He had to warn them, help them. They didn't know what was coming. Although they sensed the devil riding in, they didn't know *how*. They didn't know the instrument of the world's destruction. But Jack did.

His angels had told him *everything*. They were frantic for him to get away; he'd never seen them so panicked. They buzzed around him like a swarm of bees trying to protect their hive.

"*If they find out what you are, Jack,*" they kept telling him, "*the White will be lost!*"

"*What? What am I?*"

"*They must not know, Jack!*" was all they would say as they fluttered around him, faster and faster. His angels could not affect the physical world, but Jack understood that their swarm was creating a barrier around him. It was protecting him from detection, blinding the Priests to the truth of whatever he was. He understood something else, as well: his angels were getting tired. He wasn't sure how much longer they could protect him. He had to get away. And he had to get to the red-haired girl.

She needed his help, but time was so short.

Too short, it's too short!

He pushed the thought away. There was no giving up. He had to try.

Jack pushed harder, his legs trembling from exertion. There was an opening ahead of him, a vastness, a place where the trees surrendered. He didn't know what lay beyond the forest, but if he could get there, maybe he would be safe.

"*They're close, Jack. They're so close!*" his angels called.

By the time he realized his mistake, it was too late to stop. And the Priests were there; they were upon him and his angels were wailing. His feet found the edge and he teetered over the sudden drop, feeling the emptiness reaching up to him from below.

He knew the blow was coming before he felt it.

Batter up!

He heard the whistle of the shovel as it moved in a perfect arc toward his skull. He could just make out the neat rows of farmland below him in the moonlight, laid out like a checkerboard.

Craaaaack!

And then he was flying. He turned and twisted like a dove. He saw the stars above him. Millions and millions of stars. Specks of glorious light that hid the promise of the end within their twinkling beauty. If he looked closely enough, would he be able to see them coming?

Those devil's horsemen, trailing their carriages of fire?

CHAPTER THIRTY-ONE

"Noooooooooooo!" Sumner screamed as he watched the boy cartwheel out over the dark fields, arms spread as though he might fly. But he didn't fly; he dropped. *He dropped.*

Sumner sat bolt upright in bed, wailing. It was that boy, Jack. He was certain of it. As certain as he was that it was not a dream. It was real.

Oh Jack. My fault. *My fault!*

His keening brought them running. The light flared on above his head and he shielded his eyes. He was in the spare bedroom of Ora and Lexy's apartment in downtown Houston.

"What! What is it?" Ora shouted.

"Sumner? What's wrong? Are you okay?" Lexy was grabbing at him. Only Phoenix stood in the doorway, dour and silent.

"It's Jack! Oh *shit*, poor Jack. *Poor Jack!*" He rocked back and forth, tearing at his eyes in an attempt to rip the vision of Jack Barbetti's last moments from his sight.

"Who?" Ora asked.

"Who's Jack? Sumner, calm down and talk to us!" Lexy shouted.

"Shut the fuck up!" Phoenix hollered. He strode into the room and backhanded Sumner across the face. His hand was as hot as a poker straight out of the fire, and it was the heat rather than the shock of the impact that silenced him.

Why was his hand so hot?

Lexy's eyes widened in panic and she jumped up, grabbed her brother by the shoulders, and pushed him out the door.

"Igloo, Phoenix! Think igloo!"

Sumner watched their retreat, perplexed. Why was the room so hot? There were beads of sweat breaking out on his forehead and dampening the back of his neck.

"Oh, shit!" Ora bounded out of the room after them, and Sumner managed to find his feet and follow.

At the doorway of the living room, he ran straight into a wall of heat. He staggered backward, hit the wall behind him, and slid down to the carpet. The air inside the living room was rippling in the same way it would above the pavement on a hot summer day.

"What the hell?"

"Igloo!" Lexy screamed.

Phoenix was crouched in the middle of the room. His hands were fisted against his face, and he was snarling and roaring, spittle flying from his mouth. He looked like one of those demonic statue dogs from *Ghostbusters*.

"Holy *shit*." Sumner's heart had lodged itself in his throat. "Hang on, Zuul, while I find the Keymaster!"

They ignored him.

"Phoenix! The fireplace!" Ora yelled as she crawled toward him. Crawled, because the room was too hot to stand in.

Phoenix lifted his eyes and, for a moment, Sumner could have sworn they were the orange of a bonfire. Ora shrank back from his gaze, lifting an arm reflexively to shield her face. With sudden ferocity

Phoenix stood upright, knocking Lexy to the floor. He turned to the fireplace, where a pile of logs was stacked into a pyramid.

Whooooooooosh!

The interior of the fireplace exploded, white-hot flames leaping forth as though the pits of hell had suddenly opened. The bricks surrounding the rim of the fireplace blew out like missiles. One caught Ora's arm a glancing blow and she screamed. Another just missed Lexy's head.

"Get water!" Ora yelled, scrambling toward the kitchen. Sumner rolled over onto his belly and crawled to the bathroom, away from the merciless heat that threatened to bake him like a human kebab.

There was a vase on the bathroom counter filled with wilting roses. Sumner dumped them on the floor and filled the vase from the tap in the tub. Dripping water, he ran back down the hall and staggered into the living room.

The water hit the flames licking the edge of the carpet. The fire roared up in angry response. As he watched, wide-eyed, the curtains caught fire. The flames hungrily chewed their way toward the ceiling.

Lexy screamed, and Ora dropped her pot of water and stared. Phoenix, too, was staring, his mouth open in shock.

"We have to get out!" Sumner screamed, pulling at Lexy's arm. "Ora! Phoenix! We need to get the hell out of here! *Now!*"

Ora blinked, coming out of her daze. She grabbed Phoenix, who seemed paralyzed by the vision in front of him.

"I'm sorry, I'm sorry," he was muttering.

"It's okay, baby," Ora said, pushing him away from the flames. "It's okay, but we need to get out."

They scrambled down the hallway, Sumner in the lead, and tore through the door into the blessedly cool corridor beyond.

"Close it!" Sumner shouted, and Lexy pulled the apartment door closed behind them.

"We need to get out of here before the fire department shows up!" Ora said.

They made a beeline for the exit stairs. Sumner pulled the fire alarm as they crowded into the stairwell, and they descended six stories surrounded by the echo of the alarm and the hollow thunder of their feet pounding the stairs. As they fled into the cool night, they could hear the wail of the fire trucks, still several blocks away but closing in.

They ran in the opposite direction.

***

"Dammit, Phoenix! You have to control yourself!" Lexy was standing over her brother, who was slumped forward on the white leather couch, cradling his head in his arms. They had made it the five miles to Phoenix's gleaming white penthouse on foot. From this height they could see the inferno in the distance, spewing black smoke into the predawn air.

"Don't you think I know that? Lay off me, Lexine. I couldn't help it." His voice was muffled against the white silk of his sleeve.

They were an interesting contrast, Sumner thought absently as he watched from the wing chair. They were opposites in every way: where one was light, the other was dark.

Phoenix was tall and muscular. Lexy was petite, no more than five feet tall. Phoenix had Aryan features; white-blond hair, pale skin, and pale eyes. Lexy's skin was the color of caramel. She had dark curly hair, and eyes the color of coal. He would never have pegged them as siblings.

Of course, they would have had different mothers. The *Amante* system at its finest.

"You couldn't help it?" Lexy was clearly furious. "My apartment is in ashes! Because you couldn't control your temper. *Again.*"

"I said I was sorry!"

"We could have been killed! Do you even *care* about that?"

"Of course I do! I'm not a monster!"

"Oh no? Then what are you?" she spat.

"Lexy, that's enough!" Ora jumped in, grabbing Lexy's arm and pulling her away from her brother. She pushed her into a seat at the other end of the room, where Lexy sat fuming.

"Phoenix." Ora sat beside him on the couch, stroking his arm. "What happened?"

"He lost his damn temper. That's what happened!" Lexy shouted.

"Enough!" Ora said, before turning back to Phoenix. "Tell me what happened."

He looked up, grabbing her hands. "You know I didn't mean it, Ora. I'm so sorry."

"I know you are, honey. It's okay." He crumpled into her, cheek to ample chest. Even Sumner, an outsider to this weird little group, could see his motivation wasn't entirely pure. But instead of pushing him away, Ora wrapped her arms around him and rocked back and forth, murmuring words of comfort in his ear.

"Like that, is it?" Lexy pouted.

Ora shot her a look over the top of his pale head, and Lexy snorted and turned away.

"You know what? I'm really getting sick of the lot of you," Sumner piped up. "Is anyone going to tell me what the hell is going on?"

No one responded. Lexy continued pouting, Ora continued comforting, and Phoenix continued nuzzling his face into Ora's cleavage.

"Hello?" He could feel his temper rising. He'd been with them less than thirty-six hours, and already their narcissistic immaturity had driven him to the brink. He'd made a game-changing decision when he'd joined Ora for that plane ride to Houston. He had expected to meet up with people who had knowledge and resources, and some kind of *plan*. Instead, he'd thrown his life away to join the cast of *Beverly Hills, 90210*.

"That's it! I'm out of here. You can continue your stupid little rebellion without me!" He was almost at the door when Ora's voice stopped him.

"You ever see the movie *Firestarter*?"

He turned slowly. "The one with Drew Barrymore? Yeah."

"Well, that's what he is. A firestarter. If he gets mad, or upset . . . well, you saw."

"Holy shit. Is that for real?" Even growing up at The Ranch, Sumner had never known anyone to have that kind of power.

Phoenix met Sumner's eyes. "I'm really sorry. Most of the time I can control it, but . . ." He shrugged.

"So, what? You got mad because I had a bad dream, and burned down a building?"

"It wasn't a dream, and you know it."

"What are you talking about, Phoenix?" Ora asked.

"It wasn't because he had a bad dream. I'm not that volatile, no matter what *you* think, *Lexine*." He looked pointedly at his sister, who smirked in return.

"Then what was it?" Ora was stroking his arm, and it reminded Sumner of gentling an antsy horse. Another lesson learned at The Ranch.

"I saw what they did to that boy. To Jack. I saw what you saw, Sumner."

Sumner sat back down. "You did?"

"Yeah. I mean, when I came into the room I could see it, like, *replaying* in your head. They killed him, right?"

"I think so."

"Killed who?" Lexy asked.

"A little boy. He was trying to escape and . . ."

"Someone took a shovel to his head," Sumner finished, and both Ora and Lexy winced.

"He fell off the cliff above the farm," Phoenix said.

"No way." Lexy was shaking her head. Phoenix turned on her.

"What do you mean, 'no way'? I saw it! *He* saw it!" He jabbed a finger at Sumner.

"They wouldn't do that."

"Lexy . . ." Ora reached out to her.

"No! They wouldn't *do* that. They wouldn't *kill* a *boy*. I don't believe it."

"That's because you're a naïve little—"

"Phoenix!" Ora cut him off.

"Stop it!" Sumner yelled, and all of them turned to look at him, like kids in a classroom. Damn, they were young.

"Jack is . . . *was* . . . one of the latest kids to be kidnapped. He was still in The Hut, being reprogrammed or whatever you want to call it."

"How do you know that? That he was kidnapped?" Lexy asked.

"Wow, you really are naïve. Or brainwashed. Where do you think all these kids have been coming from?" Sumner asked.

"I told you," Phoenix said smugly.

"Oh, shut up!"

Phoenix opened his mouth to reply, but Sumner cut him off. "Enough! Both of you!" He turned to Lexy. "I know because for the past ten years, *I've* been in charge of finding them."

She blinked at him. "What do you mean?"

"I run the public-school testing that finds these kids. The *special ones*. The ones *I Fidele* wants. I find them, and I tell *I Fidele* where they are."

"Did you know that?" she turned to her brother.

"I suspected. I knew he worked at the Department of Education."

"NCES, actually," Sumner corrected.

"Look," he went on, "there's a lot you guys don't know, being *born* at The Ranch. You get to come and go as you please, completing your assignments without anyone giving you a mind-wash first.

"You never went through what the Disciples did. You weren't ripped from your homes. You didn't have your memories of life *before I Fidele* scrubbed clean, and then at seventeen scrubbed clean *again* so they could send you out into the world on some mission you weren't even aware of.

"You didn't have to go through the hell of awakening! Of receiving a note and losing your implanted memories when *I Fidele* decided it was time to fuck with your head *for the third time* so they could bring you home!" At this point he was yelling, and all three were staring at him with wide eyes.

"Shit!" He turned and punched the nearest wall, leaving an impressive fist-shaped hole in the pristine white surface. He blinked at it in admiration, ignoring Lexy's gasp behind him.

"It's okay. Sumner, calm down." Ora was moving toward him, her hands out in front of her.

"It's not okay! You don't think they're capable of killing a boy? Ever see what happens to Chosen children born without any powers? And what do you think happened to your mom?" he asked Ora, and then pointed at Lexy. "Or yours?" He turned on Phoenix. "Or yours? Maybe they're out there following their mission, practically lobotomized by what *I Fidele* has done to them. Or maybe they're rotting in the dirt because they couldn't stand to let their babies go!

"But even if you don't know anything about that, you know they are preparing for some kind of Holy War! For the 'End of Days'! Isn't that what you guys are trying to stop? Or are you just a bunch of teenagers pretending to rebel against your daddies?"

"No!" Ora jumped in. "It's more than that! But we don't know *what* we're trying to stop! We don't know *what* they're *planning*. Do you?"

"Shit, no! Don't you think I would have said by now, if I did?"

"*Nobody* knows, except the Fathers," Lexy said. "And they've built walls around that information so strong not even the best mind readers can breach them."

"Somebody knows." Sumner slumped back into the chair. "Or did."

"Who?" Ora asked.

"Jack," Phoenix answered, and Sumner nodded.

"Jack? The boy they . . . ?" Lexy asked quietly.

"That's right. He knew. He was trying to get to me. Well, me and some woman with red hair. He was trying to warn us. Maybe they knew that and that's why they killed him."

"No," Ora said. She was shaking her head, and a small smile was spreading across her face.

"What?"

"If that's true, they wouldn't kill him. Even if they weren't sure about him, they wouldn't run that risk."

"What do you mean?"

"If he dies, he becomes even more powerful, right? How easy would it be to get to you, *Summoner of Spirits*, if he's no longer tied down by his own flesh?"

"I guess. But I saw . . ."

"It doesn't matter what you saw. They wouldn't want him *dead*, but they would have to incapacitate him. So what would they do? Maybe keep him locked up there, or something? Drugged up? Or in a coma?"

"He went off the *cliff*, Ora."

"Well, let's test it," she said to Sumner. "Call his spirit. If you *can't* find him, then I would bet he's still alive. And if that's the case . . ."

"Then we're going to have to go get him," Sumner said, beginning to smile.

CHAPTER THIRTY-TWO

"Are you all right?" Agent Metcalf asked. "I thought I heard you cry out."

His head poked hesitantly through the doorway. His black hair stood up in ragged spikes and his eyes were bleary and red. He didn't look at all like an FBI agent. His wild appearance brought me out of the horror of the dream, and the vise loosened its grip from around my chest.

"What?" he asked. "Why are you smiling?"

"You look like a porcupine."

He rubbed a hand over his head, smoothing the hair down. "Are you in pain?"

Actually I was, but that wasn't why I had screamed. Still, sitting up proved to be a challenge, so he anchored an arm under my back to ease me upright.

"Oooh." I swayed, eyes closed against the bolt of pain that pierced my skull. My right leg was throbbing in time with my heartbeat; my left shoulder thrummed with a more distant ache.

"Why don't we get some food into you, so you can take your next round of meds?" he suggested.

"Coffee." It was more of a desperate plea than a statement.

"Okay. I'll make some coffee."

"No."

"No?"

"*I'll* make it."

"I'm perfectly capable of making—"

"Cricket's piss."

"What?"

"You'll make cricket's piss. I can tell. I saw the face you made drinking my coffee last night."

"I think you used a whole bag of beans for one cup."

"That's the only way it's worth it."

He sighed. "Fine, let's get you to the kitchen."

Once I was up and moving around, the pain receded slightly. I went about the happy task of brewing coffee, and then stuffed a couple Pop-Tarts into the toaster before he could stop me.

I sensed his disapproval, but he remained silent. He pulled a pan out of the cupboard and waged his war for healthy eating with my knife and cutting board. He chopped up a pile of vegetables and began to sauté them in a dribble of olive oil. For a time I managed to ignore him, pouring the coffee and sipping out of my MIT mug with something close to religious fervor.

"What are you doing?"

"I'm making an omelet."

"Without the yolks? That's the best part!"

He conceded and mixed a couple of yolks into the pan. When it was done, he slid a plate and fork in front of me.

I had to admit, the omelet was pretty good. I washed it down with a second cup of coffee, and then happily ate both Pop-Tarts when he turned down the one I offered him. He poured a lot of cream into his coffee, but drank it without complaint.

"Rya . . . I mean Rowan—" he began.

"It's okay if you call me 'Ryanne.'"

"Are you sure?" he asked.

"Yeah. It . . . coming from you, it sounds right."

"Only if you'll call me 'Josh' instead of 'Agent Metcalf.'" He shook out a couple of pills and handed them to me.

Shrugging my agreement, I swallowed the pills with a mouthful of coffee.

"So, I've been thinking about this problem with your memory. I think you might have been on the right track, talking to that woman, what's her name? Selena?"

"Kahina Dokubo-Asari."

"Right. Obviously, we've got to get those repressed memories of your childhood back. I'm sure there's information locked inside your mind that could lead us to the missing children, including Ms. Doku . . . um, Kahina's granddaughter."

"Are you suggesting we go see her? Because I'm not really in the mood to be murdered today."

He smiled. "I promise to protect you from any and all violent grandmas."

"Are you expecting more than one? Besides, doesn't the FBI have people who can help with this?"

"Of course. The thing is . . ." His sudden hesitation peaked my interest.

"What?"

"Well, I'm not sure I should use them."

"Why not?"

He was cracking the joints in his fingers, one after another, pop pop pop, and peering nervously into his coffee cup.

"What's going on?"

"I'm not really sure. I've been with the FBI for seventeen years. I've trusted my colleagues, and my superior officers, with my *life*. Time and time again. There's an unwritten code of trust among FBI agents, and I've never questioned it. Never had the *need* to question it."

"Until now?" I asked.

He ran a hand across the rough stubble on his cheek, sighing. "Right. This investigation . . . well, I don't know who to trust anymore. There are a lot of kids missing."

My heart picked up speed inside my chest. "I'm not the only one? Well, Leora. That's two."

"I think she's number seven hundred and eighty, actually."

Blinking at him, I tried to process the immensity of it. "Are you serious?"

He stood and grabbed his briefcase. He pulled out a binder and slid it across the table. Inside, I found page after page of missing children. There were twelve kids per page, in two rows of six, with the picture on the left, and the name, age, date, and place of disappearance on the right.

I flipped through them, slowly at first, and then faster, until a familiar face stopped me halfway through. Ryanne Elizabeth Jervis, Elkhorn, Nebraska, June 24, 1988.

"This many? And you think they're all connected?"

"I do."

"Where did they all go?" I wondered, thumbing through the pages. There were so many.

He gave me a strange look. "You tell me."

That stunned me, and I could only shake my head mutely. I turned to the last page and gasped.

"What is it?"

"This boy! I had a dream about him!"

"What?"

"You asked me why I cried out. I had a dream about this boy, Jack . . . Barbetti." I read the name beside his profile. He'd been missing less than two weeks.

"Tell me!" Josh grabbed my good hand, looking at me with a desperate hope that made my stomach churn. I shook my head.

"I'm sorry. I don't . . . he was trying to escape. He was running through a forest, at night." I closed my eyes, partly to better visualize the dream and partly to avoid the upcoming pain in Josh's blue eyes. "He fell off a cliff, or, well, I think someone hit him in the head with a shovel. And *then* he fell off a cliff."

"No." His hand released mine, and the sudden coolness on my skin made me open my eyes. He was looking down, his gaze fixed on the image of the little boy with the pale-brown hair and crooked teeth.

"I'm sorry."

"Ah, *shit*." He rubbed his eyes and took a deep, trembling breath.

"It might not be true. I mean, just because I dreamt it doesn't make it real."

"Yeah."

"The thing is, I think he was looking for me."

"What do you mean?"

"He was intent on getting to me. Well, I *think* it was me he wanted. Or some other redhead. And he was looking for a man, too."

"A man? Could it have been me?"

I shook my head. "He was blond. I can see his face, kind of. In Jack's mind, he was both a boy and a man, at the same time. It's hard to explain."

"Why was he looking for you?"

"He wanted to warn me about something. He knows . . . *knew* something he wanted to tell me. He seemed to think there was some kind of danger coming."

"What do you mean?"

"I don't know. But Josh, I think this is way bigger than a bunch of missing kids. Something bad, I mean *really* bad, is going on. And Jack Barbetti knew what it was."

He was looking at me, eyes wide and serious.

"So, if this dream is *real*, then we need the full force of the FBI backing us," I told him.

"That would be a very bad idea."

"Why? I don't understand."

"Because I'm pretty sure some people within the Bureau are involved in this."

"You're kidding."

"I *wish* I was—you have no idea."

"Look." I leaned forward. "You've been really great. I mean, I've told you a bunch of bizarre stuff, and you haven't once made me feel like I'm crazy. So I should probably return the favor here, but . . . you're talking about the *FBI*."

"Yes, I am." And that's when he told me about the National Center for Education Statistics. About the PSST exam, and the disappearance of Sumner Macey, the man who was running the program. About his confrontation with his boss and the deputy director of the Office of Congressional Affairs, during which he was threatened off any investigation into the Department of Education. An investigation they should have known nothing about, since he had played it close to the vest for fear of leaking information to the wrong person.

"I haven't submitted a report in *weeks*, which is completely against protocol. I didn't want anyone to know where the investigation was going. But they still *knew*. How did they know?"

"What if they find out you've found me? One of the missing kids?"

"That would be very bad. That's why I told Agent Chang I had cleared you of wrongdoing in Leora's disappearance."

"And he believed you?"

"I'm a senior agent. I pulled rank on him."

"Still, they, whoever *they* are, might figure it out if they hear my name."

"That's why I'm not letting you out of my sight. It's also why we need to use civilian sources, like Kahina. We need to get to those lost memories."

I drained my coffee. "I'll go get dressed."

CHAPTER THIRTY-THREE

When she came out of the bedroom her cheeks were flushed; Josh guessed it was from the frustration of getting dressed one-handed. She'd managed to pull on jeans and a black T-shirt, and she'd secured her left arm back into its sling.

"I can't figure out how to tie my hair back with only one working arm. Do you mind?" She held out an elastic, embarrassed.

Her hair was damp from her morning shower. Up close, it was an intoxicating blend of copper and gold that deepened to the darkest ruby where the water still clung to it. It smelled like coconut and some kind of tropical flower, and it felt like a heavy blanket of cool silk. He managed to pull it all into a thick rope at the back of her head and work the elastic around it. The result was lopsided and somehow childlike.

He stepped away from her, his hands shaking. "Are you ready to go?"

She nodded. Her skin was mottled with embarrassment, and he wondered how much of his internal struggle she had picked up on.

Checking to make sure his gun was properly holstered against his side, he grabbed his bags and followed her out the door. Her yellow FJ

Cruiser was waiting beside his rental car in the driveway, and she turned to him with surprise.

"I had an officer drive it home for you," he explained.

"Thank you."

He helped her up into the passenger seat of the FJ Cruiser and then climbed into the driver's seat. The officer had left the key under the mat, as promised, and Josh started the engine and took a moment to adjust the seat and mirrors.

"So, where to?" she asked.

"Let's see if we can find Kahina at her home."

CHAPTER THIRTY-FOUR

No one answered his knock at the neat white rancher on Hoagland Road, but I could see Josh was prepared for that possibility. He climbed back into the FJ Cruiser and pulled a small notepad out of his breast pocket. He'd already written down the address and directions to the Wylie household, and he used them for reference as we wove through downtown Las Cruces southbound.

The Wylie residence was located on Monte Vista Avenue near the university. It was a nondescript, beige, one-level house with a single carport in which an old Buick was parked. The front yard had been paved, and I saw a number of children's toys and bikes strewn across the cracked concrete. The curtains were tightly drawn against the swarm of media camped outside. Parked askew in the driveway was a late-model red Hyundai Sonata with a personal plate that said "ISEEDP."

"I see DP?" I asked.

Josh drove past and pulled to a stop around the block. "'I see dead people.' Didn't you ever see that movie with Bruce Willis?"

"I try to avoid movies like that. They're too close to reality."

"I'm guessing we've found Kahina. Too bad about the media; the last thing we need is to be on the evening news."

"So, now what?"

He ignored me, pulling his cell phone out of the inside pocket of his suit jacket. He punched in some numbers and waited.

"Agent Chang? It's Agent Metcalf. Just checking in. Have there been any new developments? Right. Uh-huh." He paused, listening. "How's the family holding up?" I could barely hear the drone of the other agent's voice.

"Right. Well, I'm all wrapped up on my end. I'm heading back to DC this afternoon. I've got a few leads to follow up on back home. Yup, I'll keep you informed. Oh hey!" he said, as though he'd just thought of it. "Have you had any more trouble with that grandma?"

Watching him, I couldn't help but take a mental tally. He'd cleaned himself up since the previous day; his hair was neatly styled, his face clean-shaven. In a dark suit, he was more movie star than federal agent. He also smelled really good, like man-spice.

"Wow. Sounds like she's raising all kinds of hell. I've got nothing to do until my flight; why don't I have a chat with her? Maybe I can put her mind at ease. Sure, it's no trouble. Where can I find her? Yeah. Okay, go ahead."

Josh grabbed a pen and scribbled on his notepad. "Yeah, you can thank me later." He laughed again at whatever Agent Chang said. "All right, keep in touch." He hung up and winked at me. "Got her cell number. But we might have a little problem."

"What's that?" I asked, but he held up a finger, phone to his ear.

"Ms. Dokubo—" He looked at me in panic.

"Asari," I whispered.

"Ahem. Ms. Dokubo-Asari? This is Senior Special Agent Joshua Metcalf. Agent Chang called me in on the investigation of your missing granddaughter. I'm wondering if you could meet me somewhere? I have some information for you in regards to the witness, Dr. Wilson." He looked at me and smiled.

"That's not true, ma'am. I'm taking your allegations *very* seriously, as is the rest of the FBI. I've been investigating Dr. Wilson's involvement in Leora's kidnapping, and a few interesting details have cropped up that I would like to share with you." He paused and I could hear her questioning tone on the other side. "As you can imagine, this is a highly sensitive issue and I'd like to meet with you away from the rest of the family to discuss it. I understand you have an office in town? Could I meet you there?" He paused, listening. "Great. I'll see you then." He hung up and looked at me. "How are your self-defense skills?"

I looked down at my left arm, which was sitting ineffectually in its sling, and then back up at him. "They could be better."

"She's almost seventy." The side of his mouth was twitching.

I harrumphed. "You haven't met her. She's as tall as you are, and she hasn't been pummeled by a Ford. She might have the advantage."

"Don't worry." He opened the flap of his suit jacket so I could see the gun holstered against his side. "I'm not opposed to gunning down any grandma who looks at you funny. You just say the word, darlin'," he drawled like some kind of Old West cowboy.

"My hero. What's got you in such a good mood?"

"Are you kidding?" He looked over his shoulder and pulled away from the curb. "This is the first time since 1988 I'm actually getting somewhere on this investigation. Heroin probably doesn't feel this good."

CHAPTER THIRTY-FIVE

"Oh, what the *hell*!" The parapsychologist jumped to her feet. She was wearing a long black cotton dress, pale-blue Crocs, and an extremely angry expression on her face. Ryanne took a step back toward the doorway, hovering behind Josh.

"Now, listen Ms. Doku . . . uh, *Kahina*. Please, I have a very good reason for bringing Dr. Wilson here today. If you could just remain calm and hear me out, I think we might go a long way toward finding your granddaughter."

"Why? Is she going to tell me where her *friends* took Leora?" She turned her hot gaze on Ryanne. "You tell them if they hurt *one hair* on that little girl's head . . . she's just a *baby*."

"I had nothing to do with it!" Ryanne protested from the doorway. "I don't know *who* took your granddaughter. All I know is I risked my *life* trying to stop it! And I'm sorry . . . I'm *so sorry* I didn't succeed." Josh noticed her eyes sparkled like emeralds when she was about to cry.

"What do you mean, you don't know who took her? *You were there.* If you didn't have anything to do with it, why were you there?" Kahina spat at her.

"Yes, I *was* there. I was there to *stop* it. The question is, why weren't *you*, if you're so psychic?"

Kahina reeled back. "How dare you? I would do *anything* to protect that girl . . ."

Ryanne blew out a ragged breath. "I'm sorry, I didn't mean that. I don't know who took her, I swear. I would tell you if I did."

"Well, that's not quite true," Josh said.

"What's not true?"

"You *do* know who took her, and you probably know where they took her, too. You just don't remember yet." Ryanne looked like she'd been slapped across the face. Kahina was watching him with wide eyes.

"Listen." He turned pleadingly to the older woman. "I've been leading an investigation into a large number of missing children, an investigation that's been ongoing for more than twenty years in one way or another. There are hundreds of missing-child cases I believe are linked to the kidnapping of your granddaughter."

"How so?" she asked.

"There are a number of similarities, but the main one is all the missing children have some form of ESP. Does Leora share your gift?"

Kahina sat heavily behind her desk. "She does."

Josh took the opportunity to sit down across from her, wanting to stay on her level. Ryanne remained in the doorway.

"Believe it or not," he said, "for the first time in, well, *forever*, I can actually say that's good news."

"How is it good news?"

"Because I think I'm getting close to finding the people behind these kidnappings. I have hope we will find Leora. *Alive.* But we need your help."

"What can *I* do? Obviously, I'm not much of a psychic. As you pointed out." She eyed Ryanne.

"We don't need your psychic abilities. We need your help to unlock Dr. Wilson's memories. Just like she was asking you to do before you kicked her out of your office."

"I don't understand. What good will that do?"

"When I was twenty, I investigated the kidnapping of a young girl by the name of Ryanne Jervis. She went missing on her way home from school. The circumstances of that case were very similar to Leora's. I became, well, *obsessed* with it. In fact, that case is the reason I joined the FBI. And that led me to the discovery of hundreds of other cases matching Ryanne's disappearance, all beginning in the sixties." He turned and smiled encouragingly at her, standing battered and frail in the doorway.

"Kahina, I'd like you to meet Ryanne Jervis. Missing child number five hundred and thirty-four."

CHAPTER THIRTY-SIX

"You are a complete idiot. I can't believe we share the same genes!" Lexy shouted at her brother. Sumner could feel the temperature in the room rising; Ora seemed aware of this as well.

"Phoenix, don't listen to her." She grabbed his hand, and Sumner noticed she winced as if touching a hot stove, but held on anyway. "Lexy, *chill*."

"How can you be so *dumb*, Phoenix?" Lexy was too angry to heed Ora's warning, and frankly, Sumner couldn't blame her.

"We needed to know if the kid was still alive."

"*Without* letting them know we're interested!"

"They don't know. I only talked to Mannix, it's not like I announced it to the whole Ranch!" Phoenix was red to the tips of his ears.

"You only talked to Mannix? *Only?* He's being ordained into the *Priesthood*!"

"He's my *friend*, Lexy."

"Not anymore, he's not," Ora chimed in, but gently. "Phoenix, we can't trust anyone Inside anymore. Especially not someone who has committed to the Priesthood."

"He didn't know anything, anyway," Phoenix said.

"That's even worse! Now they know we're interested, and we didn't get anything out of it, either!" Lexy was stomping, too angry to stay still.

"Okay, Lexine! I screwed up! Are you happy now?"

"Why would I be happy? I'll be happy when you start using your brains! And not the ones you keep in your pants, Phoenix!"

"How dare you! My sex life is none of your business!"

"You make it my business when you try to sleep with my girlfriend!"

"Hey!" Ora jumped in. Phoenix looked like he'd been slapped. The air in the room was starting to ripple alarmingly.

"You think I don't know, *dear* brother? I know everything!"

"Then you know nothing has ever happened." Ora moved toward Lexy, reaching out for her.

"Don't lie to me, Ora! I know about the *kiss*." Ora froze. "What's worse, I know you *liked* it."

"Okay, Lex. I'm sorry. *I'm sorry*, I should have told you. But I swear, that's all it was. It was just a *kiss*. Nothing else has ever happened."

"Not yet, but it will! It *will*!" Lexy burst into tears, great wailing sobs that shook her tiny frame.

Ora wrapped Lexy in her arms and buried her face in Lexy's soft cloud of curls. Sumner could hear her murmuring endearments and reassurances, and Lexy folded into Ora's chest, fingers twisting into her blond locks.

Phoenix turned away. "Get a room."

Sumner might have found the sight arousing if he weren't so infuriated with all of them. "Can we all calm down and work out the problem? We have more important things to deal with here."

The girls slowly untangled, flushed and damp from Lexy's tears. Ora pulled Lexy down onto the couch beside her, cuddling the smaller girl up against her side.

"Sumner's right," Ora said.

"Thank you."

Phoenix was still turned away from them, but the air had cooled. "Phoenix?"

"Fine," he sighed and turned to his sister. "And for the record, I'm sorry."

"Sorry for what? For being an idiot or for trying to fuck Ora?"

"Lexy!" Ora sputtered.

"You see what I have to deal with?" Phoenix said to Sumner. "I'm sorry for both, Lexine."

"Whatever," Lexy muttered, looking away from her brother. Sumner could see Phoenix's temper beginning to rise, and broke in to head off another fight.

"Okay! So . . . we don't know if Jack is still alive, but we do know I couldn't find his spirit. Right?" He waited a moment, but no one was responding, so he answered himself.

"Right! I think we've got to assume they're keeping him somewhere on The Ranch, alive but unable to reach us." He paused again. This time he got a small nod from Ora. Encouraged, he continued. "So, what do we do?"

They responded with more silence, so he jumped in with both feet. "I'm going to try to break the kid out."

"They'll see you coming from a mile away. You'll never make it," Ora said.

"Yes. But would they see *you* coming? Or know what you were planning?"

The three of them looked at each other, contemplating.

"Maybe not," Phoenix said thoughtfully. "We're pretty good at shielding our minds from them. We might be able to do it."

"We can't go back before they've called for us. They'll be suspicious," Lexy said.

"And they won't be calling us back for at least another week," Ora agreed.

"What if I create a distraction?" Sumner suggested. They all turned to him.

"What do you mean?" Lexy asked.

"Well, they know I've gone AWOL by now, I'd imagine."

The first thing Sumner had done upon landing in Houston was throw away his cell phone; he didn't want them using technology to find him. With Ora, Phoenix, and Lexy shielding him, it was unlikely they knew where he was. They must have known he hadn't gone back to DC, as promised.

"So I'm already on their radar. What if I head back to The Ranch, guns blazing, so to speak, to draw their attention to me?"

"And we try to get to Jack while they're focused on you?" Phoenix was smiling. Sumner nodded.

"They'll kill you," Lexy objected.

"Probably."

"I don't like it." Lexy was shaking her head.

"Can you think of a better idea? I'm no hero. I'd really rather not be killed. I just can't think of any other way to get Jack out of there."

"Maybe we don't need him," Lexy muttered.

"We do, Lex," Ora said softly.

Phoenix nodded his agreement. "The boy knows stuff. I don't know how he knows, but he does. I got a sense of him when I was plugged into Sumner's dream. That kid is . . . different."

"Different than what? We're all different, Phoenix," Lexy said.

"I know. But he's . . . *special* somehow. I felt it. It's hard to describe, but . . . well, you know how the Chosen usually have stronger powers than the Disciples?" They all nodded in agreement.

"Well, this kid goes way beyond that."

"But he's not—I mean—are you saying that genetically . . . ?" Ora couldn't seem to find the words for the question she wanted to ask, but Phoenix understood anyway.

"No, he's not one of the Chosen. Genetically, he should be in league with the Disciples. But he's not. He's powerful . . . like something I've never seen before. I think with proper training he'd be more powerful than all of us put together."

"Are you serious?" Lexy asked.

"How is it he knows *everything*? Whatever the Fathers are planning, he *knows* about it. He has the *whole picture*. The group of us, with all our powers combined, has never been able to get *close* to figuring it out."

"They guard that information too well," Ora said.

"Right, exactly. But somehow *he* knows. We *need* this kid."

"Okay, I'm convinced," Lexy sighed. "But can't we figure out a way to rescue him that doesn't get Sumner killed?"

They all stared at each other blankly.

"What about the woman he was looking for?" Ora asked. "Does anyone know who she is? I mean, is she from The Ranch?"

"I don't know; I haven't given her much thought," Sumner admitted.

Phoenix looked pensive. "Did you actually see her in Jack's mind, Sumner? All I could see was the red hair, but everything else was a blank."

Sumner shook his head. "It's the same for me, just the red hair. I don't know how old she is, or what she looks like, or anything."

"But she was the one he really needed to get to, right?" Lexy asked.

"Yeah. In fact, I think he feels a connection to me because we had a moment of communication at The Ranch, but it's really her he needs to find."

"So that means we need to find her, too," Ora said.

"You're right," Sumner agreed. "Are there any redheads at The Ranch?"

"There's Ashlyn, but she's only eleven," Phoenix said.

"I think she's twelve or thirteen now," Lexy corrected.

"Who is she?"

"She's one of the Chosen," Ora answered. "She's Father Gabriel's daughter, very powerful. She's the only person I've ever known who can draw forth water."

"She's Phoenix's shadow when he's on The Ranch. We call her his fire hose," Lexy joked.

"It's because she has a crush on him," Ora chimed in, and Phoenix blushed.

"When you say she can draw forth water . . ." Sumner prompted.

"Just that," Ora replied. "She can create water the same way Phoenix makes fire. It's very useful when you've got a hot-tempered firestarter running around."

Phoenix seemed to take the teasing in stride. "She's come in handy more than once," he admitted. "But she doesn't need to get angry to bring forth water, the way I do with fire. She has more control over her gift than I do."

"Well, most of the time," Lexy said, and the other two paled.

"What?" Sumner asked.

"Lex." Ora gave her a warning look, and the smaller girl seemed to shrink back into the couch cushions.

"What is it?"

"Let's just say there was an incident," Phoenix said.

"What kind of an incident?"

"Well, she doesn't always have control over how much water she produces. And water can be dangerous. People can drown."

"Phoenix," Ora said sternly, and he looked down, chastened.

After a moment of silence, Lexy chimed in. "Anyway, I doubt she's the one Jack is looking for. She's too young. And she's on The Ranch; don't you think this redhead would be Outside?"

"Probably. Anyone remember a Disciple with red hair?" Phoenix asked. The girls both shook their heads.

"Sumner?" Phoenix asked.

"I . . . don't know. Maybe. I think there was a little girl, a new Disciple who was brought in just before I left. I don't remember her name or anything, though; I just have the impression of red hair."

"Just before you left? So you were eighteen?"

"Seventeen. It was just before I went into the Cocoon. After that, I don't remember much," he said bitterly.

"Any idea how old she was?" Lexy asked.

Sumner shook his head. "I didn't pay much attention; if it weren't for the red hair I probably never would have noticed. I'd say anywhere between five and eight. So I guess that would make her . . . in her early thirties?" he calculated.

"Wait, if she's in her early thirties, then that means she's, what . . . ten to fifteen years older than us?" Ora said. "Are you sure you don't remember her? Phoenix? Lexy?"

"I don't think so," Phoenix said, shaking his head.

"Nope, me neither," Lexy agreed. "We would have been pretty young when she went into the Cocoon."

"Or became an *Amante*," Sumner said tersely.

"Right. So if—" Ora was cut off by the sudden shrill of Phoenix's cell phone. They all jumped. He pulled it out of the pocket of his robe and looked down at the screen.

"*Shit.*" His pale face had gone gray.

"Who is it?" Lexy whispered.

"Father Narda," Phoenix's voice was grim. Sumner's heart plummeted.

"Oh, shit!" Ora moaned.

"What do I do?" Sumner could hear the hammer of Phoenix's heartbeat in his voice.

"Answer it," Sumner said through gritted teeth.

On the fifth ring, Phoenix tapped the answer button and held the phone up to his ear. His hand was shaking violently. "Hello, Father."

They sat, white-faced, watching Phoenix.

"She's fine. She must have turned off her phone or something," he said, and then swallowed audibly. "No, she's right here. Hang on a sec." He held out the phone to Ora like it was a bomb. "Your dad wants to talk to you."

Dad? It struck Sumner like a crowbar to the chest. She was Father Narda's daughter? The younger sister of Adelia's twin girls?

"Hi Dad," Ora said. To give her credit, she sounded calmer than she looked. "Uh-huh. Right, but . . . *now?* It's . . . but we're still processing orders, and we haven't finished clearing the accounts yet." Her eyes widened in panic. "But we've got at least another *week* of work to do . . . Okay, fine. I said *fine!*"

She clicked off and closed her eyes. "He's calling us home. We're to report to The Ranch ASAP."

CHAPTER THIRTY-SEVEN

Josh watched as Kahina prepared Ryanne for hypnosis, helping her settle comfortably on the couch and dimming the lights. She covered her in a plush green blanket, tucking it gently underneath her legs, but Josh noticed she avoided touching Ryanne. After the last time, Josh couldn't blame her.

"Okay, Ryanne. Are you comfortable?" Kahina asked, her voice melting into a soothing hum.

"I'm a bit nervous," she admitted.

"That's to be expected. But I'm here, and Agent Metcalf is here, and nothing bad can happen to you on our watch." She sat in the chair near Ryanne's head.

"We're going to explore your memories, and as we do, I want you to keep in mind that a memory is something in the past. As I guide you into hypnosis, which is nothing more than a deep state of relaxation, I'm going to keep reminding you to take a step back from it, to be an observer only, as though watching everything on a movie screen inside your mind. You will not be reliving it with the same intensity as you did the first time." Her voice was slow, soothing, and Josh could feel himself relax under the weight of her words.

"Okay," Ryanne said, leaning back against the cushions. "What do I do?"

"Just listen to my voice. Let it be your guide, and allow yourself to appreciate that you can relax . . . deeply . . . and calmly . . . and let your eyes close now . . . as you feel wave after gentle wave of relaxation . . . lapping over you . . . soothing the muscles and ligaments in your body . . . that's good, Ryanne . . ."

Josh blinked and sat upright, fighting against the tug of Kahina's voice as she continued to draw Ryanne down into a hypnotic state. He watched her face relax, her brows unfurl, the lines around her eyes smooth out, and her jaw loosen as she responded to Kahina's slow prompts.

"And you know that a very deep part of you can start to feel very soothed . . . and reassured in such a comforting way . . . as you continue to *relax* . . . so beautifully and serenely . . . like the surface of beautifully calm water . . . so clear and calm . . ." she continued softly, her voice slowing more and more with each thought, each word.

Josh shook his head, fighting against the desire to close his eyes. He watched Ryanne's pale face, smooth and unlined in relaxation, as Kahina continued. Time seemed to have slowed to a crawl, each moment punctuated by the slow inhale and exhale of Ryanne's breath.

"And now I'd like to focus . . . on the movie screen in your mind . . . and notice how it is big . . . and white . . . and unlit . . . but in a moment . . . when you are ready . . . a picture will begin to emerge . . . and you will watch . . . with calm . . . peaceful . . . detachment . . ."

Ryanne let out a soft moan, and her brow tightened.

"Can you tell me what you are seeing?"

"Butterflies." Ryanne's voice startled Josh out of his drowsiness. It had the pure, high-pitched tone of a child. Gone was the deeper huskiness he had grown accustomed to. "Yellow and orange and black. So pretty."

"And is there anything else?"

"A man."

"Can you describe this man?"

"He's wearing a black robe, like a priest. He's got gray hair."

"And what is he doing?"

She let out a squeaky giggle that made the hairs on the back of Josh's neck stand up. "He's dancing."

"He's dancing?" Kahina prompted.

"They think he's funny."

"Who are 'they'?"

"The kids watching him."

"And why do they think he's funny?"

"Because his dancing is silly. He's dancing with the butterflies. They are flying around his head. Landing on his hands, and shoulders, and one even lands on his nose. It makes him sneeze." She giggled again.

"Who are the kids watching him dance?"

"Mmmm. Lots of kids. Young ones."

"And is Ryanne watching the man dance?"

"No. *Rowan*," she corrected, a slight frown creasing her brow.

"Of course. Rowan. Is Rowan there?"

"Yes. She's very little. She's the newest Disciple."

"The newest what?"

"Shh. He'll hear you."

"Who will hear me?"

"Father," she whispered.

"Father? The priest? I promise he can't hear me."

"Then why is he *looking* at you?"

Kahina took in a sharp breath. Josh's stomach flipped over.

"He's . . . looking at me?"

"Oh yes," she said in a singsong voice. "He has a message for you."

Kahina looked questioningly at Josh. All he could do was shrug. "What's the message?" she asked.

"He says you're weak. You can't stop them. He says you'll die with the rest of the cockroaches."

"What . . . *who* can't I stop?"

Ryanne shook violently, like an earthquake was rumbling through her whole body. Her eyes opened and focused on Kahina with bitter hatred. Her eyes were black. Kahina froze.

That's not Ryanne, Josh thought. He jumped to his feet and pulled his weapon.

The voice that emerged from her throat was deep and gravelly, a man's voice. *"Stay out of her head, charlatan."*

"Who . . . who are you?" Kahina stuttered.

"I am the New World. Who are YOU to stand against me?"

And then those black eyes turned on Josh.

Josh raised his weapon.

"Shoot her, Agent Metcalf. Kill her! Leave her choking on her own blood."

Her head cocked to the side, red hair sliding across her face as she examined him with something close to amusement.

"Can you do it again, Metcalf? I promise, killing gets easier the more you do it." And with that, she reared off the couch and lunged at him, teeth bared and snarling like a rabid dog.

CHAPTER THIRTY-EIGHT

"Ryanne! Ryanne . . . fight back! Can you hear me?"

I was in the black. It wasn't the black of nighttime, or what I'd imagine one would find in the depths of the earth. It was a sightless kind of dark, one without any hope of light.

"Baby girl, you need to *fight*." She sounded distant, anxious.

"I can't, Mama. I've been swallowed by the whale." The voice that emerged from my throat was young, childlike.

"You need to find your way back, Boo. He can't keep you here unless you let him. Do you understand?"

"Yes, Mama. But I don't know what to do!" I was so tiny, so insignificant against the vast sea of darkness.

"The jail is your mind. Find the wormhole, Ryanne. It's there! You just need to find it."

"The wormhole . . ."

"That's right, baby girl. The one that will bring you home."

"But I'm not little anymore, Mama. That's *ago*, that life with you and the sunshine. I can't go back there."

"No, no. That's not your home anymore, Ryanne. Don't you see?"

"See what, Mama?"

"It's Josh. *Josh* is your home now, Boo. You have to save him!"

"Save him? From what?"

"From *extinction*, Ryanne."

"What? I don't understand!"

"You will, Boo. In time, you will. For now, you must go! Listen to him! He's calling you. Follow his voice, it will lead you home."

She was right, I *could* hear his voice, so distant but so very insistent.

"Okay, Mama."

"That's a good girl, Boo. You're a good, brave girl."

I took one step, and then another. His voice grew louder. I couldn't make out what he was saying, but there was desperate fear in his voice. I started to run. Down and down into the wormhole. Away and toward, all at the same time.

"I'm coming Josh! Hang on, I'm coming!"

***

He was flattened out on top of me like a lead blanket. My hands were pinned between our bodies. My injured left shoulder, twisted at an odd angle, was on fire. I could barely breathe.

"How much do you weigh?" I wheezed, trying without success to wriggle out from under him, at least enough to fill my lungs.

"Ryanne?" he shouted in my ear. I winced away from him, head pounding savagely.

"Well, who else?"

"Ryanne?" he shouted again.

What the hell was the matter with him?

"Are you . . . trying . . . to kill me?"

He lifted himself up enough to allow me a full breath. His eyes were huge and panicked, and he was breathing in sharp, shallow gasps, like a locomotive trying to make it up a hill.

It was disconcerting to be so close to him. His blue eyes were pinwheeled with slate gray and framed with squint lines.

"It was more the other way around." He was staring at me so intently I started squirming.

"What?"

"Your eyes are green."

"Um. Yeah. They are."

"Are you Ryanne?"

"I thought I was the one with a concussion."

"This is no time for jokes. I almost killed you."

"What a way to go. Steamrollered by an FBI agent."

The corner of his mouth twitched, but his eyes remained serious. "A bullet to the head might have been worse."

He hoisted himself off me and plunked down on the carpet by my side. That's when I noticed the gun in his hand. And Kahina, who had backed up against the far wall of her office and was standing there with her hands cupped over her mouth.

"What . . . happened?"

"Some guy tried to get me to kill you." Easing an arm under my back, he helped me to a sitting position, wincing when I moaned in pain.

"What guy?"

"You tell me." Another penetrating look, as though confirming I was indeed Ryanne, and he holstered his gun.

"What? I have no idea what you're talking about."

"Kahina? Can you help me?"

Her hands had dropped to her sides, but she was still propped against the back wall. I suspected if she weren't she would have fallen. "I've . . . never seen anything like it."

"Like what? What happened?"

"I . . . your regression was going beautifully. You followed my guidance perfectly, and went under like a dream. You were telling us about a priest, and some kids who were watching him dance . . ."

"With butterflies. I remember that."

"Do you remember what happened next?" Josh asked.

"I . . ." I closed my eyes, thinking back. "He stopped dancing and turned to look at me. He had black eyes. And then . . ."

"Then what?"

"Everything went black." I opened my eyes. "What happened?"

Josh looked at Kahina. She shrugged uneasily. "I've hypnotized hundreds of subjects over the years, and there has never been anything close to this. This was more like a . . ."

"Possession." Josh finished when she couldn't.

"Possession? You mean like *The Exorcist*?"

Josh met my eyes, and I could see that whatever had happened, it had disturbed him to the core of his being. "Exactly."

"It was a man," Kahina added. "He told me some horrible stuff. That I would die with the rest of the cockroaches. And then he tried to goad Agent Metcalf into killing you by attacking him."

"I came *this close* to shooting you. I knocked you off your feet and pinned you. I'm afraid I might have hurt you, but you were doing your best to rip my heart out of my chest."

"I . . . can't believe it. I'm so sorry, Josh."

"It wasn't *you*, Ryanne; there's no need to apologize. But if you weren't weakened by your injuries, I don't know what might have happened."

"Are you okay?"

"Nothing that a boatload of whiskey won't fix," he tried to joke.

Kahina pushed herself off the wall. "I'll make a calming tea." She plugged in the kettle and started digging through the tins on her coffee table, pulling out assorted herbs and dumping them into a teapot. Her hands were shaking. She poured in the steaming water, set the pot to steep, and helped Josh get me back to the couch.

My right leg was throbbing, as was my left shoulder. The worst of it, however, was my head. It was like someone was taking a chisel to my temples. Without having to be asked, Josh shook a couple of pills into my palm. I swallowed them with a gulp of hot tea, fragrant with chamomile and mint. Why did tea always smell better than it tasted?

"Is there anything else you can remember, Ryanne?"

"I could draw you a picture of what the priest looked like, but I'm not a very good artist. I assume a stick figure won't help you much?" I shrugged. "He had gray hair and black eyes, like I said. He was younger in the beginning, when he was dancing with the butterflies. Maybe in his fifties. But when he looked at me, it was like he suddenly aged twenty or thirty years. Like he traveled up through time from that memory to the present, all within the span of a few seconds. His face thinned out and developed more lines. His hair became more white than gray."

"Do you remember anything about the surroundings? Or the other kids?"

"The kids were a blur. I heard them laughing, but I didn't actually see them. As for the surroundings? It was a clearing, or maybe a meadow. There was forest all around, and I think there were mountains in the background. I couldn't see them, but I could feel them out there. It was nearing dusk. Everything was hazy and tinged with gold."

"What about smells? Do you remember any particular scents?"

I thought back, closing my eyes. "Forest smells, you know. Pine trees and greenery and flowers. And horses."

"Horses?"

"Yeah, I could smell horses and hay and bran mash."

"What's bran mash?"

"You feed it to horses. It has a kind of sweet, earthy smell once you mix it with hot water."

"How do you know that?" Josh asked, and my eyes popped open.

"I . . . don't know."

"Have you spent time around horses? I mean, as an adult?"

"No. Never."

"Well, then. There's a clue," Kahina chimed in.

"Forest and horses," Josh mused.

"And mountains," I added.

"Right. That doesn't narrow it down much, does it?" He seemed so despondent, I reached out and grabbed his hand.

"It's a *start*. We're getting somewhere Josh."

"I know. You're right."

"I'm sorry I didn't get more information for you. But this is just the beginning."

"You can't be hypnotized again!"

Kahina agreed. "It's too dangerous. You almost got killed. The both of you."

"Are you serious? That's *it*? Just because some weird guy comes through and spouts off a bunch of filth?"

"It was more than that. He was dangerous, and he wanted you dead," Kahina said. "What did he do to you? Where did you go?"

"Into the black. But I fought my way back out."

"How?"

"I had some guidance." I shrugged uncomfortably.

"Who guided you?" Kahina asked.

I looked at Josh. "My mom." I realized we were still holding hands when I felt the tremor of his within my grasp.

"And Josh, too," I continued. He looked at me in surprise. "My mom told me to follow your voice down the wormhole."

"The wormhole?"

"It's an image I used when I was kidnapped. It helped me to remember. I guess they were trying to make me forget my life before."

Kahina drew in a shaky breath. She must have been thinking about her granddaughter, wondering what was happening to her.

"She told me I had to save you, Josh," I admitted.

"Save me from what?"

"From extinction."

"What?"

"That's what she said. And I can't think of any other way to do that than to figure out who kidnapped me." I looked at Kahina. "And Leora. If we can figure that out, maybe we'll learn what this greater danger is, as well. And how to stop it."

"What if you don't make it out of the black the next time?" Josh asked.

My mom had called Josh my home. Not a place, like Las Cruces, or even a moment in time, like the present or the past, but a person. And one I had just met. But I wasn't ready to think about that, let alone discuss it. "I think I will, as long as you're there to call me back," I said simply.

"I will be. You're very brave, Ryanne." The echo of my mom's words made me feel very young and small. I was surprised to feel my eyes prickle with tears.

"All right, if we're really going to try this again, I think Ryanne should have a rest first," Kahina said.

"I'm fine," I protested.

"You're not fine," Josh disagreed. "You have a concussion. You're supposed to be resting so you don't make it worse. You heard what Dr. Sanchez said."

"All right, fine. Why don't we go home and I'll rest for a couple of hours. Maybe Kahina can come over later?"

Kahina and Josh looked at each other in sudden discomfort.

"Going home might be a bit of a problem," Josh said.

"Why?"

"It's my fault," Kahina admitted. "I was so angry, and so desperate to find Leora. I really thought you were involved in her kidnapping."

"I know you did. So, what's the problem?"

"I spoke to the media." Her cheeks were flushed. "I told them I thought you were involved in Leora's kidnapping, and the police and FBI weren't doing their job. I said I thought you knew the kidnappers, and where they had taken Leora. I told them I thought the FBI should be bringing you in for questioning, at the very least. And then I gave them your name. And your address."

"Holy shit. They're probably swarming all over my house right now!"

"I'd imagine so. I think going home would be a very bad idea," Josh said.

"What about my house?" Kahina offered.

"Not secure enough." Josh shook his head. "They know where you live, too. They could show up there at any time. I think we're going to have to find a hotel."

**

Americas Best Value Inn was located on West Picacho Avenue on the western edge of Las Cruces. Josh eased me into a seat in the lobby and went to check in. The lobby was done in neutral grays and whites. A couple of statement walls were painted in pool blue and hot pink, and the whole space was airy and clean.

"I got us a suite," he said, helping me up. "But it's on the second floor. Are you up for some stairs?"

"No problem."

Actually, the stairs were more of a challenge than I might have thought, and I was winded and weak by the time we reached the second floor. Josh guided me down the long hall, eventually stopping in front of a door and using the key card to gain access. I didn't even pay attention to the room number. My mind was shutting down, drifting into sleep, while my body desperately tried to remain upright.

He helped me into the living room and was just about to close the door when one of the hotel staff appeared in the doorway with a smile and a plate piled high with nachos. I perked right up at the sight of them and my stomach let out a low rumble of anticipation.

"Compliments of the hotel," she said as she handed them over to Josh, along with a couple bottles of water.

"Thanks," he managed, and then closed the door and turned the dead bolt. "Well, that's unusual."

"Bring 'em here." I was already sitting at the table.

"I thought you were going to rest."

"There are *nachos*, Josh. Rest can come later."

CHAPTER THIRTY-NINE

While Ryanne rested in the back bedroom, Josh remained in the living room and caught up on his work, grateful he'd had the foresight to bring his laptop when they left Ryanne's house that morning. His phone had been on silent during the meeting with Kahina, and he'd missed several calls from his boss.

It wouldn't take long for Executive Administrative Director Dean Forster to realize Josh had ignored his directive to back off the case. He chose not to retrieve his messages.

Rubbing his eyes, he tried to wake himself up. Although he wasn't planning on submitting them, he'd been filling out reports, and his eyes were burning from staring at the computer screen for so long.

Though it was for his eyes only, he felt the need to document everything that had happened. Laying everything out in writing helped. It both clarified and solidified the events of the past couple of days, allowing him to take a step back and reflect on what he'd learned without as much emotion.

There were so many questions, and he suspected most of the answers lay buried within the mind of the woman snoring in the back bedroom.

Josh was a basket of nerves, giddy with the exhilaration of finding Ryanne (One of the missing children! *Found!*), and all the possibilities that came along with such a huge break in the case. But overshadowing his excitement was an overwhelming sense of danger and impending doom.

Ryanne had said there was something much bigger going on than the kidnappings. After witnessing the evil that had come through her during hypnosis, he was convinced. One word kept haunting him, tightening his chest and loosening his bowels. The word was *extinction*.

***

"Why didn't you tell me you'd been attacked?"

Josh jumped at the sound of her voice. He'd been in a half doze in front of the computer, his mind wandering through the tangled web of his unanswered questions. Ryanne was standing in the doorway. Her hair was mussed and there were pillow creases on her right cheek.

"Attacked?" He shook his head, uncomprehending.

"The man that was trying to break into your home." She limped into the room and settled into the armchair facing him. With everything that had happened since, he had completely put that incident out of his mind, and he told her so.

"It's not a big deal," he insisted, but she was already shaking her head.

"It wasn't just some random guy trying to steal your baseball cards."

"How do you know about my baseball cards?" he asked, but she waved off the question.

"That guy was sent to kill you, Josh."

"I can't believe that."

"It's true. Remember, you told me about your boss, what's his name, Foster?"

"Forster. Dean Forster."

"Right, that guy. The one with the nasty case of erectile dysfunction."

"What?"

She waved dismissively again. "He and that other guy, the bigwig with the fancy suits." He hadn't told her about Warner's clothing, either.

"Deputy Director Michael Warner."

"Right, him. He's a really bad guy, Josh. I mean *really* bad."

"You don't have to tell *me* that."

"He ordered a hit on you."

He sputtered, "You can't be serious!"

"That guy was breaking into your house to kill you. It was pure luck you were leaving to fly here, instead of lying asleep in your bed, when he broke in. Didn't it ever occur to you to wonder why some guy was breaking into your home with an arsenal of weapons?"

"Damn it! Of course that's been bothering me. But I've barely had time to think about it since I got here."

"Well, I'm glad you made it here. And it looks like we have something in common."

"We're both on someone's hit list?"

"We're on the *same* someone's hit list." Her mouth was curling up at the corners.

"And that's a good thing?"

Her smile grew. "Hell, yes. It means we're rattling the right cages."

He had to laugh. "You're nuts."

"No, just sick of being scared." She picked up his cell phone and handed it across the coffee table to him. "Call Kahina. I'm ready to do some more cage rattling."

***

She answered her cell on the fourth ring, sounding out of breath and nervous.

"Kahina? Are you all right?" Josh asked.

"I'm fine," she said, but his heart had already kicked into high gear. Something was off.

"What's going on? Where are you?" he asked.

"I'm at home. I'm fine. Just tired." She sounded anything but tired.

"Is the media there?"

"No, I'm alone." But he heard someone in the background. Was that a man's voice?

She was lying. And her voice was shaking.

"Kahina, listen very carefully. I'm going to bring over some food. What would you like? Say 'pizza' if you're in danger. Say 'Chinese food' if you're safe."

There was a long pause.

"Pizza sounds good. Thanks." And she hung up.

***

He was amazed Ryanne was able to keep up with him, but she did. She was wheezing as she flung herself into the passenger seat of the FJ Cruiser, and still trying to put on her seat belt when he squealed out of the parking lot.

It took less than ten minutes to get to Kahina's home on Hoagland Road. They drove in tense silence; there was nothing to say.

It was dark by the time they reached her neighborhood, and Josh parked on the opposite side of the street and several houses down, cursing himself for choosing Ryanne's bright-yellow FJ Cruiser that morning rather than the rental car. How much more conspicuous could he get?

"Wait here," he said, but she was already out of the car and hobbling across the street. "Shit!" He jumped out and followed her, pulling his gun free of its holster. He caught up to her on the far sidewalk and grabbed her good arm.

"Where the hell do you think you're going?" he hissed.

"Hurry, Josh!"

He considered his chances of convincing her to go back to the car, and gave it up as a losing battle. Why hadn't he left her back at the hotel?

But he knew why. He couldn't stand to have her out of his sight. He was terrified she'd disappear. Again.

"Stay behind me and don't do anything stupid!"

She followed him up the path to the front door. From the outside, all appeared normal. Kahina's car sat silently in the driveway. The lights were on inside the house, the curtains drawn against the evening chill. There wasn't any media around. He debated knocking on the front door, but his nerves were at "code red" levels, so he tried the handle instead.

The door was unlocked.

He motioned for Ryanne to get down and stay put, and then walked across the threshold, gun first. The TV was on in the living room. It was tuned to the evening news, which was covering Leora Wylie's disappearance. The camera panned over the front of Ryanne's house. His rental car sat sedately in the driveway.

"Dr. Wilson was first hailed as a hero for her attempt to stop the kidnapping. But I had a chance to speak with Leora's grandmother this morning, and she paints a much different picture." Kahina's face filled the screen. She was standing outside the house on Monte Vista Avenue, her cheeks wet with tears.

Josh turned away, easing through the living room. It was tidy and undisturbed. The kitchen on the right was spotless save for a pot of tomato sauce cooling on top of the stove.

"Hey!" he hissed as Ryanne passed by him, moving toward the back of the house.

"They're gone," she called back over her shoulder.

He caught up with her and pushed her aside, moving into the point position.

"Stay the *hell* behind me." He cleared the bathroom and the guest bedroom, and then moved toward the back bedroom with Ryanne close at his heels.

The first thing he saw was the blood. Wet and fresh. He tried to push Ryanne back, both to protect her from the sight and to protect the chain of evidence. She was having none of it, though. She slipped under his arm and through the doorway.

Ryanne gasped when she saw the blood spatter, reeling back against his chest. And then she was moving forward again, like a woman caught in a nightmare that, no matter how horrific, still had to be seen through to its conclusion.

Kahina was on the floor on the far side of the bed. Her throat had been slit from ear to ear, leaving an angry purple gash. Her skin was gray, her eyes open and staring sightlessly at the ceiling.

"Don't touch her!" Josh called, to no avail. It was obvious she was gone. But Ryanne knelt down in the blood and placed a trembling hand over Kahina's eyes.

"Ryanne, she's dead. You have to move away from her; you're disturbing the evidence."

"She was trying to protect us." Her voice was hoarse, shaky. "They were looking for us. She wouldn't tell them where we were."

"Who? Who was looking for us?"

"She thought they were federal agents. They showed her badges, so she let them in. But then she realized something was wrong. She refused to answer more questions, tell them anything more about us." She gulped back a huge sob and continued.

"She ran. But they caught up with her here. She fought them, but they were too strong." The tears came. *"It's my fault. I'm sorry, I'm sorry,"* she keened over Kahina's lifeless body.

He grabbed her around the waist and hauled her upright. She was covered in tears and blood.

"Come on," he said, pulling her back down the hall to the front door. "We've got to get out of here." He was going against his training, against every instinct he had.

Secure the scene. Gather the evidence.

All the old rules, the ones around which he had fashioned his very existence, no longer applied.

"Where are we going?" she managed as he lifted her into the FJ Cruiser.

"We're about to become ghosts."

CHAPTER FORTY

"Sumner, you're going to have to trust us," Ora said, touching his arm gently.

He wanted to keep arguing, but there was no point. She was right. Lexy, Ora, and Phoenix had been called home. He could either go with them to his certain death, or he could go rogue.

"Sumner, find the redhead," Lexy said, coming up beside Ora and looking up at him earnestly. "If we can't get Jack away from The Ranch, then we might still have a chance if you can find her. That redhead, whoever she is, is the key. We all sense that."

"Jack is key, too," Sumner argued.

"Yeah. He is. And we'll do our best to get him. I promise," Ora said.

"Sumner, if you come with us, it will put all our lives in jeopardy," Phoenix added. "They can't know we've joined forces."

"Your lives might already be in danger," Sumner said. "There's a very real chance he's calling you back early because he's been tipped off."

"I know." Lexy gave her brother a look. "Mannix probably told Father Narda that Phoenix was poking his nose where it didn't belong."

Phoenix's cheeks reddened. "Once again, I'm sorry."

Ora shook her head. "It doesn't matter now. If he's been tipped off, we'll have to deal with it. My dad isn't going to kill me over it. The punishment might be harsh, but it won't be deadly."

"Not for you, but what about us? *Our* dad isn't the High Priest," Lexy said.

Ora met her gaze. "Honey, I would never let my dad hurt you."

Sumner felt a stab of jealousy. That was the difference between the Disciples and the Chosen, in a nutshell. The Chosen were the true children of *I Fidele*. The Disciples were expendable. They didn't have fathers who would protect them, and that created a chasm between the two groups that could never be bridged.

Could he trust this group of spoiled kids? Their hearts might have been in the right place, but they were so *young*. He'd already witnessed enough in the short time he had spent with them to know they were guided more by raging hormones and teenage angst than by logic. They were narcissistic and overindulged. Was it wise to lay such a huge responsibility at their feet?

Ora squeezed his hand. "We'll give you a head start, and shield you as long as we can."

"It won't be for long. Once we separate, it will be difficult to protect you," Phoenix added. "You need to stay well hidden."

"I know," Sumner said.

"They're going to hunt you," Lexy warned.

"I know," Sumner said again.

"And they won't ask questions. They'll kill you on sight," Lexy added.

Sumner nodded, swallowing hard. "Any idea where I should go?"

Lexy closed her eyes briefly, as though assessing an internal map. "North and west," she said with certainty.

"Okay." That was as good a direction as any, he supposed—except The Ranch was also to the northwest. Phoenix left the room and returned with a wad of cash. He pushed it into Sumner's hands.

"Here's thirty grand. Use it to stay alive."

"I can't take your money," Sumner protested.

"It's not my money. It's *I Fidele*'s money. And as you well know, it's just a drop in the bucket."

Sumner did know that. Without further comment, he shoved it into the front pocket of his jeans.

"Be careful," he told them, surprised to feel the sting of tears in his eyes. Would he see any of them again? Ora hugged him.

"You too," she whispered. "Call me if you need help." He knew she didn't mean on the phone.

Lexy hugged him, and then Phoenix gave him a manly clap on the shoulder. Sumner turned and left, refusing to look back as he closed the apartment door behind him. He had been alone for a long time, and had gotten just a taste of what companionship felt like. It was hard to leave, hard to walk away from the relative comfort he had found in their presence.

***

Sumner took a Greyhound bus to Austin and spent his first night in a hostel off East 6th Street, in the high-crime Entertainment District. He purchased new clothes: underwear and warm socks, blue jeans, and black T-shirts. He also picked up a puffy green coat that would keep him warm and distort his shape, personal hygiene products, and a duffel bag for storage. He also bought a bottle of brown hair dye and electric clippers, which he made use of back at the hostel.

With his newly shorn dark hair, Sumner wandered along East 6th Street. Psychic abilities sometimes came in handy. It wasn't long before he found exactly what he was looking for: an operation that made decent fake IDs. It was a thousand dollars to get a full set, which included a California driver's license that would pass all but the closest of inspections, a new birth certificate, and a prepaid MasterCard.

New papers in hand, he purchased an iPhone and set up an unlimited data plan, paying for a year in advance. He spent the rest of the evening searching Craigslist for a suitable vehicle. He slept as well as could be expected of someone being hunted, and was in a taxi by six the next morning.

Seventy-five hundred dollars bought him a white 1984 Westfalia camper van. It was loaded with a kitchenette, a two-person table, and enough room to sleep four if he ever decided to open the pop-up roof. It had been well loved and ran smoothly, although it took him a good hour to get used to the manual transmission, something he hadn't operated since his early twenties.

The old man he bought it from was kindly, and he'd stocked it with blankets and towels. His plump wife took pity on Sumner's slender form and piled the fridge with goodies, despite his protests.

Why did kindness make him feel so guilty? Sumner blinked back tears, thanking them for the tenth time. If they only knew the things he'd done, the pain he'd caused.

But as he found his way out of Austin's maze, he had a thought, and it eased the heaviness in his chest: Maybe it wasn't too late to save his blighted soul. And maybe the road to redemption was north and west in a VW van, in search of the redhead.

CHAPTER FORTY-ONE

"It's my fault! It's my fault!" I was both wailing and sobbing, tears and snot mixing in a disgusting stew of phlegm.

Josh had cleared us out of the hotel room in less than five minutes, and was weaving silently through the light evening traffic on I-25, his grim face ghostly in the dim light of the dashboard.

His jaw was tight, his eyes methodically switching focus like a man watching a tennis match. Forward to the windshield, up to the rearview mirror, left to the wing mirror, right to the passenger wing mirror, and repeat.

Around Caballo Lake, I ran out of steam. My wails turned to soft sobs, my sobs to snuffles and hiccups. I closed my eyes against the searing pain in my head and tried not to replay the image of Kahina's bloody corpse in my mind.

My head was splitting open, so I dug through my purse for my pain meds and dry-swallowed a couple. The next thing I knew, Josh was shaking me awake. I startled out of the blackness, good arm flailing, fighting an unseen enemy.

"Shh! It's okay!" he hissed. His face swam into focus. I could barely make him out in the dark; he had turned off the engine and all was silent except our labored breathing and the ticking of the engine as it cooled.

"Where are we?"

"Truth or Consequences. We need to change vehicles. This FJ Cruiser is like a beacon." He wasn't looking at me, but rather beyond me through the passenger window. I swiveled to look. It was a used-car lot, dimly lit and gated off.

"Looks like they're closed for the night," I said, stating the obvious.

"Yes." Hard determination was pinching the corners of his eyes.

"I'm pretty sure it's frowned upon for a federal agent to steal a car."

He looked away from the lot long enough to trap me with his gaze. The cold steel behind his eyes caused a ripple of fear in me. Perhaps it was the tears he had shed in the hospital, or the gentleness with which he'd taken care of me. Whatever the reason, I had wrongly pegged him as a soft man. In the darkened car, there was nothing soft about him. He was all sharp edges and blunt force, ready to cut and bludgeon to get what he needed.

"I'm not a federal agent. Not anymore." Josh jumped out of the car and slammed the door behind him, giving me one last piercing look that pinned me to my seat. I understood the silent order to stay put, and I wouldn't have left the car if it caught fire around me.

Then who the hell are you? I wondered.

***

I waited in the ticking quiet of the FJ Cruiser for what seemed like an eternity. Finally, the dark shape of a fast-moving car appeared from the back of the lot. It aimed straight for the chain-link gate, breaking through with a shower of sparks and a horrible screeching sound as metal scraped against metal. The car swung around, fishtailing, and pulled to a stop in front of me.

Josh jumped out of the driver's seat and trotted back to me. The engine was off, so I couldn't lower the window. I opened the passenger door instead, and as soon as I did, I caught the dull bleating of the dealership's alarm.

"Do you think you can drive?" He was huffing, a sheen of sweat visible on his cheeks and brow.

"I guess so," I said without confidence. The pain had eased to a distant throb, but between my left arm and my right leg, I wasn't really in my prime.

"Great. It won't be far. But we need to get out of here. Fast."

Well, duh.

He helped me out of the car and I limped around to the driver's side. I needed a boost in, and he turned on the engine and adjusted the seat and mirrors back to my position.

"Just follow me," he ordered, and trotted back to his stolen car, which was a silver Ford Fusion. He'd pulled off the price stickers, but there were no license plates.

Josh took care of that problem with haste, stopping in a residential neighborhood a mile away and lifting the plates off a late-model Subaru. Within minutes, he had them attached to the Ford and we were weaving out of Truth or Consequences northbound.

I trailed him past Elephant Butte Lake State Park, following the signs toward the municipal airport. He entered the long-term parking lot and stopped at the far end. I pulled into the stall beside him and cut the engine.

He opened my door. "Leave the key in the ignition."

"Are you serious?"

He hauled me out of the car and pried the keys out of my hand.

"Wait a minute! I'm not abandoning my car!" I argued.

He stuffed me into the passenger seat of the Ford, then yanked the Toyota key off the ring and handed me the rest.

"Hey!"

"Ryanne." His voice was terse. "If they don't know what you drive by now, they will soon enough. That car will get us killed."

Without waiting for further argument, he slammed the door in my face and emptied the trunk of the FJ, which had held his laptop bag and a metal briefcase. He yanked my purse out of the front, dumped his bags in the trunk of the Ford, and handed over my purse as he slid behind the steering wheel.

We took off with a screech of the tires, and I turned to get one last look at my FJ as we sped out of the parking lot. I felt like I was abandoning a faithful friend.

We stopped again in a quiet neighborhood in Socorro, and Josh switched the stolen plates for ones off an old Mercedes. We were back on the road within five minutes.

"Why did you attach the first plates to the Mercedes?" I asked.

"So it takes longer for them to notice their plates have been stolen."

In Albuquerque, he switched out the plates for a third time before picking up the I-40 eastbound toward Texas.

***

The sky was just beginning to lighten as we approached Amarillo. Josh had insisted on driving the whole way, and he looked exhausted. There were dark-purple smudges under his eyes, and the five o'clock shadow on his face couldn't hide the pale skin underneath.

He hadn't relaxed his vigilance behind the wheel one iota, and drove through New Mexico like a man being chased by the demons of hell. Which perhaps he was. He changed lanes frequently, and several times he abruptly exited the freeway, only to pull back on again, watching the rearview mirror intently.

"What are you doing?" I exclaimed the first time we careened, kamikaze-style, down an exit ramp.

"Countersurveillance." His voice was curt, angry even, and after that I kept my mouth shut.

While he didn't lose the intensity of his vigilance, his shoulders relaxed a bit when we crossed into Texas. We pulled into a dismal-looking motel on the outskirts of Amarillo, and bounced across the cracked pavement to the back of the two-story building.

"Wait here while I get us a room," he said as he shut off the engine.

"I want to come with you!"

"You're covered in blood."

"What . . . oh, shit!" I mewled in horror. In the first light of dawn, I could just make out the dark streaks on my shirt and jeans. There was blood smeared on my hands and crusted under my fingernails. "Why didn't you tell me before?"

"Because there was nothing you could do about it. Wait here. Lock the door."

Josh returned within minutes, and led me to a room at the far end. He helped me across the threshold like an unenthusiastic groom.

The room was drab and faded, and smelled like the last occupant enjoyed slaughtering cats while chowing down on Chinese food and beer. I hobbled directly to the dingy bathroom, which had mold rimming the cracked tiles and a burn mark on the sink counter. It looked like the perfect place to wash off blood, and I wondered how many people before me had done just that.

The shower was a tepid drizzle, and the bar of no-name soap was whittled down to a thin sliver. I wrapped the towel around my torso for modesty, rinsed my sling and hung it to dry, and left my disgusting clothes in a sodden heap on the bathroom floor.

I emerged clutching the towel against my chest, but I needn't have worried. Josh had wrapped himself in the bedspread, and was lying on the drab carpet against the door with his head on a folded-over pillow.

He was snoring softly, like a faithful guard dog. His gun was tucked up against the pillow, his hand at rest a foot away.

After a careful inspection for bedbugs and gross stains, I eased under the blankets and laid my head against the lumpy pillow. Sleep pulled me down with its powerful undertow, and I succumbed gratefully to the dark waves of unconsciousness.

***

I awoke from a restless sleep filled with knives and blood. Josh was watching me from the depths of the armchair, three feet from my head. He was holding the gun loosely in his right hand, his suit crumpled, tie askew, and hair standing on end. He looked like a frat boy after a rough night of bingeing. Or maybe after a weekend in Vegas.

"What?" I asked.

The unblinking intensity of his stare made me squirm. Painfully aware of my state of undress, I pulled the sheet up to my chin. The towel was loose and twisted around my waist, and I wondered how much skin I had inadvertently exposed.

He blinked and sat back. "What size do you wear?"

"What?" I could feel the blush rising up my neck and warming my cheeks.

"You're very small. Size two? Four?"

"Next you'll be asking me how much I weigh. Didn't your mom ever teach you manners?"

He blinked again, and a slow smile spread across his lips. I was surprised at how much I liked seeing it; vigilante Josh was kind of scary.

"Sorry, let me start again. I'm going to find a Walmart. We both need new clothes. If you write down a list of toiletries I'll pick those up for you, too." He ripped a page out of his pocket notebook and handed it to me with a pen.

I couldn't very well argue. Until I had some clean clothes to wear, I would be stuck in this room. I wrote down my clothing, bra, and panty sizes, added my list of toiletries, and handed it back to him without meeting his eye.

"Um . . . do you prefer bikini, or thongs, or . . . ?" His skin was competing with mine to see whose could get the reddest.

"Bikini is fine."

He grunted in response and left with mumbled instructions to lock the door behind him.

An hour and a quarter later, there was a gentle knock on the door. I dutifully peeked through the curtain before letting him in. In one hand, he was carrying several overflowing Walmart bags; in the other was a tray with two giant Starbucks cups.

"Coffee. You're my hero." Towel clutched around me, I stepped back from the door and watched him set everything down on the Formica table.

"I figured you wouldn't let me back in without it." He handed me a couple of bags and I retreated to the bathroom to wash up and get dressed. When I emerged, he was sitting at the table sipping his coffee and leafing through a newspaper.

"How do the clothes fit?" he asked.

"Fine, except . . . well, I think the top is a little low-cut." I didn't bother to mention that baby pink was the last color I would ever choose to wear.

"It looks good to me," he replied, and then hastily looked back down at his newspaper, but not before I caught the flash of male heat in his eyes.

Oh, I thought.

After a moment of awkward silence, I grabbed my coffee and sat across from him. "So, what now?"

"Now, we eat," he said, nodding at the bag on the table. With my good hand, I pulled out blueberry-bran muffins, raw cashews, yogurt, and bananas.

"Seriously?"

The corner of his mouth was twitching, but he didn't look up from the newspaper. "Bon appétit."

CHAPTER FORTY-TWO

Josh watched her eat over the top of his newspaper, trying not to grin every time she grimaced or sighed over the healthy breakfast he had provided. Although she managed to scarf down two muffins, a couple of handfuls of the nuts, and two bananas, one would have thought she was being tortured. She turned her nose up at the yogurt, claiming she couldn't stomach the texture.

Josh couldn't help but laugh at her look of childish glee when he presented her with the doughnuts he'd kept hidden beside him. She actually bounced up and down in her seat, as though he were a magician producing a rabbit out of a hat. He grabbed one of the honey-glazed and pushed the other three in her direction. She dug in with enthusiasm.

When she was on her second doughnut, Josh addressed her earlier question. "So, the first thing we have to do today is get our hands on as much cash as possible."

"You're not going to rob a bank, are you?"

"No, smart-ass. But we are going to have to clear out our accounts. Any idea how much you have?"

She shrugged. "A few thousand in my checking. Probably another five in savings."

"Good. I've got about six grand I can lay my hands on. That should do, for now."

"And then what are we going to do?"

"Well, I've been thinking about it. I don't like being on the run; I don't play well on defense. I'd rather be on offense, if you get my meaning."

"Sure."

"So the way I figure it, we could hole up somewhere and work on recovering your memory. See where that leads us. But I'd rather push forward on all fronts."

"Right, that makes sense." Her lips were glistening with sugar and he had to look away in order to concentrate.

"I want to go back to DC."

"You mean where hit men are waiting to snuff you out?"

"It's where all my leads are. Sumner Macey, the Department of Education. And there's a certain deputy director I'd like to pay a visit to."

"You can't be serious."

"Oh, I am," he said with grim determination. "Deputy Director Warner has some explaining to do."

"Josh, I told you before: he's a dangerous man."

"So am I." He didn't know what she saw in his eyes, but whatever it was caused her to swallow hard.

"Okay," she conceded. "So, what? You're just going to go storming into his office?"

"No. We're going to have to fly under the radar from here on out. We're being hunted; there's no doubt in my mind about that."

"I know." Her face was grim.

"Ryanne, from now on, you need to follow my orders. Do you understand that?" Her eyes were so big, doelike, and full of anxiety. He continued anyway.

"You have to trust me, and do *exactly* what I say. This is not some macho bullshit. I've been *trained* for this. You have not." He took her hand across the table, wanting to somehow soften the blow. "What you did yesterday, in Kahina's house, was extremely dangerous. It could have gotten us killed."

Her eyes filled with tears. "I'm sorry."

"I won't always have time to explain things to you, so you can't question me like you did about dumping the FJ. I need you to trust me, and follow my orders immediately and without question. My top priority is your protection; the investigation is secondary. But I need your help to keep you safe."

"I need to learn how to protect myself, too," she said quietly.

"You're right. I'll teach you what I can."

"Okay." She snuffled back the tears. "So what's our first move? After getting the money, I mean."

"We're going to need help, and I only know one person I can trust."

"Who is that?"

"His name is Phil Lagrudo. He was the sheriff in Elkhorn when you went missing."

***

Their first stop was at a Bank of America on the west side of Amarillo, where Ryanne withdrew all but five hundred dollars from her accounts. Josh explained that withdrawing every last cent would raise eyebrows, and it was best to avoid that. The next stop was a Wells Fargo near the airport, where Josh withdrew his cash. Then they drove south through Amarillo and filled up with gas just off the freeway on the edge of town.

"Why are we doing this?" Ryanne finally asked.

"We're about to go dark," he said. "I want it to seem likely that we headed south from Amarillo."

He was marking out the winding route to Nebraska on a map he'd purchased at Walmart. "It looks like it will take about eleven hours, plus stops," he muttered, pen in his mouth as he folded the map and smoothed out the page so Ryanne could easily refer to it along the way. There were a lot of twists and turns along rural routes until they reached Kansas, and he would need her to guide him.

"You know, I have Google Maps on my phone. Wouldn't that be easier? Especially in the dark?" The sun was already low in the sky. They only had another couple of hours of daylight left.

"Shit! Turn off your phone. They can track you that way." He had turned off his phone while leaving Las Cruces the previous evening, but hadn't thought about Ryanne's.

She pulled her iPhone out of her purse and turned it off without further comment, but he saw her gaze dart around the gas station, looking for danger.

"Let's get out of here," he said gruffly.

***

They watched the sun rise over the Platte River in silence, both lost in their own thoughts. Josh was remembering fishing trips with his father, camping by the river on summer nights, and, in later years, male bonding over bonfires and beer.

He wondered what Ryanne was thinking, if any memories were sparking for her. Her expression was unreadable, deep and sad, as the gold light of dawn kissed her skin through the windshield. Josh opened his mouth, and then closed it again without speaking.

When the last streaks of pink gave way to morning light, he started the car and drove slowly into Elkhorn.

t S.M. Freedman

It was just before seven a.m. when they pulled to a stop in front of Phil Lagrudo's beige stucco house on Honeysuckle Drive, less than two miles from where Ryanne had disappeared over twenty years before.

S.M. Freedman

It was just before seven a.m. when they pulled to a stop in front of Phil Lagrudo's beige stucco house on Honeysuckle Drive, less than two miles from where Ryanne had disappeared over twenty years before.

CHAPTER FORTY-THREE

Phil Lagrudo had aged since Josh last saw him. His hair, once salt and pepper, was wispy and white. His chest was smaller than Josh remembered, his midsection rounder.

"Hey, boss," Josh said, and watched the former sheriff do a double take.

"Holy shit on a shingle. *Metcalf?*"

They went through the typical male greeting, ending with a manly clap on the back.

"Son, you look like hell."

Josh could feel the grin spread across his face. "Can we come in?"

"Of course!" He shuffled back from the doorway to let Josh and Ryanne pass. "Damn, it's good to see you! What's it been, five years?"

"Five or six," Josh replied. "It's good to see you too, boss."

"Is this your lady?" Lagrudo extended his hand. "Phil Lagrudo, ma'am."

Ryanne blushed but shook his hand.

"This is Dr. Rowan Wilson," Josh said.

"Doctor?" He winked at Josh. "Well done. Would you like some coffee?"

"Oh, yes please," Ryanne said.

"If it's not too much trouble," Josh agreed.

"No trouble at all." Lagrudo was already moving into the kitchen, and they followed. He filled the pot with water, ground some fresh beans, and set the machine to brew. "Please, have a seat. Have you had breakfast?"

"We didn't come here to be a bother," Josh said.

"It's no bother! It's not every day I get a visit from one of my favorite officers and a beautiful young doctor. Speaking of which, you probably get this all the time, but I've got this thing on my foot—"

Josh coughed.

"I'm a doctor of astronomy, actually," Ryanne said. "And I'm starving, thank you."

"Have we met before?" The former sheriff asked. Ryanne looked stricken by the question, and Josh jumped in.

"It's a long story, boss. One best told on a full stomach."

"I'm intrigued," Lagrudo said as he pulled open the fridge door. "I'm sure you remember Marcy O'Donell?"

Josh could feel his cheeks warm.

"She's Marcy Johnson now," Lagrudo continued. "Married Matt Johnson about fifteen years back."

"I heard," Josh said, and the tone of his voice caused Ryanne to look at him curiously.

"Had themselves a few kids, too. Anyway, this is her quiche. She's taken it as her mission to keep me fed since Aileen passed last year."

"I'm sorry, boss. I didn't know."

Lagrudo shrugged. "How would you? She lived a good life, and didn't suffer at the end. Just went to sleep one night and didn't wake up the next morning. I hope I'm that lucky when my time comes."

As the quiche was warming, he washed some grapes to go with it. He poured the coffee into mismatched mugs and set down the cream and sugar so they could doctor their coffee as they wished.

Lagrudo served up three wedges and handed over forks and napkins. Josh and Ryanne dug in with enthusiasm. The quiche disappeared quickly, and they polished off the grapes as well.

When they all had a second cup of coffee in hand, Lagrudo sat back and, with a tone that said "Let's get down to brass tacks," said "So what's the deal, Metcalf? You in some kind of trouble?"

Josh gave him a wry smile of acknowledgment. "You could say that."

"I figured as much. What I'm wondering, though, is what kind of trouble would lead you away from that fancy office in DC and land you on my doorstep instead."

"If you saw my office . . ." Josh joked, but then turned serious. "The truth is, we're in some serious danger, and you're the only person I know for sure I can trust."

"Well, I'm flattered."

Josh knew what he was thinking. If he couldn't trust the Bureau Boys, as Lagrudo called them, then whatever danger they were in was serious indeed.

"What's this about, Josh?"

They had worked together for nine years, and Josh could only remember a handful of occasions when the sheriff had called him by his first name. One was at Josh's dad's funeral.

"The case. It's always been the case. All those missing kids. Almost eight hundred of them now."

"You're still just as obsessed as you've always been." It was a statement, not a question. His old boss knew, perhaps better than anyone, how that blood-covered backpack had changed the course of Josh's life.

"I'm much worse, actually," Josh said. "But I've finally had the break in the case I've been waiting for all these years."

"No kidding?" The sheriff's eyes settled on Ryanne with newfound interest.

Ryanne's skin had turned ghostly save for two spots of color high up on each cheekbone, like stoplights. She looked so much like Sherry, it made Josh's heart squeeze painfully in his chest. Another moment and Lagrudo would put the pieces together, but Josh beat him to it.

"Boss, say hello to Ryanne Jervis."

CHAPTER FORTY-FOUR

Sheriff Lagrudo was looking at me across the table as if I'd sprouted a nose in the middle of my forehead. He'd gone gray around the mouth, and I silently wished for a doctorate of medicine. My ability to calculate the speed of a main-belt asteroid would be of little use if he had a heart attack.

An older man, he had the bony shoulders and thick paunch of someone no longer in the best of health. I watched him nervously for signs of medical distress, only half listening as Josh brought him up to date on the investigation, explaining how he had figured out the kidnappers were using the PSST to find kids with ESP potential.

Josh told him about Jack Barbetti and Leora Wylie. The former sheriff settled into Josh's story; there was clearly a sharp mind ticking behind those faded-blue eyes.

"And that's how I found Ryanne," he said. "She tried to stop Leora Wylie's kidnapping, and got herself run over in the process."

"Then you know who the kidnappers are!" Lagrudo exclaimed.

I shook my head. "I don't."

"Then how did you know this girl was going to be snatched?"

"She has ESP, boss. She had a dream . . . or a vision, or whatever you want to call it. And you're right, I think she does know who the kidnappers are, but she doesn't remember."

"I don't understand." Lagrudo frowned.

"Her head's been seriously messed with. She doesn't remember anything before the age of eighteen, when she started at MIT. Obviously, she must have been well educated wherever she was, because she was able to get a degree in . . ." He stopped, embarrassed, and looked at me.

"I got a master's from MIT in aeronautics and astronautics, with a minor in astronomy, and I just completed my doctorate at NMSU." Phil Lagrudo whistled in admiration and Josh nodded in agreement, which made me squirm.

Clearing my throat, I told him about my loss of memory, my visit to Kahina, and Leora's kidnapping. Josh jumped in and explained how he found me in the hospital, and described the hypnosis session with Kahina. It was the first time I had heard in detail what had happened while I was in the black. When he finished, I described the hit man Josh had subdued. Lagrudo's bushy eyebrows became one with his hairline at that little nugget of information.

Josh finished with the details of Kahina's death, squeezing my hand under the table. He mapped out his plan to head back to Washington, and his desire to find Sumner Macey, the missing director of the PSST Division.

"I really want to find him; I suspect he holds a huge piece of the puzzle. I also want to pay Deputy Director Warner a visit."

"I'd imagine you do," Lagrudo said with a grim smile. "I'm guessing this is where I come in. Do you want me to watch over Ms. Jervis while you head back to DC?"

"I'm going with Josh!" I chimed in, afraid this had been Josh's plan all along. If he thought he was going to stick me out of the way with a retired sheriff as a babysitter, he had another think coming, and to hell with following his orders!

Thankfully, Josh shook his head. "No, I need Ryanne with me." He squeezed my hand again—a gentle promise that we were in this together—and I relaxed marginally.

Lagrudo seemed to think poorly of the idea. "You're putting her in danger by bringing her with you, Metcalf."

Josh shrugged. "She's in danger no matter where she is. Don't worry, boss, I'd lay down my life to protect her."

Lagrudo looked at him strangely. "I'm sure you would, but . . ."

"I need her with me. She knows things, and at any time she might remember something crucial."

Lagrudo looked like he was going to continue arguing, but he nodded instead. "All right. So what do you need?"

"I need a vehicle, something untraceable. And I need you to get rid of that Ford Fusion out there. I also need a couple of bulletproof vests, some more ammo, and at least one more gun. Really, any kind of weaponry would be great." As he spoke, his jaw tightened and his eyes became hard.

"I also need any kind of surveillance gear you can get your hands on, and some untraceable cell phones. I've got the money to pay for most of it. Well, maybe not the car."

"I've got deep pockets," Lagrudo said with a dismissive wave. "You know what they say about old dogs and new tricks? It ain't true. I've been sharpening my teeth on PI work since retirement. It keeps me up on all the latest and greatest. Let me see what I can do." With that, Lagrudo eased himself up from the kitchen table, purpose straightening his spine, and left the room.

I looked at Josh. "Are we supposed to follow him?"

He shrugged, and then smiled at me. "Why don't you finish your coffee first? You look like you need it."

"You're one to talk." But I did as he suggested.

***

The former sheriff of Elkhorn proved to be an excellent source for semilegal and contraband stuff. By lunchtime, he had amassed an arsenal of surveillance and countersurveillance equipment, most of which looked like weird doohickeys attached to tangles of wire.

He laid it all out on the coffee table in his living room, along with several guns of varying sizes. Josh seemed pleased with what he saw, and they began an in-depth discussion about the benefits of one caliber versus another.

"Have you seen this one before?" Lagrudo was stroking the barrel of a big black handgun.

"Oh, look at that." I could hear the reverence in Josh's voice.

"This beauty is a Fabrique Nationale Five-SeveN semiautomatic. It works on delayed blowback, and it's got a twenty-round detachable box magazine and sound suppressor. It uses a five-point-seven by twenty-eight-millimeter cartridge, so it's got less recoil and better accuracy. It's designed to have excellent penetration and range, so it's ideal against Kevlar protection."

"What does that mean?" I asked.

"It means it can better penetrate a bulletproof vest," Josh answered, sighting down the length of the barrel.

"Oh. Great," I said faintly.

"This one's for you." Lagrudo picked up a smaller pistol from the table. "It's a Glock twenty-seven Gen-four, in forty caliber. It's lightweight and easy to use, and it has a grip that can be adjusted to your hand. Many people in law enforcement use it as a backup weapon. This one is brand-new, courtesy of the Elkhorn Sheriff's Department."

"Great. Thanks," I said, but made no move to take it from him.

He smiled. "It's not loaded, but I'll let Josh teach you how to use it." Josh nodded in agreement.

"Here, try this on." Josh approached me with a dark-blue vest. He helped me to take off the sling before securing my vest, tightening the Velcro straps until it was snug against my chest.

"Sexy," I commented, and he smiled.

"Alive is always sexy." He eased my arm back into the sling. "It's better worn underneath your shirt, but I figured you might not want my help with that." He returned to the table with the excitement of a kid at Christmas.

I tuned them out as they continued to work their way through the contents of the table, and snapped to attention only when they left the living room.

"Hey! Where are you going?" I jumped up and hobbled after them.

Apparently, they were going to the garage, which was off the kitchen. I found them standing in the doorway, admiring whatever was in there. Josh turned, overcome, and hugged his former boss. The two men disappeared into the dimness, and I followed, stopping in the doorway.

It was a black Chevy Suburban with tinted windows, a bit dinged up but still in decent shape. It was a nice vehicle, but I couldn't quite understand Josh's extreme reaction.

"Are you absolutely sure?" he was saying.

"Of course I'm sure. It's a 2005, but it runs well. I bought it a few years ago; it's just been sitting here collecting dust."

"But it must have cost you a small fortune!" Josh was protesting.

"I got a good deal on it. I cashed in on a favor. It only cost me twenty grand."

"Twenty grand for a 2005 Suburban?" I couldn't help but chime in. "You got ripped off."

"It's not just a Suburban," Josh corrected. "It's an armored vehicle."

"With all the gadgets," Phil Lagrudo added, and I got the feeling he hadn't enjoyed himself quite this much in years. "It's got a navigation system, front and rear cameras, an outside listening device, hidden strobe lights in all four corners, front and rear stealth buttons, and a remote starter. It's also got a pretty good stereo."

"Seriously boss, this is too much. I can't take it."

"You can and you will. What good is it going to do me sitting in the garage, when it could be saving your life, and that of Ms. Jervis here? You said you'd do anything to protect her," he pointed out.

Josh met my gaze. "You're right, I did."

"Well then, discussion over. Let's get your gear loaded in."

CHAPTER FORTY-FIVE

Before they left Elkhorn, Josh took Ryanne on a tour of the area, hoping to spark her memory. He drove slowly down Main Street, pointing out the businesses that would have been around in 1988. They wove their way to Westridge Elementary School and parked in front of a "Children Crossing" sign.

Ryanne got out of the vehicle and made her way toward the school grounds, her hair aflame in the afternoon sun. He caught up with her at the chain-link fence and gently placed her new coat over her shoulders, hiding the Kevlar vest underneath.

Her fingers were curled around the chain link, and she was gazing at the playground, her expression distant and unreadable. The image struck a chord deep within him. The girl on the outside, forever looking in.

The bell rang and kids swarmed down the steps, laughing and chattering. They made their way to the bike racks, or wandered in small clusters to the sidewalk for a short walk home, or made their way to a waiting parent parked at the curb.

Had any of those parents been Ryanne's classmates, once upon a time? Did they pick up their children out of convenience, or because they remembered the girl with the red hair? Were they haunted by her, as he was? Ryanne watched them, and Josh watched her.

Finally, he had to ask. "Do you remember anything?"

At first she didn't answer, and he wondered if she had heard him. He followed her gaze until he saw what had transfixed her. A lone girl, sitting on a bench, knees pulled up to her chest. Her hair was blond instead of red, but even from a distance, Josh could see the knots in her hair and the dirt that smudged her sleeves.

"I remember being alone." She pulled away from the fence, turning her back on Westridge Elementary School and the childhood she'd never had.

***

The house where Ryanne had spent the first seven years of her life had been torn down, leaving nothing but overgrowth in its place. He pulled to a stop, remembering the day he had bounced across the side yard in his 1978 Ford Fairmont, kicking dirt up into the hot summer air. He had been so young then, about to take that first step along a path filled with twists and turns that would eventually circle him back to this very same spot.

"Keep going," she hissed.

He turned to look at her, pulling himself back to the present. "What?"

She wasn't looking at the property where her childhood home had once stood, but rather across the street to Mt. Calvary Cemetery.

"Get me out of here!" Her voice caught in her throat. Her breath was coming in ragged gasps, her skin bathed in sweat.

Whatever was going on, she was terrified. A healthy dose of adrenaline thundered through his veins, and he slammed the Suburban into gear. They shot forward and spun the wheels, angling back onto Skyline Road.

"What's going on?" he asked once he had the Suburban under control and they were barreling away from the cemetery. His heart was roaring inside his chest, a beast trying to escape.

"Oh! Oh! Oh!" Wheezing, she rolled herself into a ball, her face on her knees, her back trembling.

"You're going to hyperventilate! Ryanne, calm down and tell me what's going on!" He realized the irony of shouting at her to calm down, but he couldn't help it.

With concentrated effort, she slowed her breathing and eventually sat back up, eyes closed and head leaning against the headrest. Her skin had a faint gray tinge to it, and was shiny with sweat.

"I'm sorry," she managed. "I can't believe that's where I lived! I hate cemeteries."

"Why?" he asked, although he could feel the back of his neck prickling.

"Do you really want to know?" she asked.

His laugh was strangled, strange to his ears. "No. I don't."

***

Their final stop was at Papillion Creek, where her bike and backpack had been found. He held her by the arm as they made their way toward the brush surrounding the creek, not because she needed the support, but because he did.

"This is where we found your bike," he said quietly, pointing to a thicket of undergrowth. "It was half hidden in the bushes right there."

Her face was pale and drawn, her eyes wide as she took in her surroundings. He led her into the dappled shade, explaining as they went how he and the sheriff had searched the area. He helped her down the bank toward the creek.

"Your backpack was right here." He showed her. "It was covered in blood. Of course, we later determined it was from a lamb."

"Lamb's blood?" Her voice was faint, fragile.

"Are you all right?" He held her arm tighter, searching her face. Was she going to pass out? But no, she was calm, almost unfazed.

Josh could see that the place held no meaning for her. It was he who was haunted by it, and haunted by the girl within the woman. A ghost in a Kevlar vest.

He marveled at the exquisite mystery of her. The woman who stood in perhaps the very spot where the girl had been taken. She was battered, damaged in ways he didn't yet understand, and yet still she stood. A spark among the shadows. A ghost no more.

CHAPTER FORTY-SIX

Sumner rolled into Amarillo the day after Ryanne and Josh cleared out their bank accounts. To his misfortune, the *I Fidele* agents who were hunting Josh and Ryanne also converged on Amarillo that day. It was pure coincidence they found him instead, and the irony of the situation was lost on him until much later. He came upon them in, of all places, the same Walmart Supercenter where Josh had shopped the day before.

Sumner had purchased a Smith & Wesson M&P Shield 9mm handgun from a pawnshop in Fort Worth and had spent the last few days visiting various shooting ranges as he traveled north through Texas.

The manager of the first one had taken pity on his obvious ignorance. He patiently demonstrated how to strip the gun down, clean it, and put it back together. He gave Sumner pointers on firing it, and then taught him a sequence that began with the gun tucked up against the small of his back. He had to pull the gun out of his belt, aim it with precision, fire off all the rounds, reload, aim, and fire again. Sumner's efforts had been sloppy at best. He secretly wondered if, under pressure, he'd be able to manage it without lodging a bullet in his butt cheek.

Although the manager had snickered at Sumner's choice of gun (apparently anything less than a .45 was a "chick's gun"), he recommended buying better-quality bullets, and wrote down the name of the ammo on a scrap of paper.

Sumner was paying for the ammo, along with a sandwich and lemonade, when he felt the warning buzz of a bogey approaching. He stopped short while reaching for his change, his hand frozen in midair.

He didn't know the real names of any of his bogeys, if they even had names, but over time he had christened them according to their personalities.

Coach hounded him any time his feet were dragging on an important task. In Sumner's mind, he was thick necked and red faced, all booming voice and bulging veins.

Loretta was a motherly type who appeared whenever he was upset or angry. She was soothing green light and the smell of meadow grass, a cool kiss on a fevered forehead.

Soapy, dubbed after the famous American con man Soapy Smith, was the trickster. He liked to pop in at inopportune moments and drop knowledge-bombs that were twisted versions of the truth. *Soapy* was a smirking swindler, always trying to cause trouble, and Sumner did his best to avoid contact.

The one who approached in the Walmart was *Redlight*. Rarely seen, *Redlight* was an alarm in a nuclear plant, all bullhorns and red-hot strobe lights. To ignore *Redlight*, even for a second, was to risk death.

Sumner grabbed his change from the cashier, pulled the plastic bag off the carousel at the end of the checkout line, and beat a hasty retreat toward the automatic doors. All the while, his eyes were scanning the people around him, searching out the danger.

There were moms with toddlers tucked into shopping carts, a rangy old man in the self-serve aisle buying a six-pack, and some construction types standing in line at the Subway. But *Redlight* was still blaring.

Danger! Danger!

If anything, *Redlight* was growing more strident. Sumner's mouth flooded with a bitter taste, like pennies. What? What was it?

The sun blinded him as he raced through the automatic doors, and he collided with the *I Fidele* agent who was on his way in. *Redlight* disappeared, leaving Sumner alone in the deafening silence.

They did the dance two strangers do when they collide, shuffling around each other with mumbled apologies. He was sure there was a joke in there somewhere: a couple of psychics collide outside a Walmart and fumble around like two of the Three Stooges.

Maybe he should have clunked him over the head with his sandwich. Bet you weren't expecting that, my psychic friend! Nyuck nyuck nyuck!

The moment before the agent's eyes registered recognition stretched in front of Sumner with all the hope a driver standing on his brakes must feel just before the inevitable, jarring impact of the crash.

And there was the third Stooge, approaching from the parking lot right on schedule. He was big and beefy and looked like he could snap Sumner in half with the twist of one tree-trunk-sized arm.

The agent Sumner had collided with was smaller than his beefy companion. He looked a lot like that T-1000 dude from *Terminator 2*, the one who looked like no match for Arnold Schwarzenegger until you saw him run down a car on foot.

And his focus was sharpening in recognition. Another moment and it would be too late. Beefcake would be upon them and Terminator would raise the alarm.

Hysteria bubbled up inside Sumner. With insane joviality, he clapped Terminator on the arm. "Time to split! Say hi to Skynet for me!"

He was lucky enough to get a bit of a head start, but he was pitting a thirty-year-old VW against a cherry-red V8 Camaro.

Oh yeah, he thought, this is going to end well.

He veered out of the parking lot onto Amarillo Boulevard eastbound, nudging into traffic and ignoring the irate honking of nearby drivers. The Camaro butted in about ten cars behind him, raising another ruckus.

They bobbed and weaved through traffic, jockeying for position, pausing at red lights and pushing through stale yellows. There was no way he could outdistance a Camaro under different circumstances, but the traffic put them on equal footing. Bit by bit he pulled away from them, gaining two car lengths and then losing one.

His break came when the Camaro got stuck at a red light at Western Street. Sumner pulled away, cackling madly as traffic flooded in behind him from the cross street. When he took the on-ramp for US 287 northbound, the Camaro was nowhere in sight.

Within a few miles, the traffic thinned out and the world spread out around him in a yellowed expanse of scrubland. The road was straight and flat, providing no place to hide. There wasn't a chance of him outpacing the agents if they chose the same route.

His only hope was that they turned south, and he watched the rearview mirror with morbid fascination. He pulled open a box of bullets with his right hand and wedged the gun between his thighs to load it.

"Hey Sumner, how'd you lose your ballsack?" He cackled wildly. And sure enough, there was a flash of red behind him.

"Shit!" Braking hard, he swung right onto Gravel Pit Road. Shockingly, it was covered in gravel. The car fishtailed when he pounded the gas pedal. Almost immediately, he realized what a bad decision he'd made, but it was too late. Nothing to do but bounce along at a teeth-rattling pace, kicking up a wild trail of gray dust.

"Do you think they'll notice me?" He couldn't stop laughing. The horror of the situation somehow seemed to call for it. It was either laugh or start screaming.

Sure enough, that telltale streak of red appeared through the dust in his rearview mirror, and he watched it grow bigger with a gruesome eagerness he couldn't explain.

Instead of the advertised gravel pit, Sumner caught a shimmer of blue-green through the dust. Was that a lake?

"Hey boys, care for a swim?" he said to his rearview mirror.

Veering toward the water, he tucked the gun into his armpit, wrapped the Walmart bag around his wrist, and opened the driver's-side door.

Sumner did his best *Mission: Impossible* dive, skidding and rolling across the loose gravel and feeling nothing at all like Tom Cruise. The gravel seared his skin like a million tiny daggers, but at least the gun didn't go off.

Dripping blood, he stumbled to the brush surrounding the lake and dove headfirst into the thickest bramble, hoping he wasn't awakening snakes or other vile creatures.

A second later, there was a surprisingly undramatic splash. The Westfalia rolled forward, nosing its way into the water. The driver's-side door eased shut.

By the time the Camaro pulled to a stop, spewing gravel from underneath its tires, the driver's compartment of the Westfalia was completely immersed and the tail was sticking up, back wheels spinning.

Sumner placed the Walmart bag on the ground beside him, wiped the sweat and blood out of his eyes, and positioned his hands on the gun. He took aim and waited.

Seven rounds—that was all he had. There was no chance he'd be able to reload before one of the agents was on top of him.

Beefcake was driving, and was therefore the closest. Sumner watched him get out of the Camaro. He could see the cocky smile on his face.

Sumner's hands were shaking violently. He took two deep breaths, sighting down the shaft of the gun, and waited for his moment.

He shouldn't have worried about whether he would be able to shoot another human being. Cornered as he was, the instinct for survival kicked in with stark clarity, peeling away his fragile human mask. He would kill or he would die. It was that simple. And he didn't intend to die.

"Not today," he growled, and pulled the trigger.

Of course he missed.

Beefcake roared and flew toward him like a tornado of muscled fury. Sumner closed his eyes and squeezed the trigger again. This time he didn't miss. Beefcake dropped with all the grace of a wild buffalo. One eye was open in shock; the other looked like raw hamburger and was spurting blood.

Terminator flew out of the passenger seat toting an enormous assault rifle that made Sumner's gun look like a dainty teacup.

He had five bullets left.

Sumner had the advantage of being hidden in the scrub while Terminator stood brazenly out in the open, trusting in his rifle to do its job. He laid down a spray of bullets, the closest of which missed Sumner's nose by several feet. The rifle was huge and obviously hard to control. It pulled Terminator in an arc from left to right.

The dumbass has his eyes closed, Sumner thought, conveniently ignoring the fact that he'd killed Beefcake with a lucky shot while his own eyes were closed.

It took four of the remaining five rounds before Terminator went down, and a new Sumner was born.

CHAPTER FORTY-SEVEN

Ora was in deep shit. It was entirely her fault for underestimating the Fathers, and if she could have kicked her own ass she would have, but it would have been quite the trick while drugged and strapped to a bed in the Priest's quarters.

Stupid! How could she have been so stupid?

She wondered where Lexy was. And Phoenix. Were they still on The Ranch? Were they still *alive*? She couldn't get a sense of them, either way.

Things had gone badly from the very start.

She should have run when she'd had the chance. Maybe stayed with Sumner. And speaking of Sumner, something big had happened Outside. She'd picked up only fragments of it, but whatever he'd done had caused a flap within the Priesthood the likes of which she had never seen.

They weren't used to losing, and they didn't take it well. Disquiet simmered beneath the calm surface. But rather than feel satisfaction over the stir Sumner's actions had caused, she was nervous. They were on a witch hunt.

And guess who would look superhot strapped to a burning stake?

Ora hadn't seen her dad since arriving at The Ranch. That was the first clue things weren't going to go well. She couldn't remember a time when Father Narda had not been waiting on the porch for her. Father Thanos, Phoenix's and Lexy's dad, was also missing.

Fathers Gabriel, Zaniel, and Palidor had greeted them instead, with their dour faces and cold eyes. A perfect trifecta of doom.

She had no idea how, but they knew about her relationship with Lexy. They knew about their foolish little rebellion. Strangely, the only thing they weren't aware of was their interest in Jack.

He was alive.

While it was only an educated guess before, or perhaps an instinct, now that she was back on The Ranch she could feel him. They were linked.

And the boy was strong. Phoenix was right about that. Jack was . . . *special.* Special *how*, she couldn't tell, but he was being well protected by some kind of spirit barrier around him. It was like nothing she'd ever encountered and she didn't know quite what to make of it. Any time she tried to reach out to him, she was blocked by a rising swarm of angry spirits. They bit at her like gnats until she backed off. Yet she could feel his pull in her blood and bones; his magnetism made her teeth ache just as much as the simple boy-ness of him made her heart ache. Because, despite his otherness, he was just a boy. He was scared and lonely and more than anything he wanted his dad.

"That makes two of us, kiddo. But I don't think either of our dads is riding in to save the day."

She kept trying to get through to Jack, but they were on a one-way intercom. All she was getting in return was dead air. He never responded to her, or gave any indication he was picking up what she was sending.

Was he being drugged? Was he in a coma? She couldn't figure it out, but she suspected there was more than just that spirit barrier breaking their communication.

Ora's mind was painfully clear, but they were giving her a drug that prevented her from moving objects telekinetically. She kept testing her binding straps, but to no avail. Whatever they were injecting her with, it was serving the purpose of keeping her a prisoner.

Her thoughts were interrupted by the jingle of keys on the other side of the door. Ora quickly shut down her mind and closed her eyes. It was better to feign sleep, safer somehow. And, strapped down to a bed, she had no other protection left.

She couldn't help the silly little hope-flutter that started up in her chest, the little-girl wish that this time it would be her father.

But it wasn't her father, who carried with him the unmistakable scent of oats and horses. It permeated his skin, even after a shower. It also wasn't the heavy tread of Father Palidor or the nervous shuffle of Father Gabriel, there to bring her food or help her to the toilet.

Whoever it was had entered silently. Her breath caught in her throat. Was she finally going to be questioned? Would she feel the prick of the needle next?

Was it Father Barnabas?

This thought sent shock waves of terror through her, and she couldn't help it; she cracked open an eyelid.

Oh, hell. She let out her breath and dropped her head back onto the pillow. "Ashlyn! What are you doing here?"

The girl's red hair was tied back in a ponytail, and she had a smudge of dirt across one pale cheek. She'd grown since Ora had last seen her, and the tiny buds of her breasts were poking out against the thin fabric of her shirt.

"Phoenix sent me." Even the mention of his name was enough to make the girl blush.

"Is he all right?"

"He's fine. He's being held the same way you are."

"Ashlyn, you shouldn't be here; you'll get in trouble!"

The girl rolled her eyes. "Let me worry about that."

"It's not a joke. There's some seriously bad sh—uh, *stuff* going down. I don't want you getting mixed up in it."

"I'm old enough to make my own decisions," she said with a belligerent pout, and Ora rolled her eyes. She remembered what it was like to be twelve.

"All right. Hurry up and give me his message, then. One of the Fathers could be in at any minute."

The girl smiled. "I doubt that."

Ora eyed her. "Ashlyn, what did you do?"

"Let's just say they've got their hands full with some plumbing issues right now."

"You flooded the toilets again?"

"Only the ones in the Priests' quarters." She smiled in satisfaction, and Ora had to laugh.

"How did you get in to see Phoenix?"

"How do you think?"

"They put you on fire patrol?" Obviously they hadn't found a drug that could stop Phoenix from lighting fires. Ora was perversely pleased.

"Yeah. He's really mad. They're keeping me nearby in case he decides to start burning stuff." She shrugged. "Guess I'm useful for some things."

Ora watched her carefully, an idea forming. Ashlyn was smart and powerful, but more importantly, she loved Phoenix. She would risk a lot for him. Was it right to involve her? But apparently Phoenix had already made that decision.

Ashlyn said, "Phoenix thinks he knows where the boy is being hidden."

"You know about that?"

Ashlyn nodded. "He says you guys need to get him off The Ranch." Her small chest puffed with pride. "I'm going to help. We've worked out a plan. And Phoenix promised I can go with you when you leave."

Shit! What the hell was Phoenix thinking? Ora bit her cheek until she was under better control. "All right. So what's the plan?"

"Phoenix said it's best if you don't know the details right now. Father Barnabas is coming in from Italy. To talk to you."

That was bad. That was about as bad as bad could get. To most people on The Ranch, Father Barnabas was a figurehead. He was a statue to be kissed, a name to be uttered with reverence during the daylight hours but never to be mentioned in the dark.

Whoever had carved the statue had portrayed the High Priest in a beatific light, as more saint than demon. But Ora had quickly realized the real man was quite the opposite. The first time she met him, when she was five, she had peed her pants when those pale eyes met hers. She suspected she would soon do it again.

"Oh man, that's so bad," she whispered.

"That's not all." Ashlyn's usually pale cheeks were flushed. "They're really mad about your . . . *relationship*. Father Palidor wanted to terminate Lexy. A few of the other Priests agreed."

"*Her?* Why not me?"

"Because you're Father Narda's daughter," she said simply, as if that explained everything. And perhaps it did. After all, Father Narda was the Ranch's High Priest. Father Thanos was much lower on the food chain. Which led to the obvious question, the one she had been avoiding. Was she being detained on her dad's orders?

But that was something to worry over later. "Are they going to kill her?"

Ashlyn shook her head. "Father Thanos pleaded with Father Narda. Begged him to spare her life, and Father Narda agreed."

"Oh, that's good." But her relief was short-lived.

"They made . . . an agreement." Ashlyn's entire face was aflame.

"What kind of agreement?"

"Do you remember Angeni?"

"The Native American girl? The one who can spirit-travel?"

"Right. Well, she became Father Narda's *Amante* a few months ago."

Nausea crept up Ora's throat. "She's younger than me!"

"Seventeen," Ashlyn agreed matter-of-factly. It was nothing new, of course. Especially not when it came to Father Narda, whose appetite for young female flesh was legendary. Ora should have been used to it by now.

"Horny bastard," she spat.

"Yeah. Anyway, he's given her up. He's taking Lexy as his *Amante*."

"What?" Ora sputtered. "He can't do that! She's one of the Chosen!"

"Father Thanos gave his permission. Fathers Palidor and Zaniel are furious. So is my dad. They say it sets a bad precedent. I guess they don't want their daughters, *you know*, with one of the other Priests." Ashlyn shuddered.

Ora's head was spinning. "He can't do that to her!" And she would probably rather die.

"He already has," Ashlyn said. "I saw her wearing a red robe at breakfast this morning. She looked like it was . . . rough."

"Oh, Lexy." Ora was weeping, and Ashlyn looked like she wanted to disappear through the floorboards out of mortification.

"Ashlyn, you need to get me out of here!" Ora reached for the girl. *"Please?"*

"I can't. I . . ." Ashlyn's eyes widened in horror, and for the first time Ora noticed how green they were.

"What is it? What's wrong?"

"I think . . . he's here."

"Who?" Ora asked, although she was very afraid she knew the answer to that question.

"He's just arrived. Can't you feel it?"

Ora could. It felt like the color black.

"I've got to go!" Ashlyn hissed, and bent over the bed to give Ora a hasty kiss on the cheek. "Stay strong, Ora!"

And with that, she was gone, leaving Ora alone. To wait.

CHAPTER FORTY-EIGHT

The drive from Elkhorn to Washington, DC, was surprisingly uneventful. Josh kept up his vigilant countersurveillance throughout the drive, and finally admitted he kept expecting to see someone on our tail. He couldn't believe we had slipped through the net as easily as we had.

No matter how bleary-eyed he became, he flat-out refused to let me take a turn at the wheel. I had to nudge him awake several times, but he still wouldn't budge from the driver's seat. Even after I lost my cool and accused him of being a macho control freak.

So I chose the path of maturity, doing what I could to get under his skin in return. I gorged on every junky food item I could find, and when I wasn't eating, I either napped or pretended to.

The irritation was coming off him in waves as he crunched his trail mix and guzzled his coffee, but at least it was keeping him awake.

By the time we reached the outskirts of Chicago, he was weaving and misjudging distances. It was midmorning and a light drizzle was falling, making the world around us hazy and gray.

"Josh," I said gently, my earlier frustration easing into pity. He looked like a boxer who knows he's been beat, but keeps getting up to face another pummeling anyway. "You need to rest."

I expected more of his macho BS, but instead he nodded, rubbing his face. "I know. I don't think I can manage the Chicago traffic without getting us killed."

"I'm okay to drive," I suggested, as though it was the first time I had offered. As expected, he shook his head.

"I won't be able to rest if you're driving."

"I'm not a bad driver, I'll have you know."

The corner of his mouth twitched. "I didn't say you were. But you're not used to countersurveillance."

"Keep looking behind you. I think I can manage that."

"It's not just about watching. It's about doing the right things if you spot someone following you, or if you're under attack. It's taken years of training for me to become proficient. And no, it's not something I can direct you on from the passenger seat, before you ask."

I shut my mouth.

"A lot of countersurveillance is counterintuitive. It takes time and practice to be able to go against your instincts."

"All right." I gave in. "So what do you want to do? Find a motel?"

He shook his head, studying the GPS map on the dashboard. "I'd like to stay invisible."

We exited the freeway onto First Avenue in Maywood. I thought for a moment he planned to pull into the Cook County Sheriff's Department, but we passed that by and continued north. Several miles later, he turned right onto Chicago Avenue and we were suddenly in the woods.

The traffic eased and he slowed, scanning the forest on either side. Josh nudged the Suburban through a break in the trees and into the woods beyond, easing over tree roots and small bushes until we were out of sight. He made a big, slow circle until we were facing back toward the road, and killed the engine. He depressed the button to roll down the windows an inch, and the smell of damp greenery trickled in on the cool fall air.

"You'll be able to hear anything coming."

He was right. The occasional passing vehicle some fifty feet away broke the silence of the forest. I would have plenty of warning if another car approached our position. "Can you stay awake?" he asked.

"No problem."

"Wake me up if you get drowsy." And with that, he reclined his seat, closed his eyes, and was gone.

I wrapped my jacket around me as a blanket and put my feet up on the dashboard. For a while I watched him sleep, studying his features. There was no doubt he was a handsome man. Although he'd been a mess when I first met him, by the next day he'd gone back to being the perfect picture of an FBI agent: clean-shaven, hair neatly styled, and dressed in a crisp suit. He had looked young and fresh, perhaps a bit too perfect and baby-faced with his bright-blue eyes and disarming smile.

He looked older now, more haggard. His beard was scruffy and had almost as much silver in it as it did black, his skin was pale, and there were dark-purple smudges under his eyes. His hair was a mussed-up mop of black and silver, and he had a coffee stain running down the front of his shirt and trail-mix crumbs in the folds of his jeans. I somehow liked this version of him better.

He stirred and cracked open his eyes. They were more red than blue and puffy with exhaustion.

"It's hard to sleep when someone's staring at you."

I blinked and turned away from him, heat inching its way up my neck. "Sorry," I mumbled.

"Creeper," he accused, grinning at me, and then turned onto his side and closed his eyes, his back to me.

***

I managed to let him sleep for almost four hours before my bladder couldn't take it anymore. It was the first chance I'd had to sit quietly and think, and I spent most of the time replaying the last few days and weeping quietly over poor Kahina.

The guilt I felt over her death was overwhelming, and I munched my way through the rest of the snacks in the car in an attempt to soothe myself. As a result, I was feeling uncomfortably full and cross-eyed from carb overload.

"Josh," I whispered, gently nudging him in the back.

He was immediately awake. He pulled himself up and blinked at me owlishly, as though trying to place me.

"Is everything okay?" He looked around, surveying our surroundings.

"Fine. It's just . . . I have to pee!"

He helped me out of the Suburban and insisted on coming with me as I made my way through the trees.

"That's as far as you're going, mister." I raised a hand to stop him when he seemed inclined to check out the bushes I had chosen for my toilet. "Do you seriously think there's somebody in there waiting to murder me? Now turn that way and don't look. Or listen," I said gravely, and he grinned and deliberately turned his back on me and plugged his ears.

Even with my left arm in a sling, I managed to relieve myself without getting pee on my shoes. It was a feat I was quite proud of, and I returned to him in a slightly better mood.

"Now plug *your* ears," he teased, before disappearing behind a tree. He emerged to find me dutifully waiting with my right hand cupped over my right ear, and my left ear awkwardly pressed against my left shoulder.

He had a nice laugh. It eased the heaviness around my heart.

***

Twelve hours later, we were approaching Washington, DC. The first stop he wanted to make was his own home.

"Are you sure that's a good idea?" I asked.

"I'll check it out before we go in, but who would think I'd be stupid enough to go home?"

"Um, yeah."

It was a little after four in the morning when we approached his townhouse, which was in a neighborhood called Falls Church, on the Virginia side of the capital. After circling the area without seeing anything unusual, Josh parked the Suburban against the back fence and slid in between the seats to the back.

He dug through the equipment in the cargo area and pulled out something that looked like a pen attached to earbuds. The buds fit snugly into his ears, and he pointed the other end toward the townhouse, moving the wand in slow circles. "I can't hear anything unusual."

He strapped a second gun against his side and slid a knife into his sock. He tightened his Kevlar vest, and then rummaged in a duffel bag until he came out with a couple of black caps. One went on his head, and then he turned to me.

He tightened the straps on my vest and pulled my hair up into the cap, tugging it down and tucking any loose strands up inside it.

"How do you feel about taking your sling off?" he asked.

"Are you kidding? It's driving me crazy; take it off!"

He did. "How does your shoulder feel? How much can you move it?"

I shifted my arm up and down, and then rotated my shoulder in its socket. It was tender, but not as bad as I had expected. "It's okay."

"Good. Your balance will be better without that arm tied down. How's your leg? Can you warm it up a bit? Get the blood flowing? I need you to be as limber as possible before we go out there."

I followed him through a series of calisthenics and stretching exercises, feeling slightly ridiculous in the cramped confines of the

Suburban. But as my muscles warmed up, the pain in my leg and shoulder eased, and my headache became nothing more than a dull throb.

Finally, he deemed it good and wrapped a utility belt around my waist. It held a nasty-looking blade, and I practiced pulling it out until he was satisfied I'd be able to do it with speed and without slicing my hand.

"What about my gun?" I asked, feeling a strange sense of possessiveness over it.

"Not until I've had the chance to teach you how to use it. But here, stick this in your pocket." He handed me a small spray can. "It's pepper spray. Try to aim it the right way, okay? And don't spray me."

I tucked it into the pocket of my jeans.

He pulled some weird-looking goggles over his eyes and then looked at me. "Ready?"

"What are those?"

"Thermal-vision goggles. We're going to climb up onto the roof of the Suburban. I'm going to have a peek into the yard, and if all is clear I'll jump over the fence. Count to five and lean over. I'll help you down."

"Seriously?"

"Hold on to the back of my vest as we cross the yard. When we go through the back door, I want you to stay low. If there's any trouble, run. If there's gunfire, get down, or get behind something. Okay?"

My mouth had gone dry. "Okay."

He smiled at me. "Don't look so worried."

Josh opened the back gate of the Suburban, looked around, and hopped out. I followed behind him with less enthusiasm. He monkeyed up onto the roof, then grabbed my hands and pulled me up beside him. My left shoulder started throbbing, but I did my best to ignore it.

I tucked myself up against him as he scanned the yard, trying to keep my breathing slow and regular. And then he was gone. There was a soft thump as he landed, and I began my count.

On five I closed my eyes and leaned over. His hands wrapped around my waist and eased me down. When he let go, my leg buckled. I landed hard on my butt, biting my tongue in the process. He wrapped an arm around my waist and hauled me upright. My mouth was filling with blood.

"Graceful." He tucked my fingers around the strap of his vest. I skulked behind him across the yard, stumbling a couple of times on the uneven paving stones. We made it to the back door without incident, and I hunched down while he unlocked the door and opened it.

We weren't greeted by wild gunfire, as I'd half expected, and I waited while he punched in the code to disarm the security system.

"We're going to take this one room at a time. Stay with me." I followed behind him as he cleared the kitchen, dining room, and living room, as well as the downstairs bathroom. He checked the front door, which was locked tight, and then we climbed the stairs.

The master bedroom looked untouched, save for the rumpled blankets on the king-size bed.

"Don't you make your bed?" I whispered.

He ignored me and moved on to the master bathroom. There were no boogeymen hiding behind the shower curtain. The last room was a spare bedroom he'd turned into his office. It had either been ransacked or he had a very strange filing system.

"Shit. They've got my files. I kept a spare set on the kidnappings at home." He didn't sound as upset as I would have expected.

"Is that all we came here for?"

"No. But it would have been nice to grab them."

"What else are we here for? And just so you know, if you came here for your baseball cards, I'm pulling out the pepper spray."

He shoved the desk up against the far wall and rolled up the area rug underneath. Using a screwdriver, he pried up one of the floorboards and pulled out a fat leather envelope.

"Here." He handed it over to me. "Tuck that inside your shirt."

"What's in it?"

"Ten grand. Might come in handy, no?"

I was following him back down the stairs when it hit me. "Josh!" I whispered, pulling at the back of his Kevlar vest. He stopped abruptly, frozen halfway down the stairs, hand on the butt of his revolver.

"There are two armed men at the front of the house, and a third in the backyard."

CHAPTER FORTY-NINE

"Get back up the stairs!" Josh hissed at her, and by some miracle she turned and did exactly that. "Get in the master closet, and stay down!"

He eased down the stairs. Two in the front, one in the back. There was no reason to doubt her. They must have been alerted when he disarmed the security system.

The front door was locked and dead-bolted. It would take them some time to get in. The back door was unlocked, left slightly ajar for ease of escape. He made his way toward the back, unholstering the FN Five-SeveN.

It was a risky choice, given that he had yet to fire the gun. But it had a sound suppressor, which his Glock 22 didn't have, and it would give him twenty rounds instead of the Glock's fifteen. Worst-case scenario, he could have his trusty Glock unholstered and ready in less than a second. It was worth the risk to keep the element of surprise. The FN felt at home in his hand.

Josh was waiting behind the door when it eased open. The guy wasn't a complete moron; he came in low, gun up. That was just what Josh was hoping for.

The intruder never saw the blow coming. Josh swung sideways, hitting the guy's temple with the butt of the gun. It had the desired effect, dropping him to the floor like a sack of grapefruit.

It took less than a minute to disarm and truss him, and Josh left him propped against the fridge. He could hear the other two working the locks on the front door.

"Congratulations," he whispered. "You're the one who gets to live. At least for a little while."

He exited through the back door, adjusting the thermal-vision goggles over his eyes. In his opinion, they were far superior to night-vision goggles, which produced an eerie green glow and required ambient light to display the area properly. But too much ambient light, or some other barrier like smoke or fog, and it was almost impossible to see properly. A person could easily hide in plain sight. Thermal goggles lit up anything that produced heat. A human turned into a light bulb, perfectly visible against the surrounding darkness.

There were two light bulbs standing on his small front porch, and both were focused on jimmying open the door. He shook his head in disbelief. Whoever they were, they weren't FBI trained. One of them should have been working the door while the other stood guard.

Josh was under no illusions as to their intent. It was kill or be killed. But he almost wished they had presented more of a challenge.

Pfft! Pfft!

The gun was quiet and effective. He climbed the steps and nudged both of them with his foot, even though he was certain neither would be jumping up to challenge him. Josh unlocked the door and pulled the bodies across the threshold one at a time, laying them out on the carpet beside the hall closet. He was just closing the door when Ryanne screamed.

"Josh!"

He turned, but he was too slow. The FN was halfway out of its holster when the guy behind him fired. With the goggles he actually saw the bullet coming, a white-hot streak like a shooting star. It seared a path across his left deltoid, knocking him sideways into the doorframe.

Ryanne flew down the stairs and threw herself at the intruder, screaming like a banshee. She landed on his back, knocking him to the floor just as he fired a second time. The bullet meant for Josh's head went wild, lodging into the ceiling above him instead.

They clambered around on the floor, Ryanne hitting and kicking at the intruder. However, he quickly recovered from his surprise, and Ryanne was no match for him in terms of strength. The man flipped her off his back and jumped on top of her, pinning her so he could raise the gun. With a satisfied grunt he pressed the business end to her forehead, and she went still.

But two could play at that game. Josh placed his gun against the back of the intruder's skull. The man froze much the same way Ryanne had.

"Shoot her and it's the last thing you'll ever do."

The man didn't budge, so he tried again.

"Drop your weapon, *now.*"

The man pulled his weapon back as though obeying the order, but his finger tightened against the trigger. Josh saw the fake for what it was, and he fired.

"Should have listened."

Ryanne was, understandably, screaming. The man had collapsed on top of her and his blood was all over her face. Josh hauled the body off her and pulled her into his arms. She clung to him, sobbing.

"Shh. Shh. Are you all right?" he asked, stroking the tangle of hair that had come free from her black cap.

"I'm sorry! I'm so sorry!" she sobbed.

"What? Why are you sorry?"

"I didn't know there was a fourth. I almost got you killed! I'm so sorry!"

"Ryanne." He shook her gently. "You saved both of our lives by warning me about them in the first place. And then you saved my life again by jumping on this guy's back. You have nothing to be sorry about!"

He grabbed a hand towel from the bathroom, dampened it, and carefully mopped the blood off her face. "I know this is a lot to take in, but I need you to calm down, okay? There's still work to be done."

She nodded, but couldn't seem to move. He wrapped his good arm around her and tucked her face into his chest, leading her away from the massacre in the front hall and into the kitchen.

The first intruder lay just where Josh had left him, propped up against the fridge. Josh flicked on the undercabinet lights and pushed the goggles up to the top of his head.

"Ah, shit!"

"What?" Ryanne asked, pulling away from his chest.

"It's a woman."

She turned to look at the crumpled figure on the floor. "So what?"

"So, nothing. I just . . . do better with men." The woman was still unconscious. She would have a killer headache when she came around, judging by the goose egg on her temple.

"Josh!"

"What?"

"You're bleeding!"

"Oh." He looked down, assessing the damage. "It's okay. The bullet just grazed me." He saw her eyes get bigger and cut her off at the pass. "I'm fine, really. I can hardly feel it." The last part wasn't quite true, but it sounded good.

Ryanne seemed unconvinced. She pulled up his blood-soaked sleeve and examined the wound.

"This should be cleaned right away. Do you have anything I can use to stop the bleeding?"

"Rowan?"

Ryanne froze. It was the woman who had spoken, her voice slurred and wobbly. "Rowan?" she asked again. "Is that you?"

Slowly, they both turned.

"What did you say?" Ryanne asked.

The woman was struggling to sit up, her eyes pinched in obvious pain. She managed to wrestle herself to a sitting position against the fridge, her arms tied behind her back and her feet, which were also tied, tucked to the side.

Instead of looking frightened or worried, as Josh would have expected, she looked relieved. Maybe even excited. Although she didn't know the fate of her three companions, he still found it strange. Josh cocked his head to the side, watching her curiously.

"What are you doing here, girl?" she asked. "And what are you doing with *him*? Don't you know who he is?" She nodded in Josh's direction.

Ryanne opened and closed her mouth several times before she managed to find her voice. "Do I know you?"

"What do you me—" And then realization seemed to wash over her. "Oh, I get it! You haven't been awakened yet." The woman was studying her with new intensity, judging Ryanne's every facial expression. Or so Josh thought, but perhaps she was doing more than that.

"So you received the note but you haven't remembered much yet."

Ryanne shied away from the woman's scrutiny and grabbed Josh's good arm. "How do you know that?"

"How do you think?"

"Who are you?" Josh chimed in.

"Shut up, cockroach. I'm not talking to *you*," the woman spat at him.

"Talk to him like that again and I'll rip your tongue right out of your mouth!" Ryanne shot right back at her, and Josh blinked at Ryanne in surprise.

The woman looked at her knowingly. "Oh, like that, is it?" She eyed her for a moment, and then smiled. "I always did admire your spunk, Rowan. And that redheaded temper, too. But this time, you're on the wrong side. It's not your fault. This . . . *man* . . . manipulated you when you were weak and confused. But trust me, you're making the wrong choices. And if you keep it up, you're going to die for them."

"And why, exactly, should I trust you?"

The woman leaned forward. Her lips were smiling, but her eyes were cold. "Because I know who you really are, and what you were trained to do."

"Care to enlighten us?" Josh asked, but the woman ignored him.

"I can see you don't believe me. Well, you'll learn the hard way soon enough. In the meantime, it's been great catching up with you, old friend." And with that she sprang to her feet. The ropes that had secured her wrists and ankles tumbled to the floor in a harmless coil.

Josh aimed his gun at her, thankful his instincts had kicked in despite the shock. "How the hell did you do that?"

But she wasn't done. The gun he had taken off her earlier was lying on the kitchen table. Casually, she reached out a hand. The gun sprang to life, flying across the kitchen toward her as if attached to an invisible wire. The next moment she had it trained on Ryanne.

"It's called telekinesis," she answered smugly. "Look it up, cockroach. Last chance to save your life, Rowan."

"If I see that finger tighten on the trigger, I'm going to blow your brains out," Josh warned.

"Don't worry, I don't need to waste a bullet on her. If she stays with you she'll be dead soon anyway. Along with the rest of the world." She tipped her head to the side, studying Ryanne. "Not coming with me? Oh well, don't say I didn't warn you." And with that, she ran toward the front of the house. Toward her three dead companions.

A moment later they heard the screaming.

"Guess you weren't expecting *that*, were you, bitch?" Ryanne yelled as Josh lifted her over his right shoulder and hauled her out the back door. As he ran across the backyard, Ryanne's knees jabbing him in the chest, she called back to the screaming woman inside the townhouse.

"Maybe you don't know everything after all!"

CHAPTER FIFTY

It had become a game to Sumner. Hunt them down, sneak up on them, and take them out. He didn't kill all of them, of course. If they were redeemable, or even if there was just the slightest possibility they were, he let them live. The trusty 9mm (aka "chick's gun") was Sumner's new BFF. His aim was usually off, sometimes by a country mile, but he was getting better at it all the time.

He was a bumbling assassin, at best. But in this hunt, it was the monumentally stupid leading the merely foolish.

Doing his John Wayne impression, Sumner said, "And life is pretty tough when you're stupid." Take the first two bozos buying a red Camaro for a covert mission. Clearly no one at *I Fidele* had thought to invest in special-ops training.

Sumner now drove it. His satire on wheels.

"Howdy, my psychic friends! Didn't see me coming? Aw shucks, sorry about that. I rolled right in here in the most obvious car I could think of! Now let me introduce you to my BFF. I call her 'Chicky.'"

He told himself he was serving a higher purpose, and to an extent, he was. But it was also revenge. Revenge for the life that was stolen from him when he was six years old. Revenge for the boy they had shaped into a kidnapper.

It was surprisingly easy to pick up their thoughts and track them. They were chasing the redhead and their orders were to terminate her. So he killed them when he found them, and each kill led him closer to his target, and his own redemption.

Sumner was eighteen hours behind the redhead, and closing in.

CHAPTER FIFTY-ONE

"Who the hell was *that*?" Josh asked as we careened away from his townhouse. He sounded as jumpy as I felt.

"I have no idea!" For some reason, we both found that hysterically funny, and we cackled away. It was a much-needed release of tension.

"How did she get free like that? And did you see what she did with the gun? It freaked me right out!" Josh said.

"Obviously you've never seen *Star Wars*."

"Are you kidding? I only watched it a million times when I was a teenager!"

"From the dark side of the Force was she." I did my best Yoda impersonation, which wasn't very good, but we howled some more anyway. Our laughter took us across the Theodore Roosevelt Bridge and into the capital. The sun was rising, setting the city aglow with pink and gold.

"So, what now?" I finally asked.

"Now? Now we sleep."

Rather than the seedy motel I was expecting, Josh pulled into the Georgetown Four Seasons.

"I don't think we're dressed for this," I muttered as the valet approached with a welcoming smile. Josh lifted an imperious finger at the valet, signaling him to give us a minute, and the valet retreated with a tip of his cap.

"It's all about attitude, Ryanne. Celebrities are usually the worst-dressed people in these establishments. So walk in there like you own the place and no one will question you. Got it?"

I nodded.

"Now, I need to get into your shirt."

"What?"

"The leather envelope." He was grinning. "Can I have it?"

"Oh! I forgot all about that." I pulled it out of my shirt and handed it over. He opened it and pulled out a slender wallet.

"My rainy day stash. Ten grand, and a set of IDs even the FBI couldn't tell was a fake. Including credit cards. This kind of hotel doesn't do cash transactions."

"Why are we here?" I couldn't help but ask.

"Because they won't look for us here. And because a hotel like this provides a certain level of anonymity. And because you deserve to sleep in a really comfortable bed."

"Fair enough. One more question. What in the world is an FBI agent doing with fake IDs?"

"Let's just say I know a guy," he said in his best *Godfather* voice, and then shrugged. "One of my informants made it. Here, put on your jacket. It will hide the bloodstains."

"Isn't owning a fake ID illegal?"

"Using it is. I'll have to add that to the list."

We emerged from the Suburban like a couple of moles who weren't used to being out in the daylight. Maybe we would be mistaken for musicians. Josh slipped the valet a hundred dollars, asking him to keep a close eye on the Suburban, and we made our way into the hotel.

I hung back while Josh flirted breezily with the young desk clerk. His charm was clearly working on her, despite the fact that he looked one step up from a vagrant.

"I got us the Presidential Suite. Don't ask me what it cost," he said as he led me to the elevator.

"Oh," I said as we entered the suite. The place was probably as big as my house and beautifully appointed, with gorgeous views of the canal. "Can I move in here?"

Josh was smiling, clearly happy that I was pleased. "I bet they have an amazing soaker tub. How about you take a bath and I'll order up room service?"

***

"How'd you sleep?" Josh asked as I came out of the bedroom some nine hours later. He had made his bed on the couch, insisting he would sleep just fine there, and when I continued to argue, he explained he wanted to sleep where he had a clear shot at the door.

I had given up after that, and slipped between the silky sheets feeling slightly guilty, but clean and satisfyingly full. My head hit the pillow and I knew no more.

Now he was freshly showered and dressed in clean jeans and a black T-shirt, but he hadn't shaved. The look was rugged and manly, and I tried not to show my admiration. Across his left shoulder, he was sporting a large bandage from the first-aid kit he'd brought up from the Suburban the night before. He insisted it was a minor wound and would heal cleanly.

I sat across from him, tucking my legs underneath me, and pulling down my nightie so it covered my knees. "I had a really strange dream," I said slowly. "And I'm not sure whether it was a dream or a memory."

He closed his laptop. "Tell me about it?"

"It's kind of embarrassing." I could feel the heat creeping up my neck and into my cheeks.

"Why? Was it a sex dream?" The side of his mouth twitched.

"Kind of. But not a pleasant one."

"Do you want to tell me about it?" he asked more gently.

"I guess. It's just kind of jumbled. It's like a bunch of snapshots all mixed up together. I can't get them into a logical order."

"How about you don't worry about the order, and just describe them to me one by one?"

"All right. The first one is of a priest. He's standing above me, wearing a black robe, and I feel very small and vulnerable. Trapped somehow."

"What does he look like?"

"Dark-blond hair, a beard. Brown eyes. He's slender and rugged looking, sunburned like he spends a lot of time outdoors."

"How old?"

"I don't know, maybe in his thirties?"

"What else? Any idea where you are?"

I pondered for a moment, and then shook my head. "All is can see is him."

"Okay." I could hear the disappointment in his voice. "Next snapshot?"

"Well, weird. I'm in a classroom. I think I'm about eight years old. On the blackboard it says *'Tutte le verità sono facili da capire una volta che vengono scoperti; il punto è scoprire loro.'*"

"What does that mean?"

"It's Galileo. He was an Italian physicist and astronomer."

"I know who he was."

"Right. It means 'All truths are easy to understand once they are discovered; the point is to discover them.' Below the quote there are bullet points about the Tunguska event."

"What's that?"

"It's a meteorite that exploded over a forested area of Russia in 1908. It did significant damage, but to a remote area. No lives were lost, so you don't hear much about it. If it had struck a city or something it would have been a much different story."

"And you were learning about that at eight? Is that what you're saying?"

I shrugged. "I don't know."

"What's the next snapshot?"

"I'm older now, maybe in my late teens. I'm naked. Bruised. I'm weeping. There's blood running down my legs. I'm in a bedroom. The sheets are tangled, covered in blood. There's a red silk robe hanging from the bedpost, and I know I'm supposed to put it on."

I closed my mouth, unable to go on. He was silent for so long I finally looked up, wondering if he was judging me, finding me as unclean as the dream made me feel. But his eyes were immeasurably sad. Somehow that was even worse, and I looked back down at my lap.

"And the next snapshot?" he asked quietly.

"The last one is a jumble of different images. I'm riding a horse, feeling free and joyous and young. And then I'm being forced down onto a bed . . . *that* bed . . . and it's the priest again, the same one. But he's not wearing his robes anymore. And there's pain. Great waves of pain. And I'm in a different bed and I'm screaming. And then there are horses. Horses running, their tails flying out behind them. Running free . . . and I'm chasing after them."

"You were raped," he said, and his voice was a perfect blend of fury and pity.

I shook my head. "I don't think I fought. I didn't want it, but it was what was expected of me. Part of a tradition."

"That's still called 'rape.'" I could handle his fury, but his pity sliced me to the core. And I wasn't done.

"The priest? I think his name was Gabriel. And I think he got me pregnant."

CHAPTER FIFTY-TWO

Josh sat beside her while she cried. He felt helpless, and in light of her revelations he was ashamed not only of being a man, but of all the less-than-pure thoughts he'd had about her. In short, he felt like a jackass.

Eventually, she got up and splashed some cold water on her face. She sat back down next to him, her face splotchy and her eyes puffy but calm. As she opened her mouth, he braced himself for her next startling revelation.

"I'm starving."

He couldn't help it, he laughed. He was grateful when she joined in with a small chuckle of her own.

"We'll get you fed. But first I have a confession of my own to make."

"What is it?"

"I have a mother."

She blinked at him. "You need some practice with this 'shameful declaration' thing."

"You say that because you haven't met her yet," he joked. "She's a bit senile, and ornery as hell. The senility is a new thing and it comes and goes, but she's always been ornery." He was rewarded with her smile. "Anyway, she's in a nursing home about half an hour from here. I need to make sure she's safe."

"Of course you do! They might try to get to you through her!"

"Exactly."

"Josh, you need to go get her. *Right now.* Bring her here, where it's safer."

He nodded. "That's just what I was thinking. I'm going to rent a car, so you'll have the Suburban, if needed. I think you'll be safer here than with me; I'm not sure what to expect at the home. If all goes well, we should be back in an hour and a half. Will you be okay here by yourself?"

"As long as I can order room service, I'll be just fine."

"Order anything you want." He stood. "But before I go, I want to give you a quick lesson in firing your gun, just in case."

Unable to help himself, he bent down and kissed the top of her head. Her hair was silky and smelled of lavender. "Thank you," he murmured.

"For what?"

He shrugged, unable to put it into words. "For everything," he answered lamely.

***

Other than being subjected to several motherly comments about his beard and scruffy appearance, picking up his mother at the care home had been surprisingly uneventful. He'd done so under the guise of taking her out for dinner, and he drove directly back to the Four Seasons.

"Oh, Joshua! This is too much!" she crooned as he pulled into the driveway. She fluffed up her hair and smiled flirtatiously at the valet through the window. Josh helped his mother out of the car, tipped the valet, and guided her inside. He noted the look of confusion that crossed her face when they passed the entrance to the dining room.

"I have something more private planned," he said as he led her to the elevator.

As they rode up and made their necessarily slow way to the Presidential Suite, he found he couldn't catch his breath.

If anything had happened to her . . .

He couldn't even finish the thought.

When he opened the door and was greeted with her smiling, obviously unharmed face, he felt faint with relief.

"Mom," he said, guiding the older woman forward, "I'd like you to meet Ryanne."

"Oh, my!" she said.

"It's lovely to meet you." Ryanne stepped forward and kissed her on the cheek.

"Oh . . . well, likewise I'm sure," his mother stammered.

She gave Ryanne the once-over, most likely assessing her age and judging the width of her hips, trying to decide whether Ryanne was a suitable candidate for bearing her grandchildren.

"I hope you don't mind, I ordered up some dinner," Ryanne said, seemingly unaware that she was being appraised like a brood mare. She led them to the elegantly appointed dining room, where she had laid out a feast on the table for six.

"I wasn't sure what you would like, Mrs. Metcalf, so I ordered several different dishes."

Josh could see that his mother was suitably impressed. She chose the chilled corn soup to start and then the duck. Without asking, Ryanne set a spring salad and filet mignon in front of Josh, and took the tuna tartare and New York strip steak and fries for herself. She hadn't put the sling back on, and Josh was pleased to see her moving her arm without any signs of discomfort. Even her limp had improved some.

"Well," his mother said. "This is quite the treat! Tell me, how did you two meet?"

"Um," Ryanne said.

"That's a long story, Mom."

"Well, then I look forward to hearing it, Joshua," his mother said pointedly. "This is delicious! Everything they serve at Dogwood Manor tastes like cardboard. Apparently they think we lose our sense of taste along with our marbles. That's a lovely dress, dear."

Ryanne looked down, her mouth twitching. She was wearing a floral dress in shades of pink and lavender—Josh had picked it out on his shopping trip back in Amarillo. It was feminine and delicate, and Josh thought she looked very pretty with her hair piled into a bun on top of her head.

"Thank you. Your son bought it."

His mother raised her eyebrows at him, but Josh avoided her gaze. Ryanne seemed oblivious to their interplay, her attention on her steak.

"So Mom, I was thinking it might be a good idea if you stayed here tonight."

"And why would I do that, Joshua?"

"Well, this case I'm working on? There's a chance my cover has been blown. That's why Ryanne and I are here."

"And what does that have to do with me?"

"If they know who I am, then there's a chance they could find you."

"I'm sorry, Joshua, but there's no possible way I can stay here. I don't have my medications, or any of my clothes, and there's a bingo tournament tomorrow I don't want to miss. The grand prize is a lovely knitting kit."

"You don't knit."

"No, but that horrible Mabel Fenske does, and it would chafe her hide something fierce if I won it. She's been prattling on about it for weeks!"

Across the table, Ryanne covered up a smile with her napkin.

Josh took a deep breath. "Mom, I brought your medications, and I'm happy to buy you whatever else you might need. Including a knitting kit."

"Now don't be ridiculous, Joshua. Why would you buy me that? I don't knit."

"I have a clean nightgown you can borrow," Ryanne offered.

Josh jumped in before she could mention he'd also bought the nightgown. "Mom, I want to make sure you're safe. Please? Humor me?"

"Well, perhaps. Did you order any dessert, dear?"

Ryanne smiled. "Are you a chocolate-torte or an apple-pie kind of woman? Or perhaps crème brûlée?"

"Chocolate!"

"A woman after my own heart." Ryanne served them both torte, and Josh took the pie for himself. He watched in amusement as the two women dug in with matching enthusiasm.

"So, where will everybody be sleeping tonight?" his mother asked with false innocence.

"Ryanne and I won't be sleeping much, so—"

"Joshua!"

Ryanne went beet-red, and he felt the heat creeping up his cheeks. "That's not what I meant! Mom, you can take the bedroom. Ryanne and I have some *work* to do. So we'll be going out."

"Whatever you say, dear. Oh my! Look at all this leftover food."

"Don't worry, we'll stick it in the fridge. I'm sure Ryanne will take care of it later."

His mother looked up at her, but Ryanne just grinned. "It will make a nice snack."

***

"I'm surprised you didn't leave me behind to watch your mother," Ryanne said.

"Are you kidding? You're proving to be a valuable asset in keeping me alive. Besides, you wouldn't have stood for it."

"Well, that's true. But I thought I was supposed to follow your orders?" she teased.

"You are. But I'm smart enough to know when I'll lose the battle."

She was dressed all in black, as he had instructed, and he made sure her Kevlar vest was secured under her T-shirt. Her hair was tied back from her face, and her gun was harnessed at her side.

He'd given her as much training with the gun as possible, considering the time constraints and the fact that she could only practice firing it without any bullets. It was now loaded and she seemed surprisingly comfortable with it at her side. She was pretty good at pulling it out of the holster and pretending to fire off a couple of rounds, and she was able to load it quickly, but whether she'd actually be able to pull the trigger under pressure remained to be seen.

"So where are we going?"

"Deputy Director Warner's house." His jaw tightened. "That pompous ass broke into my office. It's time to return the favor."

"I was afraid you were going to say that."

CHAPTER FIFTY-THREE

Deputy Director Warner lived in an upscale neighborhood of Chevy Chase, Maryland. His home, from what I could see from the road, was a three-story brick structure covered with ivy. It was set back behind gates and ten-foot-tall shrubbery. The left side of the gate prominently displayed a sign for an alarm company.

"Well, that looks easy enough," I commented dryly as we made our first pass. Josh clenched the steering wheel, but he made no comment.

We parked on a dark side street. Josh rummaged through his pile of equipment, untangling wires and sorting through all the strange devices. He strapped on a utility vest and filled its many pockets and loops. Both guns went into their holsters and a black cap went over his head, followed by the thermal-vision goggles.

"Now you." He checked my Kevlar vest again, and made sure my gun was comfortably strapped to my side and my extra ammo was easy to access. As before, he handed over a bottle of pepper spray, which I tucked into my pocket.

"We'll put this one in your bra, and this one in your sock," he said, handing me two sharp knives. I followed his instructions, and then blushed as he adjusted them and taped each one against my skin.

"The tape will hold them in place so they don't slip, but one quick yank and they'll come free. Can you reach them easily? Practice for me."

I did, and he made a minor adjustment to the one in my sock before he seemed satisfied. He fitted the black cap over my head, tucking my ponytail up into it, and then insisted on a round of calisthenics and stretching before he allowed us to get out of the Suburban.

"Like last time, your job is to stay near me, stay quiet unless it's to alert me to danger, and try not to get yourself killed. Got it?"

I nodded silently.

"And keep breathing." He smiled at me, and I let out my breath.

We made our way up the sidewalk. I kept expecting to run into a neighbor out for a nighttime stroll with his dog, but the street was quiet.

There was a small walk-through gate hidden in the shrubbery, with a keypad set above the bronze handle. Josh tried the handle first, but the gate was locked. He shrugged and smiled at me as if to say *It was worth a try.*

Josh pulled out a small drill. Within thirty seconds, the outer casing of the keypad had come off in his hands, exposing the wires underneath. With a tiny pair of scissors, he cut a couple of wires and spliced the ends together. The lock clicked open.

"The gate isn't attached to the main security system," he whispered. "Piece of cake." He took a moment to screw the outer panel back on, then led me through the gate.

Decorative pot lights highlighted different portions of the garden, leaving the spaces between in deeper darkness. We stuck to the shadows as we crossed the manicured lawn. I followed him around the house until he found a metal box attached to the back corner. It was half hidden behind a gloriously fragrant rosebush that was still in bloom, despite the season. I stood there forcing myself to take deep breaths while Josh worked the door of the box open.

"Shit," he muttered.

"What is it?"

"This kind of alarm has 'crash and smash' technology. It sends a warning signal to the alarm company during the entry delay process. If the alarm isn't disarmed at the keypad, the alarm company assumes that the panel has been smashed, and the police are called. It's the latest in alarm technology."

"So, what do we do?"

"We can climb up to the second floor and hope he was too cheap to wire those windows into the alarm system. Or I can try to disarm it from here."

Climbing up the side of a house was not on my list of fun activities. "Yeah. Try that."

"Right. No guarantee this will work, though, and if it doesn't cut the alarm, it will likely set it off instead."

"Should we climb, then?"

He thought for a moment, and then shook his head. "I'm betting he spared no expense, and the upper floors are armed." He pulled a device the size and shape of a cell phone out of his vest and began punching numbers on the touch screen.

"I've established a link," he eventually whispered. "Now let's see if I can get this thing to disarm." A few more minutes and a number of cuss words later, he took a deep breath. "Okay, here goes nothing. This is where we might have to run. Get ready."

The device emitted a quiet beep. Josh looked up, waiting, but all remained quiet.

"Is it disarmed?"

"I think so," he replied. "Let's go find out."

Choosing an ornamental door off the patio, Josh pulled out a bag of lock picks and set to work. I bounced on the balls of my feet. My bladder was screaming, but I didn't think he would appreciate stopping so I could relieve myself in the shrubbery.

An eternity later he made a satisfied grunt, and the door swung open. He paused, waiting for the telltale shriek of the alarm, but all remained quiet. We slipped inside and Josh pulled the door almost shut behind us, stopping it just before it latched.

His goggles were in place, and I followed close behind as he made his way through the enormous kitchen and dining area, gun first. The entire ground floor was shrouded in darkness. He opened the front door an inch, and did the same with the sliding glass door that led out to the yard, and then we mounted the stairs.

When we reached the second floor, we could hear CNN coming from behind a closed door at the end of the hallway. I followed him down the hall, practically floating from all the adrenaline-laced anxiety thundering through my veins.

At the doorway, he shoved the goggles up to the top of his head and pulled me close. He bent to whisper in my ear. "Remember the exits. If you have to choose between fighting and running, I want you to run. Even if it means leaving me behind." He tucked the Suburban's keys into my pocket and gave me a quick kiss on the forehead. It felt very much like a kiss good-bye, and I didn't like that one bit.

Without waiting for me to answer, he turned and opened the door. Light spilled out into the hallway, and the TV noise grew louder. Josh stepped across the threshold and leveled the gun in front of him.

"Metcalf. What took you so long?" Just the sound of the man's voice was enough to cause my blood to freeze. "Come on in. Can I offer you a drink?"

Josh took a couple of steps into the room, and I nervously followed. It was a small study, lined with bookshelves that were stacked with leather-bound tomes I would have bet were just for show.

Deputy Director Warner was sitting in a leather recliner behind a giant mahogany desk. His silver hair was impeccably styled and he was wearing gold-rimmed glasses. His eyes were brown, cold, and dead. I could smell his cologne from across the room, spicy and cloying. He was holding an enormous revolver casually in his lap. A tap of the remote and the TV went black.

"Rowan! So nice to see you again, dear."

"Oh, you've got to be kidding me." I was really getting sick of people I didn't recognize knowing who I was. It was quite disconcerting.

"I take it you were expecting us?" Josh aimed his gun at Warner's head.

The older man shrugged. "You were more of a challenge to kill than I expected. When I heard you found Rowan, I figured you'd show up. Well done disarming the security system, by the way. I'll have to give my alarm company hell for that tomorrow."

Warner's gaze turned to me. "I must say, Rowan. You've grown into a lovely young woman. A shame you didn't continue to follow the straight path, dear. Always a risk once a Disciple is awakened, of course. But you had such promise." He pouted for a moment, and then brightened.

"Never mind that now, you did your job admirably. It's made all the difference, and I suppose at the end of the day that's all that matters." He stopped, surprised, and then chuckled. "At the end of the day. Yes, that's just right, isn't it? For the 'end of days' is most certainly upon us!"

"What the hell are you talking about?" Josh asked.

He smiled beatifically. "Your boyfriend here thinks he's going to get answers just by waving a gun in my face. What he doesn't realize is there's simply no point to any of this anymore. Even if I give him all the answers he's seeking, it's too late to do anything about it."

"Then why don't you tell me, anyway?"

Warner laughed. "Oh, Metcalf. I'm almost sad your life is near its end. I like your perseverance! I watched you flounder around *forever* with that silly investigation of yours. Most people would have given up years ago. But not Agent Metcalf. It was personal for you! I'm glad you had some career satisfaction before the end. You worked so hard, didn't you? I'd recommend you for a promotion, if there were any point."

"Why are all of you people arrogant shits?" I asked.

"Oh, Rowan." He shook his head. "How disappointing."

"So, what's it going to take for you to start talking about stuff that matters?" Josh asked. "Should I start shooting one limb at a time, or are you going to be reasonable?"

Warner leaned back in his chair. "It doesn't matter what you do to me. If I die now, it will be an honorable death."

"'I only regret that I have but one life to lose for my country'?" I mocked.

He smiled at me. "Something like that."

"Start with his kneecaps, Josh."

"Well, your timing is excellent!" Warner said, and it took me a moment to realize he was talking to someone behind me.

And then there was cold steel against my head. Again. "Oh, hell."

"Time to drop your weapon." The voice behind me was raspy, like fingernails on sandpaper.

"I'm sorry you won't be around to witness the end, Agent Metcalf. It's going to be quite the show!" Warner stood and aimed his gun at Josh.

"You want me to take the girl into custody?" said the voice behind me.

"I'm afraid she's become too much of a liability. She'll have to be terminated, too."

At Warner's direction, the man pushed me farther into the room. My legs had turned to wood. Aided by a helpful shove, I flopped awkwardly onto a love seat. He was a giant man, African American, with a shaved head and chiseled features. The gun was big and mean-looking, and the sight of it made my mouth dry up.

"You want me to shoot her, Father?"

S.M. Freedman

"Father? Dude, I think you're adopted." As soon as I said it, I winced. Apparently political correctness went out the window when you were facing your own death.

"Metcalf first. Let her watch," Warner replied.

That would teach me for opening my smart mouth.

"I'll take you down with me, Warner." Josh nodded in the other guy's direction. "And if you so much as look at her the wrong way you'll be dead."

Unfortunately, the giant didn't seem impressed with Josh's big talk.

"Howdy." And just to stack the odds against us even more, a new guy stepped into the room. He was smiling. It seemed something about our situation amused him. He had a bad dye job and was holding a gun casually at his side.

"Who the hell are you?" For once Warner looked surprised.

So this guy wasn't another one of the deputy director's cronies after all. I saw Josh focus on him, probably trying to figure out the same thing I was. Friend or foe?

Apparently the answer was friend, because the guy raised his gun and shot the giant. It wasn't a great shot; it hit him in the back of the leg, but the guy went down screaming anyway.

I was too busy watching the action in front of me to see exactly what happened next, but I heard the shots. By the time I looked up, Deputy Director Warner was slumped over his desk with a big bleeding hole gaping out of the back of his head. Josh moved in on the screaming guy on the floor, gun raised. He fired and the giant went quiet. I chose not to look.

"Holy shit!" the guy in the doorway said. "I actually got him on the first try!"

"Yeah . . . good job," Josh said.

"Thanks!" He was still smiling, and I wondered if he was entirely sane. "Of course, you did both the kill shots, but still!" He turned to me. "Now, for the love of all that is good and holy, please tell me you have red hair?"

I didn't know quite what to make of that question, but it seemed important to him. Since he'd just had a big hand in saving my life, I felt obligated to pull the cap off my head. My hair floated free, dim embers in the lamplight.

"Are you Rowan?"

"Ryanne," I answered. "I don't go by Rowan anymore."

"Right, I get that," he said, nodding emphatically. "If I knew my original name, I'd go by it, too."

"So . . . what *do* you go by?" Josh asked.

"Oh, sorry. How rude of me! I'm Sumner. Sumner Macey."

CHAPTER FIFTY-FOUR

"Hello, Ora."

She managed not to wet herself at the mere sight of him, but perhaps that was because her bladder, like everything else in her body, was frozen in fear.

"Don't get up," he joked as he pulled a chair closer to her and sat with a swish of his black robes.

He hadn't aged a bit. Not since she was five. But that couldn't be, could it?

"Well, dear. Father Narda is quite disappointed in you."

"Yeah. No shit," Ora managed, but it didn't sound half as tough as she'd hoped.

Whatever you do, she thought, don't look at him. Don't get trapped by those pale eyes.

But were they pale? Or were they black, like his robes? Like his soul? She fought the urge to look, just for one teensy-tiny second. Perhaps if she managed to keep her eyes averted, all would not yet be lost.

"People talk of homosexuality as though one were simply born that way. Nonsense, of course! But such is the cesspool of modern life. Well, not to worry. All of that will soon be lost in the inferno."

"I'd like to see my dad," Ora said quietly.

Father Barnabas cackled, except his cackle was more like a shriek. It made the hairs on the back of her neck stand on end.

"Oh, I'm afraid Father Narda is no longer permitted access to you, my dear. Such must be the punishment for bad parenting. Yes, it's very sad, isn't it?" he said as her eyes filled with tears.

"For you, anyway. Terrible to be abandoned by one's father at this time of . . . *distress*. Especially since your father is, at present, quite content. He's not giving your situation much thought. He's . . . otherwise occupied, shall we say?"

Ora's jaw tightened, but she remained silent.

Oh, Lexy, she thought. I'm so sorry.

"Your father seems to think that, in time, he'll be able to change Lexine's ways. I have my doubts, but who am I to deny him some harmless fun?"

"You call rape harmless?"

"Compared to what's in store for you? Most certainly." Father Barnabas stood and leaned close to her. He smelled of sweet cologne and rot, and she swallowed hard to avoid gagging. "Although perhaps your father has a point. You *are* lovely, my dear." One bony finger stroked her arm, blazing a trail of ice from wrist to shoulder.

He's so cold, she thought, shrinking away from him.

"It's been many years since I took an *Amante*. Do you think I could make you see the error of your ways?"

She couldn't help it. She gagged, although the gag was mixed up in a sob. "I'd rather die."

"Yes, yes. All in good time." He sat back down. "I find it *disturbing* that you have chosen to turn your back on one of our most vital pieces of Doctrine: in order to thrive, we must procreate with our own kind.

Had you come to us and been honest about your struggle, we could have found a mutually beneficial solution. Well, never mind that now! There are much greater issues to discuss, no? Issues like where Sumner has gone. And where Rowan is."

"Who?" she asked.

One moment he was sitting calmly at her side, the next he was on top of her, bony fingers closing off her windpipe.

"Don't play with me, Ora. Rowan! *Rowan!*"

She couldn't help it; she looked up at him. She was wrong. His eyes were red.

"I . . . *don't* . . ." she managed. Her vision was going dark. And then he was sitting in the chair beside her, as if nothing had happened.

Ora gasped, struggling for breath. Her throat was on fire but the skin around her neck, where his hands had been, felt like it was wrapped in permafrost.

He waited until she was back under some kind of control. "The redhead. Does that help?" His voice was calm and smooth.

"Oh."

"Yes. Oh."

"I don't know anything about her."

"Do you think he's found her?"

Why doesn't he know?

As soon as the thought entered her mind, he hurled the chair he had been sitting on across the room. It hit the wall on the far side and fell to the floor with a resounding clatter.

"Because I can't see them!" he screeched.

Ora closed her eyes, cringing, and fell back against the pillow.

"I can't see them! *Why can't I see them?*"

And then he was sitting at her side again. Sitting on the chair he had thrown across the room, as if nothing had happened. Ora's head was spinning.

"I had her once, for just a brief moment. She was with that charlatan, and the truth-seeker. I almost got him to turn his gun on her."

Ora had no idea what he was talking about, so she kept her mouth shut.

"Do you know where they are, Ora? Do you know what they're planning?"

She was grateful for the fact that she could answer honestly. "No. I don't."

Once again he was on top of her. His icy hands went around her neck. "Why don't you know? Why don't you know! Why don't you know!" he screeched at her.

Her last thought before everything went black was: Why doesn't he know about Jack?

CHAPTER FIFTY-FIVE

Sumner spoke for a long time. He spoke until he said his throat was raw. Josh got him some water. Ryanne seemed incapable of moving. She was curled into herself on the couch of the Presidential Suite, wrapped in a throw blanket and looking all of about five years old.

Josh couldn't begin to imagine the toll Sumner's story was taking on her. She listened with dry eyes, occasionally stopping Sumner for clarification, but mainly just allowing him to speak.

Josh sat on the other side of the couch, a few feet and a million miles away from her, and Sumner sat across from them in a lounge chair.

He told his story concisely, beginning with his awakening some six months before, and describing how confused and alone he felt after that note appeared in his mailbox. Ryanne nodded, obviously relating to Sumner's experience.

"But I've regained so few memories," Ryanne said.

"It took me six months to remember everything I do now, and who knows how much I'm still missing. I think it has to be a slow process so we don't lose our marbles. Which I almost did, anyway."

He spent a long time describing life at The Ranch, patiently answering Josh's questions about its location and giving him as many names as he could remember. He described the structure of the organization, both on and off The Ranch.

At Josh's request, he divulged details about the PSST: how they researched the country's public-school children, isolated the children who showed psychic potential, and collected data on those kids until a decision was made as to whether they would be taken.

"Kids would usually be watched for a year or two before a decision was made," Sumner explained. "A number of factors were considered. What kind of skills did the child possess? How much potential did they have? How much space was there at The Ranch?

"They also dealt with demographics. How many children were gathered in that particular year? Where did the child live, and had there been any recent 'removals' nearby? If so, they might either delay or forego taking that kid to avoid the scrutiny of the local authorities. No one wanted the attention that comes when something becomes 'serial.'" He shrugged, looking into his water glass. "Although all of that caution went out the window if the kid was telekinetic. That's the ability to move things with your mind," he told Josh.

"Yeah, so I gathered," Josh said, thinking about the woman in his townhouse. "Why the interest in that skill?"

Sumner shrugged. "I have no idea. But those kids were treated very differently, and they didn't stay on The Ranch for long. They were taken to—"

"The Command," Ryanne interjected, and Josh looked at her in surprise. "I remember that. I think."

"That's right. The Command," Sumner agreed.

"What's that?" Josh asked.

"I don't know. Those kids were never seen again. And before you ask, I have no idea where it is, either."

"So everyone with telekinesis was automatically sent to this place, never to be seen again?" Josh asked.

"Yes. Well, any of the Disciples, anyway. The Chosen stayed on The Ranch, even if they had that skill. Always made me think The Command must not be the nicest place to go."

"The Chosen?" Josh asked.

"Right." Sumner took a long swallow of water. "Those are the kids born on The Ranch. Most of them are spoiled brats. Skilled, but spoiled."

"Whose children are they?"

Sumner grimaced, and then explained about the *Amante* system. How a Priest could take a female Disciple as his concubine when she turned seventeen. How during her year of servitude she was relieved from all Ranch and farm duties, her sole purpose to serve the Priest in any way he found pleasing. When he mentioned the red silk robes an *Amante* wore to denote her status, Ryanne sat up, throwing off the blanket. Her eyes were wild.

"What happened if she got pregnant?" she asked. Josh had a sudden desire to grab her hand, but he couldn't move. He was frozen, locked inside his own fear. Or was it grief?

Sumner hesitated, obviously understanding the importance of her question.

"Please?" she implored. "What happened?"

"The mother was allowed to nurse and care for the baby for the first year."

"And then what?" she asked, and when he didn't answer, she asked again. "And *then* what, Sumner?"

"And then the mother was . . . removed. She was brought to the Cocoon, and reprogrammed for her mission Outside."

Ryanne was leaning so far forward, Josh was afraid she was going to fall off the couch. "And the baby? What happened to the baby?"

"The baby was raised on The Ranch. By its father, and the rest of the *I Fidele* family. The babies were always well taken care of, Ryanne." He was clearly trying to make it better, easier for her somehow.

Ryanne slapped her hands over her mouth and stumbled to the bathroom. The door slammed behind her, muffling the sound of her retching. And then she was wailing. Josh's heart felt like it was being squeezed in a vise. He sensed Sumner's eyes on him, and looked up.

"If you don't go to her, I will," Sumner said.

That unfroze his limbs, and Josh made his way to the bathroom on legs that wobbled.

"Ryanne?" He eased the door open. She was hunched over the toilet, sobbing so hard her whole body was shaking. He stood watching her, unsure of what to do. He wanted to take her in his arms, but was afraid of her rejection. After what had been done to her, he wouldn't be surprised if she rejected all men.

Finally she sat up and leaned back against the wall. "It's too much, Josh. It's just *too much!*"

Tears were streaming down her cheeks in tiny rivers. She was clutching at her abdomen, as though searching for the life that had once grown in there.

"My baby!" she wailed. *"I want my baby!"*

He sat down next to her, squeezing his large frame into the small space. Hesitantly, he reached for her, ready to pull back if she flinched. But to his surprise she flew into his arms, almost knocking him over. She pressed against him, clutching at him with a ferocity that was startling. It was as though she were trying to escape her own skin and burrow into his. Trying to stake her claim within his blood and bones.

His arms found their natural home around her. He closed his eyes and buried his face in the lavender and silk of her hair. Josh held on, losing himself in her sorrow.

***

When they emerged, Sumner was sitting in the same position, head bowed. Josh's anger erupted.

"I don't get it. How can you be responsible for kidnapping so many children! Don't you have a soul?"

Sumner looked up, his eyes bleary and full of pain. "I didn't know."

"How could you not know? I don't believe it!"

"Josh . . ." Ryanne implored, tugging at his shirt.

He pulled away from her, focusing all his anger on Sumner, the easy target. He was blind with rage. Overcome with fury for all the missing children he had chased, for the decades of his life he had sacrificed, but most of all for the woman who stood beside him.

The woman with the fault lines etched into her grown-up shell, lines that ran so deep he could see all the way down to the girl that was. To the innocence that had been stolen like a perfect rose plucked before its time. She broke his heart, again and again.

He poked a finger at Sumner. "*You* figured out which kids were worth kidnapping, and *you* sent out your minions to get them! You want to play innocent with me?"

"I gathered the information; it's true! But until my awakening six months ago, I had *no idea* why I was doing it! I had no idea what was happening to those kids, I swear!" Sumner jumped up and began to pace. "I lived the last couple of decades with blinders on. I didn't know anything, I didn't question anything!"

"You were programmed," Ryanne said softly.

"Yes! Programmed! But is that any excuse for what I've done? How many families have I destroyed? How many kids' lives have I ruined? How in the world do I ever forgive myself? How!"

Josh stood there, stunned by Sumner's outburst. Ryanne looked from one to the other, her face pale.

"I wonder what I was programmed to do," she said.

CHAPTER FIFTY-SIX

Both men turned to look at me—Sumner with deep understanding, Josh with even deeper denial.

"I'm sure there's nothing, Ryanne," Josh said.

But Sumner was looking at me like I was a puzzle that needed sorting out. "What do you do for a living?" he asked.

"I'm a scientist," I said. "I work as a space data analyst for LINEAR's Spaceguard Program. I collect, analyze, and classify data on Near Earth Objects by using ground-based, electro-optical, deep-space surveillance telescopes."

Sumner's eyes grew bigger. "You lost me after scientist."

"I look for big bad asteroids that want to crash into Earth."

There was an extended silence while both of them contemplated this.

"So, you work for NASA?" Sumner asked.

"In a roundabout way, yes. We receive funding from a number of different sources, but NASA and the US Air Force are the two biggies."

"US Air Force?" Sumner mused. "Maybe it's something to do with that? I mean, *I Fidele* is definitely planning some kind of attack. Maybe it has something to do with either using the Air Force . . . or wiping them out? Destroying the planes?"

Josh looked at him skeptically, and Sumner shrugged. "I'm just spitballing here."

Josh shook his head. "I can't see Ryanne as part of a plot to steal military planes . . . or destroy them . . . or whatever."

"I couldn't see myself as part of a kidnapping ring either," Sumner countered.

"Son, I think it's time you turn yourself in to the authorities." Josh's mom had crept out of the bedroom. She was wearing the nightie I had given her. Her white hair, tucked into a complimentary bathing cap, was falling out in cotton-candy wisps around her neck.

She had Josh's very large and unwieldy gun aimed at Sumner's head.

Sumner jumped as if he'd been goosed and stuck his hands in the air. "Holy shit, it's Annie Oakley!"

"Mom!" Josh shouted.

Josh approached his mother, his hands out in front of him. The gun was obviously too heavy for her; her hands were shaking trying to keep it aloft. I was worried she'd fire it by accident. Sumner must have been thinking the same thing. He was trying to back away without her noticing.

"Mom, put the gun down," Josh said.

"Hang on, Annie!" said Sumner. "I'll get you a deck of cards so you can show us your sharpshooting skills!"

I didn't think making fun of her was the smartest idea, under the circumstances.

"Hold yourself still, young man, or I'll shoot you right in the kisser!"

"Who is this crazy old lady?"

"I may be crazy, but I'm no kidnapper!" Her hands were trembling more by the second.

"Mom, *please*. You need to put the gun down."

"Mrs. Metcalf, it's not what you think," I tried. "Please put the gun down so we can explain."

"There's no need to explain anything, dear. I heard perfectly well what this baby snatcher was trying to convince you to do. Although stealing one of those warplanes seems a bit far-fetched. Who's going to fly it?"

"Wow," Sumner said.

"Mom, I think you've misunderstood."

"And you!" The gun made an erratic swoop, and all of us screamed and ducked. "I'm terribly disappointed in you, Joshua. In my day, if you got a girl in trouble you *married* her."

"Oh wow," Sumner wheezed. "I'm on a twisted version of *Three's Company*."

"Mrs. Metcalf—"

"Now just you hush, dear. I'm sure my son will do right by you. He's a good boy, and he'll make a good father."

I opened my mouth, but nothing came out.

"Mom! Ryanne's not pregnant. Now please put the gun down before somebody gets hurt."

"What do you mean, she's not pregnant? I heard her in the bathroom!" She turned back to Sumner with another sweep of the gun. Once again, we all screamed and ducked. "Are you dealing in the black market? What did you do with the baby?"

"I think the dingo ate the baby!"

"Sumner!" I choked out. "What the hell is *wrong* with you?"

"Mom, I promise I'll explain everything. Just put *down* the gun," Josh implored.

"Oh, phooey." She turned to Josh. "Here!"

I think she was trying to hand the gun over, but instead she fired it. The lamp beside Sumner exploded. A second later we all hit the deck.

"Holy shit!" Sumner squawked.

"Oops," Mrs. Metcalf said.

***

We made a hasty exodus from the Four Seasons and regrouped at a waffle shop on 10th Street. We feasted on platters of waffles and fried chicken, steak and eggs, biscuits and grits, and gallons of much-needed coffee while Sumner told us about Ora, Lexy, and Phoenix.

To her credit, Mrs. Metcalf sat silently through breakfast, quite contrite after the murder of the lamp.

When Sumner told us about Jack Barbetti, I could feel the stir of excitement within my overfull belly.

"I had that dream too!" I exclaimed. "Do you really think he's alive?"

Josh was looking at Sumner with equal amounts of hope and excitement.

"Well, Ora did," Sumner replied. "And I think she had a good point. Whether they'll be able to find him at The Ranch and bring him out is another story."

"And you really think he was looking for us, Sumner?" I asked.

"You in particular." He pointed a forkful of chicken in my direction.

"Why me?" I wondered out loud.

"He seems to think you're the key to everything."

All three pairs of eyes fixed on me with speculation. Well, Mrs. Metcalf seemed more confused than anything else, but who could blame her?

"Well, then. I guess we know where we need to go," Josh said.

"Josh, isn't there anyone in the FBI you can trust?" I asked.

He shook his head. "I'm sure most of the agents I know have no involvement, but how can I know which ones are clean? And this would be a big operation; FBI protocol would have to be followed. Which means my boss would be involved. I think we still need to stay under the radar. At least for now."

"Sounds good to me," Sumner said. "Besides, me and Chicky are probably on their Most Wanted list by now."

"Who's Chicky?" I asked, and Sumner patted the front of his pants and winked.

I choked on a piece of waffle, and then took a closer look and realized he had a gun stuck into the waistband of his pants. He helpfully passed me a glass of water.

***

It took Josh some time to convince Sumner to give up the red Camaro, but eventually he climbed into the passenger seat of the Suburban with a few choice words that made Mrs. Metcalf gasp. I leaned forward and patted Sumner's shoulder.

"He made me dump my yellow FJ, too. Fair warning, he doesn't share the driving, he insists on eating health food, he doesn't let you play music, and he won't even play car games."

Sumner groaned and Josh gave me the gimlet eye in the rearview mirror.

"He should know what he's in for, bossy-boots."

I leaned back against the rear seat and watched the capital slip by outside my window. I had the strange sensation that rather than moving forward, we were tumbling back. Back to The Ranch. Back to a childhood I barely remembered and guessed might be a blessing to forget. Back to a little boy from Oregon who held the knowledge that might save the world.

Back to the baby my aching body remembered nurturing beneath my heart, even if my mind did not. Back in time, twelve or thirteen years, to the beginning of that new life. The sun was streaming in the car windows, and I closed my eyes and sank beneath its gentle golden light.

Eventually, I dreamed. In the dream, there was a little bundle mewling beside my bed, and my breasts tingled and ached with engorgement. I lifted the swaddled form out of the bassinet and brought it to my breast. A late-day sun streamed through a crack in the curtains and golden light kissed the top of the baby's head, setting the red fuzz aflame. I stroked the soft head and inhaled the smell of milk and warm, doughy flesh.

They can't make me forget you, I had vowed. *One day I will return for you.*

I had broken the first promise. I wouldn't break the second.

CHAPTER FIFTY-SEVEN

"What are you doing up, Mom?" Josh asked as she slipped out of the bedroom she was sharing with Ryanne and closed the door quietly behind her. They had rented a two-bedroom suite at a Ramada Inn somewhere east of Chicago, and everyone had stumbled off to bed after a late dinner at the adjoining Denny's. But Josh was feeling restless and twitchy, his dinner sitting heavy in his gut. "It's two a.m. You should be asleep."

"So should you, Joshua."

Josh closed his laptop. "I couldn't sleep." He ran his hand across his rough beard. His eyes were burning from eleven hours behind the wheel.

"You should have let the others drive a bit."

"I can't do that."

"Can't or won't, I suppose it amounts to the same thing. Now, are you going to make your mother some tea?"

"Of course." He moved into the tiny kitchenette and plugged in the electric kettle. When the tea was ready, he sat down across from her and passed her a steaming mug.

"I'm going to be dropping you in Elkhorn, Mom."

She smiled. "That's nice, dear."

"I'm going to leave you with Phil Lagrudo. But you can't contact any of your old friends, okay?"

"Your father would be very proud of you, Joshua. Well, I suppose you know that. You always made him proud."

"Did you hear me, Mom?"

"He was such a good man. We never wanted for anything, did we?" Josh gave up with a sigh. "No."

"Do you remember after you started your FBI training, how you flew us out to tour Quantico?"

"Of course."

"And your dad got us on the wrong plane? We almost ended up in Washington State instead of Washington, DC!"

Josh smiled. "And then you got lost looking for the White House, and I—"

"Sent out a search party," she finished.

"Well, you'd been missing for six hours."

"Were we ever surprised when those armed men swooped in!"

"They sent a bunch of newbies up from Quantico," he laughed. "They used it as a tactical training exercise."

She was laughing too. "Where were we, again?"

"Trinidad. Not exactly the safest neighborhood. You were in gang territory."

"Oh, that's right. And your father said he hoped they'd scared some of those gangsters straight." She was laughing and crying at the same time. "How I loved that man!"

"I know, Mom. Me too."

"Even if he didn't know his ass from his elbow!"

"Mom!" Josh laughed.

"Well, it's true. He was a brilliant man, but he could get lost on the way to the grocery store."

"He was just easily distracted."

"Ain't that the truth." She took a sip of tea, and then patted her damp eyes with the sleeve of her nightgown. "I was happy with him. He was kind and gentle, and he always put my needs above his own." She looked up at him. "Follow his example, Joshua."

"What?"

"When you get married. Be like your dad."

"Of course I will, Mom. If I ever do."

She eyed him for a moment. "Did I ever tell you about Jesse Simpson?"

"I don't think so."

"He was my first beau. We dated all through high school, like you and that Marcy O'Donell girl. Oh, my, were we ever in love! Or at least, we thought we were. He played baseball. Handsome boy, looked like a young Paul Newman."

She took another sip of her tea, and continued. "Well, it was a couple years after high school. Jesse was working at the motor parts factory, and I was doing seamstress work. I kept waiting for his proposal. In those days folks got married young, and I was already feeling like an old biddy at twenty-one!" She laughed and shook her head. "But Jesse never could make up his mind about a damn thing, and it used to drive me batty. You might not believe it, but I was quite the pistol in those days."

Josh couldn't help but smile. "You still are, Mom."

"I gave him an ultimatum. Told him he had one month to decide if he wanted to marry me. Then I met your father on day twenty-eight."

"Really. So what happened?"

"George swept me off my feet. Not because he was handsome, which of course he was, and not because he was charming, which he was as well. He saw what he wanted and he went for it. I knew I could rely on him. That he would never let me down." She gave Josh a tearful smile. "And I was right."

"What happened to Jesse?"

She shrugged. "He was devastated by my betrayal, as he saw it. He joined the Marines a month later and he never came home. He died just before you were born."

"Why are you telling me this?"

"Come on, Joshua. You're a smart man."

He shook his head, but his gut was churning. "Mom, it's complicated."

"No, dear. It's not. Love is always simple; it's people who add in the complications."

"You don't understand."

"Oh yes. I do. Just because you're a touch older and you and her mother were friendly? Are you going to let that matter?"

"How did you know that?" he asked.

"I'm not as foolish as I may sometimes seem. I know who she is. And I know love." She leaned across the table and took his hand in hers. "I've seen the way the other one has been looking at her."

Josh nodded. He'd seen it too: the way Sumner's eyes kept finding her when she wasn't looking.

"If you love her, then it's time to go get her. Be like your father, Joshua."

CHAPTER FIFTY-EIGHT

We left Chicago near dawn. Josh looked like he hadn't gotten much sleep, and he was sullenly guzzling an enormous coffee. In the backseat, Sumner entertained me with stories and jokes. I found myself laughing far more than I should have, given the circumstances. At the first gas stop, I climbed into the front seat next to Josh.

"Are you all right?" I asked quietly, in deference to his mom who had just climbed into the backseat, but was already snoring. He hadn't said more than three words all morning.

"I'm fine," he said curtly, turning over the engine.

"Sumner's not back yet," I said when he put the car in gear.

"I know!"

His mom stirred.

"Shh. What's the matter with you?"

He rubbed both hands vigorously over his face. "Sorry, I'm just tired."

"Josh." I put a gentle hand on his arm, but he jumped so I pulled it back. "I could drive for a bit."

He looked at me with that stubborn expression I'd grown to know so well, and then his face softened. "Are you doing okay?"

I shrugged, taken aback by his gentleness. One minute he was as hard as a stone, the next he was as soft as a marshmallow. "I woke up without a headache this morning, so that's good. But it's a lot to take in, you know?"

"I'm sure Sumner's a big help with that. I mean, since he's been going through similar stuff."

"I guess that's true. He's very funny."

He nodded and turned away from me, his jaw tightening.

"Am I missing something?"

"Nope," he said as Sumner opened the rear door and climbed into the Suburban.

"Check this out!" He tossed a bag over my shoulder. "They have the best snacks at this place!"

"Homegirls Potato Chips?" I asked, laughing.

"Those are for you, *homegirl*," Sumner said. "Don't worry Josh, I found something for you, too."

"Ding Dong Mixed Nuts? Thanks."

"And check this out." Sumner yanked off his shirt—causing Josh to turn a watchful eye to the rearview mirror—and pulled on a new one. He puffed out his chest, showing off a picture of a corn dog.

"What would the corn dog do?" I read.

He looked at me sternly. "It's a valid question. Next time we're facing some *I Fidele* crazies, ask yourself what the corn dog would do. I guarantee a corn dog will never steer you wrong."

"Okay, I will," I said, giggling.

"You know what?" Josh said suddenly. "I can't drive anymore. Ryanne, will you take over for a few hours?"

"Of course!" I said, startled.

"Why don't you grab some shut-eye," Sumner suggested. "I'll keep her company in the front."

"That would be great," Josh said, although his tone was odd. He jumped out of the driver's seat and climbed in beside his mother.

"Don't worry, I'll be careful," I told him.

"Wake me up if you see anything that doesn't look right. Move over to the right before an exit every once in a while, and watch for cars that do the same behind you. Keep your eyes on your rear and wing mirrors at all times."

"Okay, boss. I've got it. Get some rest."

"Ryanne . . ."

"What?"

"I'm always here."

I glanced at him in the rearview mirror. His eyes were serious and somehow sad. "Don't worry. I'll wake you up if I see anything unusual."

"Good." He closed his eyes.

***

We made it to Elkhorn by late morning, but had to wait a couple of hours for Phil Lagrudo to return home. By the time we saw him pulling into the driveway, both Josh and Sumner were so antsy they were bickering back and forth like a couple of four-year-olds.

Josh was obviously concerned about the former sheriff's safety, even wondering aloud if he'd had a visit similar to poor Kahina's.

Sumner was growing increasingly agitated for different reasons. "It's Ora. She's in serious trouble. We need to get there pronto."

"I'm doing the best I can," Josh grumbled.

"Can't we just take Annie Oakley with us?" Sumner asked.

"That's my mother you're talking about. And no, we can't. I'm not going to put her in danger."

"I don't see why not. Any lamps we come across should be terrified just at the sight of her."

355

"You're not half as funny as you think you are, young man," Mrs. Metcalf chimed in.

"Well, at least she thinks I'm young."

The former sheriff had clearly spotted the Suburban parked across from his house as soon as he turned onto the street. His Chevy Impala slowed to a crawl. Josh quickly got out of the car and waved at him, smiling.

They went through the usual male greetings as the rest of us climbed out of the car. He gave me a kiss on the cheek. He shook hands with Sumner, his eyebrows rising in surprise when he heard Sumner's name. Josh gave his head a slight shake and the sheriff picked up on it, turning to give Mrs. Metcalf a warm welcome.

"It's so nice to see you, Anna. You don't look a day older than the last time I saw you. The East Coast air must agree with you." He tucked her arm through his and led her to the house.

She fluffed her hair with the other hand. "Stop it, you old flirt!" she cooed.

Josh rolled his eyes and followed behind them. Sumner and I took up the rear.

The former sheriff seemed amenable to taking in a houseguest. "Of course! Anna can stay as long as needed. I have a spare room with its own bathroom; she'll be quite comfortable."

He pulled Josh aside. "What's going on, Metcalf? Do you need help? These old bones maybe don't work quite as well as they used to, but I'm still more capable than most young bucks."

Josh seemed to seriously consider the offer before shaking his head. "I probably could use your help, boss. But I also need to keep my mom safe. I'm sorry to stick you with a babysitting job; please be honest if it's too much trouble."

"It's no trouble at all."

"How have things been around here? Anything of concern?" Josh asked.

"Just one incident of note, but all has been quiet ever since."

"What happened?"

I noticed Sumner was creeping a bit closer, listening in on their conversation.

"A couple of young guns were shot dead in their car a few blocks away. Strangers to the area, and it has some local folks scared that gangs are moving in. But I'm not so sure."

"Why is that?"

"Sheriff Bothwell's been keeping me in the loop. They were shot with a 9mm, which isn't the weapon of choice for the gangs around here. Also, whoever shot them did a piss-poor job of it, seriously sloppy work. Gang hits tend to be a lot cleaner."

Josh looked up at Sumner, his eyes tight. Sumner, for his part, was stifling a grin. "Is that so?"

"That's not the strangest thing. The two victims are still sitting in the morgue. Can't identify them and no one is stepping up to claim them. No ID and nothing came back from CODIS. It's like they came out of nowhere."

"Really. And the vehicle?"

"Bought with fake papers. Good ones, but fake nonetheless. I was thinking maybe it had something to do with your case." The former sheriff was watching Josh carefully.

Josh shrugged. "It might at that." The two men seemed to have a silent conversation, at the end of which the sheriff nodded. What he was in agreement about, I couldn't tell.

"Excuse me, Phil?" Mrs. Metcalf chimed in. "Could you point me to the ladies' room?"

"Of course!" Lagrudo took her arm and led her toward the back of the house, leaving both Josh and me staring at Sumner, who was grinning like the cat that ate the canary.

"I guess I owe you a thank-you for saving the sheriff's life," Josh finally said.

Sumner shrugged, smiling. "That's just how I roll. Now how about you, me, and homegirl over here hit the road?"

Mrs. Metcalf pulled me aside just before we left, much to Josh's obvious dismay.

"It's just girl talk—none of your business, Joshua!" She shooed him away when he tried to intervene. He left, his cheeks burning as he climbed into the driver's seat of the Suburban.

"What is it, Mrs. Metcalf?" I asked.

She turned to me, looking up into my face with sharp speculation. "You take care of yourself, dear, and that baby."

"I'm not preg—"

"Never mind that now. Whether you're pregnant now or you've already birthed your babe, a mother is a mother and one mother knows another. Do you get my meaning?"

"I . . . guess so."

"The time will come when you need to make a choice as to the baby's father. Make the right choice, dear. Funny doesn't put food on the table, or keep you and yours safe through the night. You get me?"

"Mrs. Metcalf, I really don't think—"

"Choose the man who loves you so much, he would die to protect you."

"I don't know what—"

"Yes you do, dear. In your heart, you do. Now, be a good girl. Protect that baby." She gave me a soft kiss on the cheek and turned away. Lagrudo helped her over the lip of the front door and waved solemnly before closing it behind him. I was surprised to feel my eyes stinging with tears.

"Finally!" Sumner said as I opened the door. "Did she give you any tips on how to kill an armchair from fifty paces?"

I climbed into the passenger seat beside Josh and glanced sideways at him, but he wouldn't look at me. His jaw was set, his eyes focused on the road as he pulled away from the curb.

"I think *you* could use those lessons," I joked. "It was just girl stuff. Nothing important."

Josh's right hand was resting on the gearshift. I placed a tentative hand on his forearm. I could feel the muscles underneath my hand jumping with tension, but rather than pull back I gave his arm a gentle squeeze.

He glanced at me shyly. His blue eyes were full of unease, but whatever he saw in my eyes made him smile.

CHAPTER FIFTY-NINE

The ropes were cutting into Ora's wrists and ankles something fierce. They were rough cordage, used for binding broken tools or tying down tarps and horse blankets.

Which would it be? she wondered. Death by hanging or death by fire?

Sumner was on his way.

She could feel him closing in, but doubted he would arrive in time to save her. And Phoenix? Where was he? She simply couldn't reach him at all, or Ashlyn. She didn't even try to reach Lexy; she was afraid of what she might find.

And where was her father? Would he really allow his daughter to be executed?

But she'd forced him to choose between her and the Doctrine. He lived for it, and he killed for it. She'd always known that, so it was time to put on her big-girl panties and face the truth. And the truth was he didn't love her enough to save her. Or he loved *I Fidele* more.

Either way, she would lose.

She closed her eyes, wishing they would just get on with it. The waiting was killing her nerves. At first she thought they were waiting for dusk, but the hours passed and some endless time later twilight gave way to dark.

The moon rose in the sky outside her window, and she watched it with avid concentration. It was full and robust, a late-autumn moon. Soon the stars joined it, cold and hard.

And she understood. They were waiting for midnight. For the witching hour.

Eventually she heard them gathering in the side yard. Her family. There was the shuffle of feet and stifled giggles, quickly hushed by the older children. She sensed their excitement and their nervousness. Something big was happening. Something new. They had been pulled from their cozy beds and asked to take part in a sacred ritual. To perform a duty.

They've been asked to gather rocks.

This little tidbit came to her as all golden gems of knowledge did: with quiet certainty. For a moment she was nonplussed, and then the meaning behind it hit her in the stomach. Like a rock.

"Holy shit—they're going to stone me to death."

Ora shook her head, mouth opening in a silent wheeze of terror. She hadn't thought of that one. Mentally she'd been prepared for fire, or for hanging. While neither sounded good, this was somehow way worse.

All those children.

She'd read them stories and kissed their skinned knees and let them crawl into her bed when they couldn't sleep. They were her family, and it was bad enough that they were going to watch her die. But to have them take part in it?

Her heart kicked up into a panicked gallop. She pulled against the ropes, straining her arms and legs in a desperate attempt to break free, but only succeeded in cutting deeper tracks into her already tender skin.

"I guess your dad made you a good deal after all, Lexy," she muttered, closing her eyes over a gush of hot tears. They rolled down her cheeks and pooled in the corners of her mouth. Salt and despair.

At that moment, she would have eagerly spread her legs for every Priest on The Ranch. She would have borne a busload of Phoenix's freak-children, or kissed Father Barnabas's ass, or blown up the entire world if it would have saved her own pitiful life.

She was embarrassed by her own weakness, and she felt like such an idiot. Her life was done before it had any value.

Ora the Spoiled. Ora the Selfish. Ora the Nothing. She would be forgotten before the first pile of dirt settled over her bones.

Then they were coming for her. The Priests. Wearing their ceremonial white robes. As one, they stood before her. Father Palidor with his dour, bearded face. Father Gabriel with his nervous, soft eyes. Behind them stood Father Cassiel, Father Zaniel, Father Thanos, and Father Manning. And behind them stood Fathers Angelo, Javan, Sachiel, Khoury, Caton, Taurin, and Mandek. Fathers Raynor and Montego stood off to the right and Fathers Tierney and Hagan stood to the left. And at the very back was the newest member of the Priesthood, Father Mannix. He looked away.

Together they formed a phalanx that surrounded two central figures, dressed in the crimson robes of the High Priests: Father Barnabas and Father Narda. Her dad wouldn't look at her.

"Well, dear!" Father Barnabas said with gritty good cheer. "Are you ready?"

Ora looked at her dad, standing hooded inside his crimson robe. His gaze was on the floor. She looked at Father Gabriel, and he turned away. She looked at Father Palidor. No help from that sour old bastard. Father Thanos had the decency to look ashamed. But he was weak; there was no help there. She allowed her gaze to travel from one Priest to the next, letting it rest on each of them individually. Assessing them. Marking them. Her Priests. Her Fathers. Her teachers.

Finally, she looked at Father Barnabas. She forced herself to meet his eyes. His black, cheery, insanely jovial eyes.

"Fuck you," she said, and spat on his crimson robe. It was quite a big loogie, and it clung to the front of his otherwise pristine robe in all its slimy glory. She was quite proud of it, actually.

There was a moment of shocked silence, and Ora waited for Father Barnabas to smash her head into the concrete floor. She welcomed it. After all, it would be far better than what he had planned for her.

But instead he laughed. And his laugh was a screech. It burned her skin and froze her blood.

"Come on then, dear! *Let's get this show on the road,* as they say."

Father Zaniel untied her. Father Angelo helped her stand, and then she was lifted and carried from the room. They brought her out into the cool autumn night, and the smell of horses and torch fire filled her nostrils. The wind tickled her cheeks with cold kisses.

Just outside the door was a wooden cart, one that was usually pulled by a horse and used to carry loads of hay. There was no horse strapped to it this evening, though. A tall wooden stake had been attached to the center of the cart, and four long chains dangled from it. The chains ended in metal cuffs.

They lifted her onto the cart, pushed her up against the rough wood of the stake, and clipped the metal cuffs around her ankles. They untied her wrists and lifted her arms above her head. The metal bracelets found their cold home around her wrists.

Once she was chained, Father Barnabas climbed up onto the cart and stood before her. He flicked one long fingernail at her blouse and the soft material fell away from her skin, shredding like confetti to be carried away in the wind.

"*No,*" she moaned. "*Please . . . no . . .*"

Her pants fell away in similar fashion. And then her bra and panties.

Father Palidor handed him a can and brush, and with giant strokes he painted her naked body with red paint. Her skin shrank away from the icy wetness, and she whimpered. The smell of copper assaulted her nostrils, and in horror she realized that it wasn't paint.

It was blood. Lamb's blood.

CHAPTER SIXTY

As each hour brought us closer to Wyoming and the *I Fidele* Ranch, Sumner's anxiety grew. By the time we reached the small town of Encampment, we were all buzzing with nerves.

"It's happening at midnight," Sumner said again.

"How much farther to The Ranch?" I asked. It was 10:48 p.m.

"Over an hour in the daylight, but the road is rough. Unpaved, unlit. At night it takes much longer."

"We'll make it. Don't worry, we'll make it," Josh said again. It had become his mantra over the last few hours. His hands were tight on the steering wheel, his knuckles ghostly white.

"She's given up," Sumner said.

"Ora? What do you mean?" I asked.

"She's ready to die. But she's scared. She's really scared." I noticed Sumner kept looking out at the moon. It was big and full. Enchanting. His hands were trembling in his lap. His eyes were distant, glazed.

"She knows we're coming, but she thinks we'll be too late."

"We'll make it! Tell her we'll make it. Tell her to hold on!" Josh said.

"I can't. She's not listening. Phoenix is trying to reach her. Lexy, too. She's not calm enough for them to get through to her."

"Where are they? Phoenix and Lexy? What are they doing?" I asked.

Sumner had no answer for me; he was silent for a long time. All I could hear was the steady beat of the tires against the pavement, marking off the miles.

"The turn is just ahead on the left," he finally said from the backseat. "Slow it down; it's a gravel road."

Josh braked and eased into the turn. We left the road behind, diving into the darkness of the forest.

"I'm going to take it as fast as I can. Hang on," Josh said, gritting his teeth as we rattled along. He flicked on the high beams and switched the guidance system to satellite. It mapped out the route in front of us, turn by turn, so he could see what was coming.

"I'm going to turn off the headlights when we get within a couple of miles, so let me know when we're close, Sumner."

"Okay," Sumner agreed, and then leaned forward to answer my question about Lexy and Phoenix. "I don't know what they're planning. They're guarding it."

"From you?"

"From the Priests, but they're sending me cryptic messages. The gist of it is this: Get your ass in gear, we need your help."

"Ryanne, get your vest on," Josh said. "Help Sumner. There's extra stuff in the duffel bag."

I maneuvered out of the passenger seat into the back of the Suburban, and then climbed over the backseat into the cargo area and started digging through the duffel bag. I handed Sumner a long-sleeved black shirt, and then strapped on my Kevlar vest and pulled a black shirt on over it. One by one, Josh called out items we would need and I rummaged through the bags, found them, and handed them to Sumner, who created a pile beside him. Sumner and I pulled on black caps and loaded and strapped on our weapons.

"There's a right turn coming up. See that gravel road twenty feet ahead?" Sumner whispered.

Josh nodded and turned. We bounced along in silence for several minutes.

In the dim light, Sumner looked like he was going to be sick. I reached across the seat and grabbed his hand.

"We're getting close," Sumner said, and the hitch in his voice was noticeable. "Might want to kill the lights."

Josh did, and we moved forward in tense silence.

"This is starting to seem familiar," I whispered.

"It's all way too familiar to me," he said breathlessly. "Damn! I'm sweating like a pig!"

Josh ignored us, all of his focus on the blackness in front of us.

"Up ahead on the left. There's a small road, you'll have to slow to a crawl."

It was barely more than a walking trail, and unmarked. Branches scraped across the sides of the car as we pressed forward, making eerie screeching noises against the paint.

"What I wouldn't give for a nice big bottle of gin right now," Sumner muttered.

"How's our timing?" I asked. The clock read 11:58, but that didn't mean much.

"I think we're okay. They haven't started yet. But they're gathering."

"Who is gathering?" Josh asked.

"Everyone. All the kids are out in the side yard. The Priests are gathering off the main building. They're preparing to bring her out."

"What are they going to do to her?"

"I don't know, but it isn't good. There's a gate up ahead. It's usually locked, but Lexy's opened it. She also disabled the camera system that covers the gate and the road to the main buildings."

We all held our breath as we passed through the gate. I don't know what we were expecting, but the silence remained unbroken.

Josh let out a shaky breath. "Okay, where to?" he asked.

Sumner seemed incapable of finding his voice, so I answered for him. "Veer left, see that rough track? Follow that. It will bring us around to the other side of the main buildings. About half a mile from where they're gathering. We'll have to walk from there."

Josh looked at Sumner and he bobbed his head in agreement. He swung left and we disappeared into the trees.

"They're going to strap her to a horse cart," Sumner wheezed, and the anxiety in his voice made me squeeze his hand. "Then strip her and paint her with lamb's blood."

"What the hell is the deal with the lamb's blood, anyway?" Josh muttered, but he didn't seem to expect an answer and he didn't get one.

"The Priests are distracted. They're all together, and they're focused on Ora. That's all good," Sumner said. "But . . . aw . . . *shit.*"

"What?" Josh asked.

"*He's* here."

"Who?" Josh persisted.

"Don't speak his name!" I hissed at Sumner. "You don't want to call him."

"Oh man," Sumner moaned. "Oh, that's *such* bad news."

"He's the High Priest," I explained to Josh.

"He's one scary mo-fo," Sumner added. He leaned his forehead against the back of the seat and took some deep, ragged breaths. "Okay . . . okay . . . okay . . . I can do this." He was panting like the little engine that couldn't. "Okay . . . okay . . . okay!"

His head popped up and he gripped my hand convulsively. "What would the corn dog do, right, homegirl?" His grin looked more like a scream.

"That's right." I squeezed his hand in return. His fear was infectious, and I swallowed hard.

"We're just about there," I said to Josh. "That big tree is about as far as we'll get by car."

Josh pulled up to it and turned the Suburban around so it was facing back toward the gate. He killed the engine and we waited in the ticking silence while he strapped on his vest and weapons.

"What's the plan?" I finally asked.

"We gonna keel us some honkies and we gonna keel them slooow," Sumner wheezed.

Josh patted Sumner on the back. "It's called 'winging it.' Let's get close and see what's going on." He hopped out of the car and unlatched the back gate to let me out.

"Why are you smiling?" The smile was more murdery than agreeable, but still. My heart was lodged in my throat and my bladder was screaming.

"It's called testosterone," Josh answered.

"Mix it with adrenaline and you've got yourself a Molotov cocktail of kick-ass macho awesomeness!" Sumner did a couple of spastic karate chops, quite hampered by the fact that he was in the backseat of a Suburban. Josh snorted.

"Men are weird," I muttered.

Josh lifted my shirt and pulled on the straps of my vest, making sure they were tight enough. "That's what makes us lovable, though. Right?"

I looked up at him and couldn't help but smile. "Right."

Sumner appeared beside him. "Hurry it up. You wanna live forever?" His attempt at John Wayne came out sounding more like Mickey Mouse.

"Stay near me," Josh whispered, squeezing my arms. "And don't do anything stupid."

"Always with the compliments." I followed him out into the night.

We fell in line behind Josh. He moved with grace through the dark forest, while Sumner and I tripped over roots and walked face first into low-lying branches and spiderwebs.

"In which the ninja master leads his bumbling sidekicks into battle," Sumner narrated, sotto voce.

I elbowed him. "Shh!" And then tripped over an unseen tree root and fell into Josh's back.

"My point." Sumner snickered nervously.

"Can it, you two," Josh hissed. A few minutes later, he reached back and grabbed my hand, pulling me forward to stand beside him. He was pointing at a gap in the trees.

"Yup, that's them," Sumner whispered.

Several hundred yards away, a crowd had gathered in the flickering torchlight. They cast tall, ghoul-like shadows up against the wall of the main building. They were milling around with hushed excitement.

"How many, do you think? Five-fifty? Six hundred?" Josh asked.

"Yeah, about that," I answered.

"That's way more than usual for The Ranch. A lot of adults, too. Father Narda said they were gathering in the troops," Sumner said.

"So the adults are Disciples?" Josh asked.

"And Chosen. I don't see any Priests. Do you, Ryanne?"

"How would I know?" I asked, feeling testy for reasons I couldn't explain.

Sumner wouldn't take the bait. "They're wearing the white robes. Except for Narda and . . . the other one, who are wearing the crimson robes of the High Priests. Good target practice, right Josh?"

"There are a lot of children," Josh objected.

"Yeah. And see those windows?" Sumner pointed at the main building. "There's a bunch of new kids up there, stashed in a converted classroom. Looks like they got them without my help."

"So that's where Leora Wylie would be," Josh mused.

"Yup."

I could see Josh's mind ticking through the possibilities and coming to the same conclusion I had. There was no way we could get those kids off The Ranch by ourselves.

"I guess she's safe enough. For now. But the ones down here, we need to be careful. I don't want any of them getting hurt."

"Of course," I agreed. My eyes were scanning the crowd, searching for a child with red hair. Boy or girl? No matter what else happened, I was leaving The Ranch with my baby.

"I'm talking to *you*, Sumner. I don't want you going off half cocked."

"I'm always fully cocked. That's why the ladies like me. Besides, my aim is getting much better," he said, and then pointed. "That's Lexy. What the hell, man . . ."

"What?" I asked.

"She's wearing a red robe." He was clearly stunned.

I spotted a small woman with a cloud of dark curls. If not for the robe, I might have mistaken her for one of the children. She turned, and her gaze fell directly on us. It wasn't more than a heartbeat before she turned casually away, but the message was clear enough; she knew we were there.

"She's an *Amante*?" I gasped. My stomach did a slow, nauseating roll.

Sumner was shaking his head. "That can't be. She's one of the Chosen . . ."

"Never mind that now. Do you see Phoenix anywhere?" Josh asked.

"Um, yeah. He's the guy hanging from the stockade."

"What!" I hissed, and then saw what he was talking about. How could I have missed him? He was hanging several feet off the ground, splayed against the wooden fence on the far side of the clearing. He was dangling by his hands, which were bound to the wood above his head, and he certainly didn't look comfortable. With his white-blond hair and pale skin, he looked like he was performing in an Aryan version of the story of Jesus. I doubted Jesus had looked quite so monumentally pissed, though.

"Here they come," Sumner said.

I heard the chanting before I saw them.

"They come with the blood sacrifice," I whispered.

"And the Faithful shall bear witness," Sumner added.

"The family will rise as one against the *Blasphemare*."

"And strike them down with the mighty sword," Sumner finished.

"Jesus Christ," Josh said, clearly horrified.

"Don't think he's anywhere near this action, bro," Sumner said.

The Priests formed a ring around the horse cart as they moved into the crowd. The two High Priests led the way, their crimson robes glimmering in the torchlight. The crowd parted before them, picking up the solemn chant and echoing it back to the Fathers. They reached the center of the yard and the cart stilled. With the precision of a well-timed ballet, the Priests stepped away from the cart. They fanned out like the wings of a butterfly opening to the night.

"That's Father Narda," Sumner said. "The one on the right."

"I know," I replied, but my gaze was on the girl. The girl in chains, laid bare and dripping blood from her flesh. Even her hair had been matted with blood. In the torchlight she sparkled like a ruby.

On the wind, I caught the collective sigh of the family. I could feel it, too. It electrified my skin and pounded through my veins. In some dreadful way, she was breathtakingly beautiful. She was ripe flesh and dripping blood, glorious in her courtship with death.

"And their children shall rise against them. With fire and with water will the battle commence," Sumner breathed, just as the first stones flew.

"What?" I turned to him, but he was gone. He ran straight out of the shelter of the trees and bounded toward the crowd, screaming like a Scottish warrior doing the Highland charge. In other words, he went off half cocked.

"Well, shit," I said, and followed him.

CHAPTER SIXTY-ONE

The flames burst forth with an explosion of light and heat that knocked me to my knees. One moment I was running for the crowd, Sumner in front of me and Josh somewhere behind me, and the next I was sliding across the rough earth like Jackie Robinson trying to steal home.

Josh tumbled over the top of me and came down hard on his stomach, managing to kick me in the face with one big shoe on his way down.

"Safe!" I muttered, rolling onto my side and shielding my eyes. The world was insanely bright. And hot.

I pulled myself upright and stumbled directly into the stampede of people fleeing the flames. They pushed me backward and knocked me flat. Someone's booted foot came down hard on my arm. Another tore across my abdomen, pounding me into the ground. I bellowed like a wounded boar.

And then Josh was there, pulling me to my feet and tucking me up against his side. His arm formed a vise around my waist, lifting my feet off the ground. He plunged forward like a battering ram, knocking people out of the way.

We broke into a clearing and stopped, hampered by the wall of flames that rose toward the sky with insatiable hunger. It encircled the woman on the cart, a perfect barricade. I caught glimpses of her within the inferno. A red goddess. Her eyes were closed against the blaze, her muscles taut and straining against her bindings.

The roar was deafening. The Priests ran about, their white robes flapping in the hot wind, yelling and gesticulating wildly.

One of them got close enough for me to hear him yell. "Ashlyn . . . out!" And then he was gone in a swirl of panicked robes.

I couldn't hear the gunfire, and doubted anyone else could, either. The first I knew of it was when a crimson bloom spread across the white robe of a Priest on my left. He fell and rolled, a look of eternal surprise on his face as he gave up his life.

I shied away from him in horrified recognition. It was Father Angelo. He had taught me Italian and French. Another Priest landed almost at my feet. I couldn't help but look. It was Father Manning. He had done the funniest card tricks. He was missing a large chunk of his head. I screamed.

Josh pulled me up against his chest, and that's when I saw Sumner. He was ambling about like a dark cowboy, a hard smile of determination creasing his face. As they swarmed around the fire, he picked them off, casually trolling for the next good shot and taking the time to do it right.

"Holy shit, it's Billy the Kid," I breathed.

"Well, he's crazy enough to be," Josh muttered against my ear. I could hear the grudging admiration in his voice. "Do you see either of the High Priests?"

I scanned the area and shook my head. There were plenty of white robes, and a number of Disciples who hadn't been scared off by the flames were herding children back inside the main building. And of course there was Ora, encased in fire.

"How are we supposed to get to her?" I asked, and he shrugged.

"What about Phoenix? Maybe we can get him down."

Josh and I worked our way around the edge of the panicked crowd. Some of them were forming a chain, passing forward buckets of water from the Main House. Phoenix was no longer pinned against the wall like a bug. He stood hidden in the shadows, his full attention on the flames surrounding Ora.

Only then did I understand that he was the source of the fire. I could just make out the small figure of a child half hidden behind him, one hand firmly gripping Phoenix's arm as though to steady him.

I caught a glimpse of red silk beside me, and my stomach lurched. It wasn't one of the High Priests, though. She was small, with dark skin and eyes, and an unruly cloud of black curls.

"Ryanne." She squeezed my arm.

"Lexy," I answered hoarsely.

"I'm glad you're real," she said. I blinked at her, unsure how to respond.

"We've got this covered," Lexy said. "Take your boyfriend and go find Jack. We'll meet you in the north woods, if we can."

"But—"

"He's underground. Do you understand what I mean?" she asked.

I opened my mouth to say something along the lines of "Hell, no" but nothing came out. To my surprise, I found myself nodding.

"Good. Now go!" She disappeared into the melee.

We faded back into the shadows like ghosts.

CHAPTER SIXTY-TWO

"Hang on Ora, you're not dead yet."

"You better keep yourself under control, Phoenix!"

Being enclosed in flames was almost as scary as being pummeled by rocks. It beat against her skin in waves of intense heat. It singed the hair on top of her head as well as her brows and eyelashes. She kept her eyes closed, afraid her eyeballs would dry up and pop out of her face like tiny raisins.

But she had a bigger problem: breathing was almost impossible. Every time she tried to gulp in some air, she seared her lungs instead. She could feel it burning a path down her throat and sizzling its way to the tips of her bronchi.

"I can't breathe! Phoenix, I can't breathe!"

"Don't panic."

"Easy for you to say, fucker! I'm a human marshmallow!"

"You really want to name-call right now, Ora?"

"Ora! Don't panic, we're coming for you!" That was Lexy. Her voice was a cool balm, and Ora tucked her face into her chest and tried to hold on.

"Lexy . . ."

Ora couldn't hear anything above the roar of the flames, and she was still afraid to open her eyes. But Lexy's words had calmed her, as they always did. She sent out her awareness, trying to gain some understanding of what was going on around her. Bit by bit, little nuggets of information came to her.

Phoenix is over by the fence, with Ashlyn. That was good.

Lexy is in the crowd. She's maybe ten feet away, on the left. Okay, that was also good.

Sumner has turned assassin. He's taken out four of the Priests so far. Ora paused there, trying to wrap her mind around it. He'd taken out Fathers Manning, Javan, Khoury, and Angelo. At that moment, he was moving in on Father Sachiel.

"Get that bastard Palidor if you get the chance, Sumner!"

He responded with a wild cackle.

The next nugget not only stunned her, but also started that infernal hope brewing within her once again.

Sumner found the redhead! Not only that, she's heading for the Underground to free Jack.

"Sumner, you're my fucking hero!"

"That's right, baby doll. I'm the stuff men are made of!"

"You do the worst John Wayne impersonation I've ever heard."

If she could have spared the oxygen, she would have laughed with relief and delight. But really, breathing was becoming a serious concern.

"Um, Phoenix?"

It was Lexy who answered. *"Can you undo your bonds, Ora?"*

Ora tried.

"No, I'm still too drugged."

Neither Lexy nor Phoenix was telekinetic, and panic clenched at her gut. But then a new voice chimed in.

"No problem." It was Ashlyn.

Click. Click. Click. Click.

One by one, the shackles released their hold. Ora stumbled forward, veering dangerously close to the flames before she managed to regain her balance.

"Get down, and hold on to something," Ashlyn warned.

Ora barely had time to obey, wrapping her arms around the bottom of the post. She heard the water before she felt it. It was a thundering answer to the fire's roar. She heard the screaming as its flooding force swept people away. And then it hit her. It wasn't like being doused by a cool gush of water—it was like being hit by a Mack truck. The only thing that saved her was the fact that she'd positioned herself with her back to the onslaught. She was pushed chest-first into the post.

The cart wasn't tied to anything, and it was swept away with her pinned to it. She held on, lungs burning.

"Oops. Sorry about that, Ora," Ashlyn chimed in.

Her head broke the surface of the water. She sucked in great, gasping breaths. And then she was sobbing with relief.

To breathe! It was glorious!

The horse cart came to a slow, spinning stop as the water released its hold. She opened her eyes and watched in awe as the torrent churned away from her. There were heads bobbing in the current as people were swept downhill.

"Holy *shit*, Ashlyn," she croaked.

And then they were there: Lexy and Phoenix and Ashlyn and Sumner. Ora was a drowned rat, but at least most of the blood had washed off. Unfortunately, she was still naked.

"Can someone lend me some clothes or something?" she managed.

Sumner handed over his shirt. Underneath, he was wearing another T-shirt with a corn dog on it.

"Thanks." She pulled it over her head. It hit her midthigh and was blessedly warm.

"Ora, are you all right?" Lexy asked. Her brown eyes were huge and beautiful in the moonlight.

"Oh, Lex. Are you?" she asked.

Lexy nodded, her face tight. But she didn't touch her, and Ora couldn't seem to reach across the distance that separated them. The silence stretched out, wounded and uncomfortable.

"Okay," Sumner jumped in. "Shall we hit the road, folks?"

CHAPTER SIXTY-THREE

Josh followed Ryanne through the forest. She didn't stick to a path, but rather seemed to be following some inner radar. He found it interesting that the girl who had clumsily trailed him not long before was walking with the grace and agility of a deer, while he stumbled over tree roots and slipped across slick patches of the forest floor.

Intermittent tongues of ground fog licked at his feet, which didn't help. They added to the dreamlike quality of their movement, and after a time he wondered if Ryanne was sleepwalking, or if he was. He followed her silently, trusting her to take them where they needed to go.

To Jack. His stomach tightened with excitement, and he almost walked into her.

"Why did we stop?"

"We're walking along untouched forest, right? And without thinking, we put our trust in what we can't see. So we trust there's nothing below us but dirt and rock. Thousands of miles of solidity, supporting us up here on the surface."

"Okay . . ."

"And so far you'd be right." She took his hand and led him forward. After ten paces, she stopped. "Does it feel any different?"

"No."

"Of course not. You never know what's just below the surface. Not with people and not with the earth. Not unless you dig a little."

"I get the metaphor. But what's below us right here?"

"A whole world."

"What do you mean?"

"There are plants growing and flowers blooming. There's a river flowing, and generators humming. There are bees buzzing and animals nursing their young. And somewhere under our feet, there's a young boy with the answers to everything."

Josh opened his mouth, but no words would form. The notion that he was standing above a secret world was so huge he couldn't cram it all into his head.

"I . . . don't understand."

"It's a giant fallout shelter, like those built in the fifties to protect against nuclear bombs. But it's huge. It's able to sustain all forms of life thanks to an underground river, which provides fresh water and is used to power thousands of generators. The generators run a grid of natural lights and thousands of air purifiers and heaters."

"But . . . why?" he croaked.

"That's the million-dollar question. Isn't it?"

"I guess it is. How long have you known about this?"

"Since Lexy mentioned it. Or most of my life, depending on your perspective."

"How do we get in there?"

"There are many ways in and out. You just have to know where they are."

"And do you?"

"Some of them. The one closest to where they're keeping Jack is right in front of you."

He looked down at his feet, half expecting to see the neat outline of a trapdoor disguised with dirt and branches.

"Not there. It's the tree. See it?"

Josh examined the tree carefully. It was an ancient ponderosa pine. It looked no different from the others.

"Look at the ground near the base. Do you see the hole?"

He bent over for a closer look. Hidden underneath a thickly gnarled tree root, Josh could just make it out. He could have passed by it a million times and missed it. Crouching down, Josh tried to get a better look.

"We have to crawl in there?" He didn't much like the idea.

"What's the problem, Agent Metcalf?"

"Um. Spiders," he admitted. "I'm not a big fan."

"Oh wow. I would have bet you weren't afraid of anything."

"I'm not *afraid* of them. I just don't like them," he said defensively.

She bent down and kissed his cheek. "It's okay. It just makes you more human." Her kiss burned against his skin long after she took her lips away.

"To hell with it," he said gruffly. "Lead the way."

Ryanne eased under the root feet-first and disappeared into the hole one inch at a time, her back scraping along the earth. Soon she was just a head sticking out of the ground.

"It looks pretty tight in there. Are you sure I won't get stuck?"

"Don't worry, I'll have Sumner shoot down the tree if you do." And with that she disappeared.

"Great. That's great." Josh followed her example, sliding his feet into the hole and shuffling forward. His legs dropped in, and then his hips. Around shoulder height, his feet hit soft ground and he had to bend his knees to continue. He took one last gulp of cool night air and slid in the rest of the way.

Ryanne was waiting for him, barely visible in the dark. It smelled of rich earth and pine needles. They were in a space about five feet across by four feet wide. She had no trouble standing, but Josh had to crouch so his head didn't touch the earth above.

That's where the spiders will be, he thought, and sucked in a deep breath. "Where to?"

She moved away from him into the black and he followed before he lost sight of her. Whatever moonlight had seeped under the tree root quickly disappeared, and he was blind. He could hear her advancing ahead of him, but he couldn't see a thing.

Josh silently wished for his thermal-vision goggles, but he'd lost them when the explosion of fire had practically blinded him. He'd yanked them away from his eyes, and then dropped them to save Ryanne from being trampled.

The ground beneath his feet was solid, though. It dipped down at a gentle slope as he followed Ryanne blindly into the cool earth. But what if the tunnel collapsed? He shook his head; surely it was reinforced. After a moment's hesitation, he reached out and felt the wall beside him. His fingers brushed over a rough wooden beam and, within several feet, another. That was good enough for him. He pulled his hand back and wiped it against his pants, shuddering.

"Just ahead. There's a door," she whispered. "Damn, it's locked."

Josh felt his way along until he was beside her. "I have key picks." He rummaged inside his utility vest until he felt the small leather package. The lock felt like a normal dead bolt. "Let's give this a try. I've never picked a lock blind, just so you know."

A simple dead bolt was quite easy to pick, even with a couple of bobby pins. Josh wiggled the wrench into place, placing light tension on the lock. He used the pick to wiggle the pins up and down, working backward until there was a satisfying click.

"Impressive."

Josh tucked the picks back into his vest, unholstered his gun, and opened the door. After what felt like an eternity in the absolute darkness of the tunnel, even the dim light that greeted them made him squint.

Ahead was a long hallway, carved out of rock and strung with long fluorescent bulbs that let off only the faintest glow, likely to conserve power.

Their feet made scritching sounds against the gritty floor, echoing off the walls in the most unnerving way. Two hundred feet down there was a T-junction. Josh hesitated, but Ryanne didn't. She turned left and he followed. At the end of that hall, there was a thick metal door. But this time there was no lock.

It led to yet another hallway, and then another. Each one brought them deeper within the labyrinth, and Josh grew nervous about finding their way back out. Ryanne seemed sure-footed and unconcerned, so he followed helplessly behind her.

Another T-junction, and this time she turned right. Several hundred yards down there was another metal door, also unmarked. Josh began to pick up a new sound. It grew in volume, becoming a dull roar.

"Is that fire?" he asked nervously. It sounded eerily like the bonfire party they had just left.

"It's the river." She opened the door. The dull roar exploded into booming thunder. He half expected the water to tumble through and sweep them away.

When they stepped through the doorway, he understood. Although the river was deep and fierce, the noise doubled or even tripled as it rolled and echoed along the arched rock walls. The water was onyx edged with silver.

Ryanne turned right and followed the shoreline, moving upriver. They passed metal door after metal door, and his curiosity began to get the better of him. What was behind all those doors? Animals, she'd said. Plants and bees. Generators and air purifiers. The place was immense, and he got the feeling they had barely scratched the surface.

Finally, she opened a door to expose another dimly lit hallway. Plain gray doors marched along either side, spaced ten feet apart. The doors were numbered, starting at Q-1 and counting up, odd numbers on the left and even numbers on the right. Ryanne stopped in front of Q-17 and placed a trembling hand on the doorknob. In the dim light she looked slightly green.

"Here goes nothing," she whispered, and opened the door.

It was a bedroom. Sparse and utilitarian, like a dorm room before any personal flair had been added. A small dresser sat against the left wall. On the right was a single bed with a nightstand and metal lamp.

The boy lay on the bed. He wasn't tied down. He wasn't bandaged. He didn't stir at their arrival.

Ryanne pointed to a metal pole beside the bed. An IV. Josh's gaze followed the line from the bag of dark liquid to the needle that disappeared into Jack's hand.

A fierce burst of anger propelled Josh forward. As gently as he could, he pulled off the tape. He slid the needle out of the boy's vein. Jack's hand was so small, and covered in bruises. His skin was ashy and his hair was long and matted.

"Jack," Josh said, his voice hoarse with emotion. "Jack, can you hear me? We're here to rescue you. We're here to take you home, to your dad."

"If only that were possible," a voice said from the doorway. "But I'm afraid that won't do *at all*."

The man was shrouded within a crimson robe. His eyes were sparkling with some dark amusement, but beneath that Josh sensed an abyss that could swallow a person whole.

Josh knew those eyes. He'd seen them bleeding through the clear green eyes of the woman next to him, tormenting and taunting him.

He'd raised his gun toward them once before, but hadn't pulled the trigger. This time, he vowed he would.

CHAPTER SIXTY-FOUR

Sumner helped guide Ora to the Suburban, trying his best not to think about the fact that she was wearing nothing but an oversized T-shirt.

They limped along behind Lexy, Phoenix, and Ashlyn. The girl had proved to be much more handy than a garden hose, and clearly expected them to take her with them in return for her help. She wasn't letting Phoenix out of her sight for a second.

It seemed to take forever to make it the half mile. By the time they saw the black gleam of the Suburban's roof, whatever adrenaline had been pumping through Sumner's veins was gone, leaving him shivering and queasy. He bent over and closed his eyes, swallowing hard against a black wave of nausea.

"Come on, Sumner." Phoenix clapped him on the back. "The day's not over yet."

Sumner shook his head, trying to clear it, and moved to the cargo area. He rummaged through the duffel bags until he found Ryanne's clothing, and handed Ora a pair of jeans and a pink hooded sweatshirt. She took them gratefully, although both were several sizes too small.

"Any socks in there?" she asked hopefully, and Sumner hunted around until he found some. He grabbed Josh's sweatshirt for himself.

Phoenix helped him hoist up the third-row seat, and Sumner sent up a silent thank-you to the designers at Chevrolet for making a truck that could seat nine. They were going to need it. He hoped.

Sumner climbed into the driver's seat. Josh had left the keys in the ignition. The Suburban's engine roared to life and he winced, hoping it hadn't attracted unwanted attention. The others piled in.

"Where to, folks?"

"North," Lexy said promptly. "Get as close to the cliff as possible."

Sumner put the car in gear and rolled across the forest floor, using the moonlight as his guide. He almost ran over the crimson-robed figure who stepped out in front of them. Sumner jammed on the brakes and the rest joined him in a communal scream.

The Suburban came to rest several feet away, and the man pulled the hood off his head. It was Father Narda. His gaze met Sumner's through the windshield.

"Shit!" Ora spat. "Run that son of a bitch over!"

"Hell with that," Lexy chimed in. "Sumner, give me your gun. I'm going to shoot him in the balls!"

"Ladies, please," Sumner said with surprising calm. He was locked in his former mentor's gaze, and couldn't turn away. He shut off the engine and opened the door.

"Bad idea, my friend," Phoenix warned. "Get close to him and he'll rip your heart right out of your ass."

"No. He won't."

"Sumner!" Ora called, but Sumner was already out of the car.

"Father," he said.

"Hello, Sumner."

Sumner's heart lurched, and acid seared his throat with bitter fire. It was too much to bear, and his voice shook. "I see you still have quite the way with the ladies."

"I'm a Priest."

"In other words, you can do whatever you want. It's in the covenant you made."

Father Narda shrugged.

"You bastard! I loved her. And you *knew* it!"

"Yes. I knew you loved Adelia," Narda said, unapologetic.

"Your selfishness killed her!"

"I understand how you could see it that way."

"And now . . . *Lexy*! How could you?"

"I did it for the greater good. To plant the seed. You know this, Sumner."

"The same way you *planted a seed* in Adelia?" Sumner spat.

"She produced two beautiful, *faithful* girls."

"That's all she was to you? She was just an . . . *incubator*?"

"A very enjoyable one."

"You fucking bastard." The gun found its way into his hand. He aimed it at the Father's head.

"In the *balls*, Sumner!" Lexy screeched from the Suburban.

Father Narda watched him, his brows lifted in curiosity. "Could you shoot me?"

"You better believe I could," Sumner said.

Father Narda looked at him gravely. "You've done significant damage, my son. I should terminate you for your disobedience, but I won't. You're free to go. I won't stand in your way."

"What? Why?"

"As horrible as you think I am, well, by your standards I'm probably worse. But I *do* love my daughter."

"You have a messed-up way of showing it."

The Father lifted his shoulders in a shrug. "Perhaps. But I don't want my daughter to die. I am grateful to you for saving her life, and in return I will spare you yours, on one condition: you must keep Lexine and Ora safe."

"Are you shitting me right now?"

"One learns such foul language on the Outside. No, I'm not *shitting* you. My daughter may hate me right now, but someday she will realize I gave her a gift."

"What?"

Father Narda smiled. "The seed has been planted. Within the womb of her lover grows a baby of Ora's lineage. I gave Lexine the one thing my daughter couldn't. I gave them a new life!"

"You . . . sick . . . *bastard.*"

"Yes, yes. All that and more, I'm sure. Will you do it, Sumner? Will you protect them?"

"From what!"

"Since they won't be safe on The Ranch, you need to pick your location very, very carefully. Do you get my meaning?"

"Shit," Sumner grumbled.

"Do you get my meaning, Sumner? *Day Zero is upon us.* I want my daughter, and my unborn child, to be safe. Will you do it?"

"Oh, hell! Of course I will, you bastard! But how am I supposed to protect them when I don't know what the hell I'm protecting them from!"

"Keep to the center of the country, away from the big cities. Stockpile enough supplies to last at least a year. Buy air purifiers and a generator to run them. Tape up doors and windows. You won't want to go outside for a while."

"What the hell are you guys planning?" Sumner asked in horror.

"I've already said too much."

"We're going to stop it, whatever it is," Sumner vowed.

"No." Father Narda shook his head. "You're not. It's too late to stop it. All you can do is save the lives of those closest to you." And with that, Father Narda turned and disappeared into the forest.

"Perhaps we'll meet again, someday." His voice floated back to Sumner on the cold wind and wrapped icy tentacles around his heart.

"In the New World we have created."

CHAPTER SIXTY-FIVE

"Your guns are of no use, Agent Metcalf." Father Barnabas was smiling, but his smile was more of a grotesque leer.

I was pretty sure I had wet myself when he appeared in the doorway, but would deal with the embarrassment of that later. If there was a later. It seemed unlikely, given the circumstances.

Josh tried anyway, squeezing the trigger with practiced ease. Nothing happened. He pulled out the gun Sheriff Lagrudo had given him, but it wouldn't fire, either. "Well, that sucks."

"Shall we get down to business?"

"I'd rather not," I managed.

"I'm afraid it's unavoidable, dear," he said. "Although why you decided to throw away your life to save this boy, I just can't fathom. What's so special about him?" He moved in on me solicitously. Although he had asked quite casually, I sensed the depth of his interest and alarm bells started going off in my head.

"You don't know?" I asked with as much confidence as I could muster. If by some miracle he had a blind spot when it came to Jack,

I didn't want to tip him off. "Guess whoever's in charge of doing the research on these kids missed a few things."

I must have blinked at the wrong moment and missed his approach. One moment Father Barnabas was by the dresser, and the next he had me by the throat. His icy claw was choking off my windpipe and my feet were dangling.

"Don't play smart with me, girl. I'm in no mood!"

"Let her go!" Josh bellowed, throwing himself at us. Father Barnabas raised a casual hand in his direction, and Josh went flying backward. He crashed into the night table and knocked the lamp over with a clang of metal.

"Why is this boy so important?" His eyes were red and his breath smelled of rot. I opened my mouth, but nothing would come out. Black roses bloomed in front of my eyes.

Just as quickly as he had grabbed me, he let me go. I stumbled away from him, wheezing and grabbing at my throat. The skin he had touched felt frozen. He pinned me against the wall. His eyes were black.

"Why?"

"He's . . . Josh's . . . nephew," I managed, desperately hoping he wouldn't see through the lie. Well, hell, he was going to kill us no matter what, so how much worse could it get?

He examined me for so long I was ready to scream and tear at my skin, if it would allow me to escape my body and get away from those eyes.

Josh was trying to get up, but without lifting a finger, Father Barnabas had him pinned against the night table. "He's my sister's son. She passed away last year, and I've been keeping a close eye on him ever since."

"How . . . *ironic.*" With those beady black eyes he reminded me of a vulture examining his prey just before pecking out the juicy heart. "You can see why I can't allow any of you to live, hmm?" He leaned in like a lover and traced one sharp fingernail down my cheek and along my collarbone, searing an icy path across my skin. I couldn't help the whimper that escaped my lips.

"It's a shame you won't be able to enjoy the fruits of your labor, but that was the choice you made." His lips were mere inches from mine. I could taste the black decay of his breath, and my stomach churned violently. "I'll give you another choice," he whispered. "Who dies first?"

"No . . ." I pleaded.

He nuzzled my neck, and my skin blistered where his lips and tongue grazed me. His teeth were daggers tracing their way up my neck. "Will you choose to go first, so you don't see them suffer?" he murmured, breath hot on my skin. "Or will you watch them die for your betrayal?"

"No . . ." I pulled away from him, stumbling, and he shoved me to the floor. A moment later he was on top of me. He smothered my mouth with his own, and his thick, maggoty tongue jabbed into my throat. I gagged, stomach heaving against his attack.

"Leave her alone!" Josh bellowed. I could see him struggling to get to us, but he was pinned.

"Mmm. Delicious." He pulled back and murmured against my lips. "I've always had a thing for redheads. They're so . . . *fiery*."

Father Barnabas tugged at my jeans, and I could feel his hardness pressing against my leg. I wailed in protest, struggling to get away. But my fear clearly aroused him, and he groaned with pleasure and redoubled his effort.

Pushing up my shirt, he tore at the Kevlar vest. My bra was ripped aside, his hands scorching my bare skin. He kneaded my breast and pinched my nipples, sending shock waves of pain through me. I screamed, which made him moan. His hips thrust forward convulsively.

"I said leave her alone!" Josh roared.

"Should we let him watch, my dear?" His voice was ragged with arousal.

"Please, *don't*," I sobbed.

My pants came free, and the cold air lapped at my exposed skin. He pushed my legs apart and rubbed an icy finger over my tender skin, pinching and hurting. I bellowed.

"Don't you dare!" Josh raged. The veins in his neck were popping and his skin was an apoplectic purple. But it did no good; he was as effectively trapped as a bug in a glass.

Father Barnabas smirked at him. He pulled his robe aside and moved over me, pressing me down with a satisfied grunt. I closed my eyes and prepared for the assault, wishing Josh would turn aside.

"*Shedim!*"

He froze above me.

The boy was standing on the bed, his hands splayed in front of him. His eyes were rolled back in his head, revealing only the whites, but they were focused directly on the Priest.

Father Barnabas howled, pulling back from me. I scuttled away and pressed against the wall, yanking at my clothes.

"*Shedim!*" Jack said again, and his voice was as pure and clean as the ringing of a bell.

"*They mingled with the nations and learned their deeds. They shed innocent blood and the land became polluted. And they became unclean through their deeds and went astray!*"

"Who . . . *are* you?" Father Barnabas gasped.

"*I am Jack, son of Emma. I am a mere boy.*" He climbed down from the bed and moved toward us. Father Barnabas shrank back against the dresser.

"*I am of the Sabaoth. A warrior for the White. You! Watcher, Daemon, Vile Being! You shall be cast aside, forever to wander the underworld in torment!*"

Father Barnabas laughed. It started out as a chuckle, and then it turned into a cackle which morphed into a screech that hammered at my brain. I covered my ears, and out of the corner of my eye I saw Josh doing the same.

The boy seemed unfazed. He moved in on the Priest, reaching out for him with his bruised hands. Father Barnabas tried to move away, but he had nowhere to go.

Jack Barbetti's hands cupped the Priest's cheeks, as gently as a parent would touch their child, and the Priest stopped screeching. The silence that descended was so abrupt I wondered if my eardrums had burst.

I don't know what I was expecting. Perhaps that Father Barnabas would disappear in a puff of smoke. Or maybe that he would melt to the ground like the Wicked Witch in *The Wizard of Oz*, leaving his crimson robe in a steaming pile on the floor. Neither happened.

A trickle of blood escaped his right nostril and his eyes rolled back in his head. Jack set him down carefully, cradling his head and laying it gently against the floor.

He turned toward me. I have to admit, I flinched; those white eyes were creepy. He climbed into my lap and wrapped his arms around my neck, burying his face against my shoulder. After a moment my arms found their way around him. I could feel each of his ribs and the small, hard nubs of his spine.

"I want my mommy," he said. And then he wept.

CHAPTER SIXTY-SIX

"Do you have him?" Ryanne wheezed.

"Yup. Got him, go ahead," Josh said. Ryanne took a deep breath and started to climb again.

The way out was much more challenging than the way in, and Josh was sweating profusely. It was a long, slow climb out of the bowels of the earth, made all the more difficult by the unconscious boy they were carrying.

Jack Barbetti had wept in Ryanne's trembling arms for several minutes, and then, without warning or wind-down of any kind, had simply returned to his comatose state.

That was when Josh decided it was time to hightail it out of there. They left Father Barnabas lying on the ground, blood pooling under his cheek. Although he hadn't bothered to check his vitals, Josh doubted he was dead. He kept expecting to feel one of those bony claws clamp down on his ankle. Would that wild, screechy cackle be the last thing he ever heard?

Stop it, he told himself. Stay focused on the task at hand. Still, he couldn't help it. He kept peeking back over his shoulder into the darkness. Josh had never been a fan of horror movies. He hadn't slept for three nights after watching *The Exorcist* at Kevin Greenwood's thirteenth birthday party. Now he was living through his own version of one, minus the creepy music, and he didn't much like it.

"How much farther?" he asked, pausing to redistribute the boy's weight to the other side.

Ryanne stopped ahead of him, breathing hard. "Another fifty feet or so."

"Good."

"Until the fork, I mean. We turn left, and then it's another hundred yards. Or so."

He stifled a groan. "Okay, let's go."

"Do you want me to take him?" she asked.

While he appreciated the offer, he doubted she could manage more than ten feet carrying the boy up the steep incline. "I'm fine. Lead the way."

"If it helps, Sumner's waiting for us near the top."

"No kidding?" That did lighten his spirits. "And Ora? Any idea if she's all right?"

"She's fine. She's with him."

"That's . . . really . . . great." Tears stung his eyes. Josh had long ago used up any extra stores of adrenaline, and he was on the brink of physical and mental exhaustion. His whole body was trembling with it.

Not too much farther, he thought. Get going.

He focused on the physical task of moving forward, one step at a time. They made it around the curve and he switched Jack back to the left side. Halfway up the final climb, there was a faint lightening around them. The pitch dark gave way an inch at a time until he could just make out Ryanne's outline in front of him. Ahead of her was a ghostly, silver light.

He switched Jack back to the right side and pushed his quivering muscles through the last few yards, eyes focused on the growing moonlight ahead of them. Ryanne disappeared into the glow, then reached down to help pull Jack up and over the ledge.

Josh pulled himself up beside her and lay with his eyes closed, panting against the cool earth. He had never been so grateful to feel open air around him.

"Is Jack okay?" Ryanne asked.

"I think so," Josh wheezed. "He's breathing."

"He's so thin."

"You're kidding, right? He weighs a ton." He opened his eyes, and his stomach did a slow roll. "Where the hell are we?"

"The cliff," she answered.

Very carefully, Josh sat up. They were on an eight-foot ledge, and below, the world dropped away. At the bottom, he could make out the checkerboard formation of farmland, gone fallow for the winter.

"It's ironic, really," she panted. "I guess this is where Jack landed when he fell over the edge."

Josh looked up. The rock face behind him climbed straight up some thirty feet. "Um, I don't see how we're going to get up there. Or get Jack up there, for that matter."

"Haven't you ever done any rock climbing?" Sumner's head poked out above him. He was grinning. "Howdy, folks! Fancy meeting you here."

Josh beamed up at him. "At Quantico. But that was a long time ago."

"Well, sounds like it's time for a refresher course."

"I also used a rope," Josh added.

Sumner's grin only widened. "Ask and you shall receive, my friend." He disappeared.

"There are climbing ropes stashed in a Rubbermaid up there," Ryanne explained. "This entrance gets used quite a bit. By the younger Priests."

Phoenix's head appeared over the edge, his pale skin and white-blond hair glowing silver in the moonlight.

"We're attaching the rope to the bottom of a tree. Who wants to climb up first?"

"I think you'd better," Josh said to Ryanne. "I'll carry Jack up after you."

"That does it. Tomorrow I'm going to start eating better," she panted. "And getting more exercise."

He refrained from commenting.

Sumner lowered a rope, and Josh followed Phoenix's directions to tie a Swiss seat harness around Ryanne. When he was done, she looked at him nervously.

"I'm not sure I can do this."

"Just take it one step at a time," he offered lamely. "And don't look down."

Ryanne moved slowly, testing out each hand- and toehold and pausing frequently with her face pressed against the rock. About three quarters of the way up, she slipped. Josh slapped his hands over his eyes.

"Don't worry! We've got you," Phoenix called.

Josh watched through his fingers as they hauled her the rest of the way. She disappeared over the ledge.

"Are you all right?" he called up to her.

"That harness hurts like a son of a bitch!" she yelled back down. "You'll see!"

Once again the rope was lowered, and Josh followed Phoenix's instructions for tying the boy securely against his torso. He started up. There were plenty of little ledges to grip and he moved carefully from one hold to the next. Hauling Jack's extra sixty pounds had his arms trembling from fatigue by the time he was halfway up. His feet slipped a couple of times, but he managed to regain his hold.

After what felt like hours, hands grabbed his wrists. Josh was hauled over the lip of rock and onto solid ground. He lay there panting while Sumner and Phoenix undid the ropes and lifted Jack off him.

Ryanne knelt down beside him and gave him a watery smile. She was grimy with sweat and dirt, and she'd never looked so beautiful. She stroked the damp hair off his forehead. "Are we having fun yet?"

"Are you okay?" he whispered.

Her tears landed silently on his cheeks, a secret between them. "He didn't . . . Jack was just in time."

He pulled her in, tucking her face against his chest and stroking her tangled hair. His eyes burned with unshed tears.

"Come on, kids," Sumner said. "The girls are waiting for us. Let's haul ass."

She pulled away, wiping her eyes, and Sumner helped her and then Josh to their feet.

"We're parked over that way." He pointed into the trees, and they followed him. Twenty feet ahead, they could just make out Phoenix, who was carrying Jack over one shoulder.

"Do you think Jack's all right?" Sumner asked.

Ryanne shrugged. "He was drugged. I'm hoping once it wears off, he'll wake up. Is everybody okay on your end?"

"We're all in one piece. And man, do I have some stories for you!" Sumner said, slowing his pace to match Josh's and Ryanne's exhausted hobble. "But I'm betting your night has been just as hairy."

"You could say that. And we're not out of the woods yet," Josh warned, and Sumner laughed.

"Good one!" he said, although Josh hadn't meant it as a joke.

They reached the clearing where the Suburban was parked. Phoenix was standing with his back against the open passenger door, arguing with a newcomer in a white robe.

"Oh hell," Sumner said.

Josh could see Jack's feet sticking out the door, and Phoenix was standing protectively in front of them. It quickly became apparent the Priest didn't want Jack, however.

"You're not taking her," he said to Phoenix. "I forbid her to leave The Ranch."

"Father Narda said—"

"I don't care what Father Narda said. She's *my* daughter, and I want her here, where it's safe!"

"She wants to come with us." Ora poked her head out of the open car door.

"She's twelve years old. She doesn't get a say!"

"Shit," Sumner said, and moved toward them. "Father Gabriel, I promise we'll keep her safe. I've already promised Father Narda—"

The Priest turned to Sumner and the moonlight danced across his face. He was in his late fifties, with thinning gold and gray hair and a bushy beard. He was fairly tall, but slender and narrow through the shoulders.

"I said *no*, Sumner!" He turned back to the Suburban. "Ashlyn, you come out here right this instant!"

"No!" the girl in question yelled from inside the vehicle. Josh could just make out her outline in the shadowy depths as she moved away from the open door.

"I'm not kidding, young lady!" the Priest said sternly.

"This is ridiculous." Josh shook his head. The last thing he had expected to impede their progress was a custody battle over some preteen. He was so busy watching the argument unfold, he didn't notice what Ryanne was doing until it was too late.

"Gabriel," she hissed, aiming the gun at his head. He turned toward her and froze. Even from a distance, Josh could see the blood drain from his face.

"Rowan . . ." he choked out.

"Give me one good reason why I shouldn't blow your brains out right now, you bastard."

"No!" the girl yelled from inside the Suburban.

"Rowan . . ." he stuttered again, raising his hands in front of him.

"My name is *Ryanne*," she corrected, and her finger tightened on the trigger.

"No!" the girl screamed as she flew out of the Suburban. She tripped over Jack's legs and fell flat on her face in the dirt.

"Please don't hurt him!" she yelled, scrambling to her feet.

Ryanne's gaze fell on the girl, and time stopped.

Josh reeled in shock, and if it hadn't been for a handy tree, he would have fallen. She had red hair, pale skin, and a heart-shaped face. Josh would have bet she had green eyes, too.

Ryanne's hands were trembling, but to her credit she kept the gun trained on Father Gabriel's head.

"You've had her for eleven years, Gabriel. I'm taking my daughter back."

She lowered the gun, aimed, and fired.

CHAPTER SIXTY-SEVEN

It was a strange ride to Denver. Sumner found himself trying to cover up the awkward silence with jokes, which naturally fell on deaf ears.

Ora and Lexy were sitting as far from each other as they could manage while in the same vehicle. Neither had said a word since leaving The Ranch, and the hurt and tension between them were palpable.

The family reunion in the middle row of seats wasn't going well, either. Sumner guessed that trying to connect with a long-lost daughter after shooting the only parent the girl had ever known was going to be a challenge.

Of course, it was only a leg shot. Father Gabriel would likely recover. Sumner had pointed that out to Ashlyn, but she failed to see the logic.

She refused Ryanne's attempts at conversation with the rudeness only a twelve-year-old could manage, curled into a ball against the door, and fell asleep.

Everyone's nerves were shot. Well, except Jack's, since he was the only one lucky enough to be comatose. The rest were either jittering like junkies coming off a three-day binge, sleeping fitfully, or lost in their own dark thoughts.

"The Magical Mystery Tour takes Denver!" Sumner said as they passed a sign that said they were forty miles outside the city. No one replied, and he shrugged and refocused on the road. The traffic was light. The morning was frosty and full of big blue skies.

"Do you think she'll ever forgive me?" Ryanne asked Josh softly. Sumner watched them surreptitiously in the rearview mirror, straining to hear their conversation over the road noise and Ora's gentle snoring from the seat beside him.

Ryanne's eyes were red and puffy, and Sumner felt a stab of compassion for her.

"I'm sure she will, just give her time," Josh replied softly. The two were squished in next to each other, giving Ashlyn much-needed space on the far side. The girl was sleeping against the door with her mouth slightly open.

Lexy and Phoenix were sharing the third row, Jack stashed between them. Lexy was watching the world pass by outside her window, her brow furrowed in thought. Phoenix was sprawled with his bare feet on the armrest in front of him, snoring.

"I don't know." Ryanne shook her head sadly. "She must feel like I abandoned her. Like I didn't love her, or something."

"But that's not true," Josh said gently. In the mirror, Sumner saw him take her hand. "You didn't choose to leave her. It's not your fault."

"I let myself forget her," Ryanne said. "How could she ever forgive me for that? I can't forgive myself for that!"

The sight of her small hand tucked inside Josh's made Sumner's stomach clench, but he refused to acknowledge it. As usual, his mouth opened against his will. "She's lived the last twelve years on The Ranch. Give her some credit; she knows what goes on. If there's something she won't forgive you for, it's shooting her dad."

Josh and Ryanne both looked up at him.

"Thanks Sumner; you always know just what to say." But her lips curled up into a tremulous smile.

"Homeboy speaks the truth," he said, and went back to driving. A little while later, he asked, "Any idea where we should go?"

Josh had been looking over a map, and he nodded. "I think we should rent a cabin. There's an area called Idaho Springs in the mountains west of Denver. It's still off-season, so we should be able to find something. What do you think?" he asked Ryanne.

She nodded. "That would be good for Ashlyn. She's never been off The Ranch. Heading straight to a city would be overwhelming."

"All right," Sumner agreed. "Which way?"

***

By late morning, they had rented a furnished log home at the top of Soda Creek Road. Past the Indian Hot Springs Resort, the road angled up into the trees, winding past the occasional home as it moved into the mountains. The property Josh had rented was miles away from its nearest neighbor. It was set on at least an acre, accessed by a small bridge that crossed over Soda Creek and became a gravel track as it curved toward the house. The best part, as far as Sumner was concerned, was that it had its own mineral hot spring, located in a cave carved into the mountain on the edge of the property.

They made it to their new, temporary home just before lunchtime. As the others piled out, Phoenix carrying Jack, Josh offered to go back to the Safeway to pick up supplies. Ryanne volunteered to go with him. Sumner nodded, but didn't move from the driver's seat.

"What is it?" Ryanne asked. "Are you okay?"

Their rental was a large, two-story log home, half hidden in the shade of the pines dotting the property. It butted up against a rocky outcropping where Sumner guessed they would find the hot springs. Tucked behind the house he saw a storage shed and a separate two-car garage. A large pile of firewood was stacked neatly against the side of the garage.

"Would you consider this far enough away from the city?" Sumner asked.

"Far enough away for what?" Ora asked, yawning.

After a moment, he shook his head. "Never mind."

CHAPTER SIXTY-EIGHT

The next few days were quiet as we waited for Jack to awaken. They were a time of rest, a time of healing, and a time for forming and testing new relationships. It was a perfect pocket of time, one I would later look back on with both gratitude and regret.

They were the last days of *before*, and in my memory they became seared in golden light, the way all good days do once they are gone. It was a perfect moment of stillness, sandwiched between crisis and chaos, and all the more beautiful because of what followed.

We had time to prepare, buying generators, air purifiers, gas masks, and stores of supplies, just in case. We had time to seal the windows and doorframes. We had time to talk, to rehash our experiences and brainstorm about what disaster might be coming. But mainly, we waited. We waited for the boy with the answers to wake from his sleep.

I was grateful, most of all, for the time with my daughter. Over those few days, the ice within her began to thaw, and we started the process of learning about each other. I listened for hours as she told me about her life on The Ranch, and she was equally interested in my life on the Outside. We would never be able to make up for the years we had lost, but a bond was beginning to form nonetheless.

And so, at the end of the beginning, or the beginning of the end, I was given this gift. I was given this perfect bubble of time with the flesh of my flesh—a chance to see her perfect beauty and to touch her cinnamon hair, to tuck her between clean blankets and to kiss her sleeping cheek. My heart swelled with the joy of motherhood, even as I feared the coming of tomorrow.

Later, I would be haunted by what-ifs. What if Jack had awoken earlier? What if I had figured out my part in it before Jack had spelled it out for me? What if and what if and what if. What if there had been more time?

***

Josh found me in the side yard. Ashlyn had gone to Denver with Phoenix to see a movie and buy some clothes at the Walmart. It was her first time going to a movie theater and she was obviously thrilled, not to mention she was going with Phoenix. She would have happily gone dump picking with Phoenix.

I was on the swing bench, rocking gently and watching the clouds roll across the late-fall sky. I was trying not to worry about Ashlyn's safety, or about the obvious adoration she had for someone who was, well, a *grown* man.

Above the burbling of Soda Creek, I heard the crunch of leaves under his shoes, and turned to watch him approach. We hadn't had a moment alone since our trip to Safeway. The house was always full, and there was always something to do.

"Come sit," I invited, patting the cushion next to me.

He sat and we started to swing.

"How are things inside?"

He shrugged. "Sumner is making sloppy joes and singing Springsteen songs at the top of his lungs. He really can't carry a tune." I laughed and he continued. "Ora finally convinced Lexy to talk to her, so I thought I'd better give them some privacy."

"Good. That's good."

"How are you doing, Ryanne?"

I shrugged. "Surprisingly well, under the circumstances. Ashlyn is . . ."

"She's a very smart and lovely girl," Josh said.

"She is, isn't she?" I agreed, my heart swelling with a mixture of joy and grief. "It's strange to go so long not even remembering I have a daughter, and then boom! There she is. And she's a real person, with her own opinions and desires . . . and everything." I shook my head. It seemed I was always on the verge of tears.

Josh took my hand, and we spent several minutes swinging in contented silence.

"Is it wrong to feel this . . . peaceful?" he asked. "We have a boy inside the house who is wasting away, a day at a time. I can't reach his dad. We know something bad is coming down the pike and we're helpless to stop it unless Jack wakes up."

"Maybe it's that whole 'ignorance is bliss' thing. Since we don't know what's coming, it's easy to forget that it's real."

"Maybe."

"Did you get ahold of Sheriff Lagrudo?"

"Yesterday. I convinced him to bring my mom here. They should arrive sometime tomorrow."

"That's great, Josh."

"Yeah." He was watching the sky intently, but I noticed his cheeks were rosy. "But that means I have something I need to take care of. If I don't want another lecture from her, that is."

"What is it?"

"And if something happens, well, more than anything I would regret not having this conversation with you."

"Okay . . ."

"I loved your mom, Ryanne. Not in a romantic way, but I really loved her. She had the ability to eclipse a person. She was somehow larger than life. She was wild and vulnerable. Reckless. But there was something about her that made you want to take care of her, something damaged and . . . weak. Broken."

He looked at me, his eyes compassionate and sad. "When I first met you, all I could see was Sherry, every time I looked at you. You look so much like her, and your voice is the same, and you have some of her mannerisms, too. Like the way you push your hair back from your forehead. Or that crooked smile when you're teasing me. Her eyes were brown instead of green, and you're smaller than she was, but still.

"I promised her I would never stop looking for you. I would keep the investigation alive until I could bring home her baby, one way or another. When she died I vowed that, if I found you, I would take care of you the way she no longer could. But in my mind, you never grew up. I mean, I knew the years had passed. I knew that, if you were alive, you were no longer a child. But I guess I couldn't picture it. Not until I found you.

"And then, there you were. So similar to her and yet so different. You don't need anyone to take care of you; you can take care of yourself just fine. You're strong and smart and funny. You prefer to eat chemicals instead of real food, and you're totally addicted to caffeine, and you're stubborn and you don't listen if you think you know better, and you're completely frustrating and beautiful and brave. And you've eclipsed me."

"You think . . . I'm beautiful?"

He laughed. "Is that all you're getting from this?" He turned to me and hesitantly touched my cheek. His fingers were cold but his eyes were warm. "Ryanne, I don't think I have the words—"

"Hey! There you guys are!" Sumner shouted from the porch. He was waving excitedly, a dish towel tucked into the waistband of his jeans.

"Sumner, can we have a minute?" Josh asked, the frustration evident in his voice. I don't think Sumner noticed.

"He's awake! Jack's awake! And he wants to talk to you, Ryanne!"

"Oh!" I jumped off the swing, making Josh sway alarmingly. "Are you serious?"

"Come on!" Sumner was vigorously waving me forward.

I turned to Josh, who was still sitting on the swing. His expression was unreadable.

"Go on, I'm right behind you."

"Are you sure? What about—"

"It can wait," he said, although I suspect we both knew it was a lie.

CHAPTER SIXTY-NINE

Jack was sitting up in bed, his face pale and thin. Ora was trying to interest him in some soup while Lexy stood in the corner nervously wringing her hands. Both women had been crying; they were sporting equally red, puffy eyes.

Jack's brown eyes fixed on me as soon as I entered the room. His pale hair was stringy and limp, hanging across his forehead in greasy strands.

"They found you."

"They did," I said, pulling up a seat beside the bed. "How do you feel?"

He smiled ruefully, exposing crooked teeth and a gap near the back where a baby tooth had recently come out. "I feel like someone hit me over the head with a shovel."

"Do you have a headache? Would you like an aspirin?" Ora jumped in.

He shook his head. "It's just a joke." He turned back to me. "I don't know your name."

"I'm Ryanne. And that's Ora and Lexy. And this is Sumner, and Agent Metcalf. He's the FBI agent who was looking for you after you . . . disappeared."

"Josh," he said gruffly from behind me.

"And there's also Phoenix, and my daughter Ashlyn, but they've gone to see a movie, so they'll be back later." I was starting to sound like a rambling idiot, but I couldn't help myself. I was eager to delay hearing the bad news.

Jack seemed uninterested in the others. His focus was on me.

"Do you know what the White is, Ryanne?"

"You mean the color?"

He shook his head. "That's okay. It knows you. What day is it?"

"November first," Josh answered promptly, for which I was grateful. I'd lost track of the days.

"Oh." The boy's response was so faint I almost missed it.

"Is that bad?" I asked.

"Well, it's definitely not good. I don't know . . ." His gaze had turned inward, and we all watched him silently. "I guess we have to try. Right?"

"Absolutely," Sumner agreed. "Try what?"

"I don't really know. It's not something they teach in school, you know? That's why I need you," he said to me.

"I'm here. I'm listening, Jack. Tell me what you know."

"They think humans are like cockroaches. Using up resources and killing the earth. Do you think that's true?"

"I guess there's some truth to that," I admitted.

"Right, I guess. But they also think psychics are a sub . . . I forget the word."

"Subspecies," Ora said quietly.

"That's right," Jack agreed. "They think that they . . . that *we*, are a new or better species. That we've evolved from humans . . ."

"It's called eugenics," I told him quietly.

"What's that?" Jack asked.

"It's why the Nazis exterminated six million Jews," Josh said darkly.

"It's a bit more complicated than that," I said to Josh. "It's a concept that was developed by Francis Galton, who was Darwin's cousin, by the way, in the late 1800s. Governments around the world practiced some form of eugenics. A lot of people were killed, or sterilized. There were forced pregnancies, and, well, you name it. But it was a recognized field of study at universities, *and* a widely accepted practice. It was the atrocities of Nazi Germany that caused a worldwide movement against eugenics."

"That's *terrible*," Jack said.

"Sure is," Josh agreed. "So this is what this cult . . . what *I Fidele* believes? That they need to practice eugenics on some kind of a global scale?"

"That's exactly what they believe," Sumner said grimly. "And they are so much bigger than any cult ever dreamed itself to be."

"I guess you're right. To have infiltrated high levels within the FBI—"

"All levels of government," Sumner interjected. "And that's just in this country."

"What?" Josh asked.

Ora answered, "*I Fidele* is a worldwide organization, Josh. We're . . . *they're* all over Europe, Asia, Africa. Everywhere."

"It was founded in Rome in 1958. You met one of the Founding Fathers in the Underground," Lexy added, and I noticed she avoided saying his name.

Josh leaned back against the doorframe, clearly stunned.

After a pause, I turned back to the boy on the bed. "Jack, do you know what they have planned?"

"Does it have to do with The Command?" Sumner jumped in.

Jack nodded. "The Telekinetics. Yes."

"Do you know where they are?" Sumner asked.

Jack motioned to the bookcase in the corner of the room. "Pass me that globe," he said, and Lexy pulled it off the top shelf, dusted it off, and brought it to him. He spun it slowly, and I watched the blues and greens and browns blur together. Finally, he slapped a hand down, stopping its motion.

"Right there," he pointed. We all moved closer.

"Victoria Island?" Sumner asked. Jack had placed his finger over a large island in the Canadian Arctic. It sat perched above the Northwest Territories and Nunavut. "You can't be serious."

Jack nodded. "See right here?" He ran his finger along the northwest coast of the island.

"That's Fort Collinson. It's an abandoned trading post that was used by the Hudson's Bay Company. That's where they are. They fly them in from Yellowknife. They fly in and they never leave," he said with certainty.

"Well, shit," Sumner said. "I guess I always pictured it in Arkansas or Nevada or something."

"What are they doing there, Jack?" Josh asked.

Jack looked at me, and my breath caught in my throat. Was that pity I saw in his eyes?

"They're doing what telekinetics do best. They're moving things. *Big things.*"

"What do you mean?" I could barely find my voice.

"What is the greatest danger to life on Earth?" he asked me, his voice barely more than a hoarse whisper. "What can bring about fires and floods, tsunamis and firestorms? What can kill all plant life and block out the sun's rays long enough to throw the planet into another ice age?"

"No . . ." I shook my head. But the edges of my vision were growing dark.

"Are you talking about a meteorite?" Sumner asked. "Like the one that killed the dinosaurs?"

"That's not possible," I argued. "We've been cataloging Near Earth Objects of that size for years now; we know most of them. We watch their trajectories for a long time. We would have a lot of warning if a meteorite of that size was coming in."

"You said 'most' of them," Sumner pointed out.

"We know of about ninety percent of NEOs bigger than a kilometer in diameter. And that's the size you're talking about for a global disaster."

"And the other ten percent?" Ora asked.

"No." I was still shaking my head. "No."

"What about the meteorite that hit Russia? No one saw that coming," Sumner said.

"That was less than twenty meters in diameter, too small to have a global impact. And it exploded above the earth's surface."

"What would happen if a smaller one *did* impact the earth?" Jack asked.

They were all watching me.

"It would be like dropping an atomic bomb. There would be a lot of local damage. If it hit in a populated area, like a city, you'd be looking at a death toll in the thousands or maybe millions. It would cause firestorms that would spew ash and smoke into the upper troposphere, or even into the stratosphere. That would temporarily block the sun, leading to local climate changes. But it would be too small to have much of an impact worldwide."

"And these smaller—what did you call them—NEOs? How many do you guys know about?" Sumner asked.

I opened my mouth, but no words came out.

"How many, Ryanne?" Sumner persisted.

"Not many," I admitted. "Our focus has been on NEOs large enough to be a global danger."

Jack sat up and reached for me. His hands were icy, and trembling almost as much as mine. "Ryanne. What if a *whole bunch* of these smaller ones, these atomic-bomb-sized meteorites, hit different parts of the earth . . . all within hours or days of each other? What would happen then?"

"That's not possible," I said. "Statistically—"

"What would happen?"

"I . . . don't know."

"Firestorms?" he asked.

"Yes."

"Tsunamis?"

"If any impacted in an ocean."

"Massive loss of human life?"

"That's possible," I said weakly.

"Changes to the atmosphere? *Global* changes?"

"Yes," I admitted. "If there were enough of them, it could have the same effect as one big one. It could cause an 'impact winter.' Another ice age."

"Oh my God," Josh said.

"That's what they've been up to at The Command." Jack leaned back on the pillow, closing his eyes. "All of the Telekinetics. For decades. They've been busy, busy bees. Such busy little bees."

"And no one noticed all of these meteorites just cruising on in?" Sumner asked.

Jack opened his eyes. He looked straight at me.

"What?" I asked. "Do you think I saw them?"

"Ryanne." He shook his head sadly. "You didn't just see them. *You hid them.*"

CHAPTER SEVENTY

"No, it's just not possible," Ryanne said again. Her voice was faint, though. Josh could see her working over the implications.

"I just *couldn't* have done something like that."

"I didn't know I was the head of a kidnapping ring, either," Sumner said.

"But this . . . I mean, hiding a global catastrophe . . ." She shook her head. Her skin had a gray sheen to it and she looked like she might topple off her chair at any moment. Josh wanted to go to her, but he couldn't seem to find his legs.

"Is it possible, though?" Ora asked. "I'm not asking *if* you hid that information, but *could* you have?"

There was a long silence. They waited her out. Jack had leaned back against the pillow with his eyes closed. As far as Josh could tell, the boy had gone to sleep.

Finally, she sighed and nodded. "I guess it's possible. I'm the first in line to see the information the telescopes gather. Those are our telescopes," she added. "Then I pass it along to the Minor Planet Center. It would be fairly simple not to report it. But . . ."

"But what?" Josh asked.

"LINEAR isn't the only company working for Spaceguard. There's NEAT and LONEOS and other smaller companies as well, and they all report their findings to the MPC just like we do."

"So maybe each of those places has someone working for them that's just like you?" Ora suggested.

"Maybe." Ryanne grimaced. "Or maybe, if these NEOs are small, they never noticed them."

"Ryanne." Josh had to clear his throat. "Do you think it's possible these meteorites are coming in?"

"I don't know. Spaceguard's focus has been on cataloging NEOs of global danger, which means larger than a kilometer. So there's a good chance we wouldn't know about a smaller one in advance. But that's just *one*." She yanked at her hair, tugging it back from her face.

"To have a whole bunch of them come down all at once—we've just never explored that scenario. I mean, it's just not possible . . . under normal circumstances."

"Apparently no one could predict hundreds of telekinetics bent on mass destruction," Sumner said, then turned to Ora with a frantically determined look.

"I know what you're thinking, Sumner," Ora said with a shake of her head. "But you're right. It took hundreds of telekinetics to do this, and it probably took them years, too. There's no way Ashlyn and I are strong enough to reverse it."

"Ryanne." Lexy had been leaning against the far wall, listening silently. "Can you find these meteorites? Can they be stopped?"

Ryanne swallowed hard, and then turned to Josh. "I need to go back to New Mexico."

"Yes," Josh said. "I'll go with you."

"What about the rest of us?" Sumner asked.

"I think everyone else should stay here. And prepare," Ryanne said.

"Ryanne. If they're real, can they be stopped?" Lexy asked again.

"First we need to find them." But Josh noticed Ryanne wouldn't meet Lexy's eyes.

***

By the time Phoenix and Ashlyn returned, Josh and Ryanne were ready to go. Josh watched as mother and daughter argued.

"I don't understand. Why do you have to go?" Ashlyn asked again.

"Sweetheart, I have to go back to where I work." This conversation had been going in circles for fifteen minutes, and Josh could see the strain it was putting on Ryanne.

"But why?"

"I . . ." Ryanne shook her head. "I promise I'll come back for you. Ashlyn, I *promise*."

"Why can't I go with you?"

"It's safer here. Please, honey. Stay with Phoenix, and Sumner, and the rest. They'll take care of you until I come back."

"I want to go with you!"

"It's not safe."

"Then why are *you* going? What if something happens to you?"

"Ashlyn, I'll protect your mom. I promise I'll bring her back to you." Josh touched the girl's arm gently.

"Then why can't you protect me, too? I want to come!"

Phoenix jumped in. "Ashlyn, stay here with me. It won't be for long."

"I promise I'll be back," Ryanne repeated.

"When?" Ashlyn asked.

"A few days."

"I don't like this." Her mouth was set in a stubborn line Josh found all too familiar, and her eyes were damp.

"You have to trust me. I will come back, but I need to make sure you're safe."

Finally the girl's shoulders slumped in defeat. "Fine." She looked up at Ryanne, tears streaming down her cheeks. "But if you don't come back, I'll never forgive you!" And with that she stomped out of the room. They heard the door to her bedroom slam, and then the sound of her quiet sobbing.

"Damn." Ryanne wiped angrily at her eyes.

"We'll take care of her. Don't worry," Sumner said.

"Do you want us to tell her what's going on?" Ora asked.

Ryanne shrugged. "I don't know. The broad strokes, I guess."

"I assume someone's going to tell *me* what's going on?" Phoenix asked.

"I'll let Ora and Lexy have the pleasure," Sumner said, and then turned to Josh. "I'll drive you to Denver."

Josh nodded. They had decided to rent a car, leaving the Suburban behind in case the rest needed to evacuate.

"Remember, my mom and Sheriff Lagrudo should arrive sometime tomorrow."

"Ducking out just in time, huh?" Sumner cracked, and Josh managed a smile.

They said a solemn good-bye to the rest of them, and then followed Sumner outside. Josh climbed into the passenger seat and Ryanne curled up in a sniffling ball in the back row. She pulled the hood of her sweatshirt over her eyes and ignored Sumner and Josh's stilted conversation.

"They're satellite phones," Josh explained to him quietly. "They'll work even if cell towers and landlines get knocked out. I've programmed my number into yours, so we can stay in contact." He handed one of the two satellite phones to Sumner. "The other number is for Jack's father, Keaton Barbetti. Please keep trying it."

"Okay. Will they still work if a bunch of smoke gets into the atmosphere?" Sumner asked.

Josh shrugged. "I don't know. I guess if things get bad enough, they might stop working, but it's better than nothing."

"Right. You promise you'll keep in touch? Let us know what's happening?"

"Of course," Josh said.

"Do you think we're safe where we are?"

"Father Narda told you to stay in the middle of the country, and you're not that far away from The Ranch. I'm guessing you guys are as safe as possible."

"Yeah. I guess," Sumner agreed.

They rode in silence for several miles.

"Josh?" Sumner asked quietly. "If Ryanne can find these meteorites and notify the right people . . . do you think they'll be able to stop them?"

Josh debated lying, but he didn't have the energy for it. "No," he admitted.

"Yeah. Me neither." They didn't speak again for the rest of the trip to Denver.

CHAPTER SEVENTY-ONE

"I've been dreaming about this for years," I finally acknowledged outside Santa Fe.

"You've been dreaming about what?" Josh asked. He switched into the fast lane to move around a long-haul truck.

"Well, not about the Telekinetics or The Command. But about a meteorite crashing into Earth. It's been a recurring dream for so long I stopped paying attention to it. I figured it was an occupational hazard, you know? Spend your life looking for asteroids and you're bound to have nightmares about missing one."

"Sure," he agreed. "I have dreams about freezing up in a shoot-out and watching my fellow agents get killed."

"I feel like I should have known."

"How could you have put it all together?"

"I don't know," I said slowly, struggling to find the words. "I guess because I'm psychic."

"But being psychic doesn't mean you're all-knowing, right?"

"Far from it. It's more like you randomly get extra bits of information."

"So, there you go." He shrugged. "I don't think you should feel responsible for not realizing the importance of those dreams."

"But what if I hid information about those meteorites? What if I could have stopped *millions* of people from dying?"

"There's still time," Josh said. "Right?"

I glanced sideways at him. His jaw was tight, his eyes pinched. "Sure."

Our uneasy silence lasted through Albuquerque, where we stopped to fill up with gas and get giant takeout cups of coffee. Once we were back on the road, Josh spoke.

"We've got another four or five hours to Las Cruces, and then however long to White Sands. It looks like we won't be there before daylight. Is that going to slow you down?"

"No. I don't need the telescopes. I need the data stored on our computers. I think I'll ask Dan to help out; it'll go twice as fast."

"That will mean explaining the situation to him. Do you think that's a good idea?"

I shrugged. "I don't like it. But two heads are better than one."

"Can you trust him?"

That stopped me. I hadn't seen Dan since he sat on my couch drinking beer and trying to help me sort out my crumbling memories. That felt like a lifetime ago. He'd volunteered to pick me up from the hospital, but I had called to let him know Josh would take me, and that I would be taking a medical absence due to my concussion. "I always have."

"Do you think he's a part of *I Fidele*?"

I shook my head. "No, I don't think so."

"But you never know."

"I guess you never know."

"Ryanne, get some rest. You need to be clearheaded when we get there."

***

Fifteen minutes before the end of his shift, I called Dan from the sat phone and asked him to wait for us. He agreed under the condition we bring him a massive cup of coffee and a box of doughnuts, so we stopped briefly in Las Cruces before heading directly into the rising sun.

I signed Josh in at the WSMR gate, where they examined his credentials and gave him a visitor's pass that would allow him to come and go as needed.

Dan was sitting on the front stairs of the trailer when we arrived. As we came to a stop he stood up and waved, a giant grin on his face.

"Be careful," Josh warned as I opened the door and climbed out.

"Red!" Dan boomed, rushing forward to lift me in a bear hug. "How the hell are you? Are you feeling any better?" He then seemed to remember I was injured, and gently placed me back on the ground. "Oops, sorry. Damn, girl, you look like you could use a month of rest. I guess I shouldn't ask when you're coming back to work? It's been pretty lonely out here without you."

Josh came up behind me and Dan's smile faded. I realized he was looking at the double guns Josh had strapped to his waist. "What's going on, Red?"

"Dan, this is Josh Metcalf. He's with the FBI."

"Is this the guy who drove you home from the hospital?" He held out a hand. "Dan Parks, I think we spoke on the phone."

"That's right. Nice to meet you." Josh shook Dan's hand.

"I thought FBI agents wore suits, and, you know . . . shaved."

Josh smiled tightly. "It's been a rough week."

"I can see that," Dan said, nonplussed by Josh's cool demeanor. "So, why did you need me to stay? Not to be rude, but I have a hot date with my pillow."

"Let's go inside." They followed me up the steps and into the trailer. I kicked aside Dan's bag with a twinge of nostalgia, and dumped my purse in its usual spot on the desk. Josh set down the box of doughnuts and handed out the coffee.

"I need your help," I told Dan.

"What else is new?" he joked, but when I didn't smile he grew serious. "What's up, Red?"

"I need to search through the sky coverage plots from the last three years."

"Since you started here, you mean? What are the search parameters?"

"I want to compare each night's findings against the MPC catalogs to see if there are any discrepancies."

He blinked at me. "That's a huge search. What are you looking for?"

"I think . . . I may have missed something. Will you help?"

"Are you saying what I think you're saying? That there's an NEO that didn't get sent to MPC for categorization?"

"Maybe more than one," I admitted. My cheeks were burning.

"Holy hell, Red!" Dan was pale beneath his bushy beard. "Talk about a CLM!"

"What's that?" Josh asked.

"Career-limiting move," Dan replied.

"Will you help?" I asked again.

He turned to his monitor. "Fast, medium, or slow movers? Can we narrow down the search more?"

"I think we better look at all velocities."

"Jesus Christ," he muttered, and started clicking away. "I'll start from last week and move backward. You start from your first day on site and move forward. Eventually we'll meet in the middle."

"Okay," I said, flicking on my computer.

"What can I do?" Josh asked.

"You can keep us supplied with coffee and sugar. We're going to be here a while," Dan said.

***

Around noon, Dan groaned and moved away from his monitor, rubbing his neck. "I need a break. And I'm starving."

"Josh should be back soon," I said distractedly.

"Have you found anything yet?"

"Not a thing. How about you?"

"Nada. I'm almost convinced you came up with this idea as a form of torture, but I don't know what I did to deserve it."

"I wish." I was only half listening as I scrolled through data, comparing the MPC records to our original findings. My eyes were burning and my back was aching.

"Rowan, are you ever going to explain what the hell is going on?"

I swiveled in my chair. His eyes were as red as mine felt, and his brow was creased with strain. "If there's time."

"What do you mean, *if there's time*?" he asked, and when I didn't answer, his eyes widened. "You think we're looking for an impactor? Holy *shit*, Red." He turned back to his computer and I did the same.

***

"Ryanne, you need to eat," Josh said quietly. His hand on my shoulder was warm and soothing.

"I will. Soon."

"You haven't eaten in seven hours. *Eat.*"

He stood above me, unrelenting, until I gave in and opened the box. It was an enchilada with a side of steamed vegetables. I worked my way through it as quickly as I could, hoping it would stay down. My stomach was sour and churning with anxiety.

Satisfied, Josh handed me a bottle of water and moved back to his station on the couch, where he'd spent the better part of the last ten hours reading through newspapers or dozing fitfully. The anxiety was coming off him in waves, and I understood it. He was a man of action, and the only thing he could do was wait.

I turned back to the monitor and lost myself in sky plots.

***

It grew dark, and the telescopes started their nightly work. I barely noticed. I ate a hamburger and washed it down with a gallon of coffee.

Dan was asleep, face cushioned on his arm as he snored into his keyboard. Josh was on the couch, a newspaper tented over his face and his feet propped on a cushion.

I made another trip to the bathroom and stretched out the kinks in my back before sitting down in front of the monitor. My eyes were gritty, and the information on the screen was blurred. I pressed my palms to my eyes and then blinked several times. Finally, the screen swam back into focus, and I got back to work. I was ten months into the data without seeing a single discrepancy.

***

"I think I found one. Red! Check this out."

I swam out of the blackness. My heart was pumping with anxiety long before my foggy brain could catch up. Dim light was streaming through the blinds; dawn had arrived. Josh was climbing groggily off the couch.

Lifting my head off the desk made me groan. Apparently, someone had replaced my skull with a vise while I was sleeping, and it was squeezing viciously against my brain. I pushed my hands into my temples in an effort to keep my head from splitting open, and staggered toward Dan.

"I'm not sure," he was mumbling. "I can't find this one in the MPC catalog, but maybe I missed it?"

"Let me see," I said hoarsely, and fell into the rickety chair beside him. A few minutes later, I leaned back. "Shit."

Only then could I admit to myself that with each hour that had passed with no results, hope had bloomed within me just a little bit more. But there it was: a slow mover that didn't show up anywhere in the MPC data.

"Okay." I scrubbed a hand across my face. "Make note of it and let's get back to the search."

"You've got it," Dan replied.

"I'll go get breakfast," Josh volunteered.

***

Twelve hours later, we had found fifteen NEOs that hadn't been sent over to the Minor Planet Center for categorization.

"I bet there are more the telescopes didn't see, too. I mean, statistically we have to factor that in, right?" I was chewing nervously on a piece of licorice. "All of these are small enough to be easily missed, so it seems likely there are others we *have* missed."

Dan looked confused. "There are thousands of small ones the scopes miss, Red. The good news is none of these are cause for global alarm. I mean, each of them could do some serious local damage . . ."

"Can you tell if any of them are going to impact Earth?" Josh asked.

"We're not there yet," Dan explained with a shake of his head. "We have to track them now. But I'm not worried; the chances of any of them being on a collision course are highly unlikely. I'm just relieved we didn't find any biggies." He turned back to his computer, so he missed the look that passed between Josh and me.

If Jack was right about what they were doing at The Command, there was a good chance *all* of them were on a collision course. Statistics no longer mattered.

CHAPTER SEVENTY-TWO

"Your mom and the sheriff made it safe and sound, not to worry," Sumner said.

Josh was standing outside the trailer where Ryanne and Dan were frantically tracking asteroids, watching the sun setting in vibrant pinks and oranges. Soon the stars would be out, and Josh would watch them with a nervousness he had never felt before.

"How are things going in New Mexico? Is it time to duck yet?" Sumner's attempted joke fell flat.

"They've found a bunch of NEOs that were never sent to the Minor Planet Center, and Ryanne says there are probably more the telescopes never picked up. They're working on figuring out the trajectory. I don't know how long it will be before we know if any of them are going to hit Earth . . . or where they'll hit."

There was a moment of silence as Sumner processed the information. "That's not good."

"No. Any luck with Keaton Barbetti?"

"I've left him several messages, but he's not returning my calls. I even left a message with our address. I hope that's okay."

"Yeah, what the hell." The risk of someone from *I Fidele* showing up on their doorstep seemed like a minor threat in comparison to fifteen or more asteroids crashing to Earth.

"Jack's been asking about him a lot."

"How's he doing?"

"Better. He's eating and getting some strength back. But he really needs his dad, and I don't know what else to do."

"Keep trying, I guess," Josh said. "How's Ashlyn?"

"She took the news pretty hard, but she's holding it together. Your mom is treating her like the granddaughter she never had. They're bunking together and everything."

"Really?" Josh's chest tightened with longing, but he quickly stifled it. He couldn't afford to imagine the four of them as a happy family. Those were dreams the new reality of meteorites and ice ages was bound to squash, and he didn't need the extra heartache when it did.

"The sheriff called his kids, too. He was careful not to say too much, but he did tell them to gather supplies and head for a cabin he owns—"

"Near Bone Creek. Yeah, okay, that's good. What about supplies?"

"I think we've got enough. I've made five more trips to Denver since you left. We've got water and canned food to last at least eighteen months. I bought a stove and propane tanks. Rifles and enough ammunition to last through the next century, blankets and clothing, and enough wood and matches to set all of Colorado on fire. We rented a backhoe to dig some outhouse pits, just in case we lose sewer service.

"Also, we've bought out Denver's entire supply of thermal clothing and snow gear, including four brand-new, top-of-the-line Ski-Doos, a towing trailer, and enough cans of gasoline to keep it all running for a long time. We are single-handedly fueling Denver's economy, and this place is a survivalist's wet dream. Let's just hope we don't have to evacuate. That would suck."

"Keep enough gas masks and a supply of food and water in the Suburban just in case."

"Yeah, good thought. What about you guys? You buying up supplies?"

"I've got the car stocked with enough to get us through a few weeks on the road, if needed," Josh said. "And extra gas cans, too."

"That's good," Sumner said.

"All right. You know where to reach me. I'll call again when I have more news."

"Take care of homegirl."

"Will do."

Josh hung up and watched the last colors bleed out of the sky. He stood there until the first stars appeared, and then he climbed the stairs and opened the door to the trailer.

***

"What the hell, what the hell, *what the hell* . . ." Dan was mumbling over and over. Ryanne shot Josh a look that spoke volumes. The news wasn't good.

"There's got to be something wrong with my math," Dan said. "I'm going to start again."

"There's nothing wrong with your math, Dan," Ryanne said quietly.

"There's got to be. This is just not possible."

"Dan—"

"No! It's not *possible*. I have the first three all on a trajectory that would have them impacting Earth within the week. That's not *possible*, Red. Let me work the numbers again."

Ryanne shook her head mutely and turned back to her computer. A few minutes later, Dan pushed back and punched the side of his desk.

"What is it?" Ryanne asked.

"My math on the first one checks out. Come see." Ryanne and Josh both moved toward him. "Look at this! This one is set to strike off the coast of Japan in forty-three hours, give or take."

"The two I've calculated so far are going to impact as well," Ryanne said quietly. She moved back to her computer and they followed. "See? This one is going to hit Al Qababt, Egypt, in about three days' time. That's close to Cairo. This one is heading for Saint Petersburg, Russia. It's going to impact in four days' time."

Dan was shaking his head. "This isn't possible." His voice was faint, wobbly.

"Dan." Ryanne grabbed his arm as if to steady him. "Let's do the rest. Okay?"

"Yeah. *Shit* . . . Yeah, okay." There was a gaping silence as they went back to work.

"Thirty-nine hours. Sao Paulo, Brazil," Ryanne called out.

A few minutes later Dan sighed. "Atlantic Ocean, about a hundred miles off Portugal. Fifty-six hours."

"Berlin. Thirty-nine hours."

"Toronto, Canada. Sixty-one hours."

"South Pacific, off the coast of New Zealand. Twenty-eight hours."

"Damn it! *New York*. Thirty-two hours."

"Mexico City. Forty-nine hours."

"Botswana. Seventy hours."

"Holy hell. Fifty-one hours. *Pacific Ocean*, five hundred miles off our coast."

"Hong Kong. Thirty hours."

"Fifty-eight hours. Stockholm, Sweden."

"Dear God. Thirty-six hours. *Atlantic Ocean*, a hundred and fifty miles off our coast. That will put our entire Eastern Seaboard from Nova Scotia to Florida under water."

"So . . . in the next *three days*, both of our coasts are going to be gone?" Josh couldn't process the information.

"Along with a lot of other areas around the world," Dan confirmed.

"And that's just the meteorites we know about. I'm betting there are more," Ryanne added.

"Can we . . ." Josh shook his head. "I mean, can NASA, or the Air Force, or *somebody* . . . can they be stopped?"

They both looked at him, their eyes wide. Finally Ryanne shook her head.

"Not anymore. I think the best we can do is notify people. Start evacuations, allow people to prepare," she said.

"I'll call the MPC," Dan said, and picked up the phone.

CHAPTER SEVENTY-THREE

"You might . . . turn . . . news." Josh's voice broke through the static.

"What?" Sumner sat up and flicked on the bedside lamp. It was just past six in the morning, and the world outside his window was still dark.

"Bad news?" he asked.

"You could . . . that." Josh's voice was cutting in and out. ". . . fifteen . . . impact . . . over . . . days."

"Jesus. What!"

"Ryanne . . . no . . . stopping . . . they . . ."

"What? Josh, are you there?"

"Evacuation . . . target areas."

"Where?" There was a large burst of static and for a moment Sumner thought they'd lost the connection, and then Josh's voice came through again.

"The . . . coasts . . . new . . . so . . . president . . . inland . . . declared . . . of emerg—"

"Dear God!" Sumner was biting his fist. "What should I do?"

". . . put! . . . house . . . okay? . . . No . . . Denver . . . it . . . dangerous . . . indoors—"

"Stay here? Is that what you're saying? How much time do we have left?"

"Yes! . . . stay . . . two . . . Pacific . . . York . . . Ryanne . . . more . . . coming . . . don't . . ." The static exploded.

"Josh? Josh!" Sumner screamed, panicked. "You're cutting out!"

". . . here!"

"Are you coming back?"

Static.

"Get your ass back here!" Sumner shouted.

There was a high-pitched electronic whine, and then silence.

***

"The foundations of our government will remain strong during this evacuation. Our first priority is to move our citizens out of . . ."

Click.

"The President addressed the nation, calling for calm in the face of . . ."

Click.

"Around the world, governments declared a state of emergency. This is the scene outside the Vatican this evening as . . ."

Click.

"Looting is rampant and officials are asking the public to remain indoors . . ."

Click.

"NASA spokesperson Michael D. Kozlowski confirmed this morning there are fifteen asteroids on a collision course with Earth. He stressed that all of these asteroids are between twenty and sixty meters in diameter . . ."

Click.

"Well, Mary. We're looking at a global catastrophe, and many people are wondering why we didn't have more warning. I spoke to . . ."

Click.

"So let's recap, for those of you who are just joining us. At six o'clock this morning, eastern time, the President called an emergency press conference . . ."

Click.

"Brazil; Hong Kong; Toronto; Saint Petersburg, Russia; and New York City. But the worst of the damage may come from the ocean impacts, experts are saying. Tsunami warnings are being issued for both the West Coast and the Eastern Seaboard, and evacuations of coastal towns are already under way . . ."

Click.

"Predictions are coming in from around the globe, and they are dire. As one NASA employee put it, 'The age of science is over, and now we must fall back on our faith. Our faith in God, and our faith in mankind's ability to rise again from the ashes.' Back to you, Janice . . ."

Sumner pressed the power button on the remote and the screen went blessedly dark. They sat in stunned silence. He could hear the ticking of the refrigerator in the kitchen.

It was Ashlyn who spoke first. "Did my dad do this?"

"Oh, honey . . ." Lexy said. Mrs. Metcalf wrapped an arm around the girl.

"What do we do now?" Ora asked.

Sumner shrugged. "Wait."

"And Josh thinks we'll be safe here?" Phoenix asked.

"Everyone is moving inland."

"What about Josh and Ryanne? Are they coming back?" Ora asked.

Sumner glanced at Ashlyn. "I hope so."

"They're going to have a hell of a time of it," Lexy said, and then bit her lip when Ashlyn gave her a fierce glare.

"Jack! Where are you going?" Sumner asked. The boy was moving toward the door.

"I'm going to get my dad."

"No!" Sumner jumped to his feet and the rest of them followed.

"You can't do that, honey; it's not safe," Lexy said.

"Jack, you need to stay here," Sumner added.

The boy spun on his heels. "Didn't you hear what they were saying? The West Coast . . . Seaside! My *dad* is in *Seaside*! Don't you get it?"

Ora fell to her knees in front of him. "I get it. But Jack . . . it's *too late*."

"The West Coast is going to be underwater in two days," Phoenix added. "There's no way you could get there, find your dad, and get out in time. You'd drown with the rest of them."

Ora gave Phoenix a hard look and then turned back to Jack. "I'm sure he's evacuating, honey. He'll be okay."

"No!" Jack screamed. *"No!"*

Ora tried to wrap her arms around him, but he wasn't having it.

"I want my dad!" he pummeled her with his fists. *"I want my dad!"*

"Son," Sheriff Lagrudo said quietly. He hadn't spoken in hours, since the first newscasts started coming in. "I have family I'm scared for, too. I have three sons back in Nebraska, and they all have wives and kids. I have six grandkids, all told. The youngest isn't even a year old yet. I wish they were here, so I could protect them. But there's not much I can do except pray for their safety."

"Don't tell me to *pray*!" Jack wailed. "My dad is all I have left, and I *need him*!"

The sheriff blinked at him, and then slowly nodded. "Then I'll go get him for you."

"What?" Ora asked.

"You can't do that!" Sumner sputtered.

Phoenix shook his head. "That's a suicide mission."

"Well, maybe it is and maybe it isn't." Sheriff Lagrudo shrugged. "But the boy needs his old man."

"I'll come with you!" Jack said, wiping his cheeks.

"No, son. You'll stay put. Your daddy would want you to be safe."

"Don't do this," Ora implored.

"Can you spare a bit of food and water?" he asked Sumner.

"Of course. Yes, of course we can," Sumner said.

Ten minutes later, they stood in a solemn line on the front porch, watching as Sheriff Lagrudo pulled out of the driveway, gave a final wave through the back window of his Chevy Impala, and turned onto Soda Creek Road. They watched until his car was out of sight and then one by one they trooped back into the house, until only Sumner and Ora remained.

"Well, you never know," she said faintly. "Maybe he'll find Jack's dad."

Sumner shook his head. "Phoenix was right. It's a suicide mission."

"Then why didn't you stop him?"

"You think I could have?"

"You could have tried."

"No," he said. "I won't kill the only thing we have left."

"What's that?"

"Hope," he said simply, and then turned and went back into the house.

CHAPTER SEVENTY-FOUR

"Ryanne, you've done everything you can. It's time to go."

I pushed my hair off my face. It felt greasy. Was it wrong to want a shower in the middle of a crisis? Josh looked as exhausted and heartsick as I felt. I opened my mouth to argue, but I knew he was right. There was nothing more I could do; the information had been passed on. We had spent hours on the phone with the MPC, NASA, and the Oval Office, all of whom wanted to hear about the end of the world right from the messengers' mouths.

Josh moved in on me, perhaps sensing that my resolve was weakening. "I made a promise to your daughter that I would bring you back to her. I intend to keep it."

Dan hung up the phone just in time to catch this last comment. "Daughter?" he asked. "Since when do you have a daughter, Red?"

I sighed. "It's a long story. Do you really want to hear it?"

After a moment, Dan shook his head. "I suppose not. I'll add that to the pile of questions we don't have time for, along with why he calls you Ryanne and how the hell you knew about these meteorites." He stood with a grimace. "But Josh is right; there's nothing more to be done here. It's time to head for the hills."

"But, what about—"

"Ryanne." Josh took my hands in his. "You've fought the good fight. You've saved thousands if not millions of lives by getting the word out, and the evil SOBs who caused this have less reason to celebrate because of you."

Dan opened his mouth, and then shook his head and closed it.

"Now it's time to go." Josh turned to Dan. "Do you want to come with us?"

"Where are you going?"

"Colorado. We have a place near Idaho Springs. It's well stocked with supplies, and it should be safe."

"If you can make it there," Dan remarked, and then shook his head. "My mom's in a home in Las Cruces. I can't leave her."

"I understand," Josh said.

"Dan, bring your mom," I urged.

"Thanks for the offer, but I think I'll hang here." He swept me up in a bear hug and I buried my head in his shoulder, muffling my sobs against the flannel of his shirt.

"Take care of yourself, Red." His voice cracked on the last word.

"You too."

He put me down gently and turned to shake Josh's hand. "Maybe we'll see each other again someday."

"Maybe," Josh said.

"Then again, maybe not." Dan made a noise somewhere between a chuckle and a sniffle.

"Right."

"Take care of her, okay?"

"I will," Josh promised.

With that, he turned and left. We heard the rumble of his car's engine and the sound of gravel crunching under his tires as he pulled out. And then there was silence, except for my quiet sobs.

***

Rather than head back toward Las Cruces, Josh suggested we drive east to avoid the major freeways. I watched the trailer disappear in the passenger mirror, straining to get one more look at the scattering of domed buildings that housed the telescopes. Would they fall away to dust? Or would they be covered in layers of ice, only to be unearthed thousands or millions of years from now like dinosaur fossils? And who would unearth them? Would they be human, or some brand-new species?

"Under normal circumstances, the trip should take ten hours or so, but who knows?" Josh was saying, but everything around me was growing dim. I closed my eyes against a wave of exhaustion, and that was the last I knew until Josh shook me awake some unknown time later.

***

"Ryanne, look!" Josh's voice was hoarse.

My eyelids felt like they were welded shut and I moaned, wanting more than anything to sink back into unconsciousness. But Josh was shaking me so hard my head was flopping from side to side like a rag doll's.

"Ryanne!" he shouted, and I finally managed to open my eyes. The world swam into focus, but it took a while for me to process what I was seeing.

"What the . . . where are we?"

"I think that's Alamogordo."

"It's on fire," I said stupidly. The fire was enormous, encompassing what might once have been the downtown area. "Do you think a meteorite did this?"

He watched it through the windshield for a minute before shaking his head. "This looks man-made."

"Who would do something like this?" Miles of black smoke billowed toward the sky, and flakes of gray ash were tumbling down around us like snow.

He gave me a look, and then shrugged. "People are crazy."

"Can we get around it?"

"I'm going to try." Josh moved us east toward the edge of the mountains along a rough side road that soon gave way to gravel. The houses were sparse to begin with and trickled off as we continued away from the fire. He found a small gravel lane that angled roughly northbound and eased onto it. We bumped slowly along, creosote and mesquite bushes scratching at the paint of our rental car.

"I wish we had the Suburban," he said, and I silently agreed. We had rented the best car available, which was a Toyota Camry. It was a decent car, but not meant for off-roading.

The lane meandered toward the fire and then retreated. The second time we got so close, I thought we were going to have to backtrack and find a different way through. I breathed a sigh of relief as we moved away again.

As we neared the center of town, I could see houses and businesses being consumed by the flames. Hundreds of people were milling about as they watched the fire crews work, but in the midst of the chaos there was a grim stillness.

Perhaps it was due to lack of sleep, but I felt emotionally disconnected from it all, as though I was watching a disaster scene play out in a movie. We passed the heart of the fire in tense silence and picked up the main road half a mile past the town. North of

Alamogordo, Route 54 was virtually deserted. We drove for miles at a stretch without seeing another vehicle.

We were passing through farmland, miles and miles of flat terrain stretching out to embrace the open sky above. We crossed over a railroad track, and then passed a white clapboard house with wagon wheels sticking out of the dirt and an American flag dancing above the front door.

A man in jeans and a white T-shirt was hammering boards up against the windows as a woman stood watching him in the dusty yard, two young children clinging to the hem of her blue dress. As we drove by, they all turned silently to watch. The younger child, a towheaded boy who couldn't have been much past his second birthday, lifted his chubby hand in a solemn wave. I lifted mine in return. A moment later they were gone, left behind in the swirling dust of another time, and I was weeping into my open palms.

"Ryanne . . ." Josh reached for me, but I shook my head.

"It's all so beautiful . . ." I choked out. "It's all just . . . so . . . *beautiful* . . ."

"Yes," he managed. "Yes, it is."

We moved past the farmland and into the empty spaces beyond. I watched the land streak by through a rainbow prism of tears. An hour later, we entered the small town of Carrizozo. Storefronts were boarded up and there were no cars moving or people about. The whole town seemed abandoned.

"This is creepy," I whispered.

"There's a Valero," Josh said. "We've still got three quarters of a tank, and gas cans in the trunk, but I'd like to fill up." But as we approached, we could see the lights were off. A hastily constructed sign informed us the tanks were empty. Across the street, an Alon gas station stood equally abandoned. He shook his head, his mouth fixed in a grim line. An hour later we drove through Corona. The Exxon was also drained and abandoned, and we continued north without a word.

The Camry began to sputter five miles before the small town of Las Vegas, New Mexico.

"No no no no no," Josh muttered. The car lurched and groaned, losing momentum. He eased onto the gravel shoulder.

"Shit!" he shouted, slamming a hand against the steering wheel, then turned off the car.

"What do you think it is?" I asked.

"Let's hope it's just a vapor lock," Josh said, opening the door and climbing out. I followed, meeting him by the side of the car. He was unscrewing the gas cap.

"If it's a vapor lock, this should fix it," he explained.

"And if it doesn't?"

"Then it's probably the fuel filter," he said grimly, screwing the cap back into place.

"And then what?"

"And then we're walking."

Sure enough, the engine sputtered and wheezed but wouldn't turn over.

"Shit!" Josh said again. He hopped out and stalked around to the front of the car. I followed him, watching as he popped the hood and inspected the engine, feeling as useless as I clearly was. He poked around for a few minutes, grumbling under his breath. I watched the road hopefully, but not surprisingly, it remained empty. The whole world felt like it had been abandoned.

The hood dropped with a bang, startling me.

"That well and truly sucks," Josh said. I couldn't have agreed more.

We packed what we could and abandoned the Camry to its fate. The sun was almost directly overhead, kissing the tops of our heads and shoulders with its gentle warmth. We followed our stunted shadows along the deserted highway, moving silently through the stillness of the last day.

CHAPTER SEVENTY-FIVE

"Sumner," Lexy whispered. "There's a man in the yard."

Sumner jumped up, motioning for the others to stay put. As one, they turned back to the doom being broadcast on the wide-screen TV, and Sumner moved through the kitchen toward the door, grabbing a rifle from the counter on his way by. Chicky was tucked into his waistband. Lexy followed hesitantly behind him. Darkness had settled many hours before, and Sumner stood blinking in the dark, allowing his eyes to adjust before he headed outside.

"Be careful!" she hissed as he cracked open the door. The moon was bright, lighting up the yard with its silvery glow.

He expected to find some tough nut standing out there, gun in hand and ready to rob them of their cache of supplies. Instead, there was a man sprawled facedown on the gravel driveway. A beaten up Ford F-150 was parked sideways against a tree at the edge of the property.

"Damn," Sumner muttered and stepped out onto the porch. "Hello?" he called, but the man kissing the driveway didn't move. Sumner followed the muzzle of the rifle down the steps and across the grass. "Hey! Dude?" he called, but still there was no response. He kept his distance, just in case the guy was playing possum.

He had dirty-blond hair that hung toward the gravel in greasy strands. Sumner could see the guy's rib cage poking out beneath his filthy white T-shirt, and inexplicably he was only wearing one sneaker. Sumner inched forward a couple more feet, keeping the gun trained on the guy's head. The wind kicked up and the unmistakable scent of whiskey assaulted his nostrils.

"Damn," he said again, wondering if the guy was dead. "Um, dude? You know drinking and driving is against the law?"

Sumner choked back a sad laugh. What did any of that matter anymore? Laws were made by a civilized world. They served as a thin layer protecting against the anarchy that bubbled just beneath the surface. All it took were a few impending meteorites, and the illusion of stability completely shattered.

Behind him the door creaked open, and Sumner shot a glance in that direction. Phoenix made his way across the grass, his own gun held casually at his side.

"Do you think he's dead?" Phoenix asked. Emboldened by Phoenix's presence, Sumner nudged a foot into the guy's rib cage. There was no response. He wedged his foot under the torso and pushed upward. The guy was light; he rolled over fairly easily. He was also covered in puke, and both Sumner and Phoenix took a step back, noses wrinkling. The man on the ground groaned.

"Well, he's alive," Phoenix surmised. The kitchen door creaked open once again, and Sumner heard the others trooping out onto the porch.

"What do we do with him?" Sumner asked.

"Is he alive?" Ora called from the porch.

"Yeah," Sumner called back. "Drunk and covered in puke. But he's alive."

Jack was the last to come out onto the porch, and he took one look at the beat-up truck and the man lying in the driveway and screamed.

"Dad!" The boy ignored the stairs and launched himself toward the man in the driveway. He skidded across the gravel and hunched over the man's prone body.

"Dad? Dad! Can you hear me?" The man groaned again, but gave no other response.

"Dad! Wake up!"

"So . . . *this* is Keaton Barbetti?" Ora asked incredulously. She had sidled up beside Sumner, and Lexy and Ashlyn weren't far behind. Only Mrs. Metcalf was missing, having fallen asleep on the couch an hour before.

"Apparently," Sumner said.

"Not quite what I was picturing," she remarked.

"And no sheriff," Sumner said quietly.

Ora's eyes widened. "Oh . . . *shit*."

"Jack, stop shaking him," Sumner called to the boy. "We'll bring him into the house and get him cleaned up. It would take a bomb to wake him up right now."

His timing was ironic. As if activated by his words, they heard the first rumble. It sounded very much like thunder, although the Colorado sky was clear and pinpricked with stars.

"Sumner!" Ora screamed, yanking at his sleeve. He turned where she was pointing, toward the south, and gaped.

It started as a sphere of light, brighter than a star but dimmer than the sun. It grew from there, becoming a column of light that angled downward in the southern sky. The distant thunder rumbled and rumbled, and the light grew so bright Sumner had to shield his eyes.

"Oh . . . *no* . . ." he breathed. It was all he was capable of saying.

The rumbling woke Keaton Barbetti. He sat up and his red-rimmed eyes turned toward the sky. "I will show My greatness," he croaked. "And My holiness . . . and make Myself known in the eyes of many nations . . ."

Sumner blinked at him dumbly. For once, he had no words. When Keaton started reciting the Lord's Prayer, Sumner turned back to the sky.

The light grew impossibly bright, a bluish-white streak that lit up the southern sky. They watched it approach the earth for an endless amount of time, frozen in silence except for Keaton Barbetti's jittery prayers and the ominous thunder of the approaching meteorite.

And then the light fanned out and disappeared, leaving them in blinding darkness. There was an eternal moment of silence, and then the ground rocked with violent force, knocking Sumner to his knees. Something like cannon fire pummeled at his eardrums with great, roaring explosions.

BOOM!

BOOM!

BOOM!

Sumner covered his head and wailed, cheek pressed against the cold gravel and eyes firmly shut. He expected at any moment to be torn to pieces. The world shook and roared, and Sumner lost himself in the chaos.

The ground eventually stilled and the booming receded, becoming a quiet knocking that slowed to silence. Sumner lay hugging the ground, afraid to open his eyes.

"Is everyone okay?" Ora croaked.

The others responded shakily, and Sumner found the nerve to open his eyes. He sat up slowly, trying to assess the damage. A couple of trees on the edge of the property had come down. One of them was lying against the wires strung toward the house. There goes the power, he thought.

The house looked reasonably unscathed, other than porch chairs being turned on their sides and a potted plant that had tumbled off the porch and landed on the bottom stair.

Keaton's F-150 had shifted sideways and was now perfectly aligned in the driveway. Sumner stared at it, awestruck.

Ora approached him, extending her hands. She had a gash across her right cheek, and the blood dripped black against her pale skin.

"Let's get inside," she said shakily. He let her help him to his feet and stood there swaying.

"They didn't know about that one," he managed. His voice was little more than a wheeze.

"No," she agreed, propping a shoulder into his armpit to steady him.

"Where do you think it hit?"

She looked at him for a moment, biting her lip. "To the south."

"Do you think . . ." But he trailed off, unable to voice his fear.

"I'm sure they're all right," she said quietly.

"Yeah," he agreed, and let her lead him toward the house.

CHAPTER SEVENTY-SIX

When the sun went down that night, we were past Ranchos de Taos, New Mexico. It lit up the sky in glorious pinks and oranges, and it was without a doubt the most beautiful sunset I had ever seen.

Darkness came bit by bit, until I could no longer see my feet in front of me as we followed along the edge of the road. We were in the high desert, and as soon as the sun went to bed, it grew icy. Biting winds nipped at our exposed skin. Underneath our feet, the earth crunched; our breath steamed in icy puffs around our faces.

"What do you think is going to happen?" Josh asked. His voice startled me; I had grown accustomed to the silence and I couldn't remember the last time we had spoken.

"Do you really want to know?"

"Yes," he insisted, although I heard the shakiness in his voice.

"Well, I don't know exactly . . ." I hedged.

"Your best educated guess is fine."

"My best educated guess is we're going to lose millions of human lives around the world."

"Right, I got that already. But what do you think will happen after? I mean, to those who survive the meteorites?"

I sighed. "Yeah. The meteorites are only the first wave, so to speak. They'll cause mass destruction and a catastrophic loss of life, but that's just the beginning. After that, there will be a second wave of casualties. Those who die in accidents, or by starvation, or freezing . . ."

"Jesus."

"I think we might be dealing with an "impact winter." That's a period of planetary cooling that can happen after a massive volcano, enormous wildfires . . . or after a meteorite strike. It happens because of all the smoke and ash thrust up into the atmosphere. The sun gets blocked and the earth cools down. It usually lasts about a year before the atmosphere starts to clear."

"You're talking about an ice age, right?"

"Yes. The first things to die out are the plants and animals that rely on photosynthesis. So most of the ocean life would either die off or go dormant. On land . . . well, plants could be kept alive with growing lights."

"Like the ones in The Ranch's Underground?"

"That's right. They have their own version of Noah's Ark going on down there," I said bitterly, and then continued. "So most plant life would die off, either from lack of sun or from the cold. And following that would be famine on a global scale. The animals who eat the plants would go first, and then the carnivorous animals, and . . ."

"I get the picture," Josh said shakily.

"Right. So . . . I really don't know where that leaves us. Assuming we make it back to Idaho Springs without being struck by a meteorite, we should be able to survive the first year and start to rebuild."

"If we don't have some unfortunate accident. Or get *appendicitis*, or something . . ."

"Welcome to the Dark Ages. Too bad none of us has a degree in medicine."

We walked in silence for several minutes as I worked through the thing that was niggling at my brain. Finally, I spoke up. "I think there will be a third wave after that."

"What? That's not enough?" He took a deep breath. "Okay, what's the third wave?"

"War," I said simply.

"What do you mean, 'war'?"

"I think they're going to wait out the year, let nature take care of as much of the human race as possible, and then they're going to swoop in and take care of the rest. Call it a 'mopping up' operation."

"Holy shit, Ryanne. Are you serious?"

Although he couldn't see me in the dark, I shrugged. "I can't see them leaving the job incomplete."

"Is this just a hunch? Or do you know this for sure?"

"Let's call it an educated guess."

There was nothing but silence and the crunching of the earth under our feet as Josh processed this new horror.

"How do we stop them?" he finally asked.

"That, my friend, is a good question. Imagine whatever is left of the human race struggling to survive in this new world. They make it through a year, but they're totally focused on doing what they need to do to survive. You know, food and shelter and all that good stuff. They would be completely defenseless against an attack. It would be the last thing they would expect or be prepared for."

"Well, you sure do paint a pretty picture," Josh said darkly.

"Yeah."

My feet, which had been aching for hours, were blessedly numb. My muscles were tight with the cold, and I moved clumsily, keeping as close to Josh as I could manage without tripping him up.

We stopped for a brief water and granola-bar break, but even a few minutes of stillness made us colder than either of us could bear and we began, once again, to move. The hours passed, or at least I assume they did, as both of us trudged along, lost in our own dark thoughts.

For all of my psychic abilities, I had no forewarning. One moment I was stumbling along in the darkness, feeling very much like a human Popsicle, and the next, I was burning up.

The heat exploded around me like a bonfire, and the world was suddenly as bright as the noonday sun. The sky ripped open above our heads, becoming blinding white fire.

I screamed, but the rushing roar of the wind sucked the air out of my lungs and scorched my mouth and eyeballs. The white-blue light streaked across the sky with a mighty roar, moving over our heads and continuing past us to the southeast.

The smoldering wind sucked me up into its angry breath and spun me like a top. It must have pulled me for at least fifty feet before deciding to release me back to the earth. I landed with a bone-crushing thud, and my left arm snapped beneath me. I screamed again, this time in pain.

I managed to lift my head off the ground just in time to see the impact. For a moment, the fireball spread outward, and then the earth around it rose up in a mighty cloud of dust and smoke and fire. The roar was deafening, and the ground thundered beneath me. Artillery fire crashed again and again from the direction of the impact.

BOOM!

BOOM!

BOOM!

I closed my eyes and held on to the surging ground beneath me.

A million years later, the world grew calm. The ground stilled, and a cool silence descended. I managed to pull myself upright. I was blind in the darkness, my retinas seared with the imprint of the meteorite.

I sensed more than heard the snuffling and grunting of animals around me. A large nose butted into my armpit, nudging at my good arm and breathing moist heat through the torn fabric of my coat.

Blindly, I reached up and touched warm silk and rough whiskers. The horse nuzzled my hair and I stroked its long nose absentmindedly. I obviously wasn't on the road anymore, but where was I?

And more important, where was Josh?

CHAPTER SEVENTY-SEVEN

In the days and weeks that followed, the sunlight dimmed. Sumner sat for hours at the kitchen window, watching the thick blanket of smoke, or dust particles, or whatever the hell it was, choke up the sky. He'd gone outside twice, simply unable to remain indoors a moment longer. The world smelled like an ashtray, and Sumner guessed those promised firestorms were raging somewhere to the south. They were all going stir-crazy, Sumner most of all.

Days passed, and the silence lay like heavy blankets on top of his shoulders, accumulating layer upon layer. Soon he would suffocate within their thick blackness, and that would be a relief.

They had no idea what was going on in the world outside their isolated little home. As far as Sumner could tell, they might be the last humans left on Earth. Well, them and all the crazies on The Ranch. He was sure they were doing just fine.

The Colorado Compound, as Sumner had dubbed their house, was kept warm by fireplaces in the living room and master bedroom, along with battery-powered space heaters.

The sat phone wasn't working, and no one in a house full of psychics could pull any valuable information out of their asshole brains, either.

"Watch out who you're calling an asshole," Phoenix said moodily from across the table, not even bothering to look up from the deck of cards he was carefully balancing into a tower. Sumner suppressed the urge to knock the whole thing over and turned back to the window.

He had no idea if Ryanne and Josh had survived the meteorite. It had struck somewhere to the south of them. Lexy thought it might have hit somewhat east as well. They spent hours hunched over maps, debating. But it all came down to a bunch of guesswork.

And as each day ended, there was no sign of Ryanne and Josh. Ashlyn grew silent, retreating to her room and having to be coaxed out for meals. Sumner had the strong urge to do the same, but somewhere along the way he had been silently elected leader of this crazy group of misfits, and he felt obligated to show a brave face.

"Do you want the stew for lunch? Or the black beans and rice?" Ora asked, holding out the cans for his perusal.

"I don't care," Sumner muttered, barely taking his eyes off the window. *Loretta* was hovering nearby with her cool green light, desperate to comfort him, but he ignored her.

"Then stew it is," she said, and he heard the grinding sound of the can opener behind him.

"I better give Keaton clear broth, though. His stomach is still not right. But he's shaking less; I guess that's a good sign."

There was an unappetizing plop as she emptied the can into a saucepan, and then a whoosh as she lit the propane stove. "Can you believe he had no idea about the meteorites? He got your message and headed straight here. I guess it's lucky—another day or two and he would have been stuck in a major traffic jam."

When her attempt at conversation failed, Ora fell silent. She placed a small bowl of stew in front of him, laying a spoon beside it, gave his shoulder a gentle squeeze, and moved away. It felt like the kind of pseudocomforting touch one gives the mourners at a funeral. He had to unclench his jaw in order to eat.

Across the table, Phoenix was staring into his bowl, stirring the contents with his spoon.

"You all right?" Sumner asked.

Phoenix nodded, not looking up. Sumner thought he might have seen a tear plop into the bowl, but he couldn't be sure. "I was just thinking about peaches," he said gruffly.

"Peaches?"

"Yeah. Man, what I wouldn't give for a nice, juicy peach."

It hit Sumner like a steamroller to the chest. The loss. It was massive, incalculable. He couldn't process it all at once; his brain just didn't have enough room inside it. Sumner had lost his appetite, but he spooned the stew into his mouth anyway. There was no wasting food.

"I think we have some canned peaches in the basement," he finally said.

"Yeah," Phoenix said, and took a bite of the stew.

Sumner finished his bowl and pushed it aside, belching quietly into his fist. He resumed his surveillance of the front yard and driveway, losing himself in a list of foods he might never taste again. It was depressing, but better than focusing on what was going on in the world outside their little hideaway. And besides, if he could miss food, it meant he was *alive*.

When the horses first appeared at the edge of the driveway, it took a moment to register. His eyes were glazed over with after-lunch lethargy, and he was more asleep than awake. Phoenix was snoring softly into the table across from him.

There were two of them, one a sleek black and the other a pretty chestnut. They were pulling a wagon piled high with hay. The person leading the horses was hobbling, wrapped in a quilt against the bitter cold. A wool cap was pulled down to just above the eyes, a scarf wrapped around the mouth and nose.

He let out a strangled cry that made Phoenix jump, and his tower of cards collapsed. Sumner ignored the clatter of the chair falling to the floor behind him. He pulled Chicky out of his waistband and moved to the door. His heart had taken up residence in his throat.

"What?" Phoenix squawked.

"There's someone coming up the driveway," Sumner hissed. "With a couple of *horses*."

"Shit!" Phoenix leapt to his feet and reached for the rifle on the kitchen counter. "Is it someone from The Ranch?" Phoenix had just voiced Sumner's own fear.

Sumner shrugged, watching the person approach through the half-moon window at the top of the kitchen door. The blanket obscured the details. He couldn't even tell if it was a man or a woman.

"Should we go find out?" he suggested with more bravado than he felt.

Phoenix pushed up beside Sumner and nervously watched the stranger approach. "Is that a cow?"

Sure enough, as the group rounded the curve in the driveway, Sumner saw the black-and-white rump and twitching tail. There was indeed a cow tied to the back of the wagon. She followed along at a morose distance, clearly displeased with her situation.

"What are you two doing?" Ora asked, bustling into the kitchen with an armful of empty stew bowls and making both men jump.

"We've got company," Phoenix explained, turning back to the window. "What do you thi—"

But Sumner was no longer listening. One dirty tangle of hair had escaped from the wool cap, but it was enough for him to know. Even the dull gray outside couldn't hide the telltale flicker of cinnamon. The door almost hit Phoenix in the nose, but Sumner didn't stop to apologize.

His feet didn't touch the porch steps. He went flying toward her, kicking up snow and skating across the icy patches like Milan Lucic coming in for a hit.

"Homegirl!"

With as much self-control as he could muster, he pulled her into a gentle hug. The blanket fell away, exposing the dirty sling on her left arm. She was thin and frail, her nose red from the cold. He bent down and kissed her grimy cheek.

"I have never been so happy to see somebody in my *whole damned life!*" He danced around her like a puppy, unable to contain his excitement, and she gave him a watery smile in return.

"Where's Josh?" Ora asked breathlessly from behind him.

"In the wagon." Ryanne's voice was raspy, almost nonexistent. "His leg . . ."

They moved to the back of the wagon. Josh was swaddled in a pile of hay and dirty blankets. He threw them aside, straining to greet them. His teeth flashed white through the black tangle of his beard. His eyes were hollow and rimmed with dark circles, like bruises. Sumner and Phoenix helped him off the wagon, mindful of his leg, which was clearly broken. It was splinted with a tree branch, which had been tied on with filthy rags.

"Josh!" Ora moved forward, grinning, but Mrs. Metcalf got there first.

"My boy! My boy! *Thank God!*" She was weeping, and Josh wrapped his arms around her and pulled her into his chest. He leaned down, black head to gray, and muttered reassurances. Sumner had to look away.

Ashlyn had found Ryanne, and the two were locked in an embrace. Ryanne's tears fell on the girl's head as Ashlyn sobbed into her mom's chest.

Sumner had to swallow several times before he could speak. "Maybe we should take this party indoors?"

"I'll take the animals to the garage," Phoenix offered, and Ryanne nodded gratefully.

"There are more horse blankets and a curry comb in the wagon. I'm sure they'll be hungry. And thirsty."

"No problem. I'll make them a nice home in there." Phoenix took the reins and guided the animals toward the rear of the property.

"Where did you get them?" Lexy asked.

"I wanted to steal a car, but apparently Ryanne is more comfortable hot-wiring horses," Josh joked.

"Better gas mileage." Ryanne smiled, her good arm around Ashlyn's shoulder. Sumner guessed it would be a long time before she let her daughter out of her sight.

"It's The Ranch in you, homegirl."

"They'll come in handy," Ora said. "If we can find enough food to keep them alive."

They trooped up the porch steps and into the house. Sumner entered last and closed the door behind him. He turned and pressed his forehead against the rough wood, leaning in like a felled tree. He listened to their chatter as they moved away into the living room, shaking with the effort to contain himself until they were out of hearing.

The tears came in a hot gush, searing a path down his cheeks. Some trickled into his mouth and others fell off the tip of his nose or the end of his chin to land softly on the floor at his feet. He stayed that way for several minutes, alone in the kitchen. Finally he managed to pull himself upright, and he scrubbed his face with the rough flannel of his sleeve.

"Thank you," he whispered. "Thank you."

He turned to join them in the living room.

AFTER

My throat was raw from speaking. The day had dimmed toward evening. The trees were spiny shadows against the gray snow.

She was tucked in beside me as we lay in the snow. Her bony limbs were emitting gentle heat, so my left side was much warmer than my right.

"Is that the end?" she asked, shifting within the blankets.

"I'd rather think of it as the beginning."

"How can you say that?"

"We're here, aren't we?"

She shrugged, clearly unconvinced.

"Ashlyn, you need to eat."

"I had some beef jerky."

"When? For breakfast?"

She shrugged again. I pushed aside the blankets, letting the bitter cold assault us, and hauled myself upright.

"Come on." I held out my right hand, and after a moment she conceded. I helped her to her feet and then gathered up the blankets. I bundled them against my chest as we made our way toward the house slowly, the snow crunching under our feet.

We came around the last snowdrift and paused, caught by the dim glow coming from the kitchen window. Sumner stood near a large pot on the stove, waving a spatula wildly as he talked. Ora was standing by the sink, laughing. Keaton and Josh were seated at the kitchen table with steaming mugs of tea, clearly amused by Sumner's antics.

Like a heat-seeking missile, I locked onto him. His hair was long, his beard bushy and thick. He must have sensed my gaze on him. He turned toward the window, his smile fading.

"Are you coming?" Ashlyn asked.

"In a bit," I said, turning back toward the trees. I was exhausted, but I couldn't bear to wait a moment longer. I moved away before she could argue.

He found me on the swing in the side yard, as I knew he would. For a moment, I was brought back to an earlier time when we had sat on its bench together, swinging and wondering at what horror might be coming our way.

He was limping badly, tea sloshing over the sides of the mug he carried. I doubted either of our breaks would heal cleanly. He handed me the mug, and I drained it in three gulps. It was barely warm, but it was wet and bitter and delicious.

"Thanks." I opened the blanket, just as Ashlyn had done for me many hours before. He sat and wrapped the end around him.

"Mmm. You're toasty," he said gratefully.

"Feel my cheeks; I'm an icicle," I responded, and he did just that. His fingers were so cold I doubted he could feel my cheeks at all. He tucked his hands inside the blanket and we started to swing.

"How did it go?" he asked, and I shrugged inside our cocoon.

"I told her everything. I hope it helps her understand."

"Yeah," he said, and we continued to swing.

"It's funny," I said. "It's deafening inside. There are always people talking or arguing or something and it's enough to drive you nuts. So you come outside to get away from it for a little while, but the silence outside is worse. I'm always glad to go back in."

His hand found mine inside the blankets, and our fingers entwined.

"You've been spending a lot of time with Sumner," Josh observed.

"He's a good friend."

"Is that all he is?"

I glanced sideways at him. His cheeks were like red apples, round and bitable. His jaw was clenched, his eyelid twitching. I couldn't help but laugh. "You're a real chickenshit, Agent Metcalf."

He turned to me, his mouth dropping open. "What?"

"You heard me. Can I give you a bit of advice?"

"S-sure," he stammered.

"Women like to be chased. It's sexy when a man knows what he wants, and he goes for it. Now, you're pretty tough. You could probably take down the entire Ranch single-handed. But when it comes to women? You, sir, are a Grade A chicken."

"I don't think that's fair," he protested.

I turned to him, gazing solemnly into his big blue eyes. "Bawk."

The corner of his mouth twitched.

"Bawk. Bawk!"

He grinned. "What are you, seven?"

"At least I'm no chicken. I can admit it."

"Admit what?"

"That I'm in love with you." I stared at him defiantly.

"You're in . . . *love* with me?"

"Well, duh. I would have thought that was pretty obvious by now." I waited. The world around us was so still.

"But I'm so much older than you."

"Thirteen years. I did the math."

"And I was friends with your *mom*, and—"

464

"Hey, king of the up-sell, stop while you're ahead."

He clamped his mouth shut, but his lips were curling up at the corners.

"And you love me, too," I coaxed. My heart was thundering against my rib cage. "Don't you?"

"I do, Ryanne," he admitted. "Oh, so much."

"See?" I said. "Was that so har—"

He leaned in, cutting me off. His beard tickled my cheeks and chin. His lips were chapped and cold, but his kiss was warm.

A NOTE FROM THE AUTHOR

Thank you so much for taking this journey. I hope you enjoyed your time with Ryanne, Josh, Sumner, and the rest of the *I Fidele* family.

The Faithful was inspired by the meteorite that exploded over Russia in February 2013, and a news article about Spaceguard that got me wondering about the meteorite-hunting profession. It somehow grew to encompass psychic children, kidnappings, and a really twisted organization. It's a strange game of association that, looking back, makes me wonder just a wee bit about my sanity.

I don't think this story is done quite yet. Ryanne and Josh still have things to say. Sumner, too—he doesn't always know when to shut up. Assuming I don't get struck down by a meteorite first, I hope to bring you a continuation of *The Faithful* sometime soon.

In the meantime, you can "like" me on Facebook at www.facebook.com/sfreedmanauthor or visit my website and blog at www.smfreedman.com. I'd love to hear from you!

Until we meet again,

S.M. Freedman

ACKNOWLEDGMENTS

I am eternally grateful to the amazing people at Thomas & Mercer for giving me and my work such a wonderful home. Thanks to Tegan Tigani for her developmental edit, brilliant suggestions, and tons of laughs along the way; to Rachel Moorhead for her eagle-eyed copyediting skills and ability to catch mistakes and plot holes, both big and small, and to Dave Valencia for helping with the copyedit as well; to Nick Allison for superb proof-reading skills; to Tiffany Pokorny for guiding me through all the twists and turns of author life; to Jacque Ben-Zekry for her brilliant marketing of *The Faithful*; to Mike Morris and Patrick Magee for finding ways to answer my questions without making me feel like a dummy; and most of all, a huge thank-you to Kjersti Egerdahl, who found and read *The Faithful* and liked it enough to want to republish it. Thank you for reaching out, for building up, and for making better. None of this would have happened without you.

With eternal love and gratitude to Jon Freedman, Sheryl Walker, Joyce Macey, and Joy Rosengarten, for reading *The Faithful* during its infancy and giving such valuable advice.

A huge thank-you to June Hutton, author extraordinaire, for sharing your wealth of knowledge. Without you, this writer would still be chewing dust. I am humbled by your greatness.

My deepest appreciation to the members of the WorldWiseWriters group: Jacky Gray, J.D. Faulkner, Andrea Domanski, and Hannah Sullivan, for your never-ending support, guidance, and friendship. You guys rock like a . . . well, you know the rest.

ABOUT THE AUTHOR

Photo ©2015 S.M. Freedman

S.M. Freedman studied acting at the American Academy of Dramatic Arts in New York and has worked as a private investigator and business owner. She lives in Vancouver, British Columbia, with her husband and two children.

The Faithful, a quarter finalist for the 2014 Amazon Breakthrough Novel Award, is her debut novel. For more information, please visit www.smfreedman.com.

Made in the USA
Monee, IL
03 May 2021